Ao Haru Ride

The scent of air after rain...
In the light around us, I felt your heartbeat.

2

IO SAKISAKA

② C O N T E N T S

S T O R Y
T H U S
F A R

In junior high, Futaba Yoshioka was quiet and disliked all boys—except for Tanaka, her first love. Their romance was cut short when he suddenly transferred schools, leaving behind an unresolved misunderstanding. In high school, Futaba has reimagined herself as a tomboy, as she was ostracized previously by her classmates for being too girly, and she's determined to never be singled out again.

One day, a boy who resembles Tanaka appears. He goes by the name of Kou Mabuchi, and it turns out that he is Tanaka, but he changed his name after his parents divorced.

Motivated by encounters with Kou and Makita, Futaba puts an end to her superficial friendships by saying how she truly feels.

Now in her second year of high school, Futaba is surprised to find that she's in the same class as Kou!

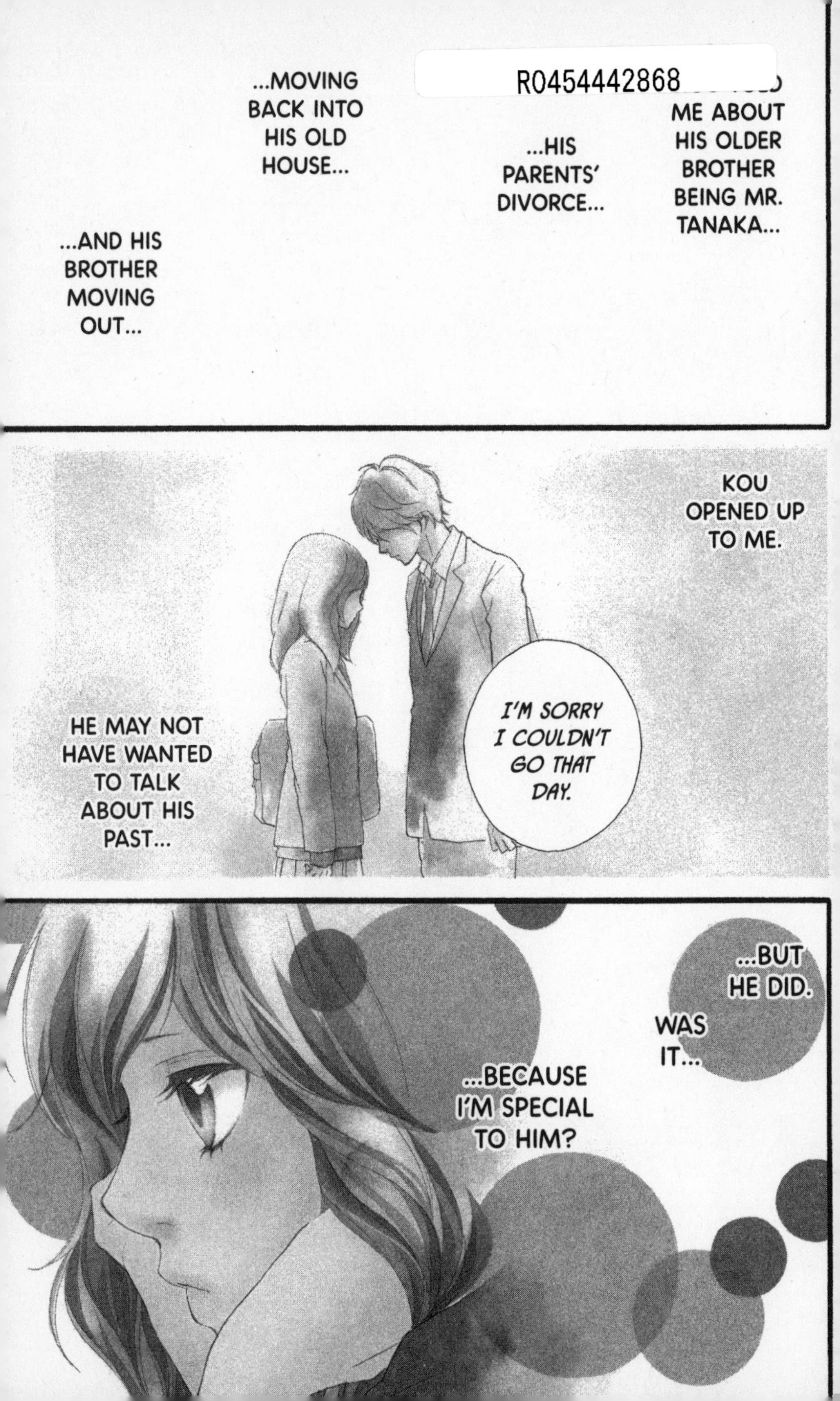
ME ABOUT HIS OLDER BROTHER BEING MR. TANAKA...
...HIS PARENTS' DIVORCE...
...MOVING BACK INTO HIS OLD HOUSE...
...AND HIS BROTHER MOVING OUT...
KOU OPENED UP TO ME.
I'M SORRY I COULDN'T GO THAT DAY.
HE MAY NOT HAVE WANTED TO TALK ABOUT HIS PAST...
...BUT HE DID.
WAS IT...
...BECAUSE I'M SPECIAL TO HIM?

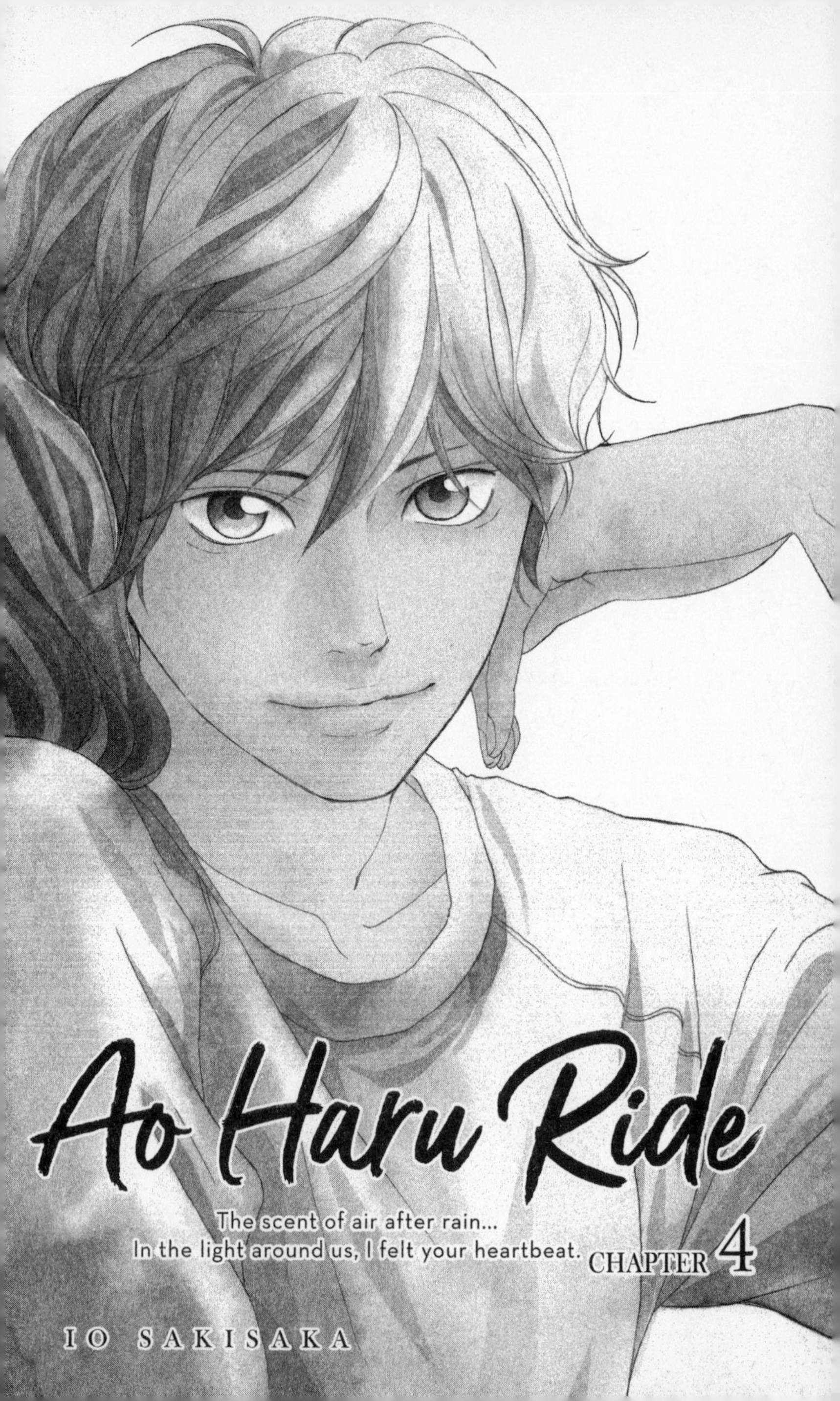
Ao Haru Ride
The scent of air after rain...
In the light around us, I felt your heartbeat.
CHAPTER 4
IO SAKISAKA

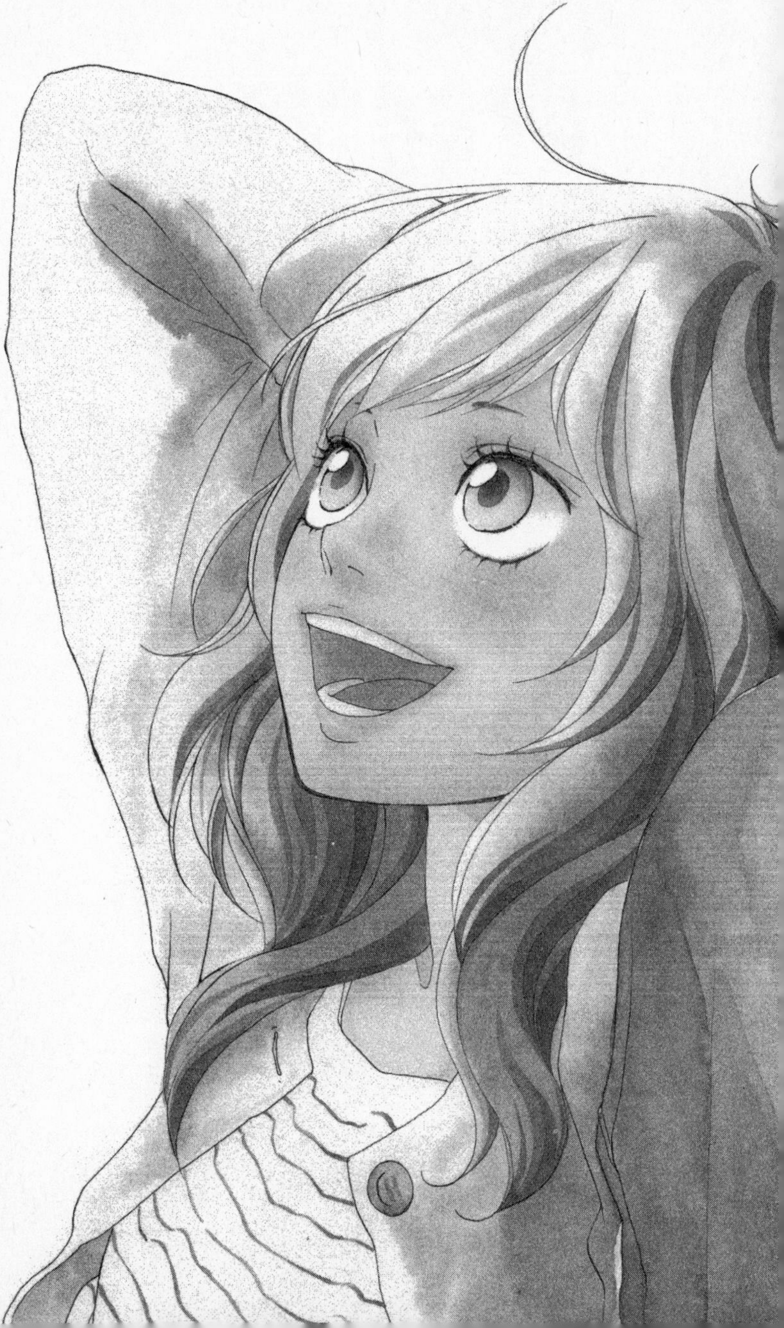

Greetings

Hi! I'm Io Sakisaka. Thank you for picking up a copy of *Ao Haru Ride* volume 2.

Ao Haru Ride is a story about reuniting with your first love years later in high school. Personally I find this concept fantastically romantic, especially when personalities and demeanor have changed completely. I can't help but get excited and imagine what happened during those lost years. (It can be aggravating not to know, I realize.) I love that bittersweet feeling of long-lost years I know nothing of, the excitement about the unknown and the realization that I will never fully know what truly happened.

In elementary school, I knew a girl who was a tomboy, and when we reunited in high school, she had become ladylike. Her story was similarly romantic, and I am sure that if she were a boy I would've had a crush on her. If she had also been my first love (like Futaba is experiencing), well, just thinking about it makes me go crazy.

I hope my romantic idealism reaches you, and I'll keep working hard to make sure it does.

On that note, I hope you enjoy volume 2, and please read through to the end!

 Io Sakisaka

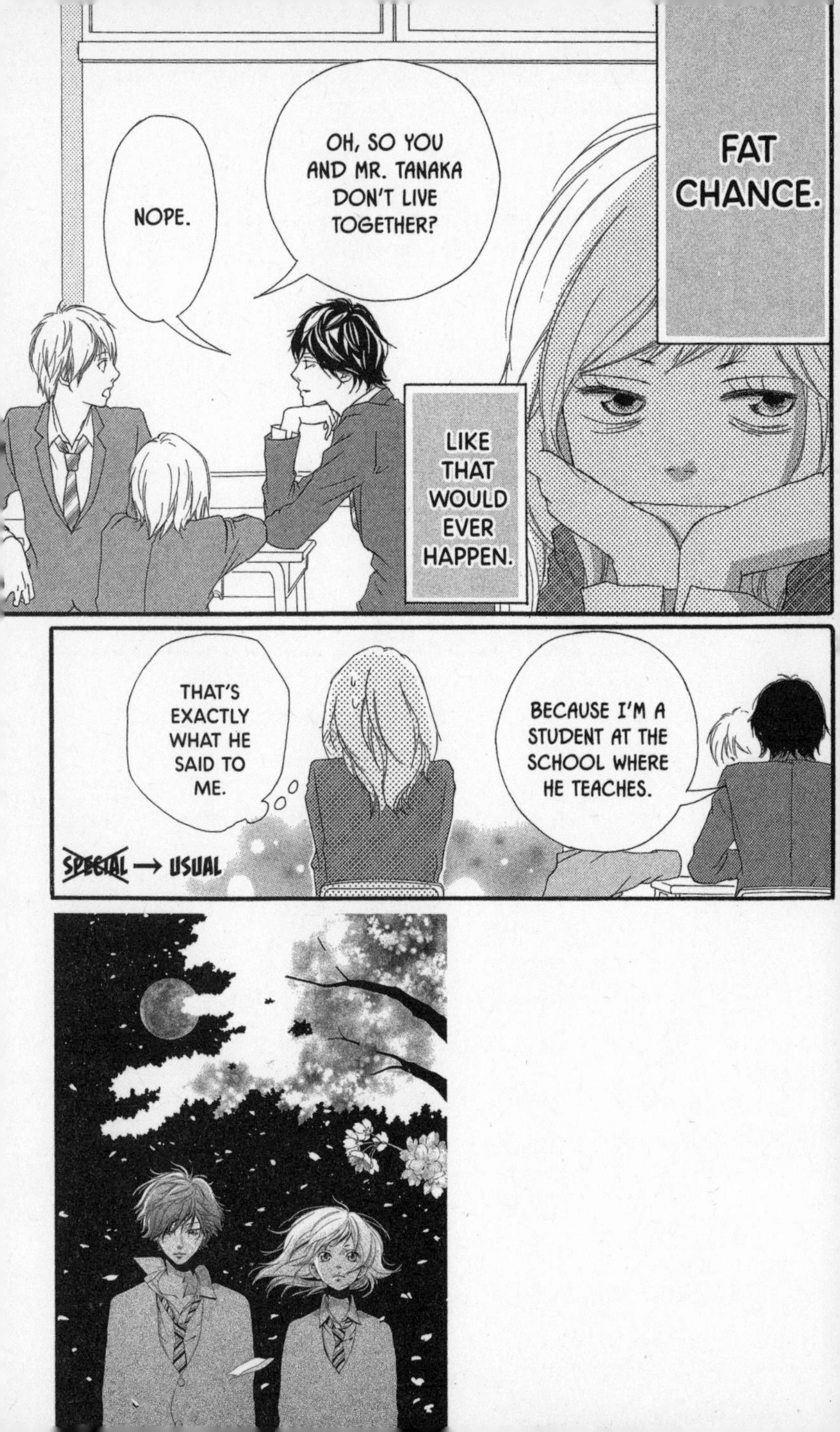
FAT CHANCE.
LIKE THAT WOULD EVER HAPPEN.
OH, SO YOU AND MR. TANAKA DON'T LIVE TOGETHER?
NOPE.
BECAUSE I'M A STUDENT AT THE SCHOOL WHERE HE TEACHES.
THAT'S EXACTLY WHAT HE SAID TO ME.
~~SPECIAL~~ → USUAL

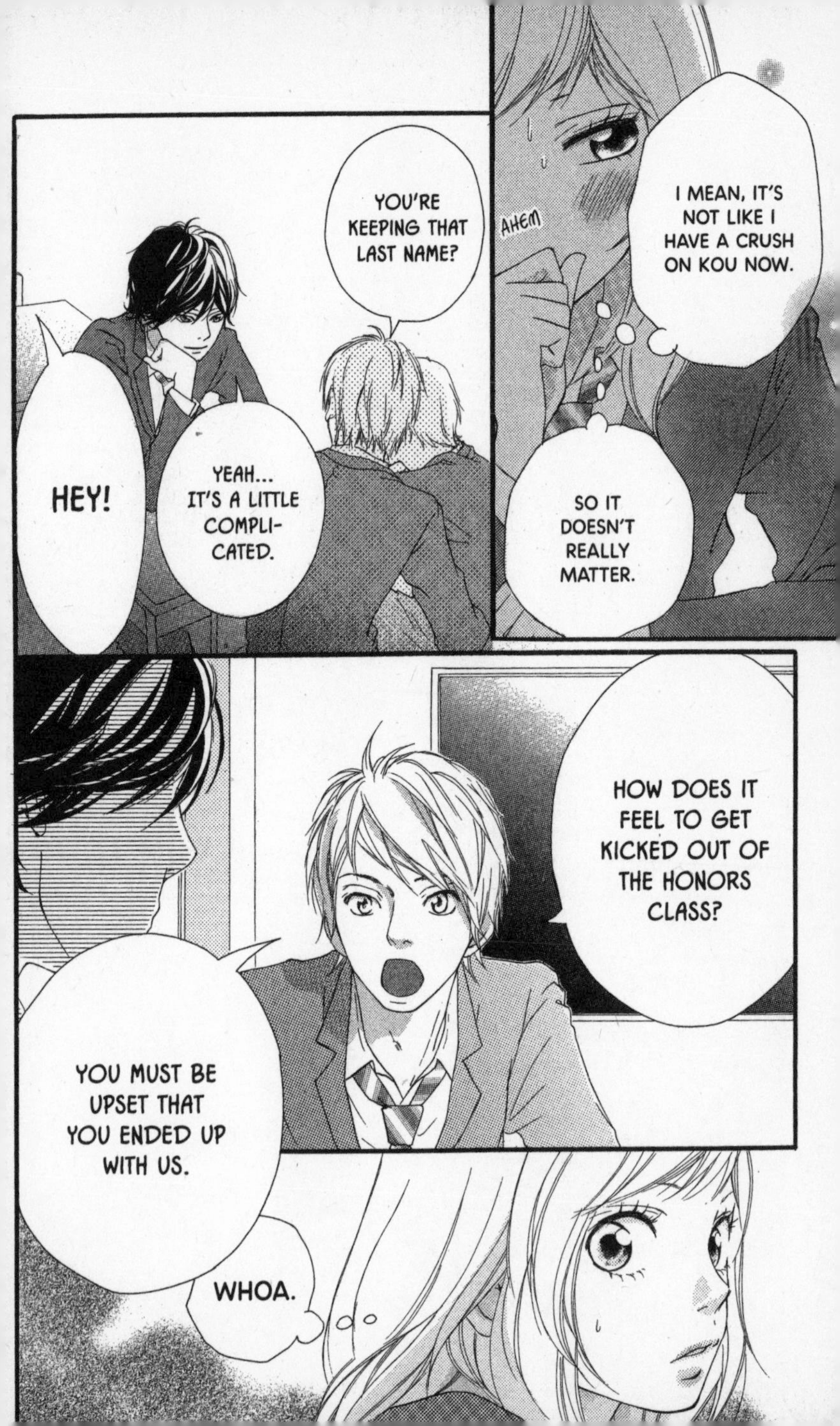
AHEM
I MEAN, IT'S NOT LIKE I HAVE A CRUSH ON KOU NOW.
SO IT DOESN'T REALLY MATTER.
YOU'RE KEEPING THAT LAST NAME?
YEAH... IT'S A LITTLE COMPLI-CATED.
HEY!
HOW DOES IT FEEL TO GET KICKED OUT OF THE HONORS CLASS?
YOU MUST BE UPSET THAT YOU ENDED UP WITH US.
WHOA.

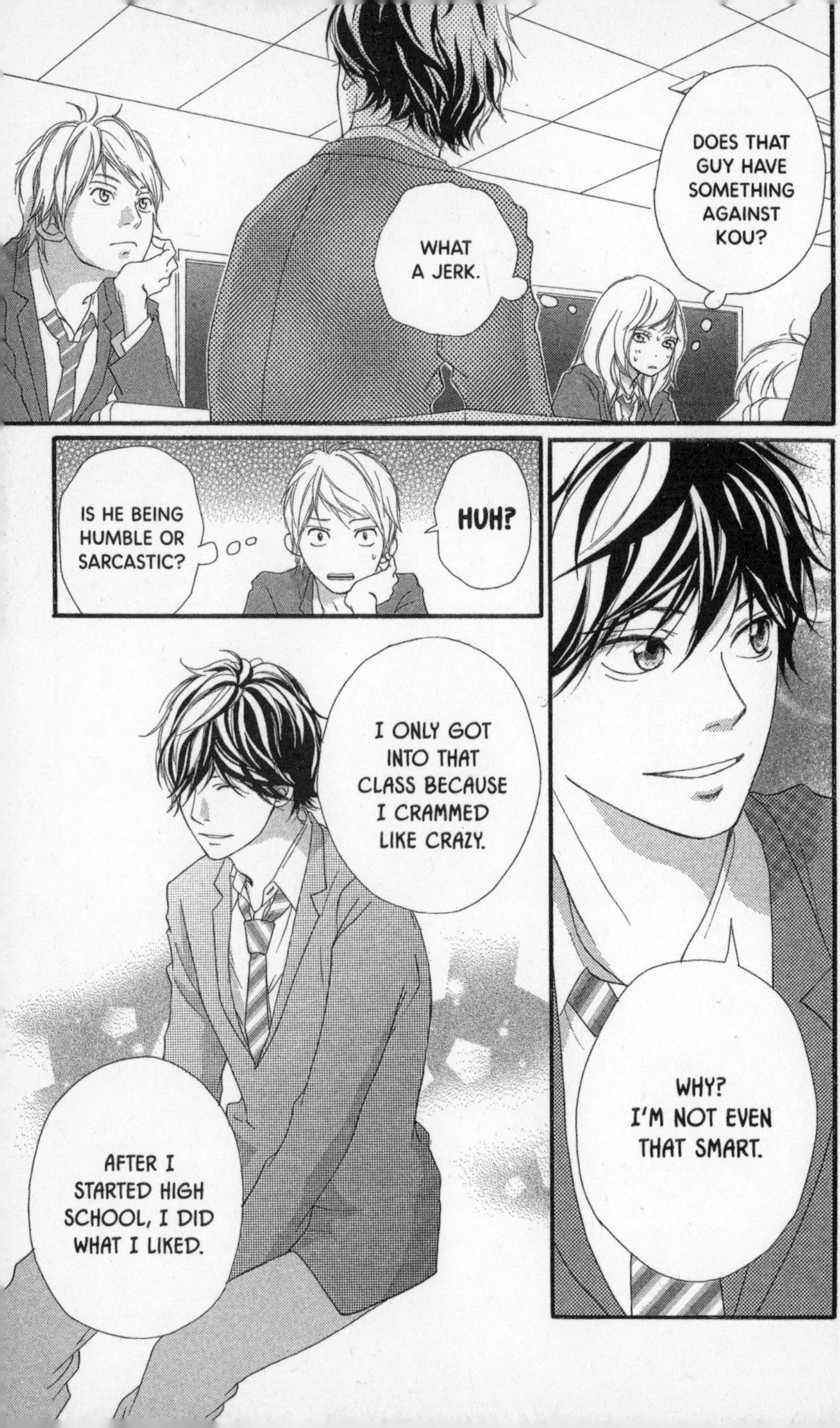
DOES THAT GUY HAVE SOMETHING AGAINST KOU?
WHAT A JERK.
WHY? I'M NOT EVEN THAT SMART.
HUH?
IS HE BEING HUMBLE OR SARCASTIC?
I ONLY GOT INTO THAT CLASS BECAUSE I CRAMMED LIKE CRAZY.
AFTER I STARTED HIGH SCHOOL, I DID WHAT I LIKED.

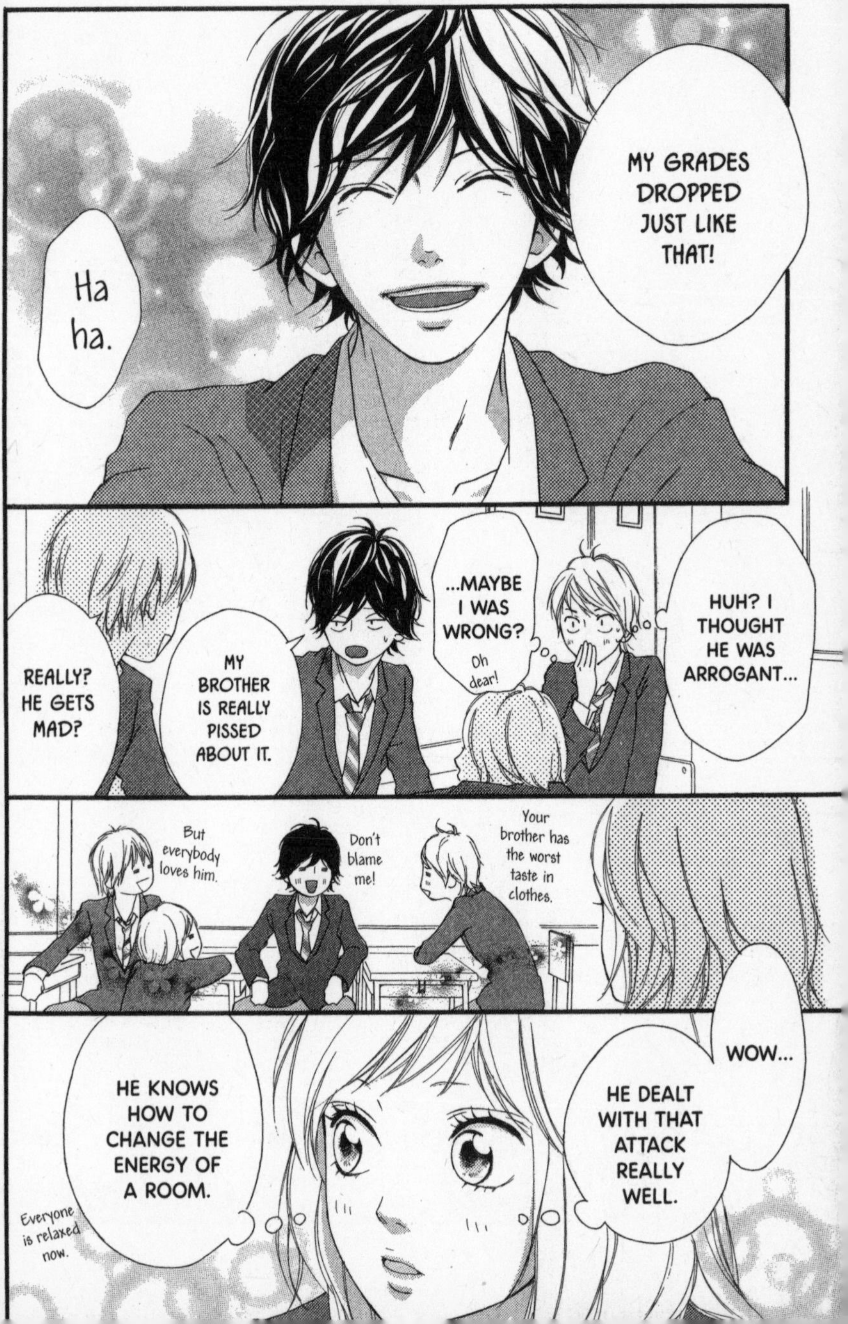
MY GRADES DROPPED JUST LIKE THAT!
Ha ha.
HUH? I THOUGHT HE WAS ARROGANT...
...MAYBE I WAS WRONG?
Oh dear!
MY BROTHER IS REALLY PISSED ABOUT IT.
REALLY? HE GETS MAD?
Your brother has the worst taste in clothes.
Don't blame me!
But everybody loves him.
WOW...
HE DEALT WITH THAT ATTACK REALLY WELL.
HE KNOWS HOW TO CHANGE THE ENERGY OF A ROOM.
Everyone is relaxed now.

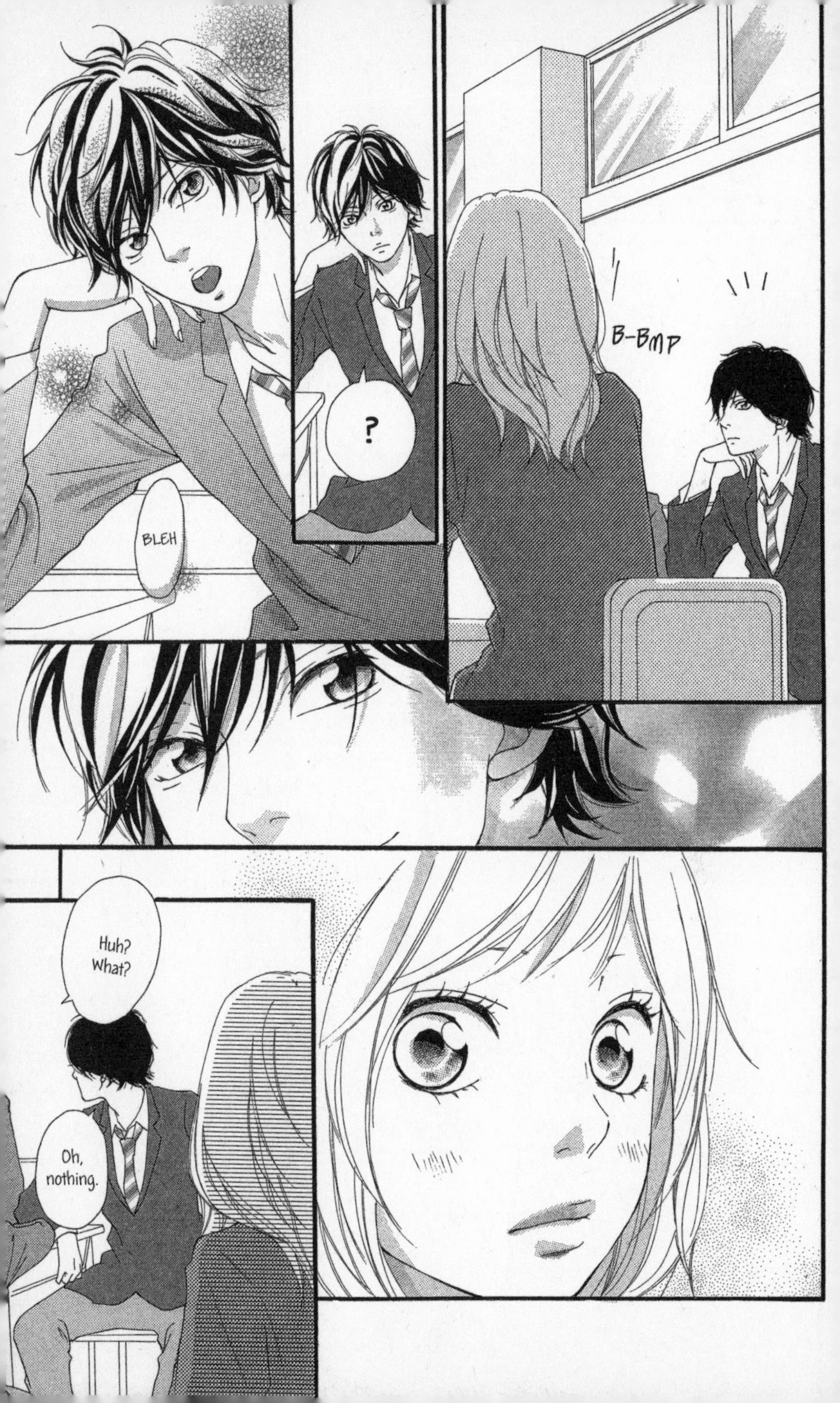
B-BMP
?
BLEH
Huh? What?
Oh, nothing.

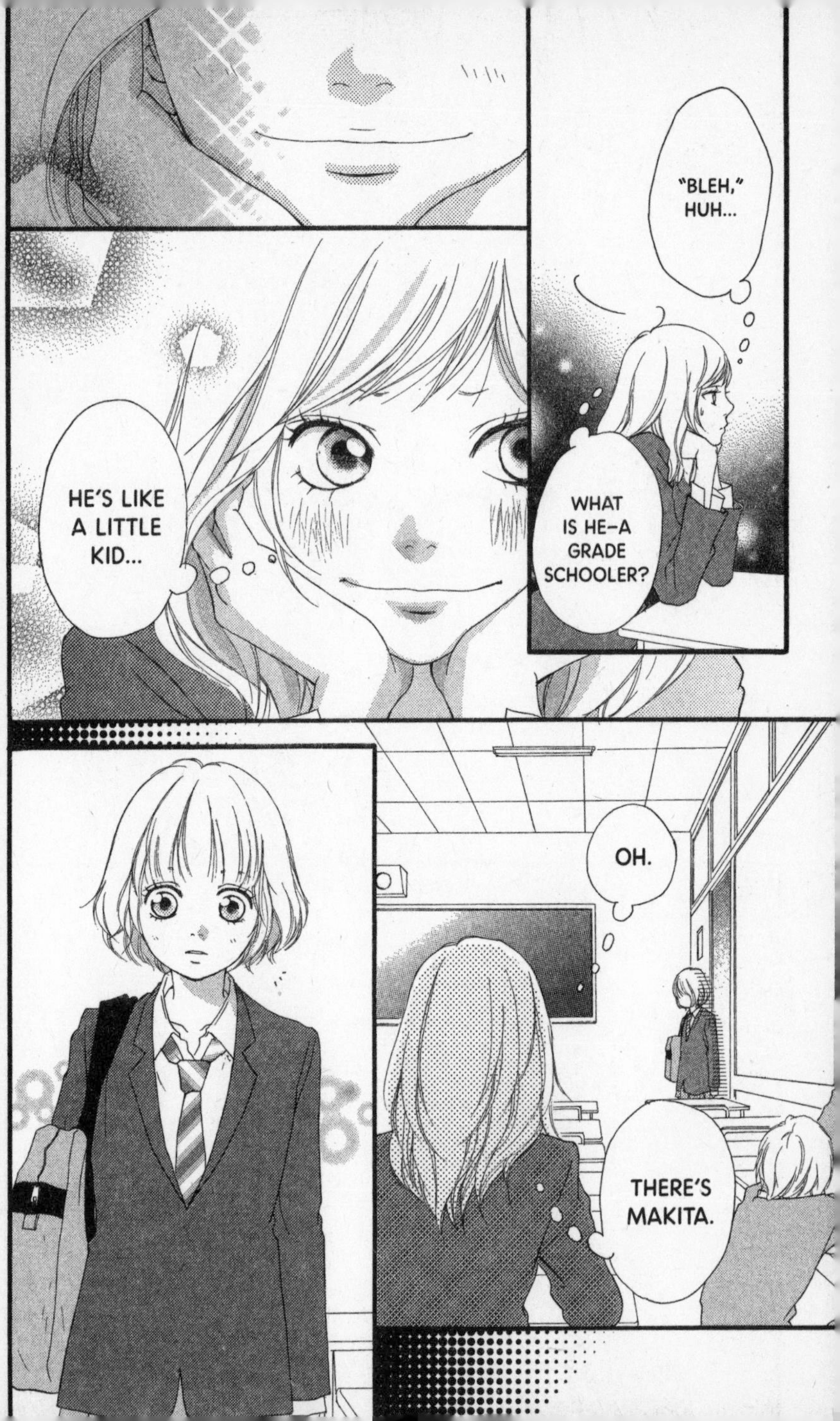
"BLEH," HUH...
WHAT IS HE—A GRADE SCHOOLER?
HE'S LIKE A LITTLE KID...
OH.
THERE'S MAKITA.

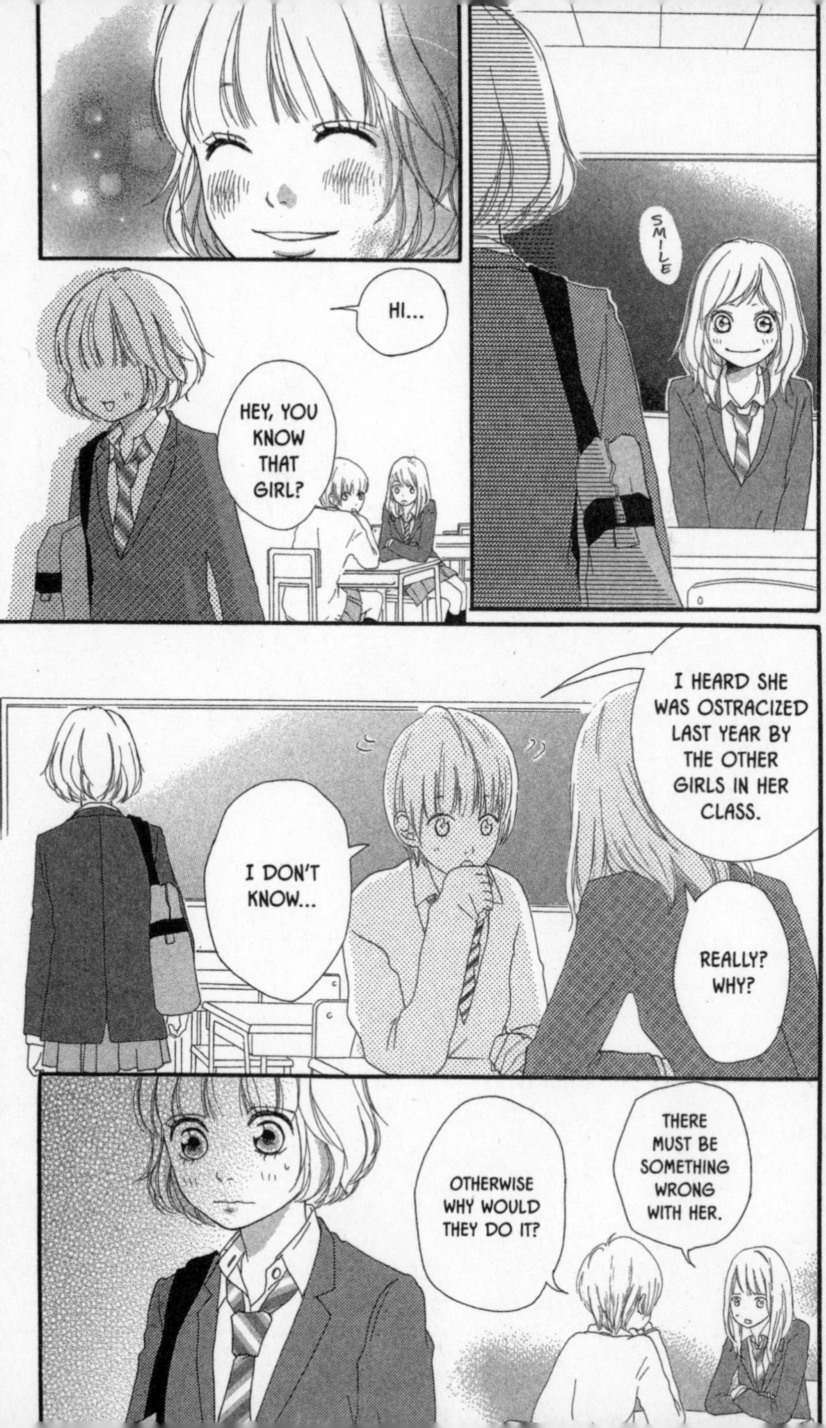
SMILE
HI...
HEY, YOU KNOW THAT GIRL?
I HEARD SHE WAS OSTRACIZED LAST YEAR BY THE OTHER GIRLS IN HER CLASS.
REALLY? WHY?
I DON'T KNOW...
THERE MUST BE SOMETHING WRONG WITH HER.
OTHERWISE WHY WOULD THEY DO IT?

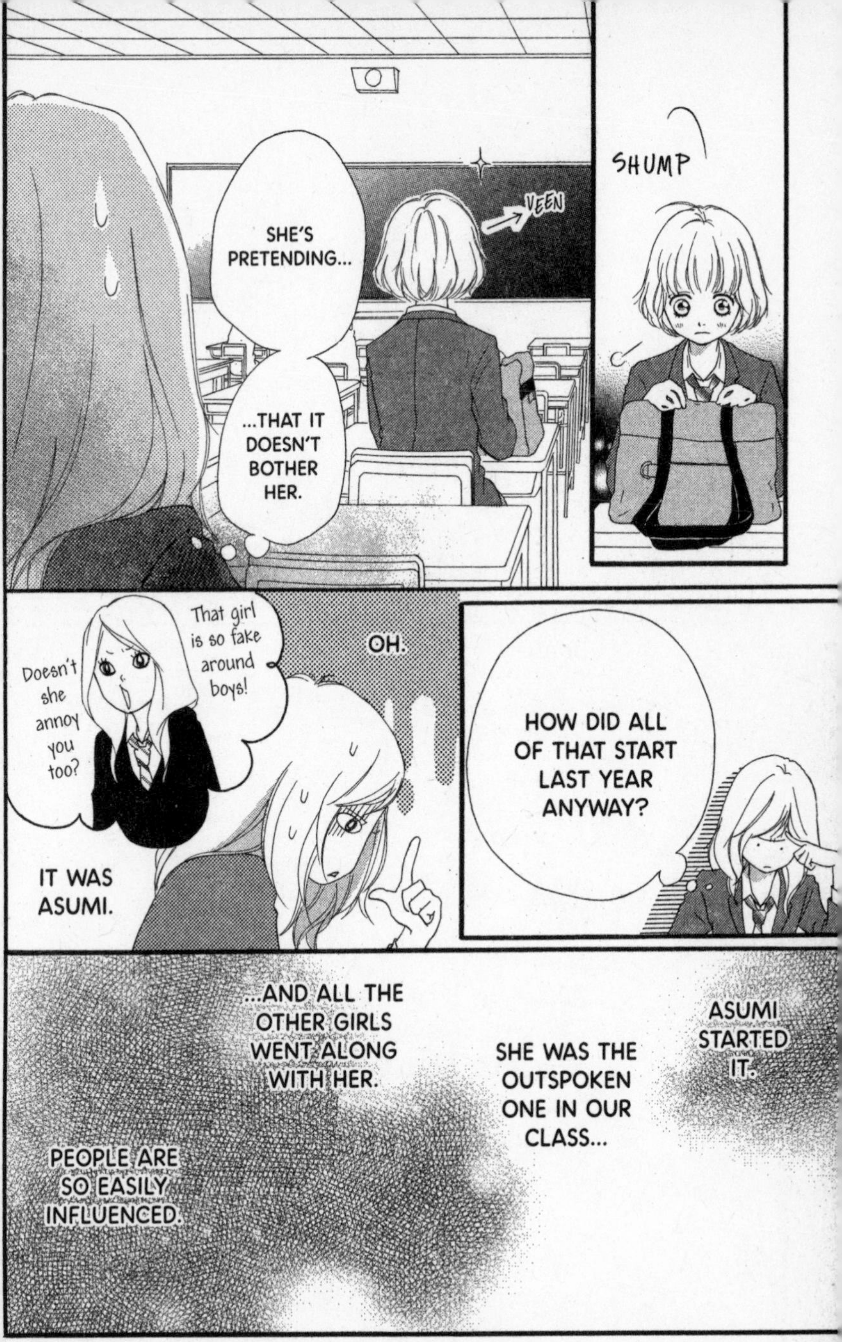
SHUMP
VEEN
SHE'S PRETENDING...
...THAT IT DOESN'T BOTHER HER.
HOW DID ALL OF THAT START LAST YEAR ANYWAY?
OH.
That girl is so fake around boys!
Doesn't she annoy you too?
IT WAS ASUMI.
ASUMI STARTED IT.
SHE WAS THE OUTSPOKEN ONE IN OUR CLASS...
...AND ALL THE OTHER GIRLS WENT ALONG WITH HER.
PEOPLE ARE SO EASILY INFLUENCED.

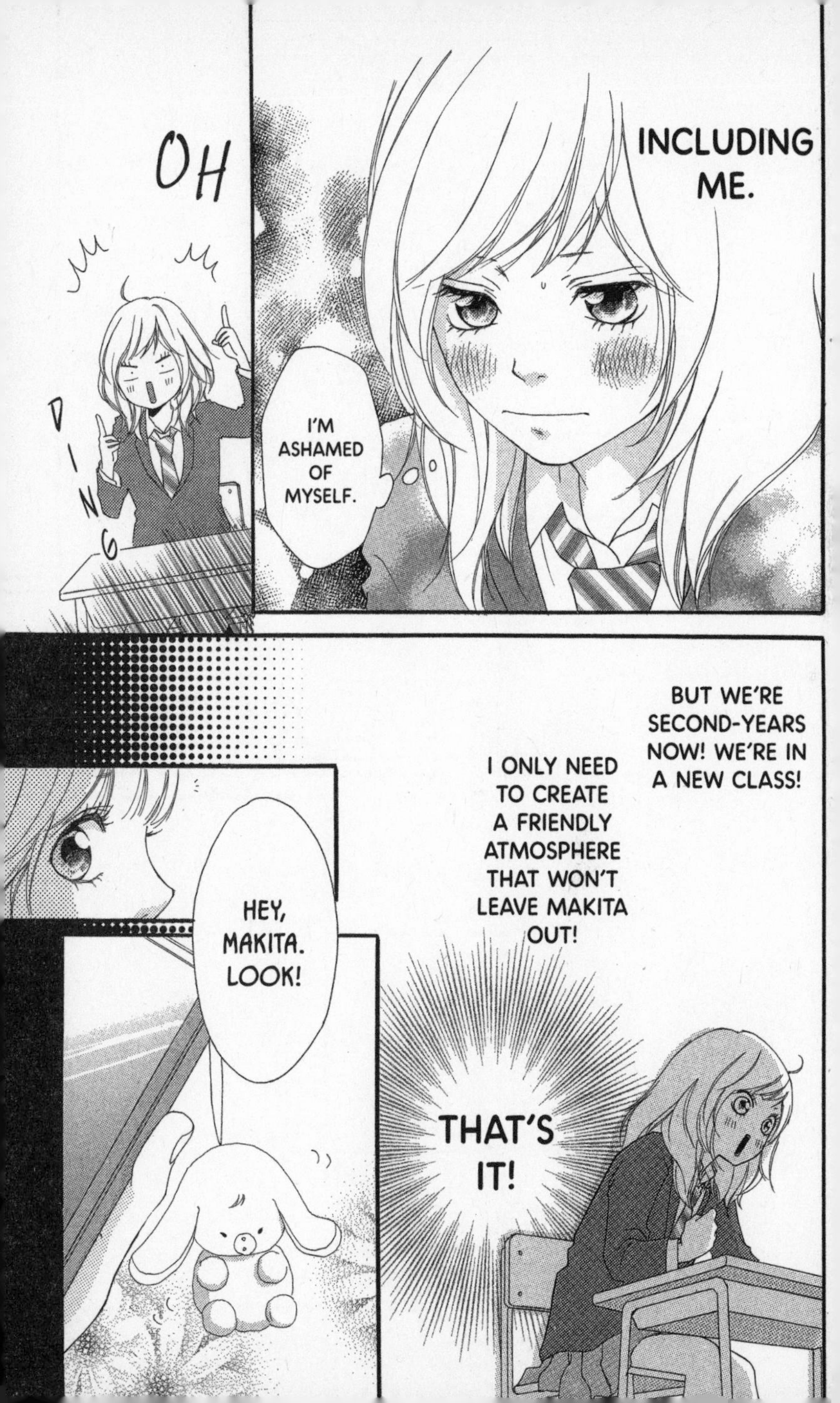
INCLUDING ME.
I'M ASHAMED OF MYSELF.
OH
DING
BUT WE'RE SECOND-YEARS NOW! WE'RE IN A NEW CLASS!
I ONLY NEED TO CREATE A FRIENDLY ATMOSPHERE THAT WON'T LEAVE MAKITA OUT!
THAT'S IT!
HEY, MAKITA. LOOK!

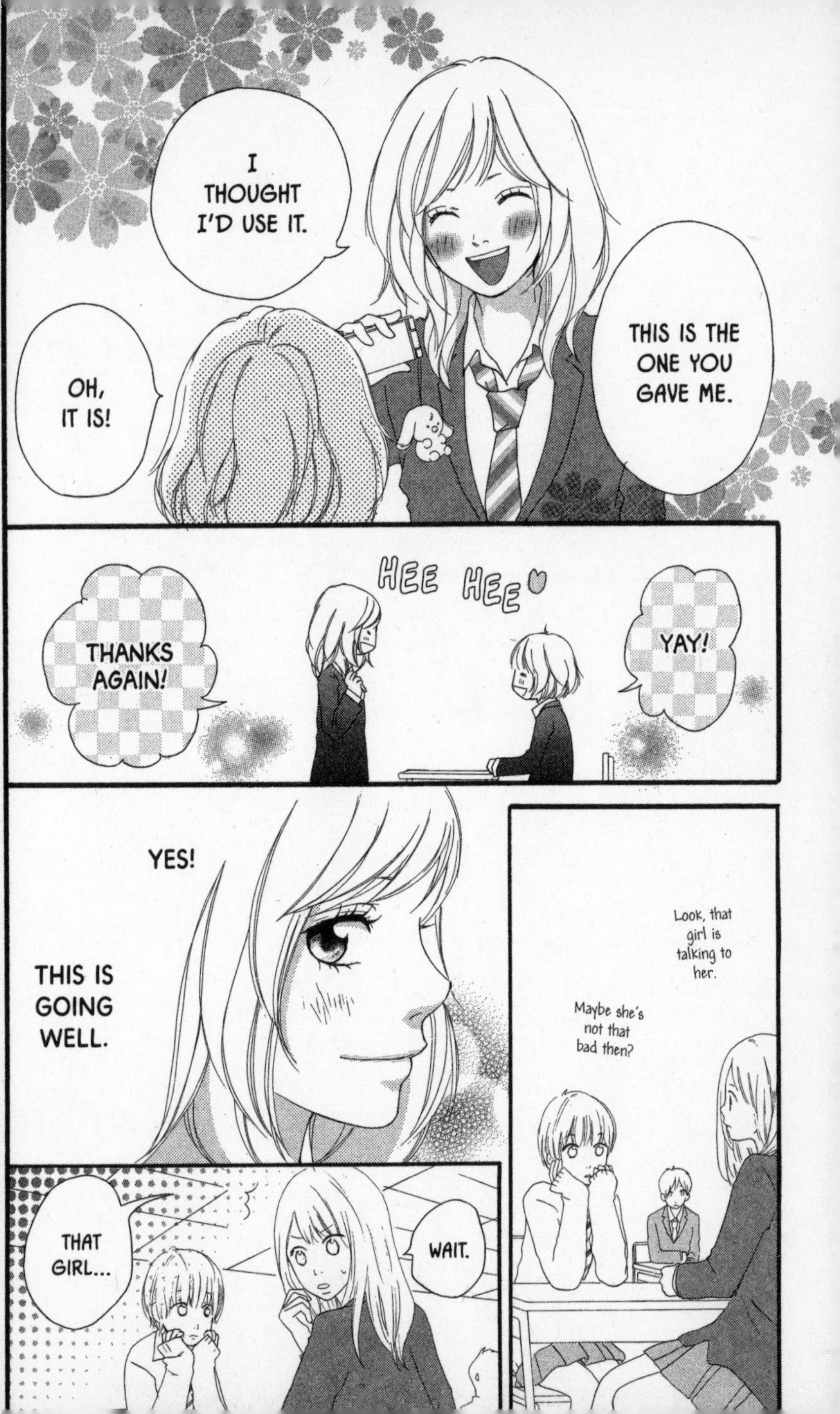
THIS IS THE ONE YOU GAVE ME.
I THOUGHT I'D USE IT.
OH, IT IS!
YAY!
HEE HEE
THANKS AGAIN!
Look, that girl is talking to her.
Maybe she's not that bad then?
YES!
THIS IS GOING WELL.
WAIT.
THAT GIRL...

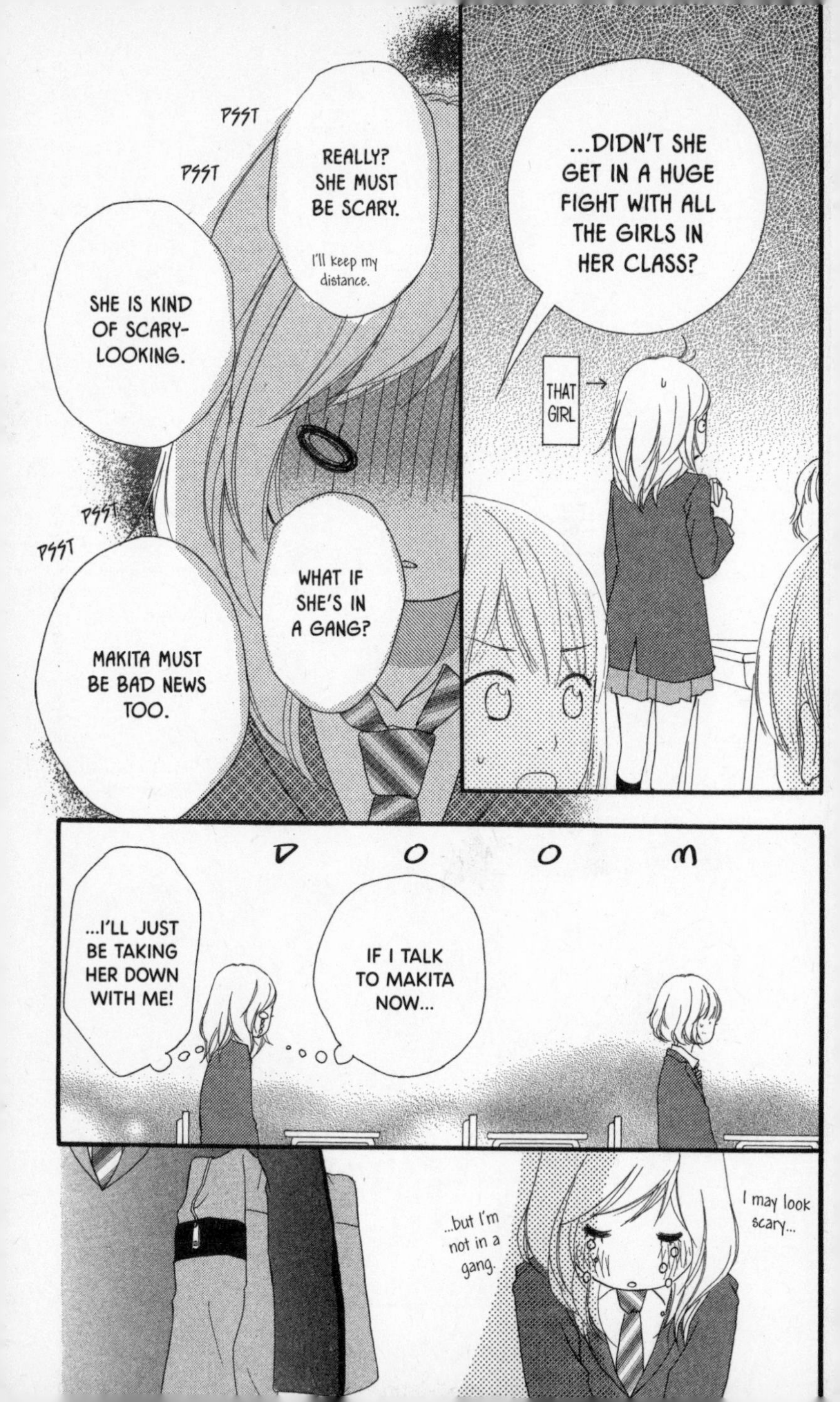
...DIDN'T SHE GET IN A HUGE FIGHT WITH ALL THE GIRLS IN HER CLASS?
THAT GIRL
PSST
PSST
REALLY? SHE MUST BE SCARY.
I'll keep my distance.
SHE IS KIND OF SCARY-LOOKING.
PSST
PSST
WHAT IF SHE'S IN A GANG?
MAKITA MUST BE BAD NEWS TOO.
D O O M
IF I TALK TO MAKITA NOW...
...I'LL JUST BE TAKING HER DOWN WITH ME!
I may look scary...
...but I'm not in a gang.

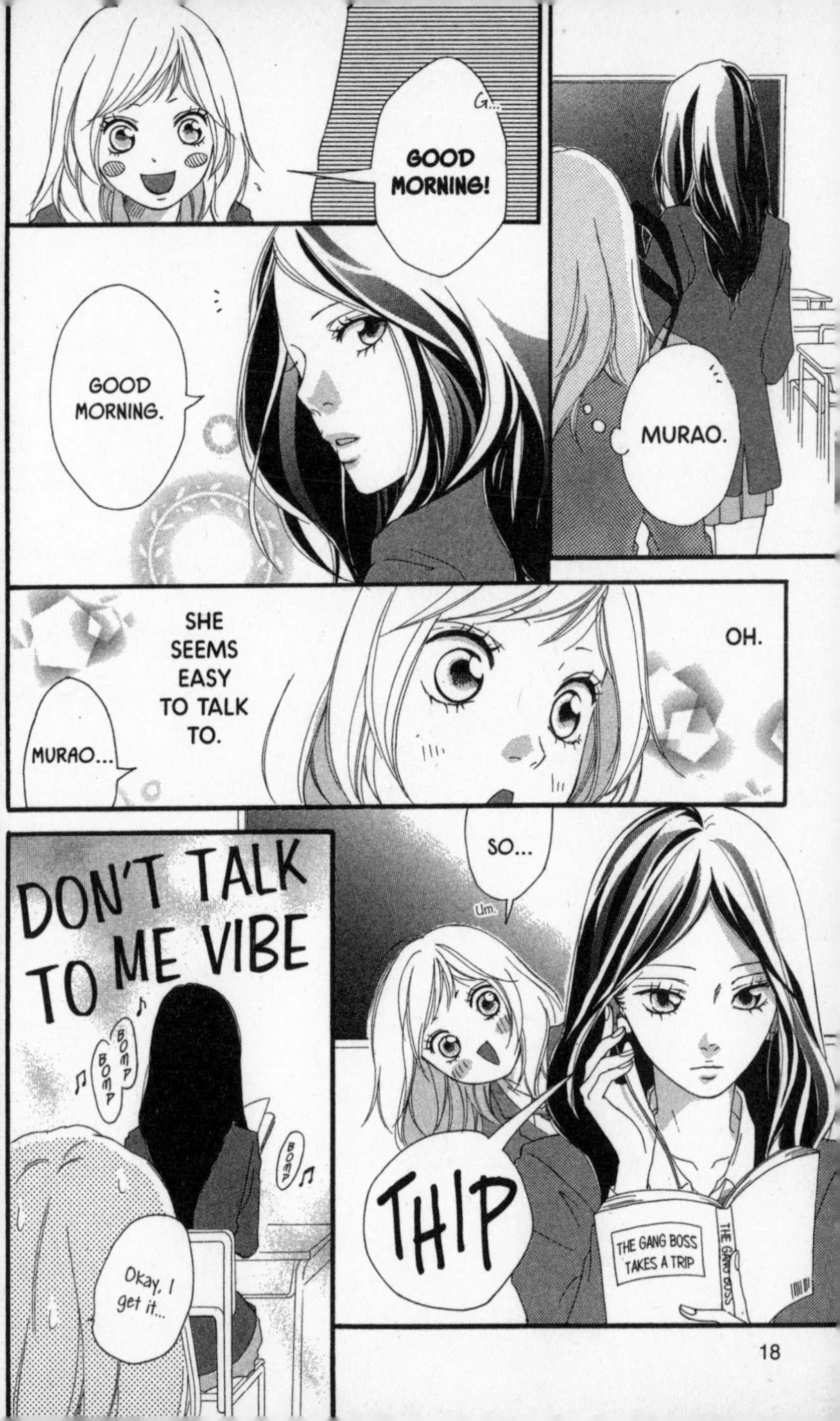
MURAO.
G...
GOOD MORNING!
GOOD MORNING.
OH.
SHE SEEMS EASY TO TALK TO.
MURAO...
SO...
Um.
THE GANG BOSS TAKES A TRIP
THE GANG BOSS
THIP
DON'T TALK TO ME VIBE
BOMP BOMP
BOMP
Okay, I get it...

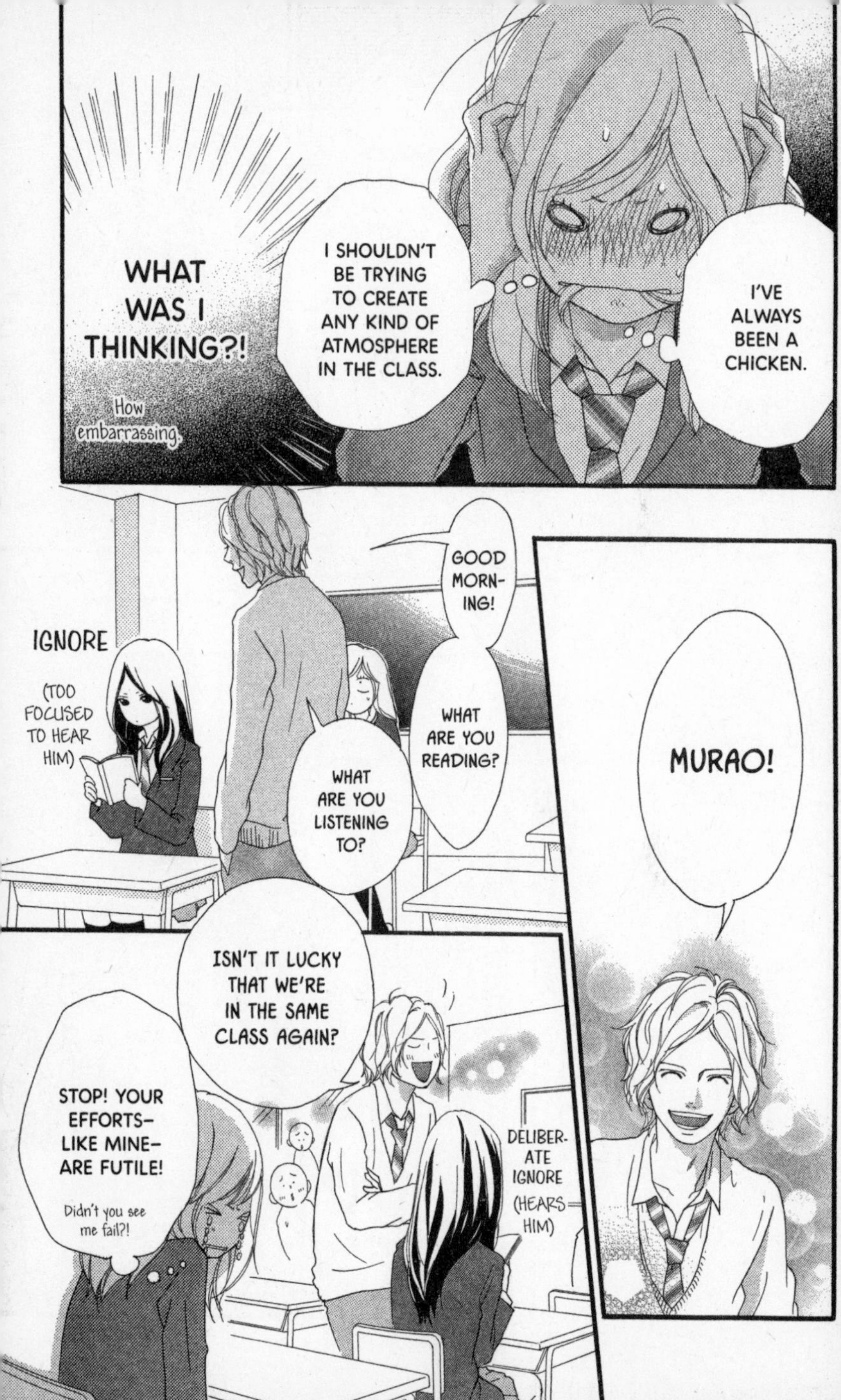
I'VE ALWAYS BEEN A CHICKEN.
I SHOULDN'T BE TRYING TO CREATE ANY KIND OF ATMOSPHERE IN THE CLASS.
WHAT WAS I THINKING?!
How embarrassing.
MURAO!
GOOD MORNING!
WHAT ARE YOU READING?
WHAT ARE YOU LISTENING TO?
IGNORE
(TOO FOCUSED TO HEAR HIM)
ISN'T IT LUCKY THAT WE'RE IN THE SAME CLASS AGAIN?
DELIBERATE IGNORE
(HEARS HIM)
STOP! YOUR EFFORTS—LIKE MINE—ARE FUTILE!
Didn't you see me fail?!

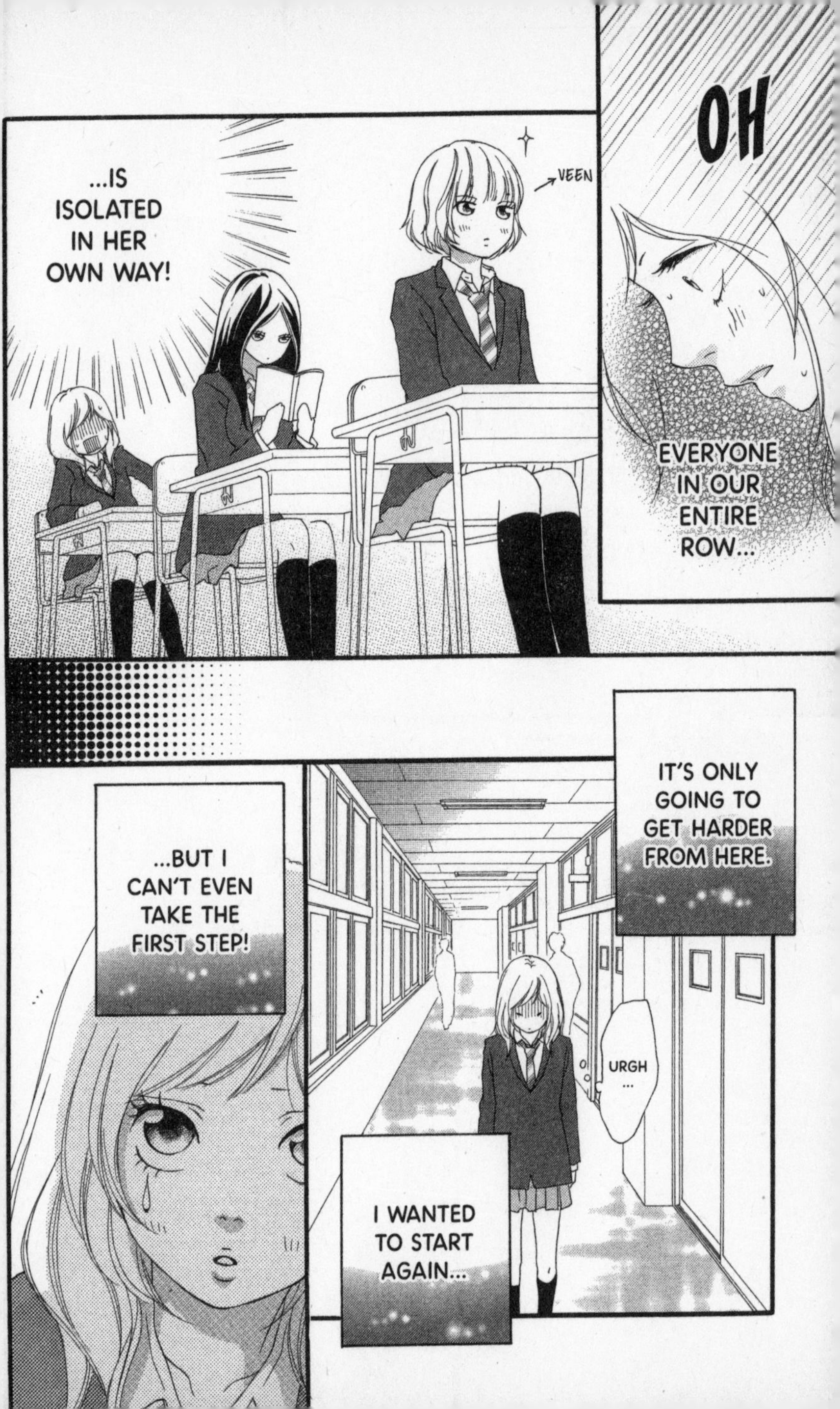
OH
EVERYONE IN OUR ENTIRE ROW...
VEEN
...IS ISOLATED IN HER OWN WAY!
IT'S ONLY GOING TO GET HARDER FROM HERE.
URGH ...
I WANTED TO START AGAIN...
...BUT I CAN'T EVEN TAKE THE FIRST STEP!
...

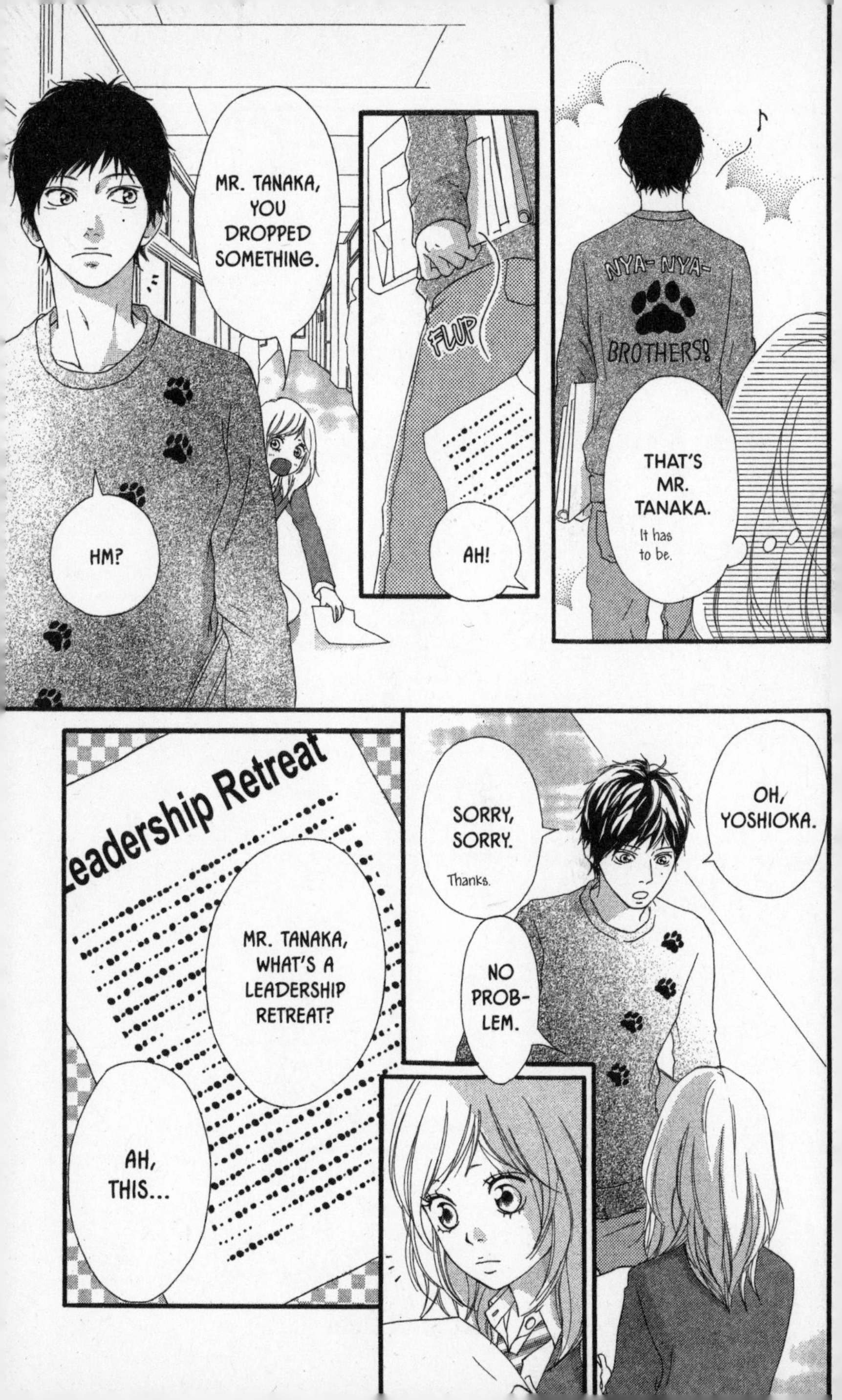
NYA-NYA-
BROTHERS!
THAT'S MR. TANAKA.
It has to be.
FLUP
AH!
MR. TANAKA, YOU DROPPED SOMETHING.
HM?
OH, YOSHIOKA.
SORRY, SORRY.
Thanks.
NO PROB-LEM.
Leadership Retreat
MR. TANAKA, WHAT'S A LEADERSHIP RETREAT?
AH, THIS...

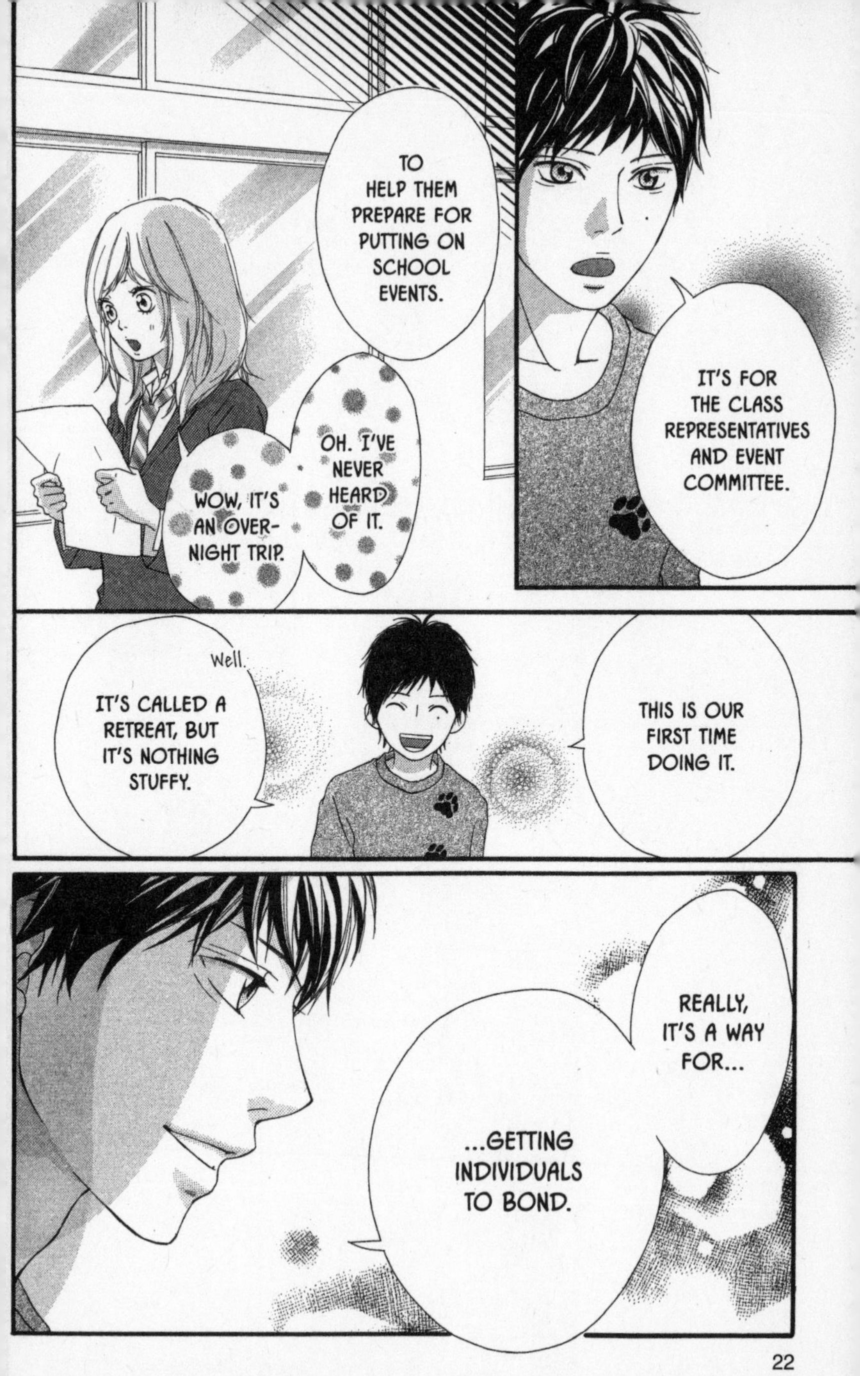
IT'S FOR THE CLASS REPRESENTATIVES AND EVENT COMMITTEE.
TO HELP THEM PREPARE FOR PUTTING ON SCHOOL EVENTS.
OH. I'VE NEVER HEARD OF IT.
WOW, IT'S AN OVER-NIGHT TRIP.
THIS IS OUR FIRST TIME DOING IT.
Well.
IT'S CALLED A RETREAT, BUT IT'S NOTHING STUFFY.
REALLY, IT'S A WAY FOR...
...GETTING INDIVIDUALS TO BOND.

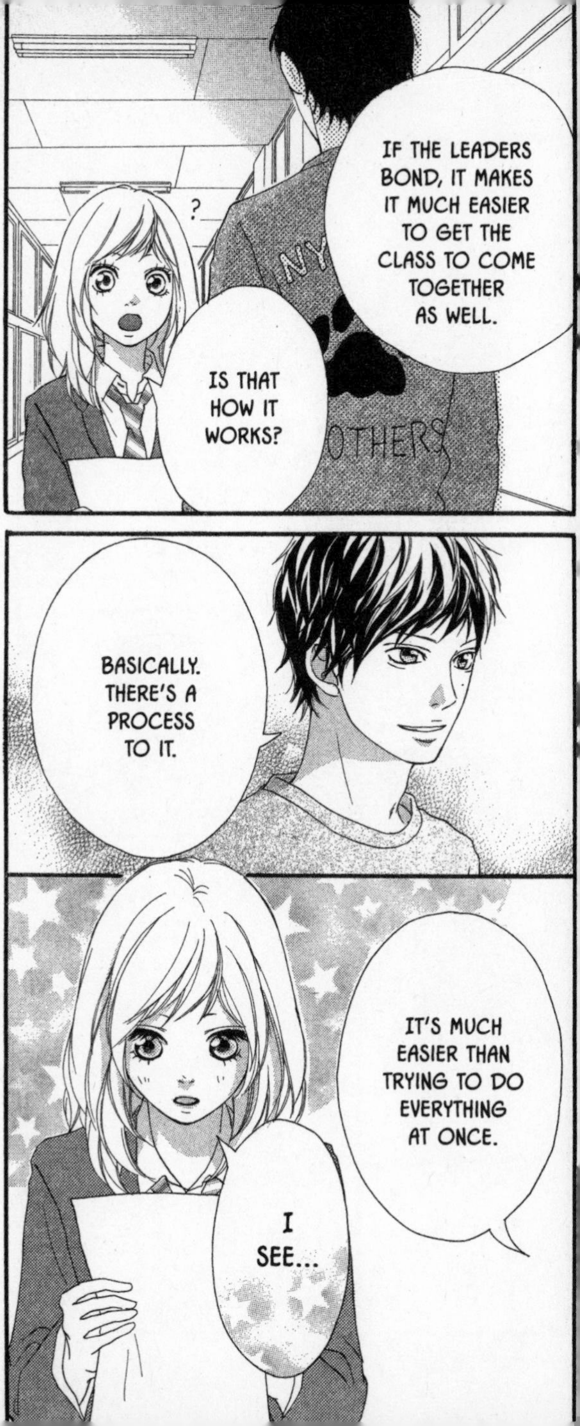
IF THE LEADERS BOND, IT MAKES IT MUCH EASIER TO GET THE CLASS TO COME TOGETHER AS WELL.
?
IS THAT HOW IT WORKS?
BASICALLY. THERE'S A PROCESS TO IT.
IT'S MUCH EASIER THAN TRYING TO DO EVERYTHING AT ONCE.
I SEE...

My Love Life

- When I was a first-year in high school, I had a crush on an older guy. I got one of his friends (a girl) to help me out, but it turned out that she'd been going out with him all along. Huhhhh?!
- A bunch of us went to a fireworks festival, and the guy and I were hitting it off. He said, "Let's watch closer up," and I agreed. We both took a step forward. It was dark, so we couldn't really see. There was a dirty river in front of us, and...SPLASH! We fell in up to our waists. Huhhhh?!
- An ex-boyfriend (we're friends now) called me after we hadn't seen each other for a while. He said he'd gained weight, and I asked him to send me a photo. He sent it. And I saw it. Huhhhh?!
- My friend stole my boyfriend. Huhhhh?!

I pulled together my not-so-pleasant stories. Thoughts?

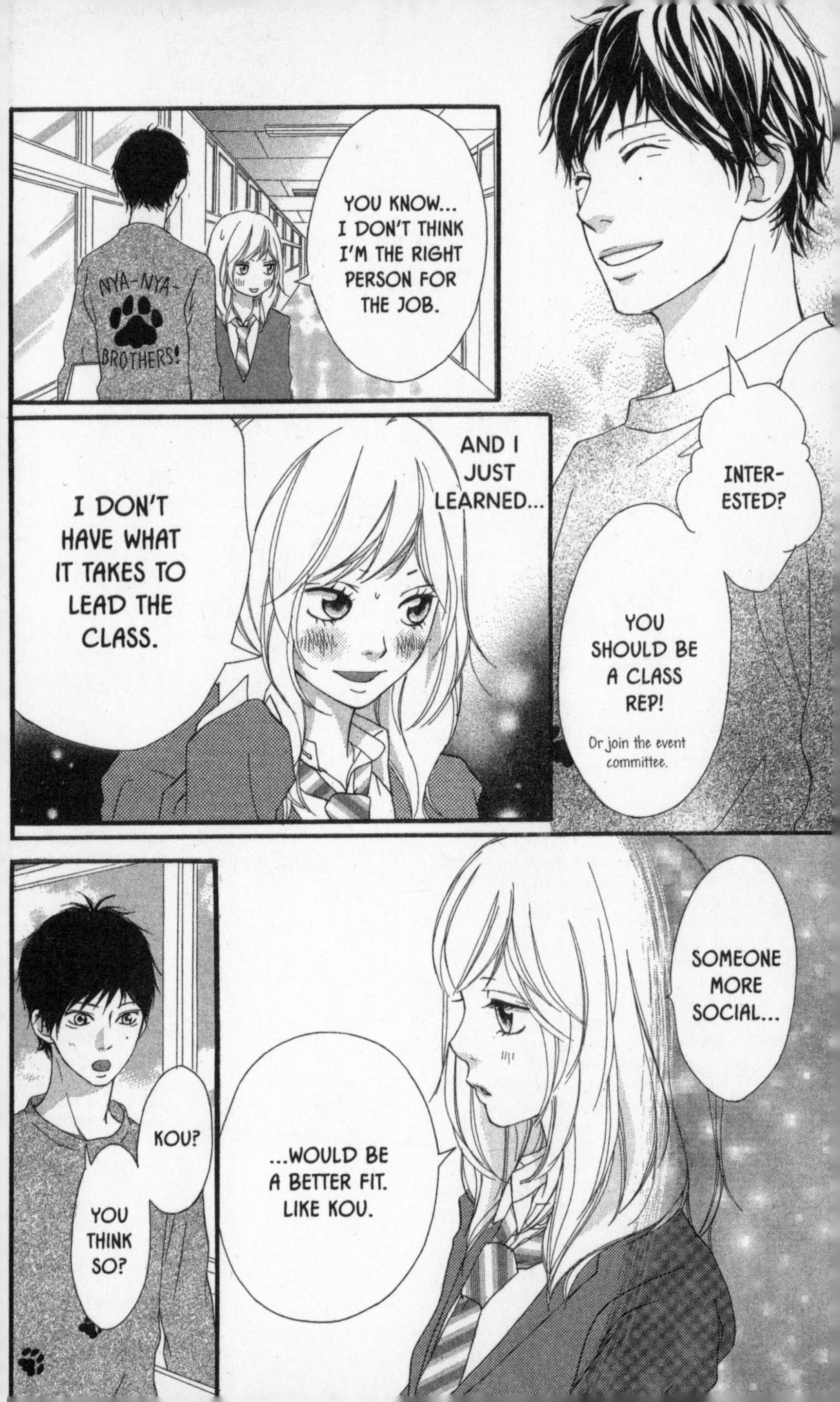
INTER-ESTED?
YOU SHOULD BE A CLASS REP!
Or join the event committee.
YOU KNOW... I DON'T THINK I'M THE RIGHT PERSON FOR THE JOB.
NYA-NYA-BROTHERS!
AND I JUST LEARNED...
I DON'T HAVE WHAT IT TAKES TO LEAD THE CLASS.
SOMEONE MORE SOCIAL...
...WOULD BE A BETTER FIT. LIKE KOU.
KOU?
YOU THINK SO?

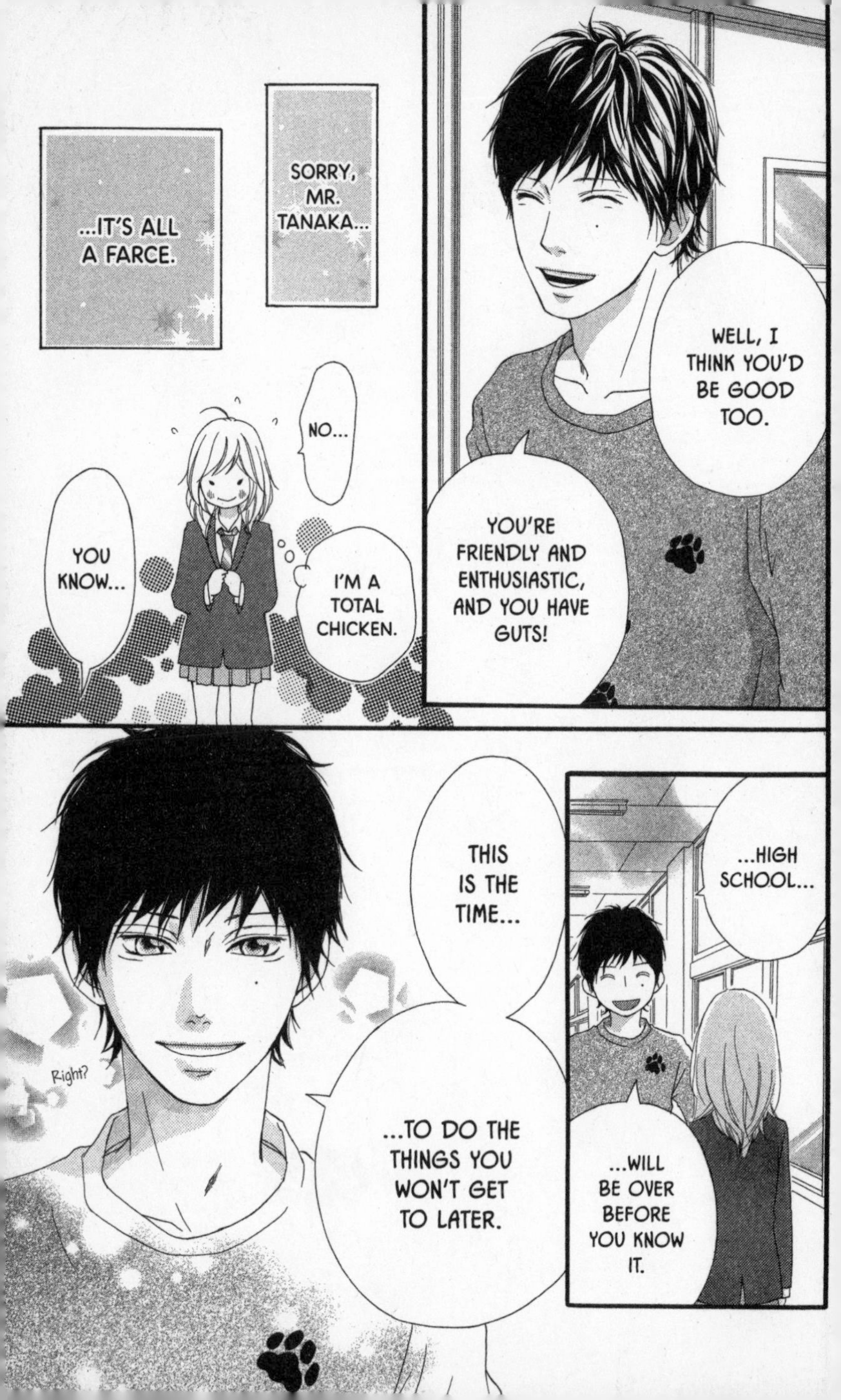

WELL, I THINK YOU'D BE GOOD TOO.
YOU'RE FRIENDLY AND ENTHUSIASTIC, AND YOU HAVE GUTS!
SORRY, MR. TANAKA...
...IT'S ALL A FARCE.
NO...
I'M A TOTAL CHICKEN.
YOU KNOW...
...HIGH SCHOOL...
...WILL BE OVER BEFORE YOU KNOW IT.
THIS IS THE TIME...
...TO DO THE THINGS YOU WON'T GET TO LATER.
Right?

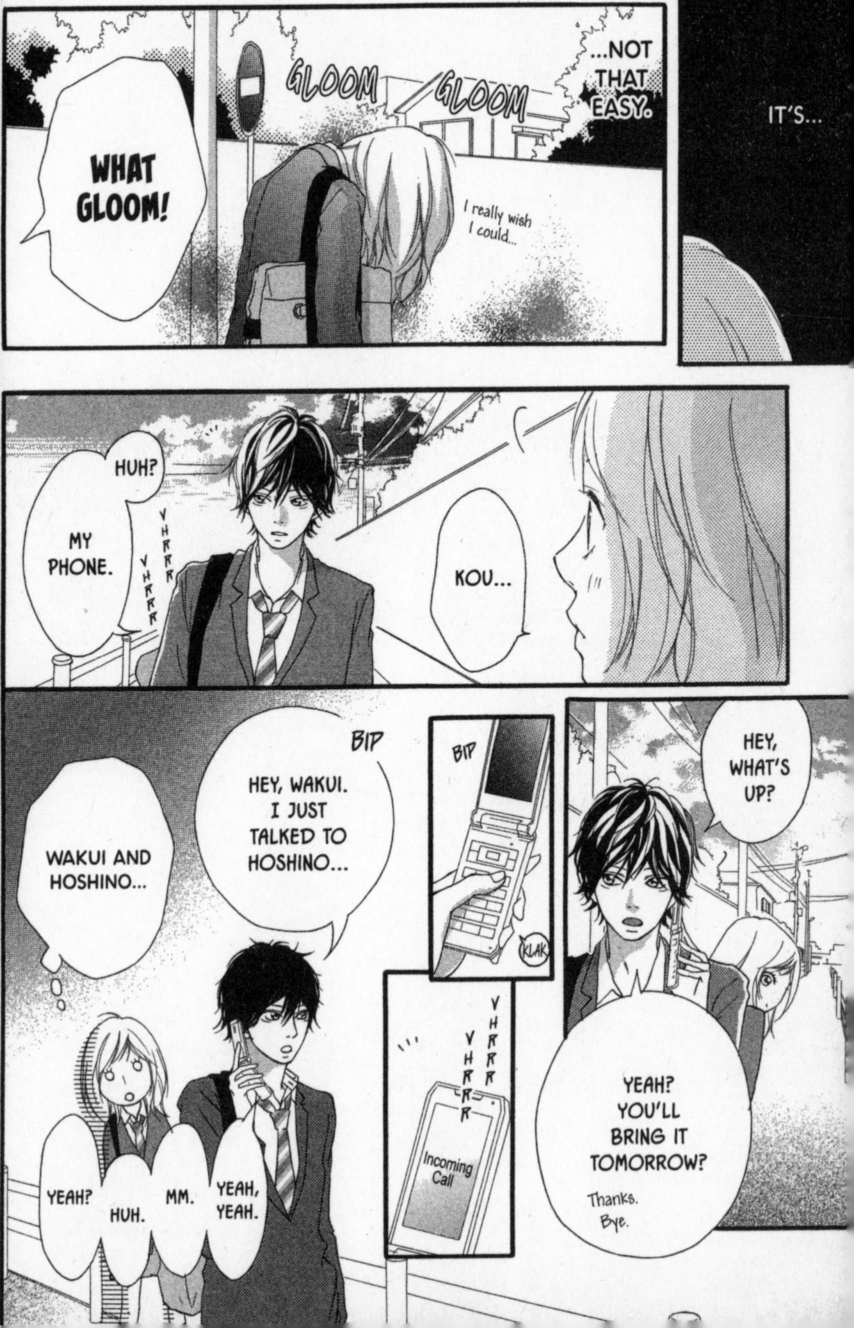
IT'S...
...NOT THAT EASY.
GLOOM
GLOOM
I really wish I could...
WHAT GLOOM!
KOU...
HUH?
VHRRR
VHRRR
MY PHONE.
HEY, WHAT'S UP?
YEAH? YOU'LL BRING IT TOMORROW?
Thanks. Bye.
BIP
KLAK
VHRRR
VHRRR
Incoming Call
BIP
HEY, WAKUI. I JUST TALKED TO HOSHINO...
WAKUI AND HOSHINO...
YEAH, YEAH.
MM.
HUH.
YEAH?

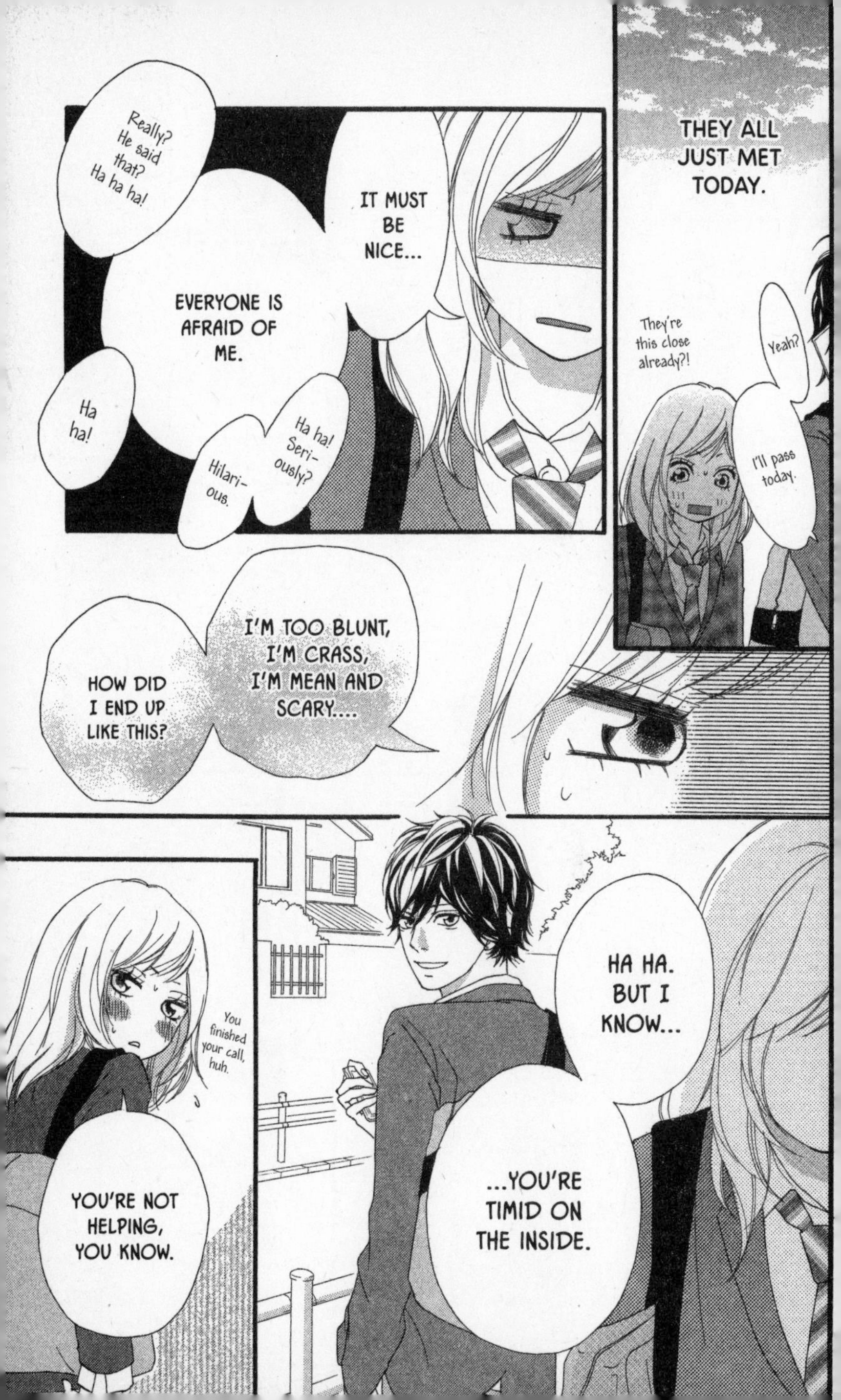
THEY ALL JUST MET TODAY.
Yeah?
They're this close already?!
I'll pass today.
IT MUST BE NICE...
Really? He said that? Ha ha ha!
EVERYONE IS AFRAID OF ME.
Ha ha! Seri-ously?
Hilari-ous.
Ha ha!
I'M TOO BLUNT, I'M CRASS, I'M MEAN AND SCARY....
HOW DID I END UP LIKE THIS?
HA HA. BUT I KNOW...
...YOU'RE TIMID ON THE INSIDE.
You finished your call, huh.
YOU'RE NOT HELPING, YOU KNOW.

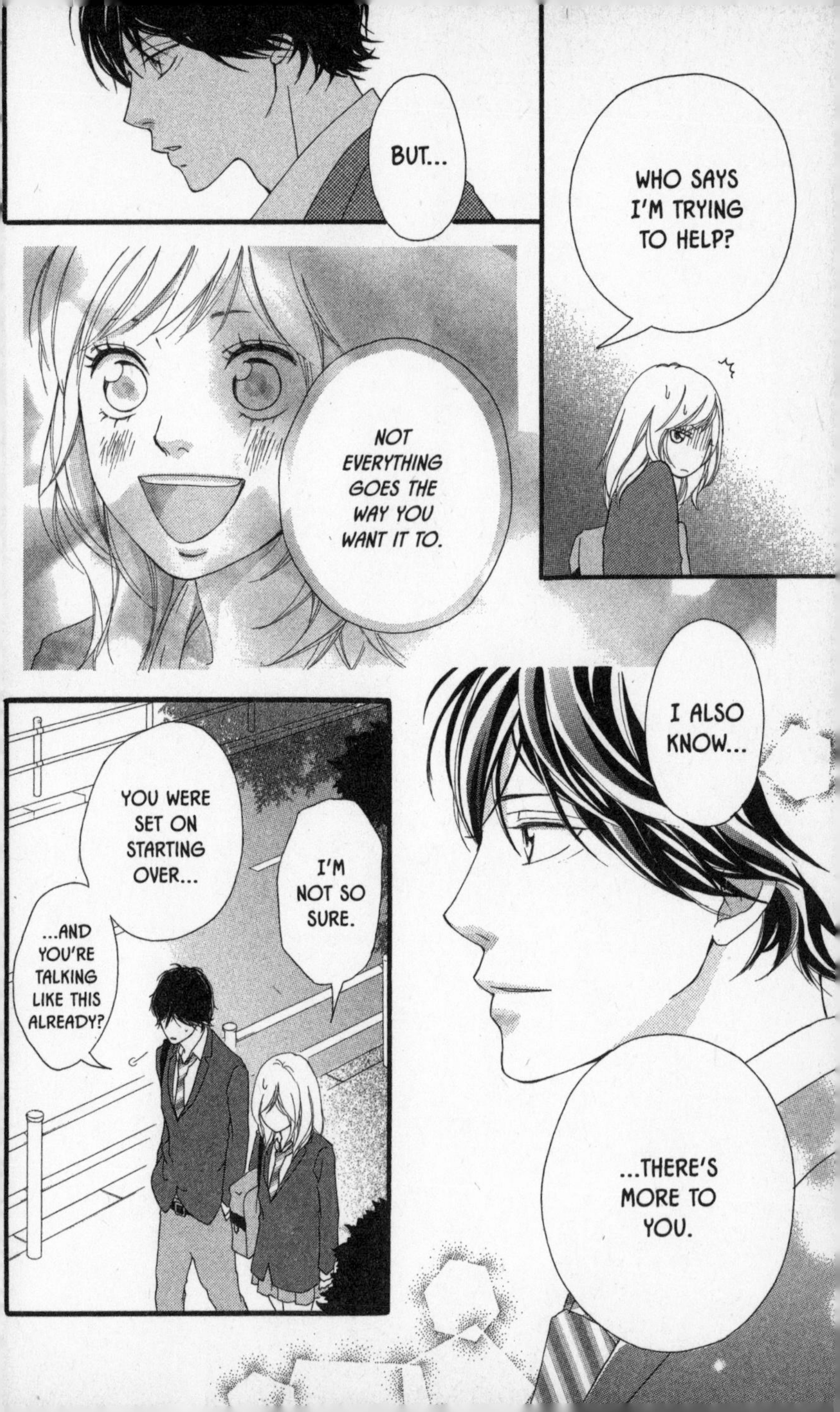
WHO SAYS I'M TRYING TO HELP?
BUT...
NOT EVERYTHING GOES THE WAY YOU WANT IT TO.
I ALSO KNOW...
...THERE'S MORE TO YOU.
YOU WERE SET ON STARTING OVER...
...AND YOU'RE TALKING LIKE THIS ALREADY?
I'M NOT SO SURE.

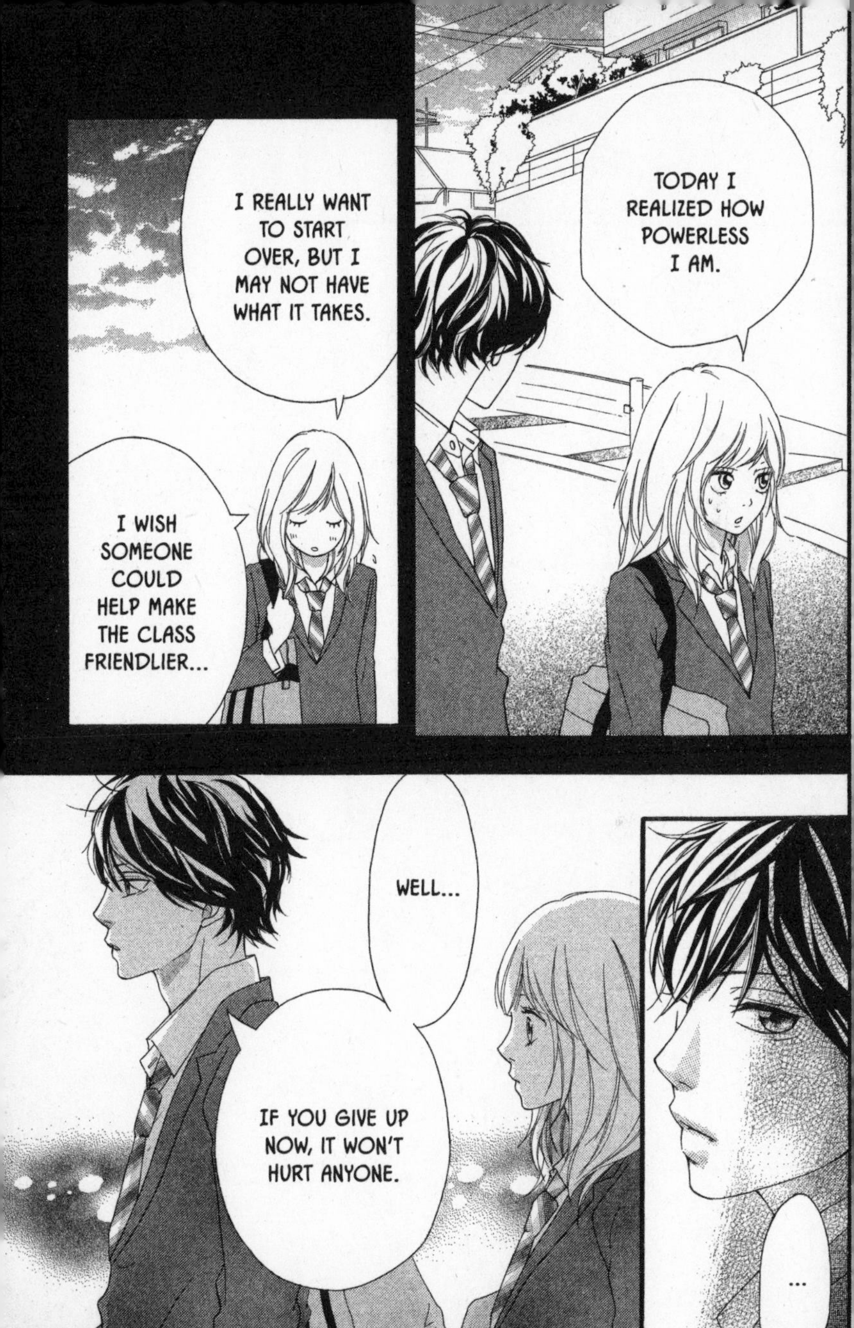
TODAY I REALIZED HOW POWERLESS I AM.
I REALLY WANT TO START OVER, BUT I MAY NOT HAVE WHAT IT TAKES.
I WISH SOMEONE COULD HELP MAKE THE CLASS FRIENDLIER...
WELL...
IF YOU GIVE UP NOW, IT WON'T HURT ANYONE.
...

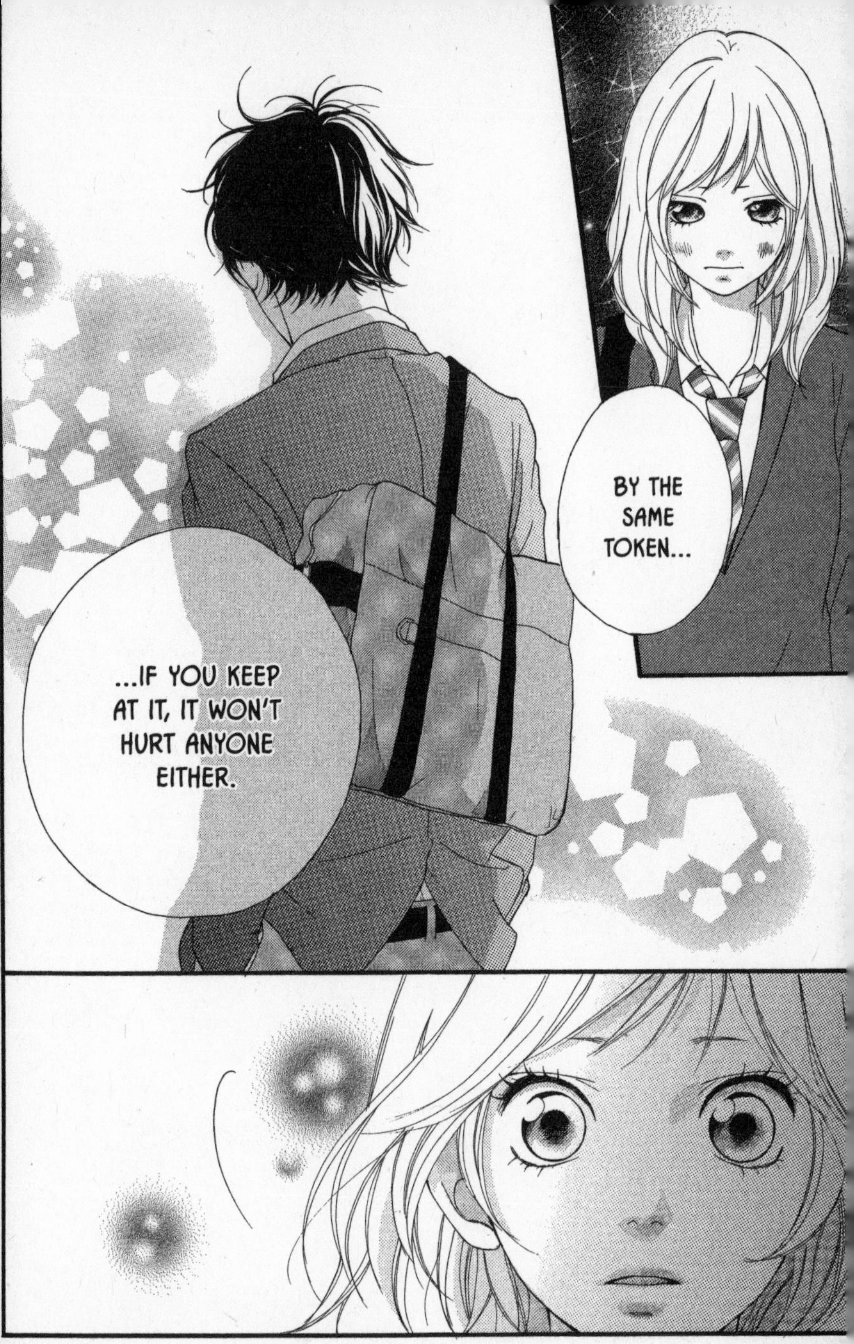
BY THE SAME TOKEN...
...IF YOU KEEP AT IT, IT WON'T HURT ANYONE EITHER.

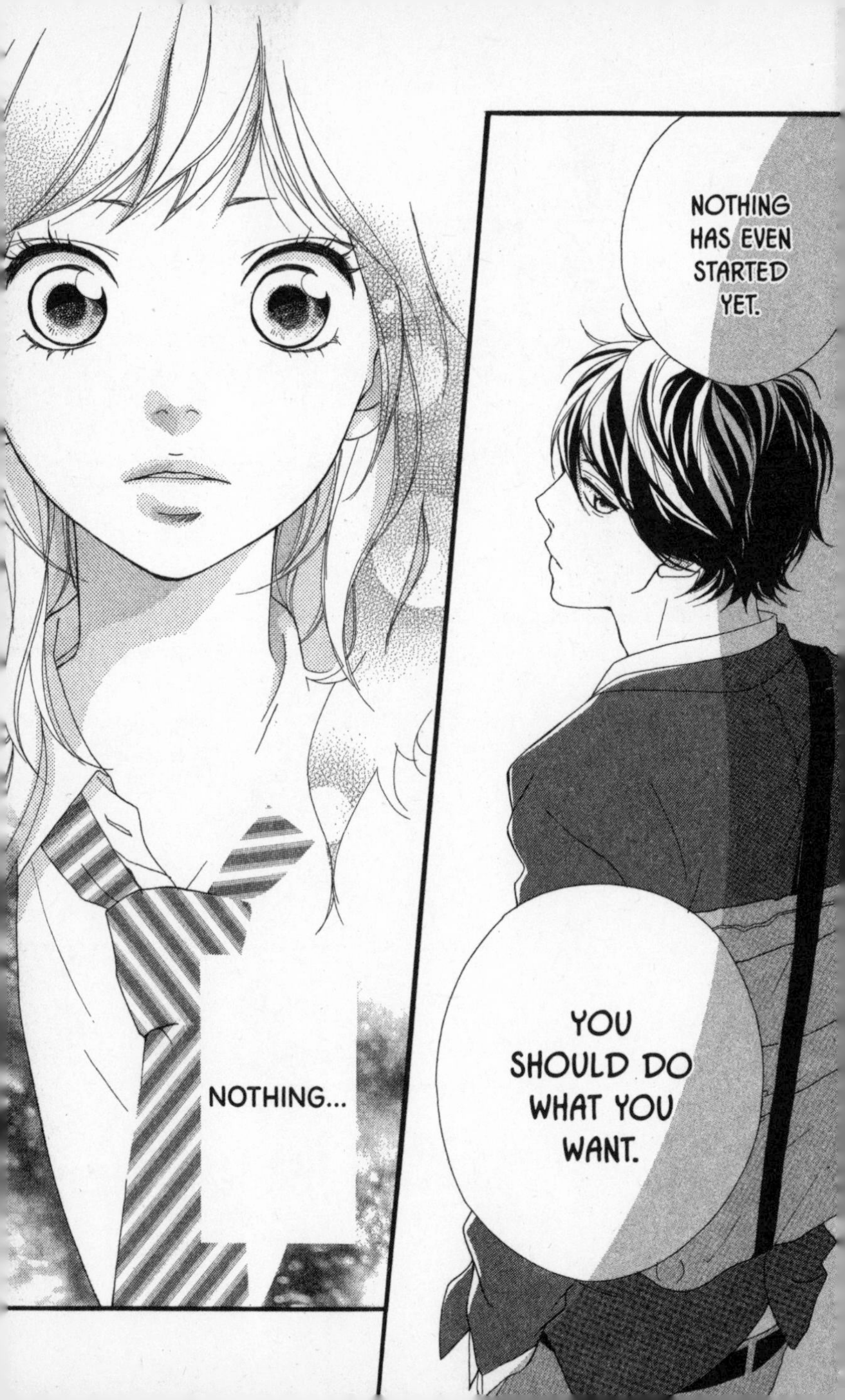
NOTHING HAS EVEN STARTED YET.
YOU SHOULD DO WHAT YOU WANT.
NOTHING...

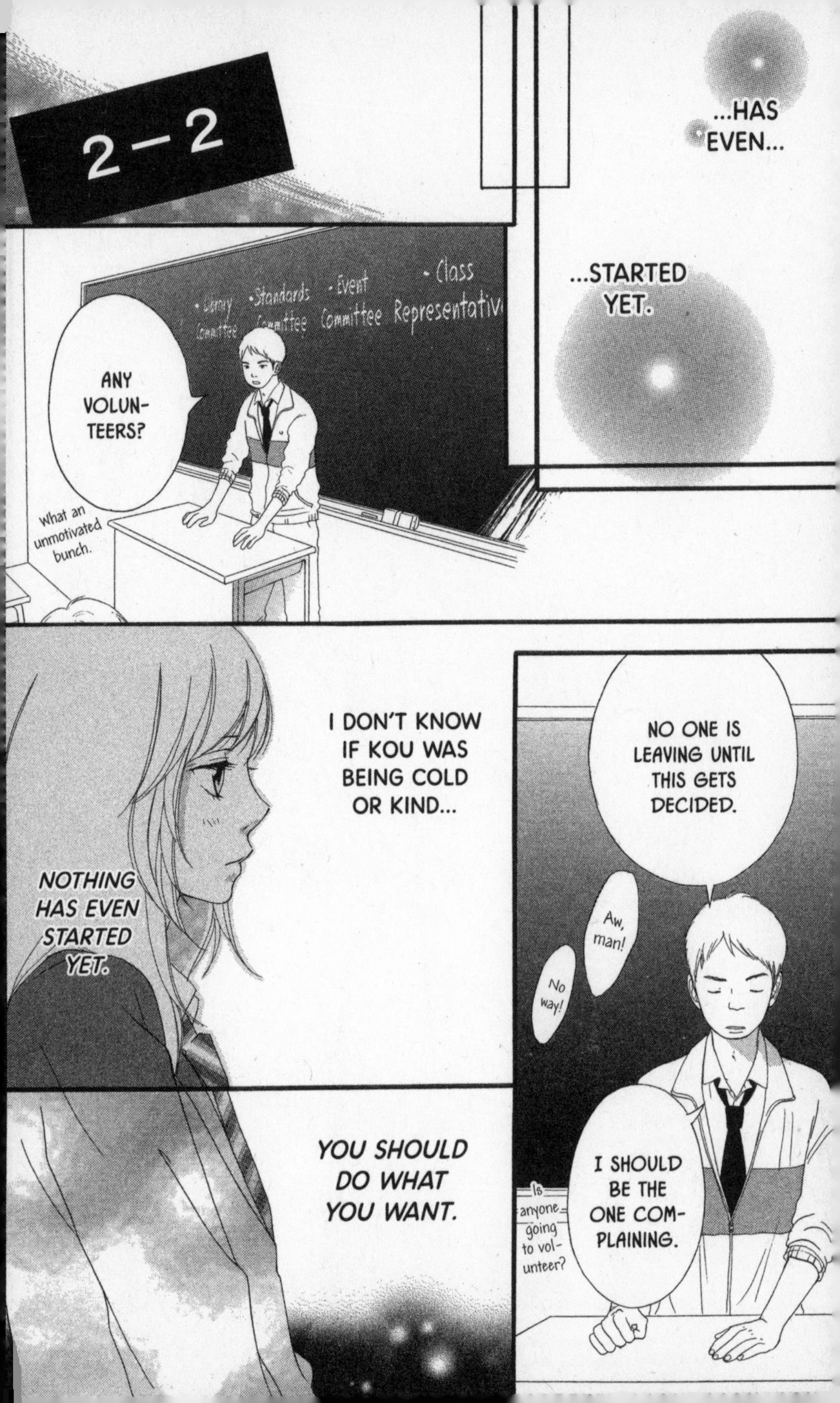
...HAS EVEN...
...STARTED YET.
2-2
Standards
Event Committee
Class
ANY VOLUNTEERS?
What an unmotivated bunch.
NO ONE IS LEAVING UNTIL THIS GETS DECIDED.
Aw, man!
No way!
I SHOULD BE THE ONE COMPLAINING.
Is anyone going to volunteer?
I DON'T KNOW IF KOU WAS BEING COLD OR KIND...
NOTHING HAS EVEN STARTED YET.
YOU SHOULD DO WHAT YOU WANT.

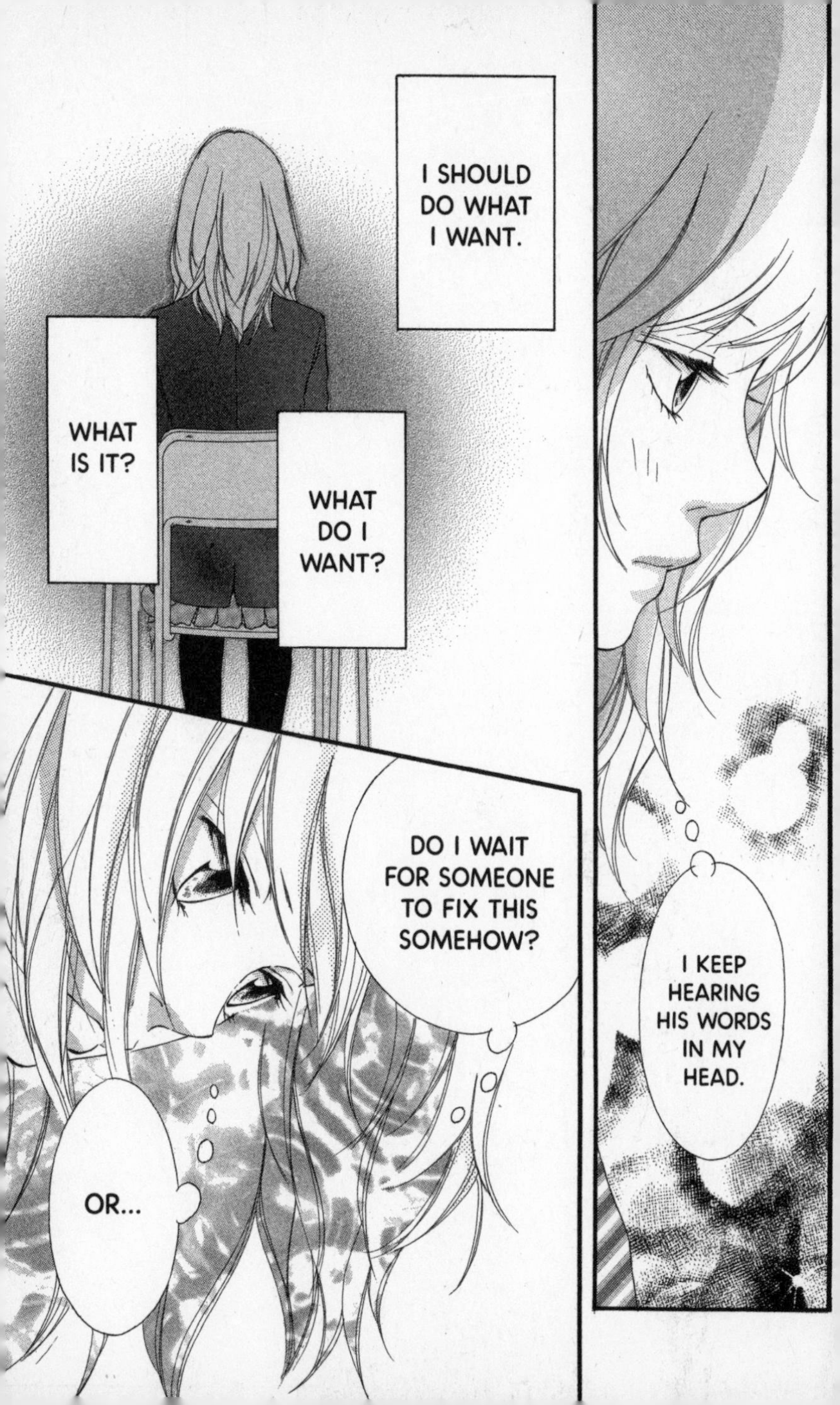
I KEEP HEARING HIS WORDS IN MY HEAD.
I SHOULD DO WHAT I WANT.
WHAT DO I WANT?
WHAT IS IT?
DO I WAIT FOR SOMEONE TO FIX THIS SOMEHOW?
OR...

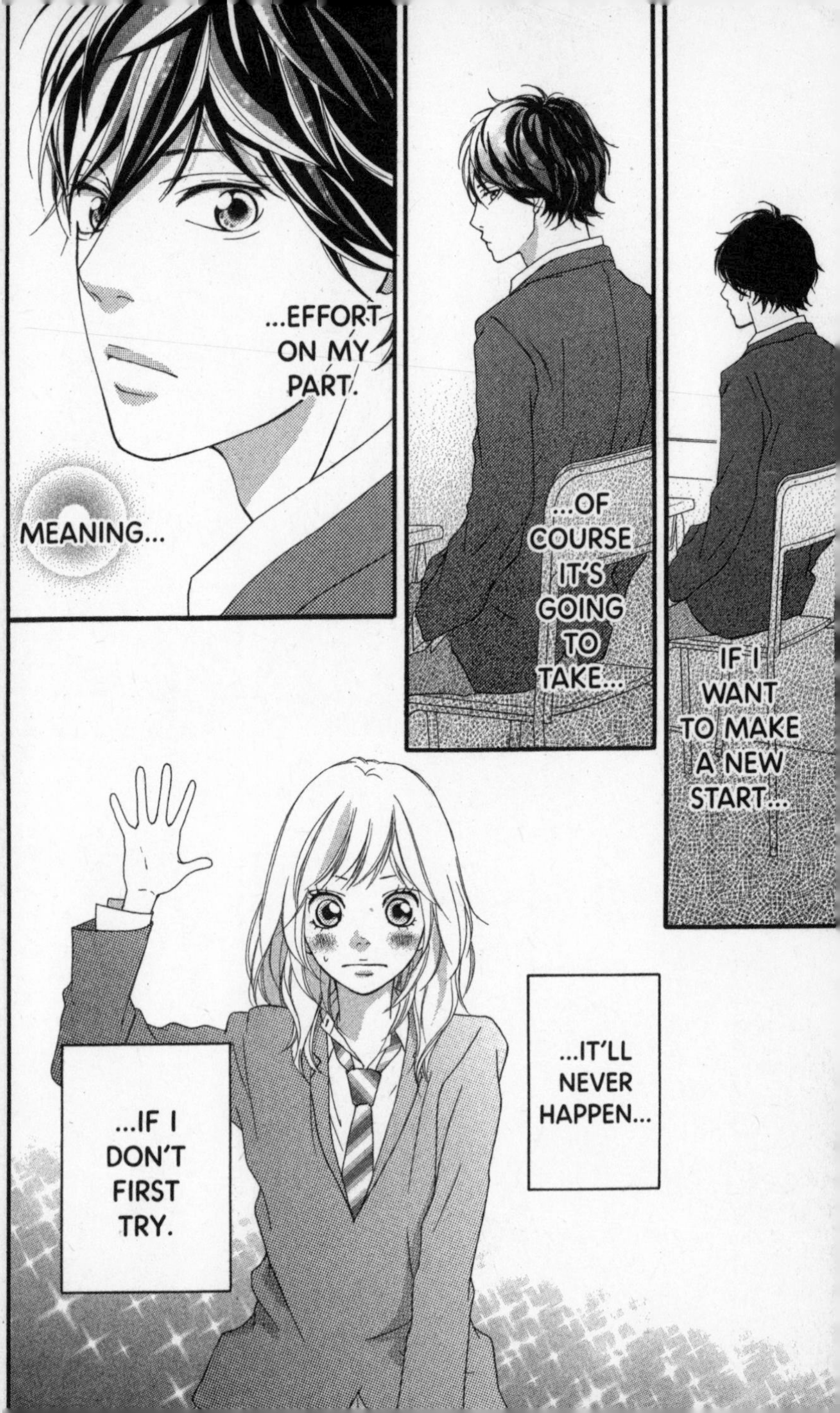
IF I WANT TO MAKE A NEW START...
...OF COURSE IT'S GOING TO TAKE...
...EFFORT ON MY PART.
MEANING...
...IT'LL NEVER HAPPEN...
...IF I DON'T FIRST TRY.

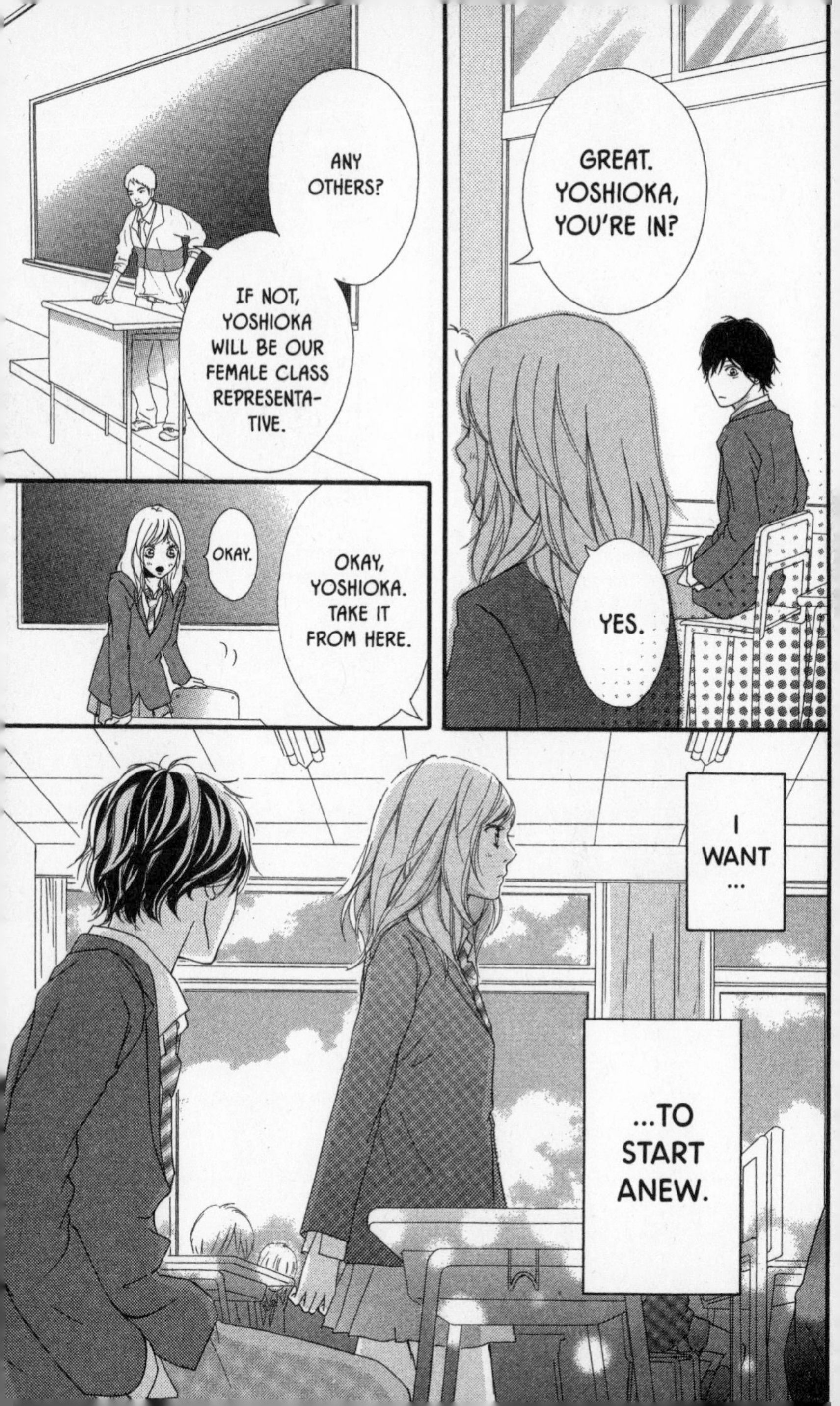
GREAT. YOSHIOKA, YOU'RE IN?
YES.
ANY OTHERS?
IF NOT, YOSHIOKA WILL BE OUR FEMALE CLASS REPRESENTA-TIVE.
OKAY, YOSHIOKA. TAKE IT FROM HERE.
OKAY.
I WANT...
...TO START ANEW.

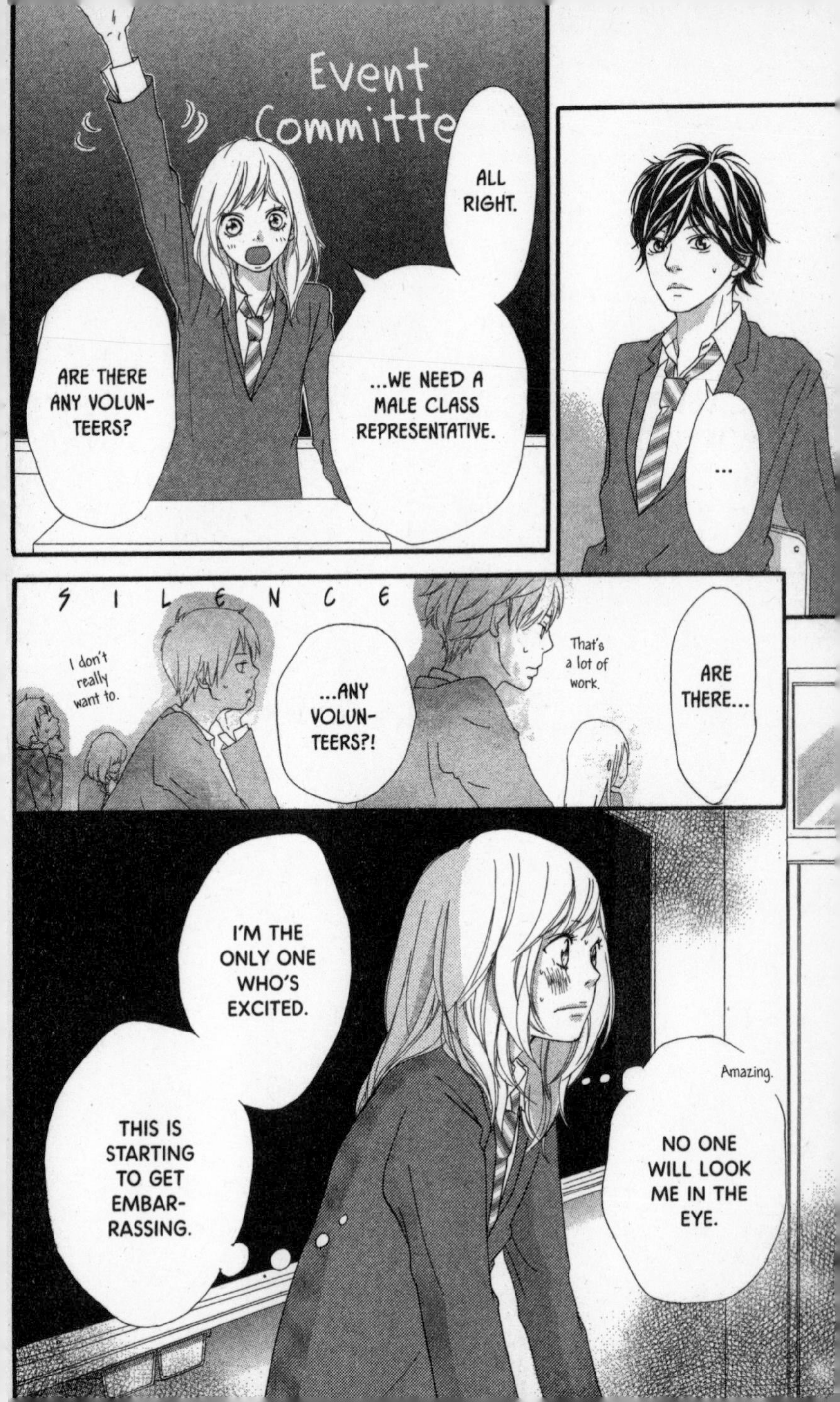
...
ALL RIGHT.
Event Committe
...WE NEED A MALE CLASS REPRESENTATIVE.
ARE THERE ANY VOLUNTEERS?
ARE THERE...
That's a lot of work.
...ANY VOLUNTEERS?!
SILENCE
I don't really want to.
Amazing.
NO ONE WILL LOOK ME IN THE EYE.
I'M THE ONLY ONE WHO'S EXCITED.
THIS IS STARTING TO GET EMBARRASSING.

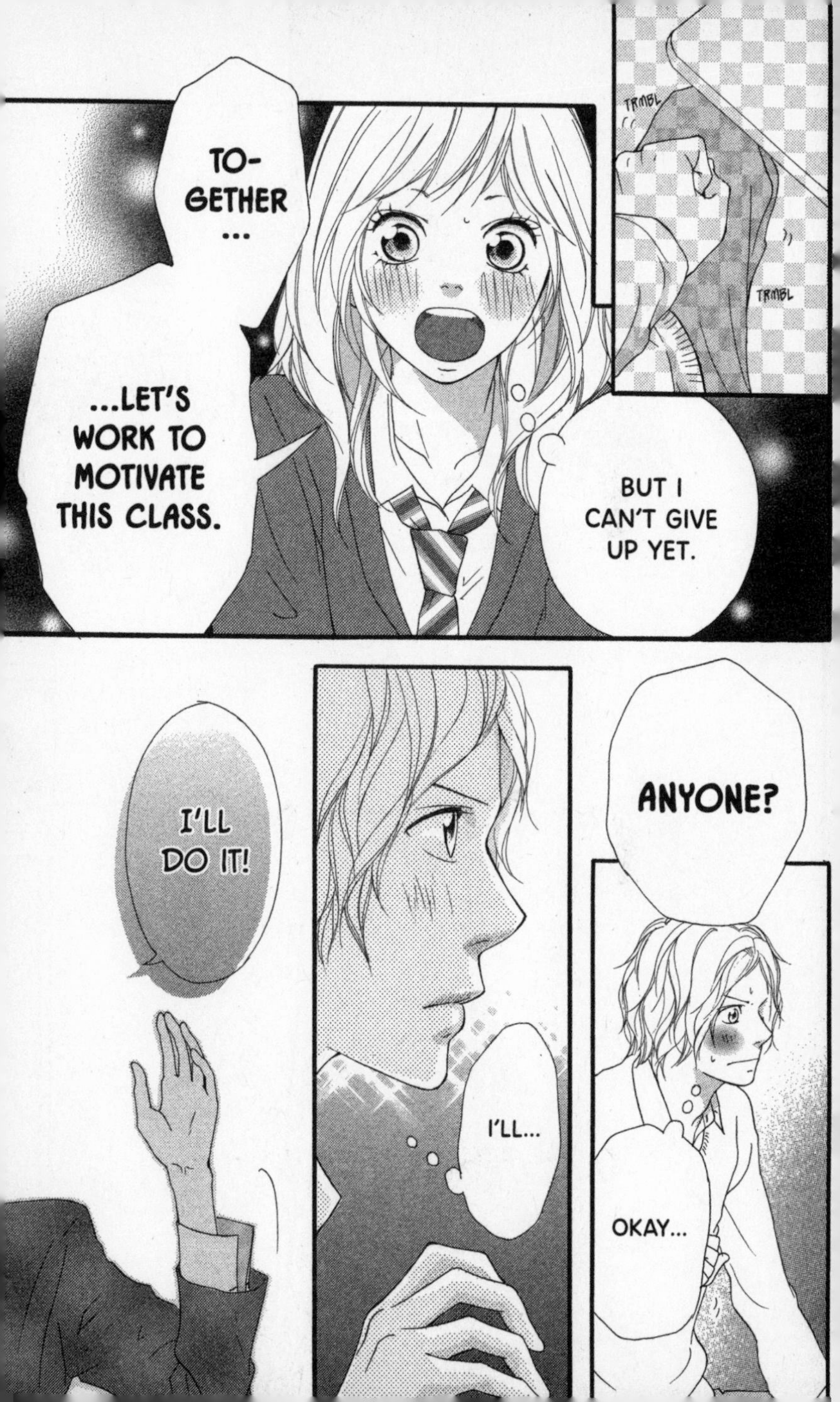
TRMBL
TRMBL
TO-GETHER ...
...LET'S WORK TO MOTIVATE THIS CLASS.
BUT I CAN'T GIVE UP YET.
ANYONE?
OKAY...
I'LL...
I'LL DO IT!

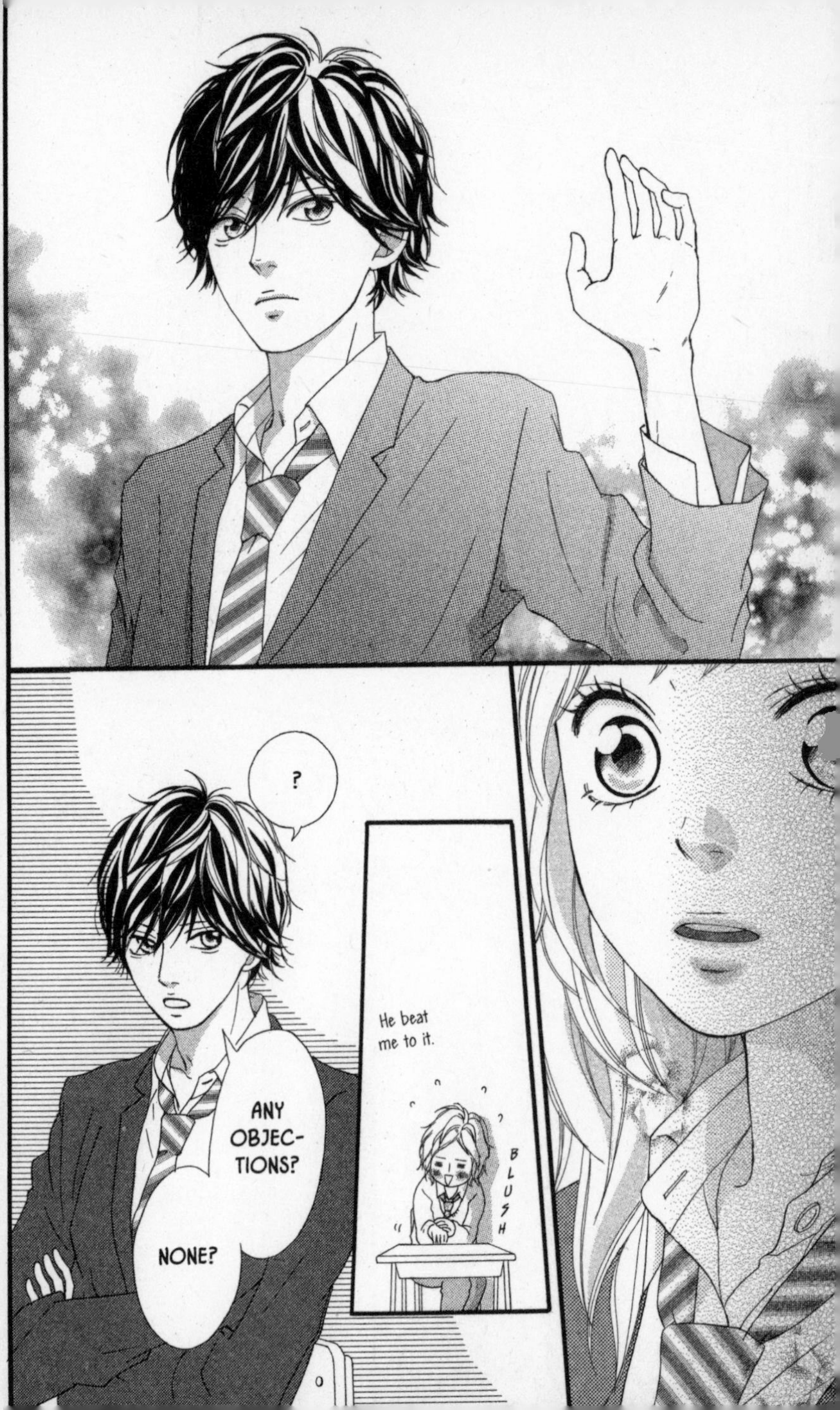
He beat me to it.
BLUSH
?
ANY OBJECTIONS?
NONE?

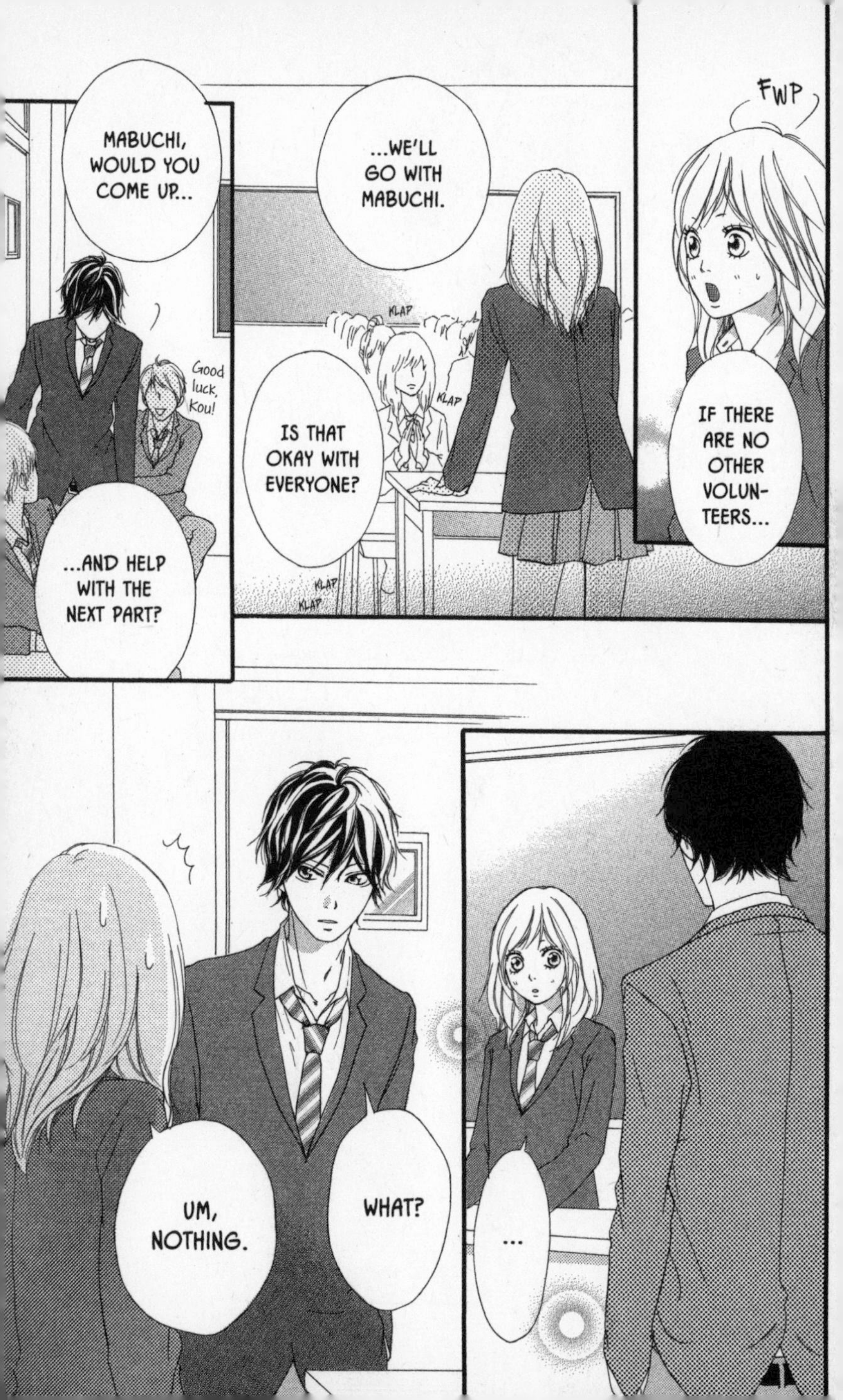
FWP
IF THERE ARE NO OTHER VOLUNTEERS...
...WE'LL GO WITH MABUCHI.
KLAP
KLAP
IS THAT OKAY WITH EVERYONE?
KLAP
KLAP
MABUCHI, WOULD YOU COME UP...
Good luck, Kou!
...AND HELP WITH THE NEXT PART?
...
WHAT?
UM, NOTHING.

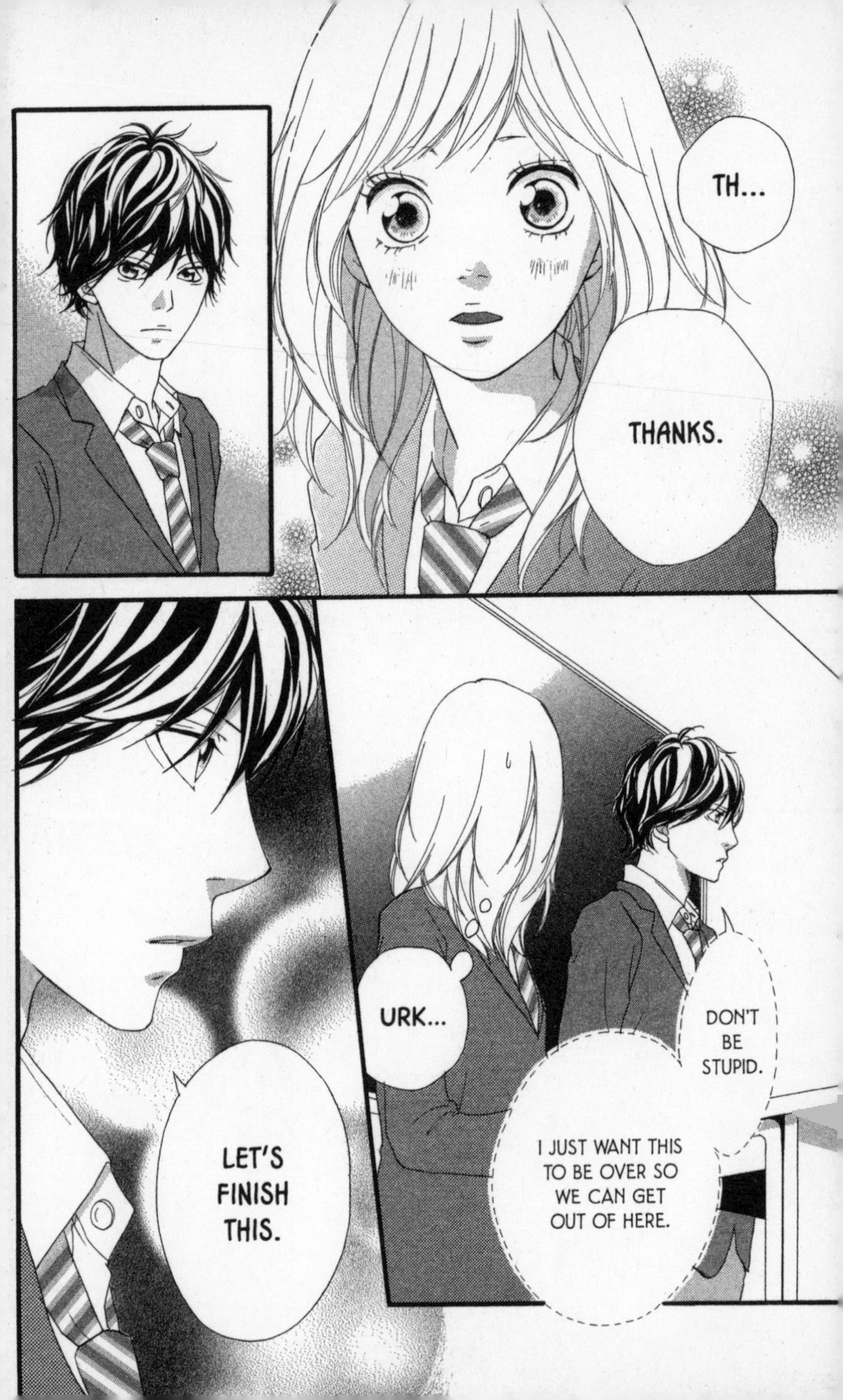
TH...
THANKS.
URK...
DON'T BE STUPID.
I JUST WANT THIS TO BE OVER SO WE CAN GET OUT OF HERE.
LET'S FINISH THIS.

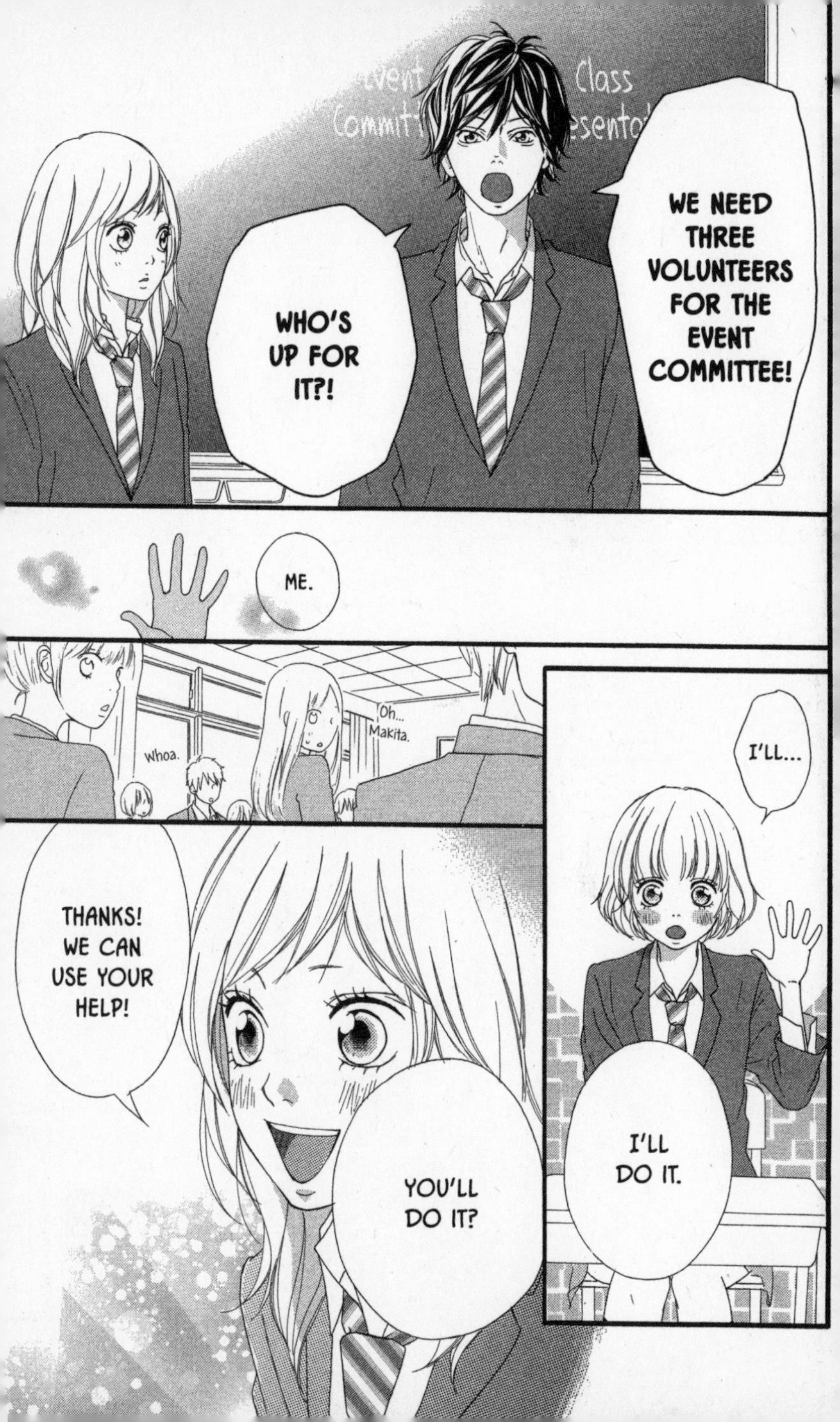
Class
WE NEED THREE VOLUNTEERS FOR THE EVENT COMMITTEE!
WHO'S UP FOR IT?!
ME.
I'LL...
I'LL DO IT.
Oh... Makita.
Whoa.
YOU'LL DO IT?
THANKS! WE CAN USE YOUR HELP!

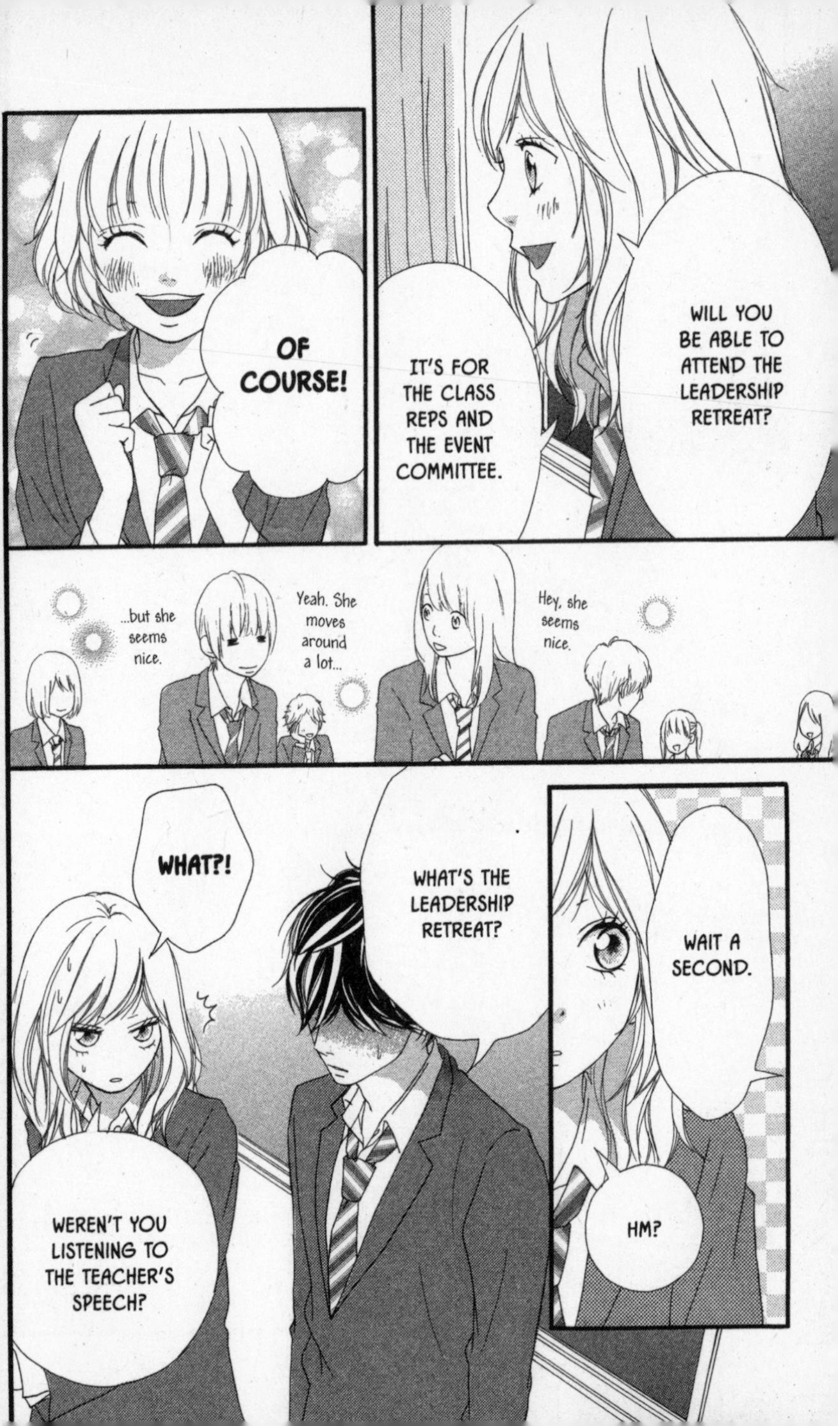
WILL YOU BE ABLE TO ATTEND THE LEADERSHIP RETREAT?
IT'S FOR THE CLASS REPS AND THE EVENT COMMITTEE.
OF COURSE!
Hey, she seems nice.
Yeah. She moves around a lot...
...but she seems nice.
WAIT A SECOND.
HM?
WHAT'S THE LEADERSHIP RETREAT?
WHAT?!
WEREN'T YOU LISTENING TO THE TEACHER'S SPEECH?

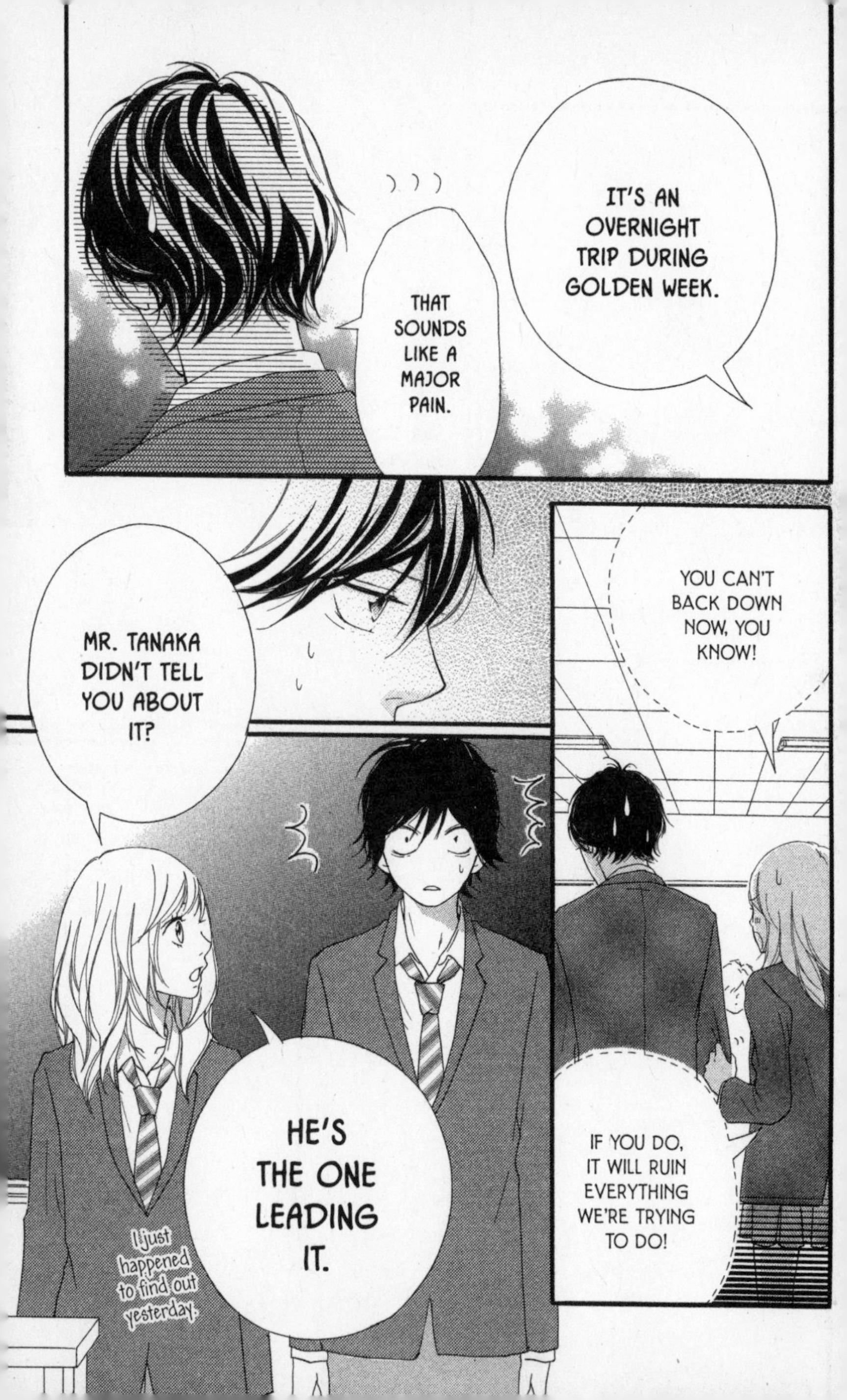
IT'S AN OVERNIGHT TRIP DURING GOLDEN WEEK.
THAT SOUNDS LIKE A MAJOR PAIN.
YOU CAN'T BACK DOWN NOW, YOU KNOW!
IF YOU DO, IT WILL RUIN EVERYTHING WE'RE TRYING TO DO!
MR. TANAKA DIDN'T TELL YOU ABOUT IT?
HE'S THE ONE LEADING IT.
I just happened to find out yesterday.

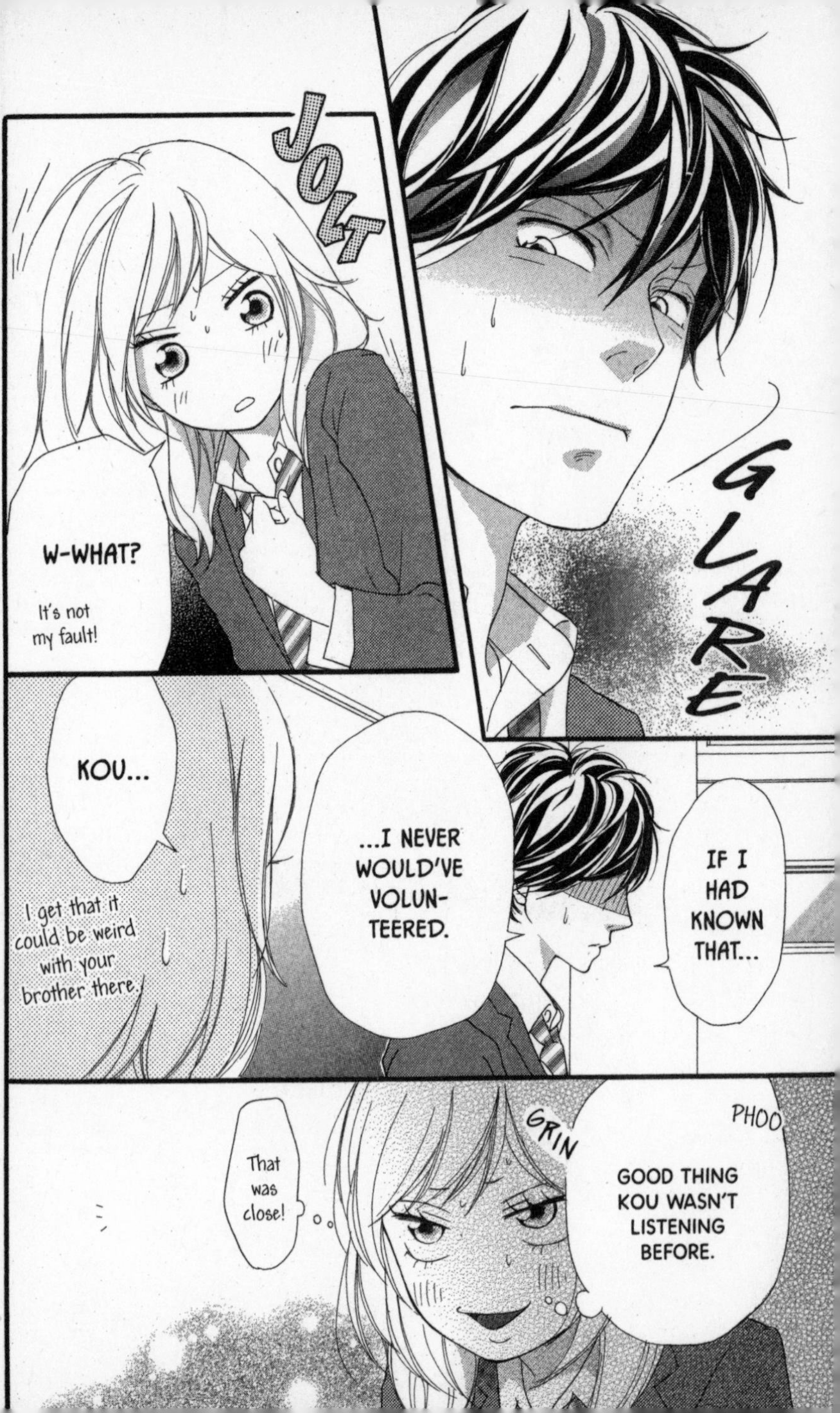
GLARE
JOLT
W-WHAT?
It's not my fault!
IF I HAD KNOWN THAT...
...I NEVER WOULD'VE VOLUNTEERED.
KOU...
I get that it could be weird with your brother there.
PHOO
GOOD THING KOU WASN'T LISTENING BEFORE.
GRIN
That was close!

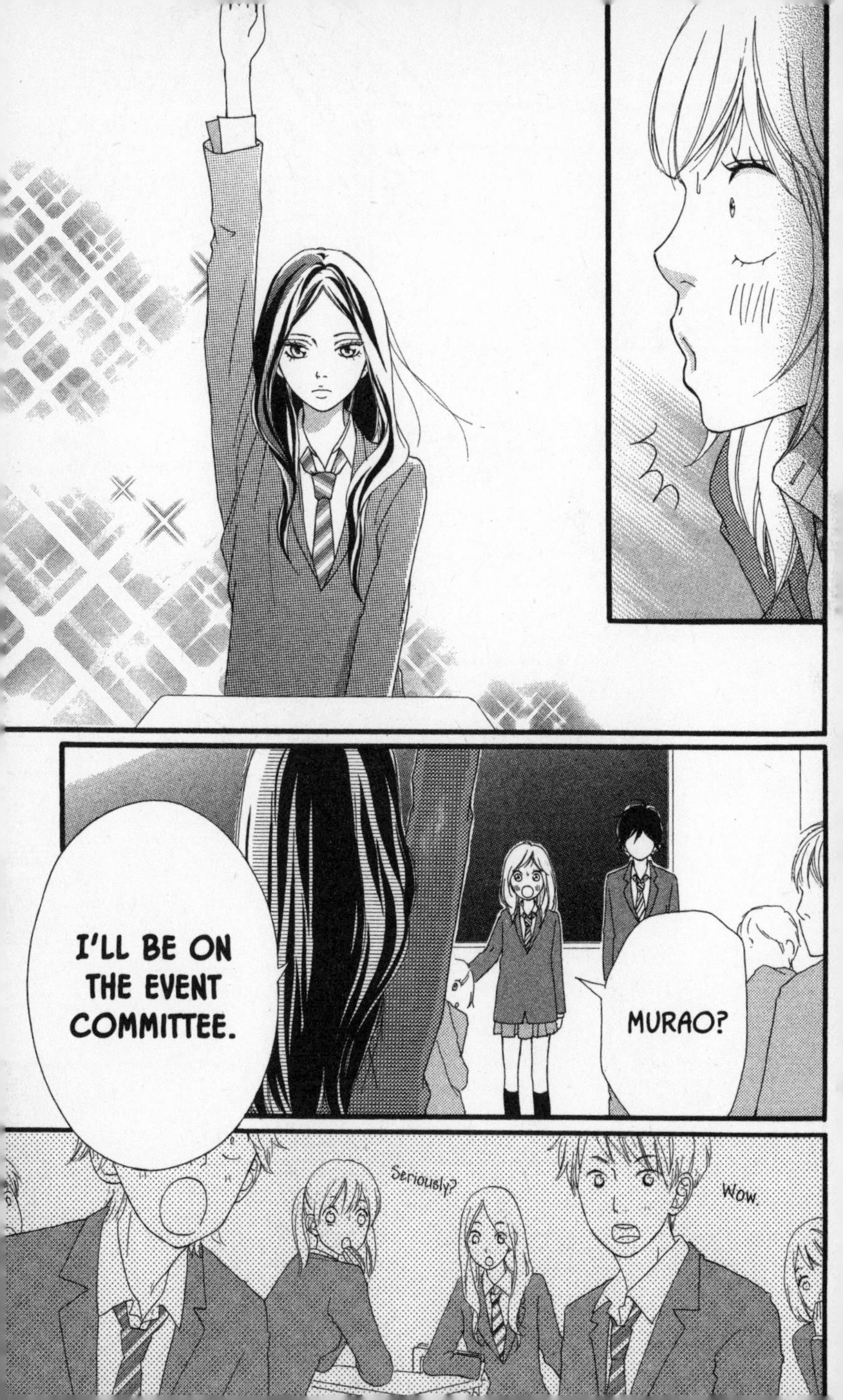
MURAO?
I'LL BE ON THE EVENT COMMITTEE.
Wow.
Seriously?

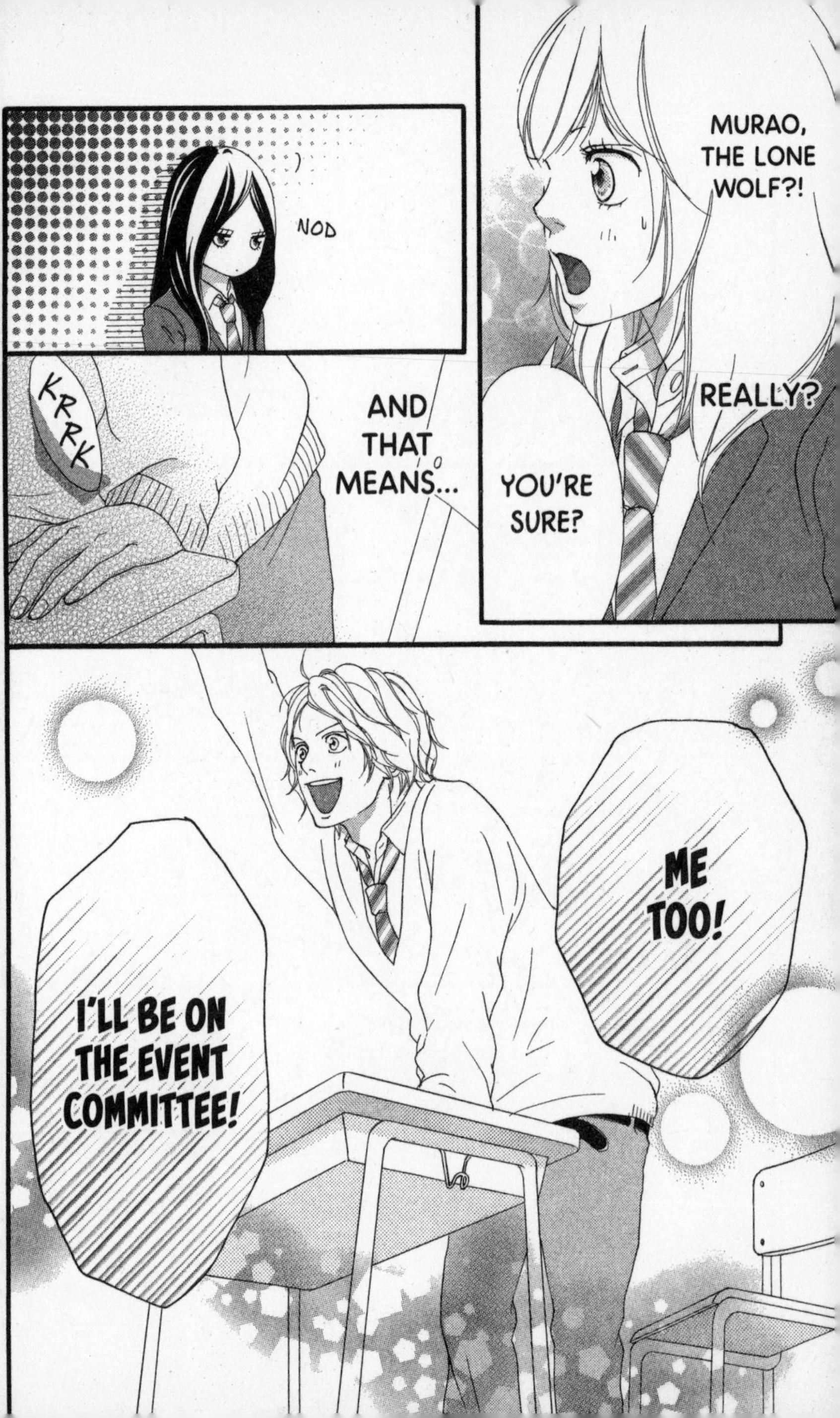
MURAO, THE LONE WOLF?!
REALLY?
YOU'RE SURE?
NOD
KRRK
AND THAT MEANS...
ME TOO!
I'LL BE ON THE EVENT COMMITTEE!

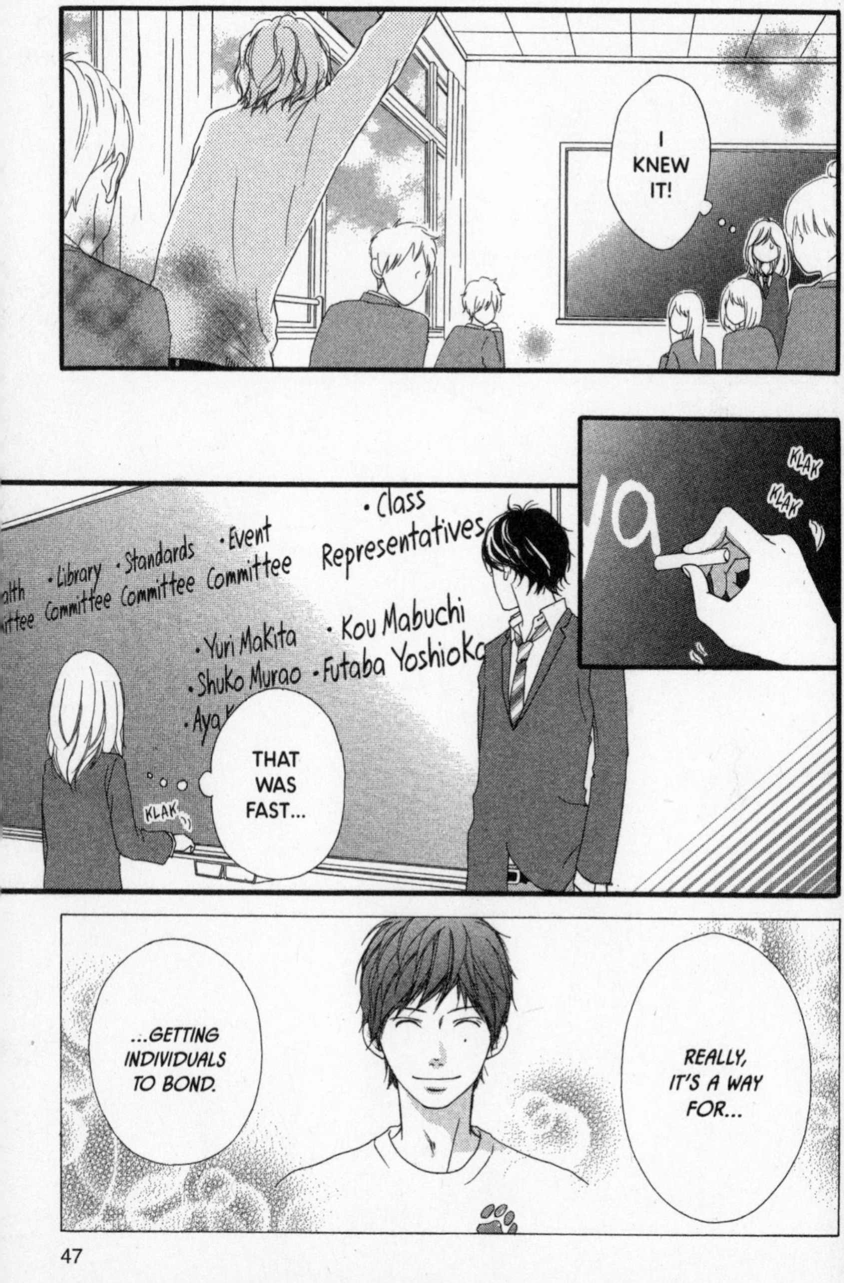

I KNEW IT!
KLAK KLAK
ya
• Class Representatives
• Event Committee
• Standards Committee
• Library Committee
• Kou Mabuchi
• Futaba Yoshioka
• Yuri Makita
• Shuko Murao
THAT WAS FAST...
KLAK
REALLY, IT'S A WAY FOR...
...GETTING INDIVIDUALS TO BOND.

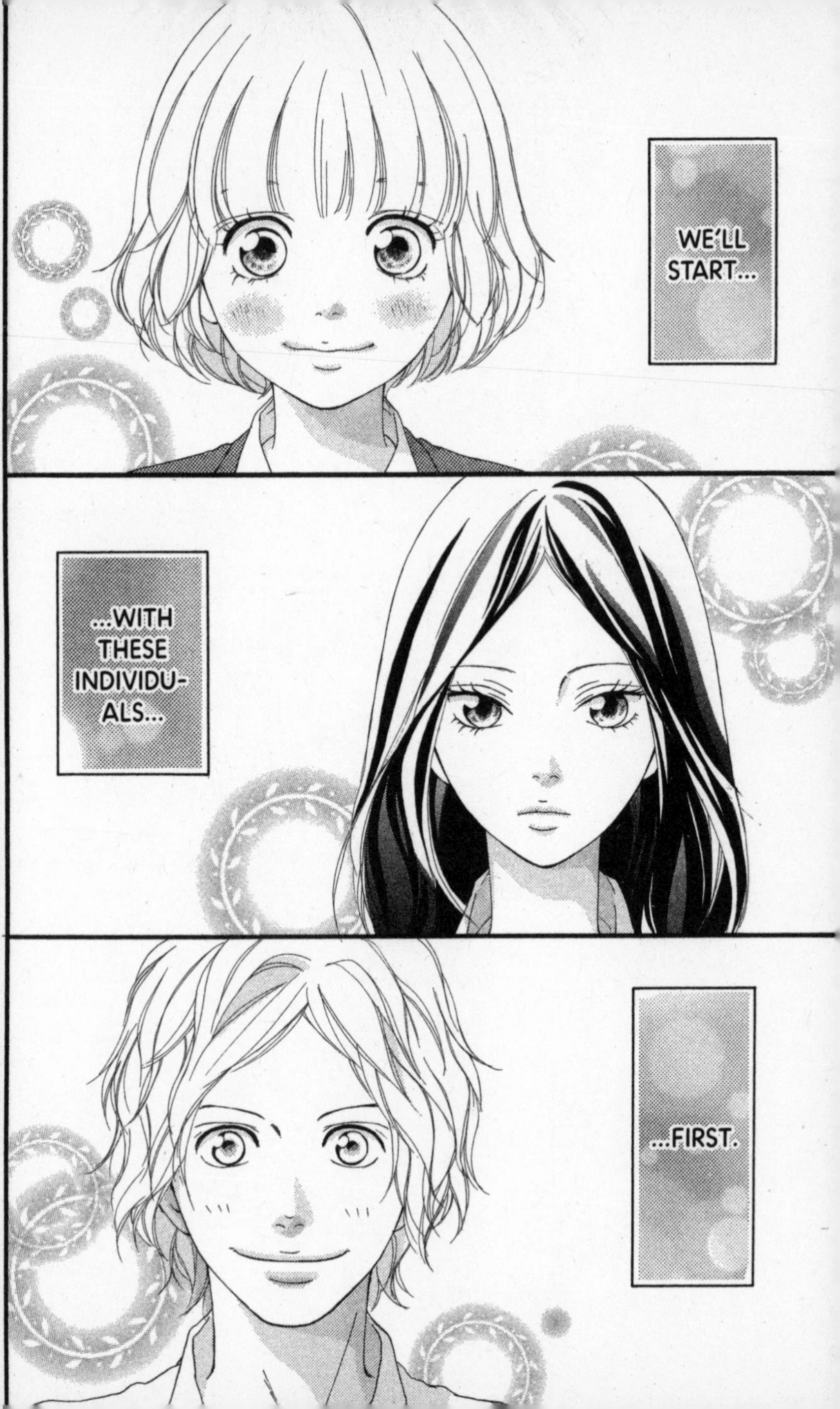
WE'LL START...
...WITH THESE INDIVIDUALS...
...FIRST.

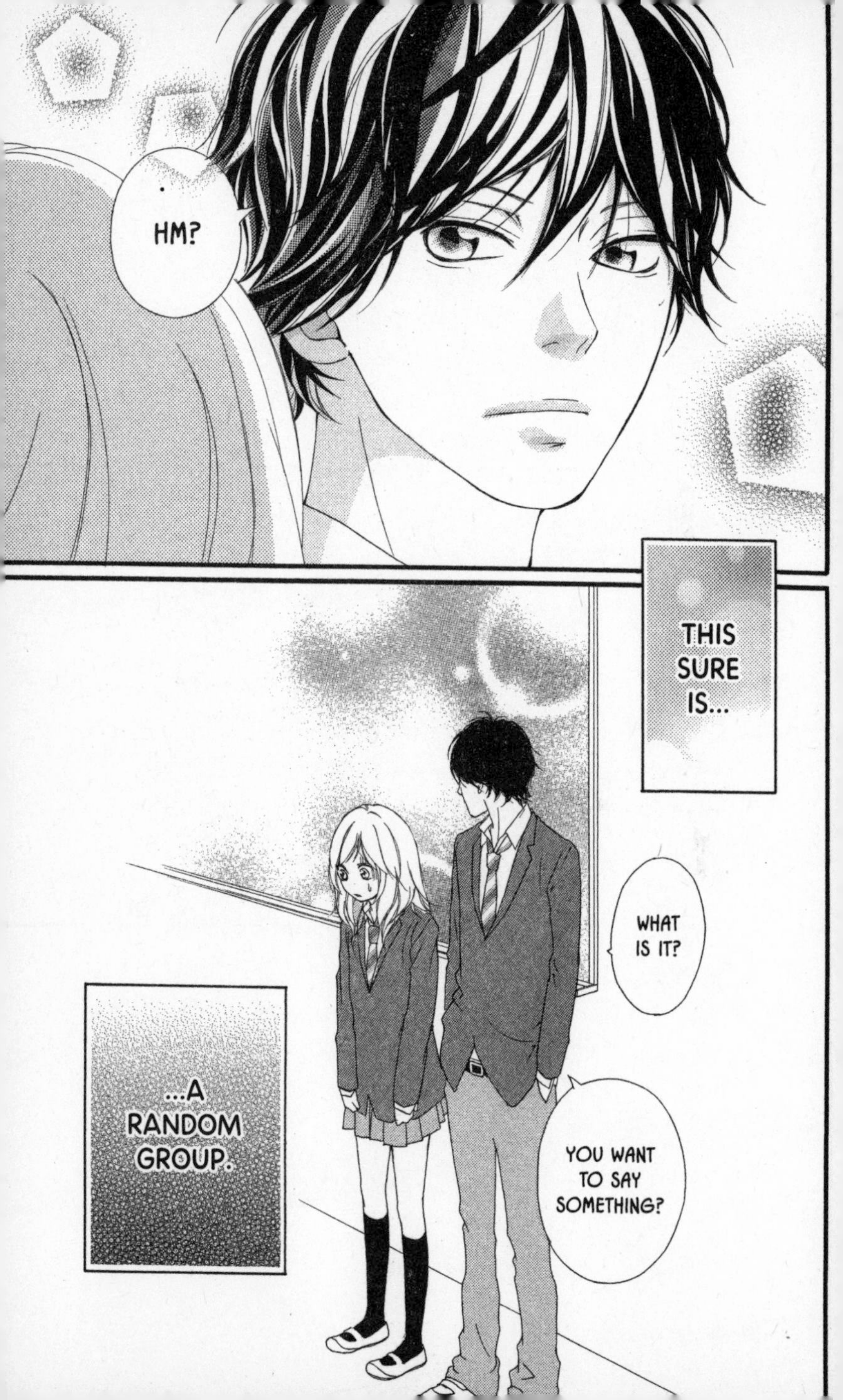
HM?
THIS SURE IS...
WHAT IS IT?
YOU WANT TO SAY SOMETHING?
...A RANDOM GROUP.

GariGarikun's sister is Garikochan.

This summer I was addicted to the pear-flavored GariGarikun popsicle. After a *Bessatsu Margaret* artist tweeted that they were delicious, I tried one and was blown away. It's the best when you get one from the convenience store and bring it back home because it's a little bit melty. I ate them pretty much nonstop. After the tenth, I got a winner popsicle stick that was good for a free one. I was walking on air until I lost that stick. Wah! When I couldn't find it anywhere, I vowed to not let my summer end until I won again. ☆ I ate and ate, but I didn't win. Before I knew it, they stopped making the seasonal pear flavor, and it quickly disappeared from the shelves at my local stores. And so, I am here to announce that my summer has still not ended, and apologies in advance as I may still be in full summer mode when Christmas comes around... At this point, I'm really looking forward to next year's popsicle release lest I be stuck in summer mode forever. To be honest, I ate so many popsicles over the summer that I really felt the summer fatigue. Now my new motto is "know your limits." Thank you.

 ★ Saki ★

*GariGarikun is a popsicle brand.

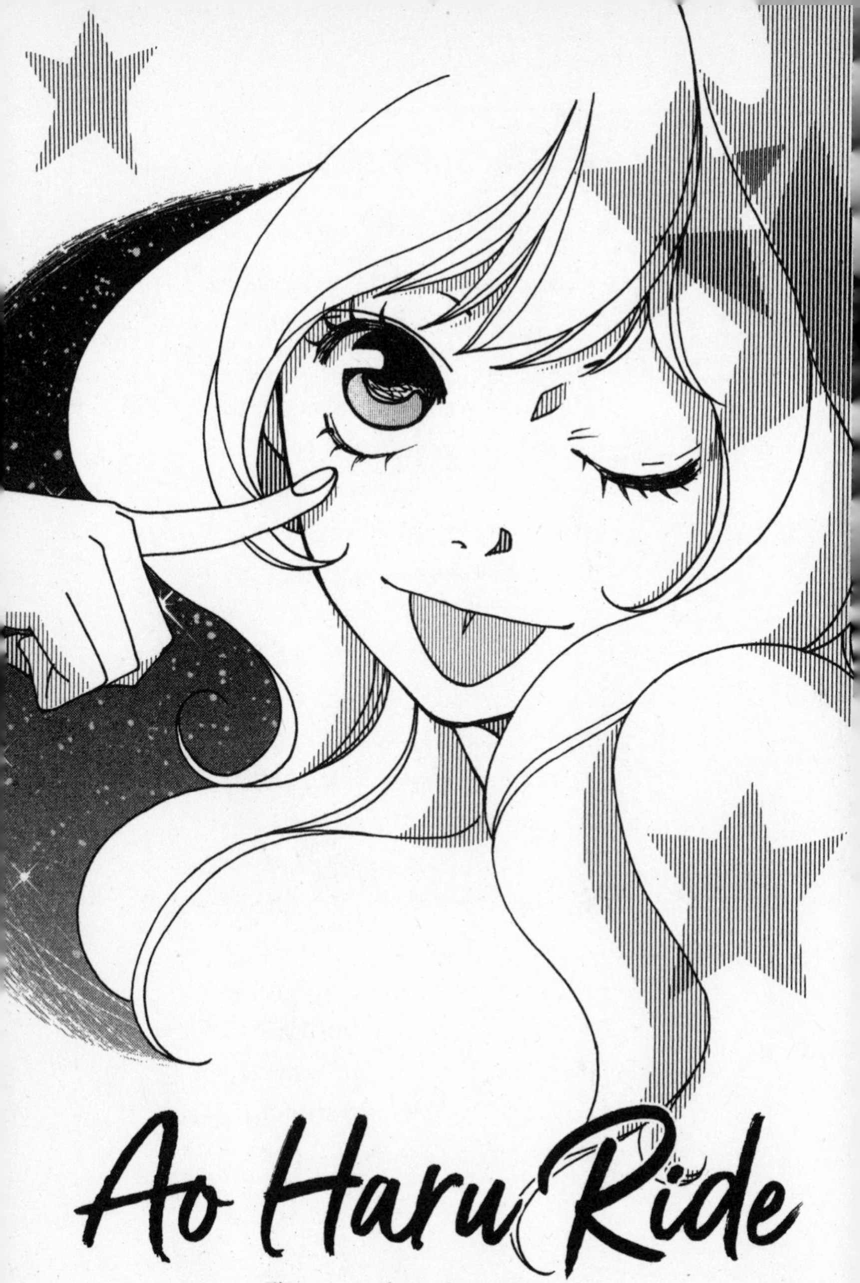

Ao Haru Ride

The scent of air after rain...
In the light around us, I felt your heartbeat.

CHAPTER 5

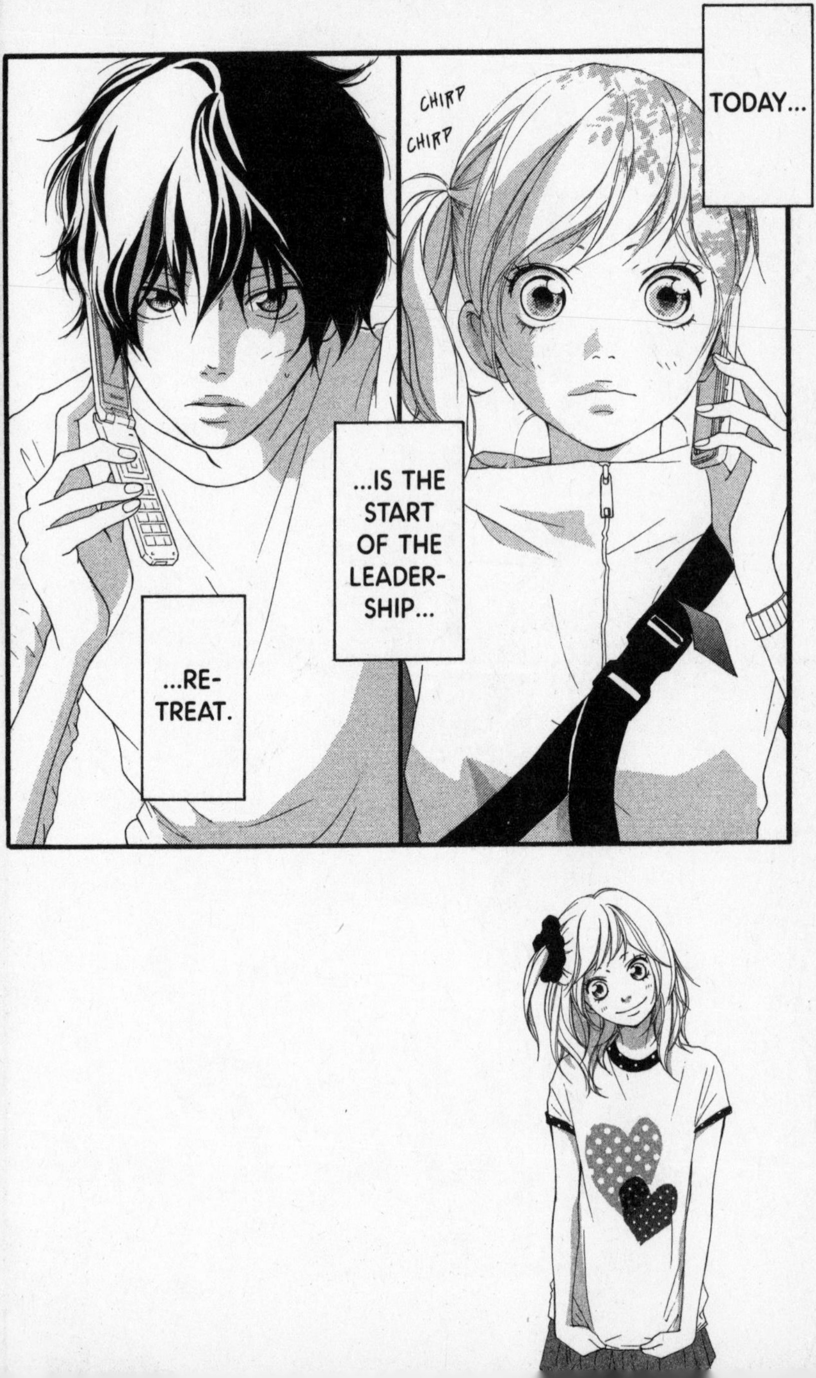
TODAY...
CHIRP
CHIRP
...IS THE START OF THE LEADER-SHIP...
...RE-TREAT.

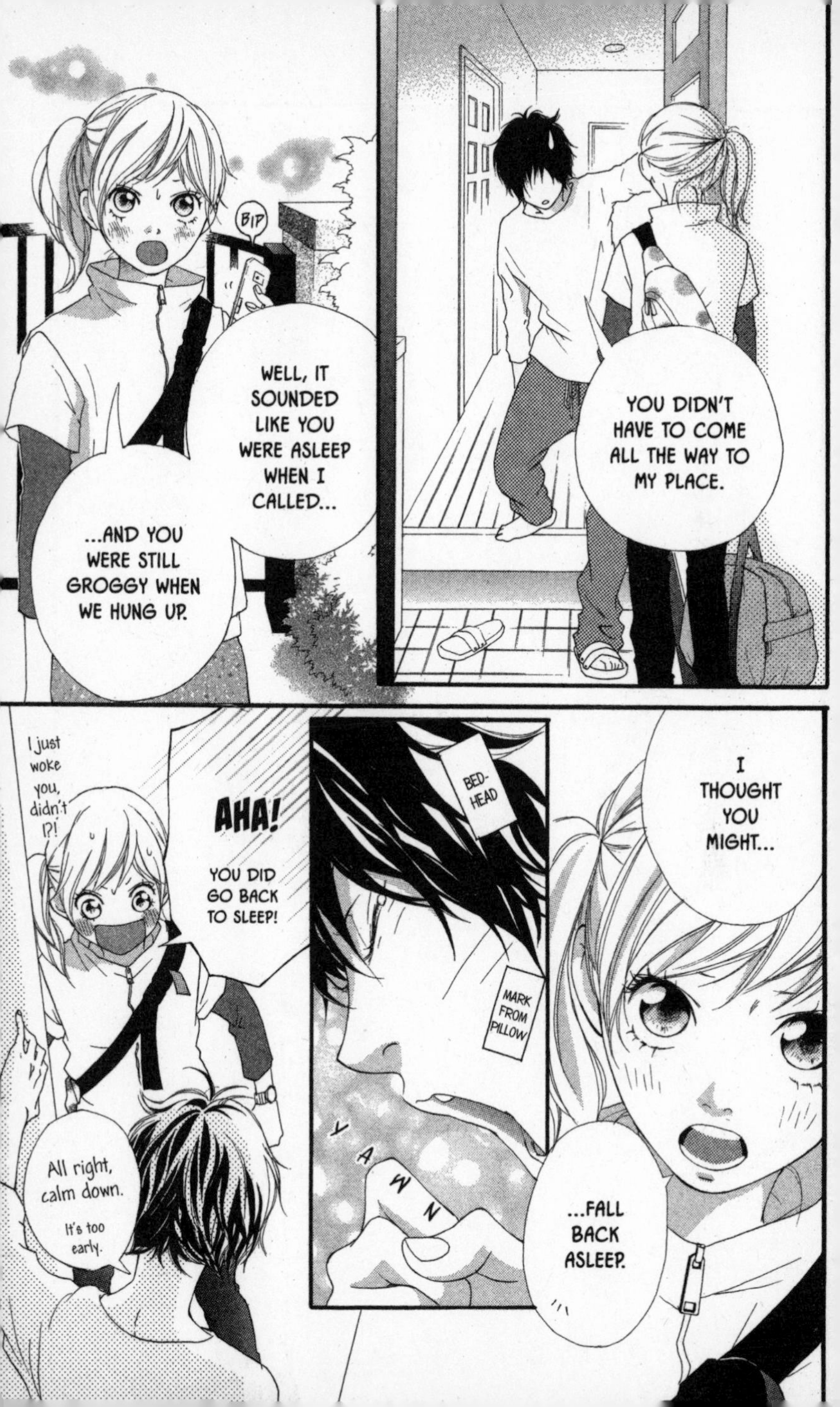
YOU DIDN'T HAVE TO COME ALL THE WAY TO MY PLACE.
BIP
WELL, IT SOUNDED LIKE YOU WERE ASLEEP WHEN I CALLED...
...AND YOU WERE STILL GROGGY WHEN WE HUNG UP.
I THOUGHT YOU MIGHT...
...FALL BACK ASLEEP.
BED-HEAD
MARK FROM PILLOW
YAWN
AHA!
YOU DID GO BACK TO SLEEP!
I just woke you, didn't I?!
All right, calm down.
It's too early.

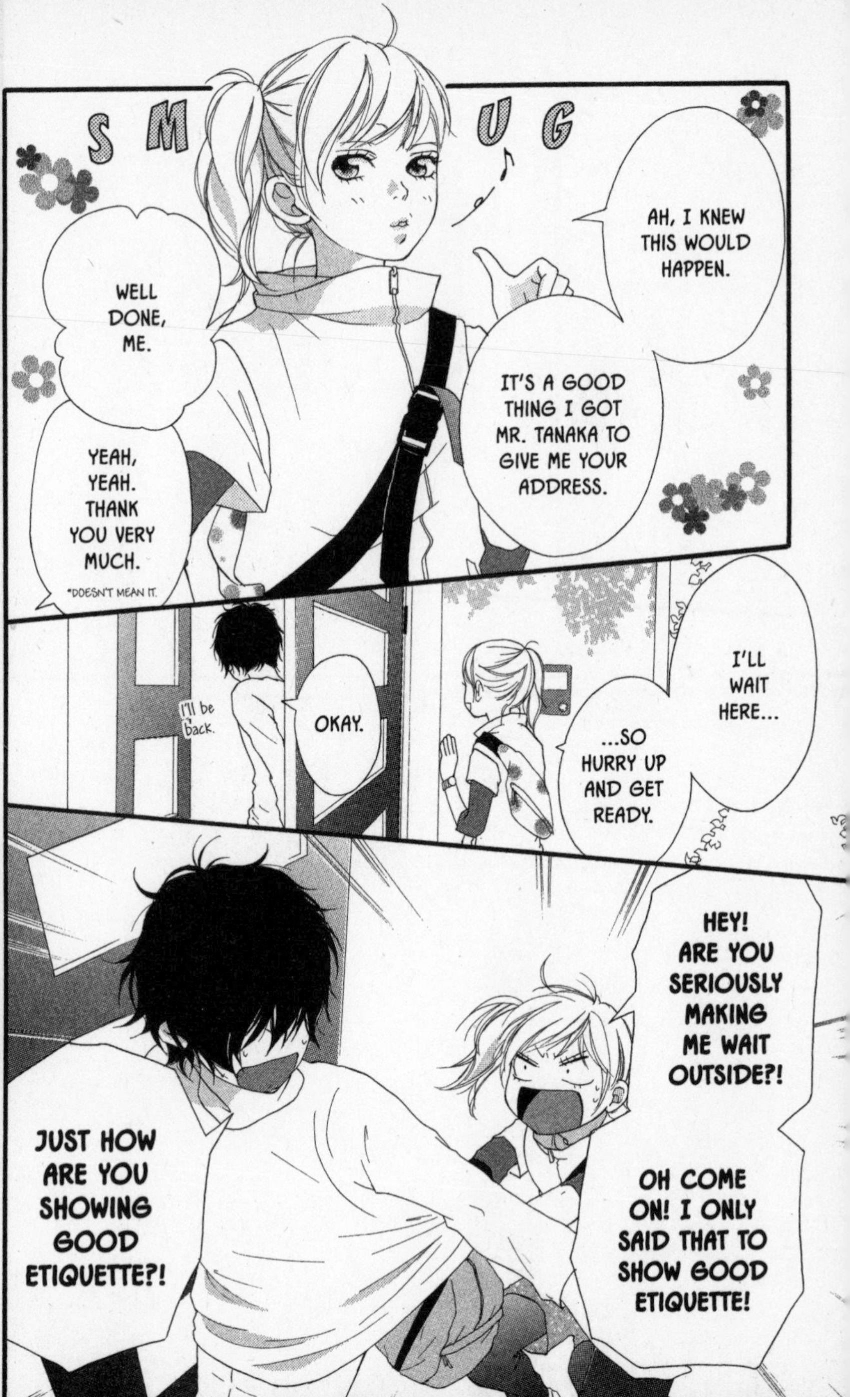
SMUG
AH, I KNEW THIS WOULD HAPPEN.
IT'S A GOOD THING I GOT MR. TANAKA TO GIVE ME YOUR ADDRESS.
WELL DONE, ME.
YEAH, YEAH. THANK YOU VERY MUCH.
*DOESN'T MEAN IT.
I'LL WAIT HERE...
...SO HURRY UP AND GET READY.
OKAY.
I'll be back.
HEY! ARE YOU SERIOUSLY MAKING ME WAIT OUTSIDE?!
OH COME ON! I ONLY SAID THAT TO SHOW GOOD ETIQUETTE!
JUST HOW ARE YOU SHOWING GOOD ETIQUETTE?!

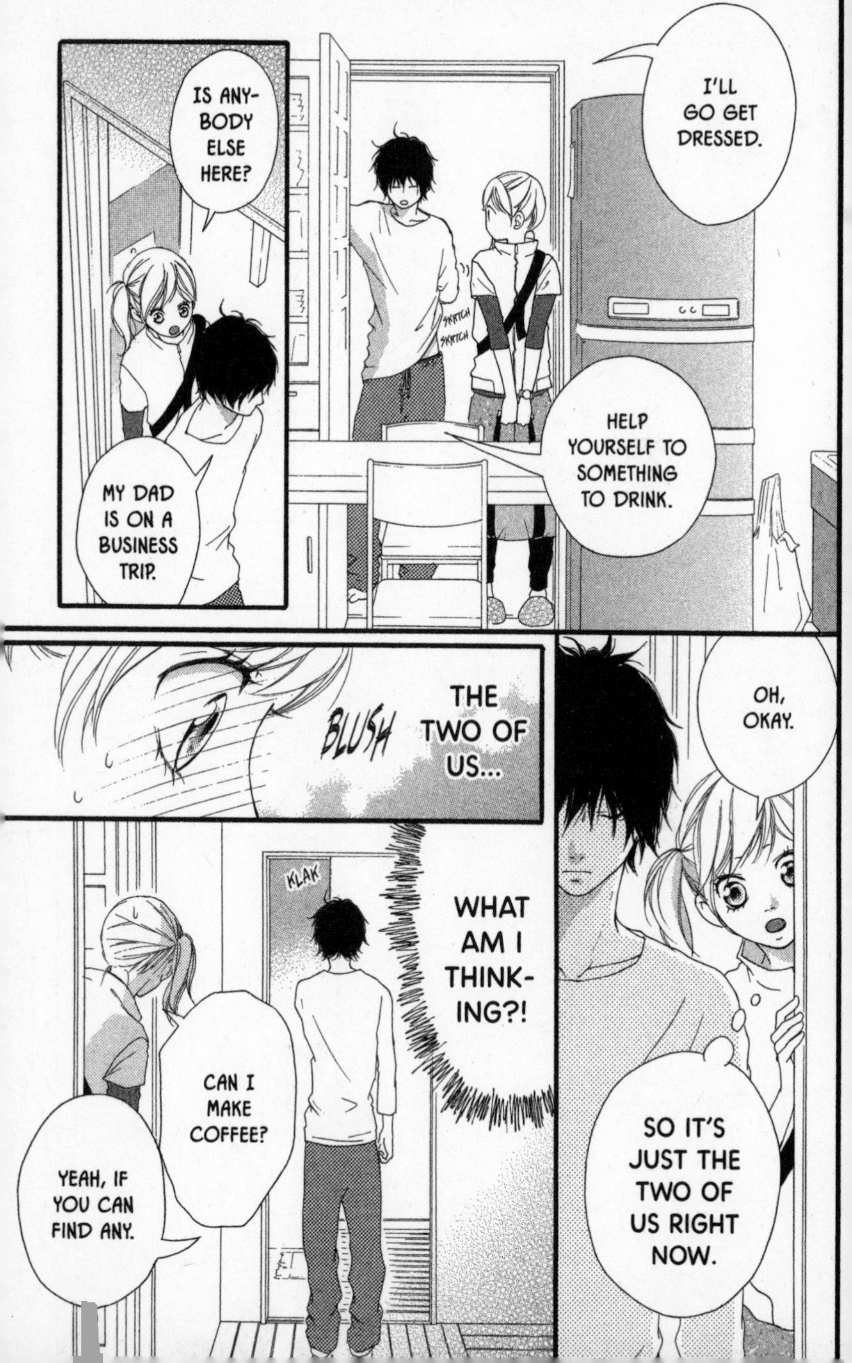
I'LL GO GET DRESSED.
SKRTCH SKRTCH
HELP YOURSELF TO SOMETHING TO DRINK.
IS ANY-BODY ELSE HERE?
MY DAD IS ON A BUSINESS TRIP.
OH, OKAY.
SO IT'S JUST THE TWO OF US RIGHT NOW.
BLUSH
THE TWO OF US...
WHAT AM I THINK-ING?!
KLAK
CAN I MAKE COFFEE?
YEAH, IF YOU CAN FIND ANY.

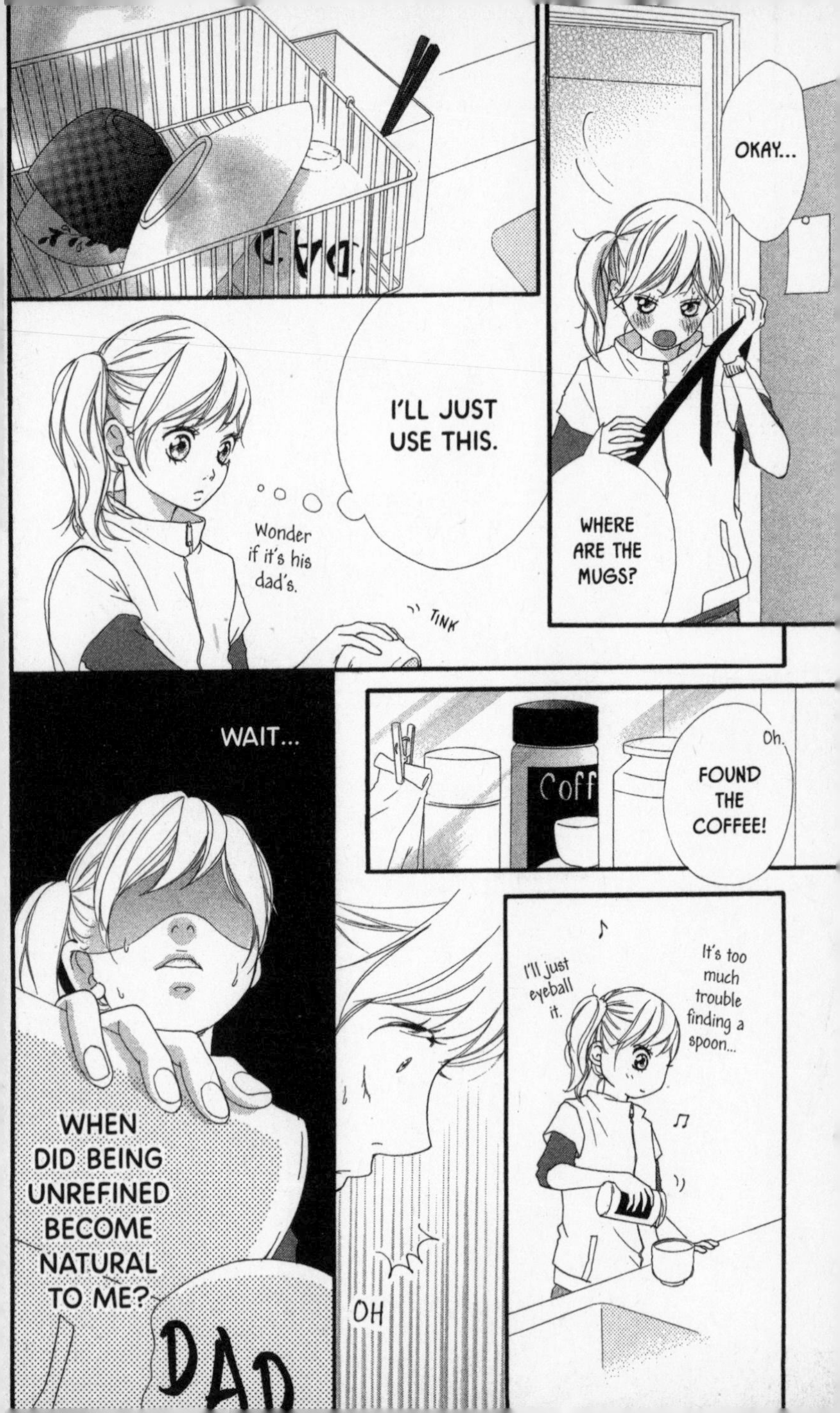
OKAY...
WHERE ARE THE MUGS?
I'LL JUST USE THIS.
Wonder if it's his dad's.
TINK
Oh.
FOUND THE COFFEE!
It's too much trouble finding a spoon...
I'll just eyeball it.
OH
WAIT...
WHEN DID BEING UNREFINED BECOME NATURAL TO ME?
DAD

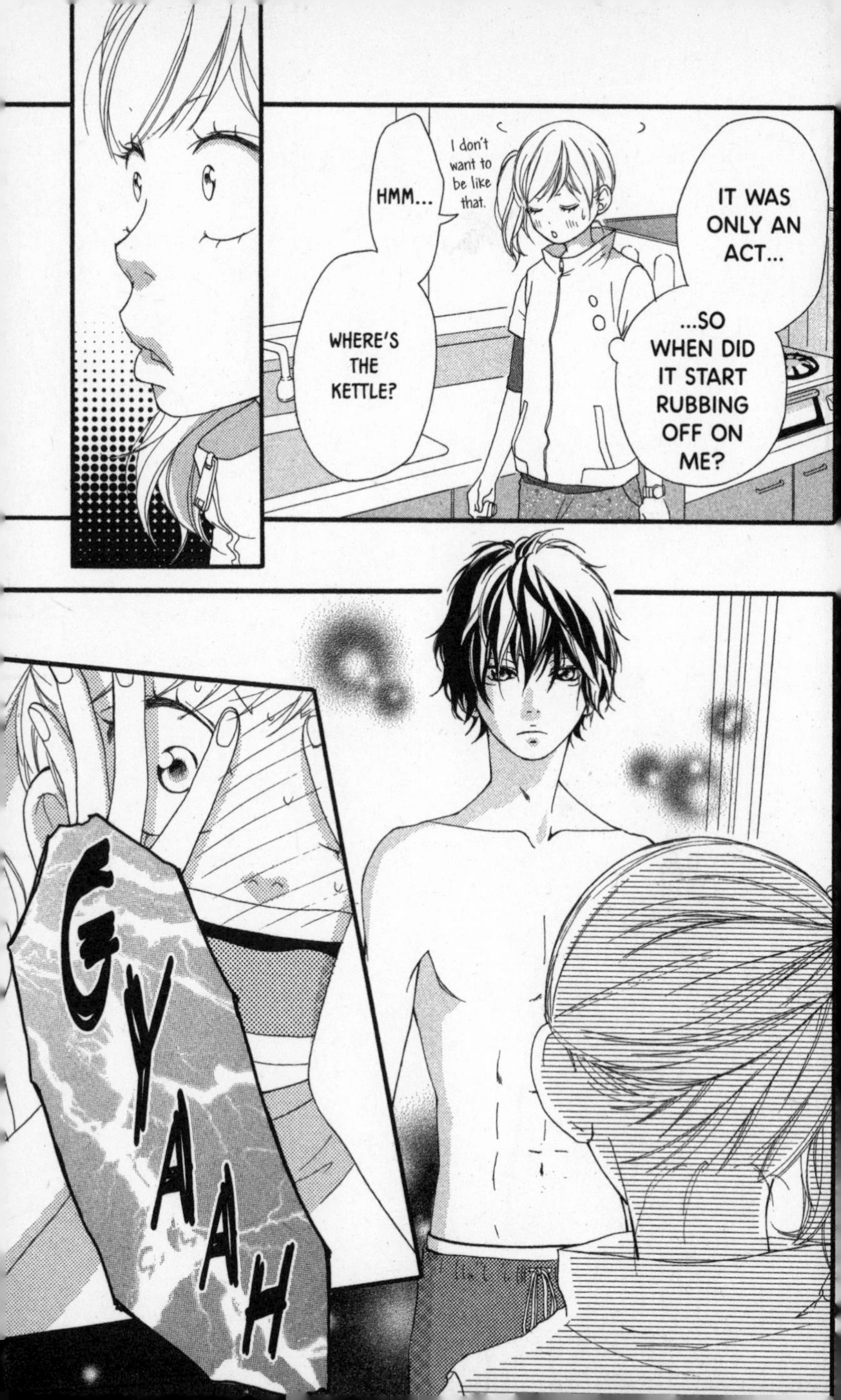
IT WAS ONLY AN ACT...
...SO WHEN DID IT START RUBBING OFF ON ME?
I don't want to be like that.
HMM...
WHERE'S THE KETTLE?
GYAAH

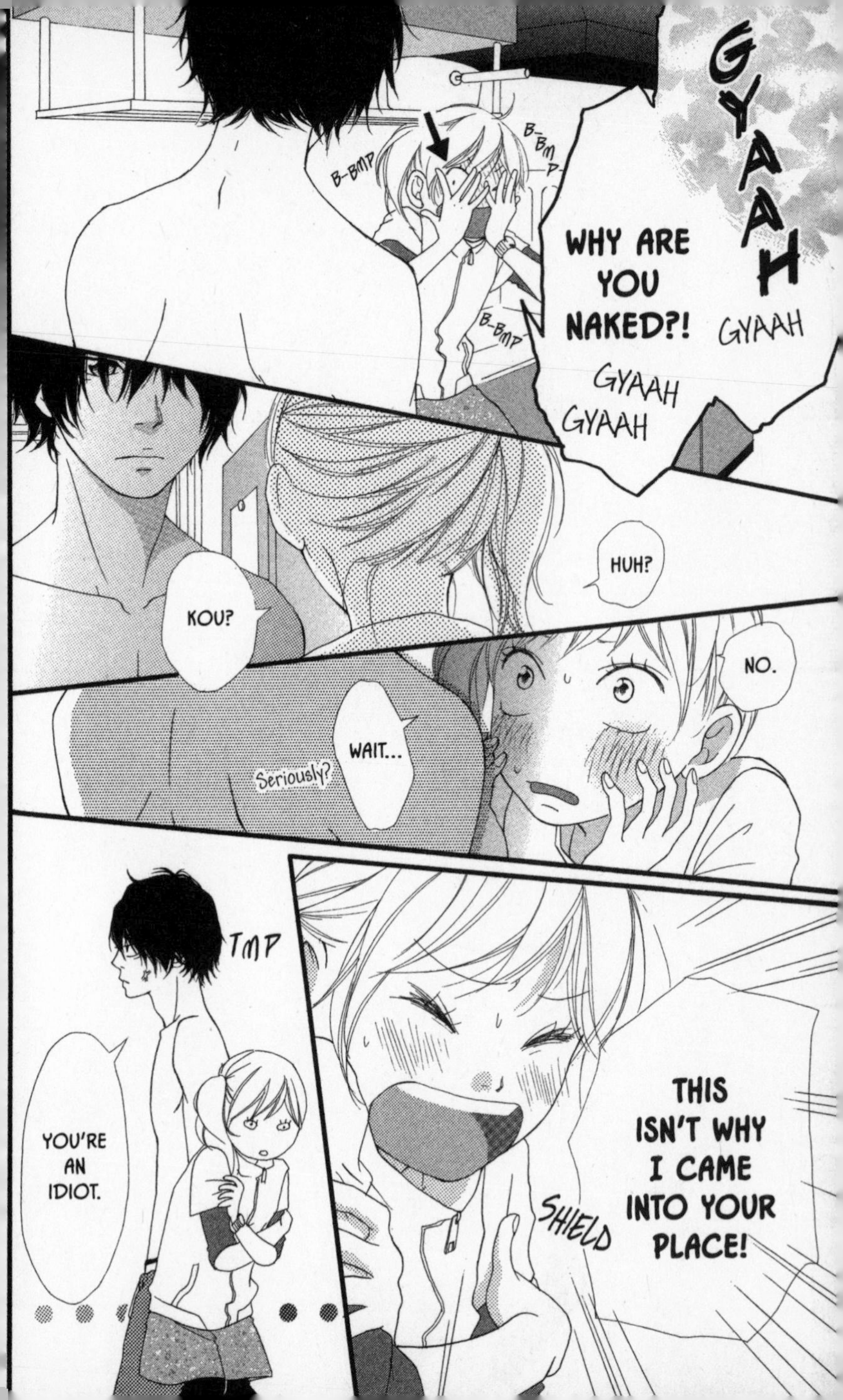
GYAAH
WHY ARE YOU NAKED?!
GYAAH
GYAAH
GYAAH
B-BMP
B-BMP
B-BMP
HUH?
KOU?
NO.
WAIT...
Seriously?
THIS ISN'T WHY I CAME INTO YOUR PLACE!
SHIELD
TMP
YOU'RE AN IDIOT.

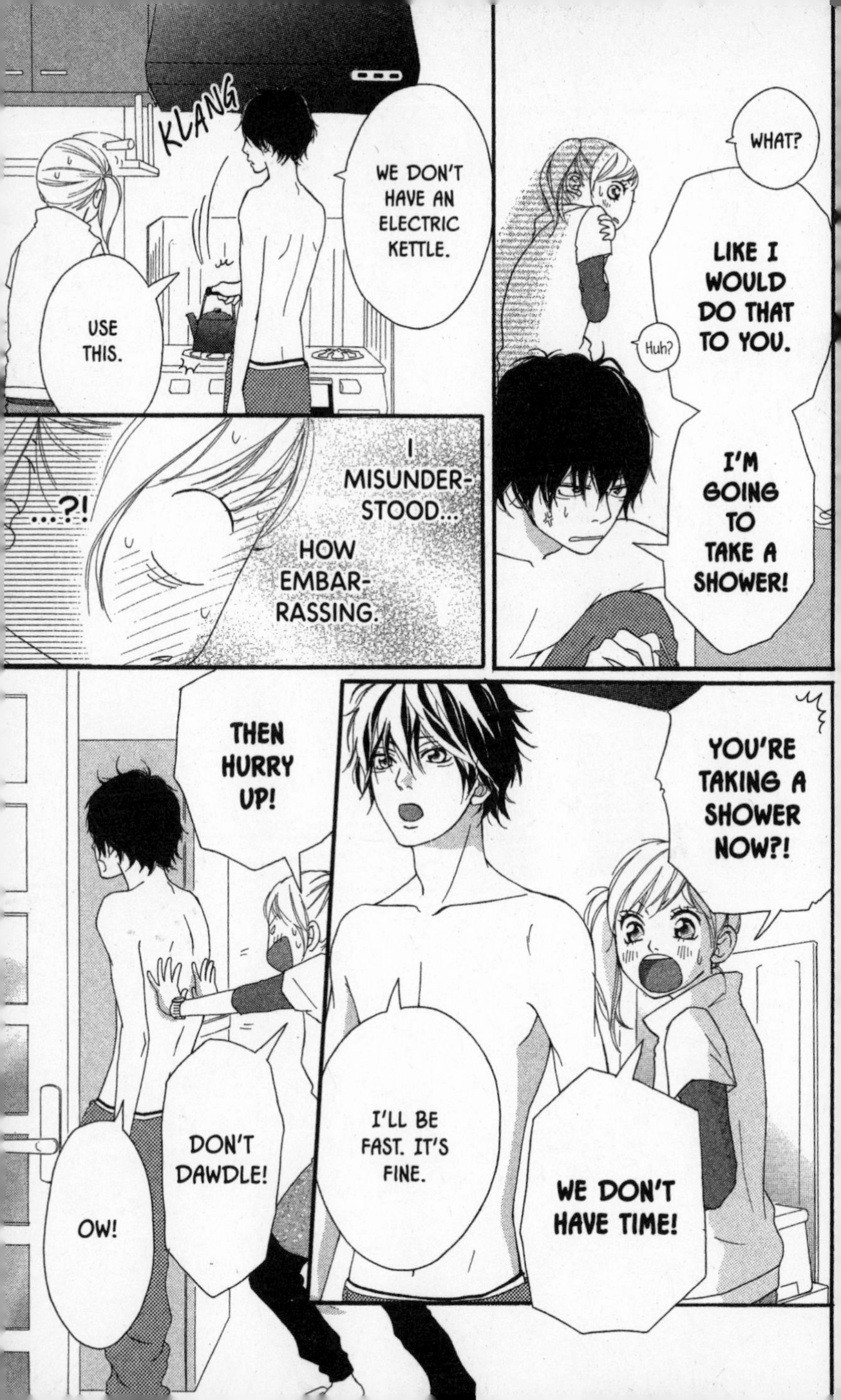
WHAT?
LIKE I WOULD DO THAT TO YOU.
Huh?
I'M GOING TO TAKE A SHOWER!
KLANG
WE DON'T HAVE AN ELECTRIC KETTLE.
USE THIS.
...?!
I MISUNDERSTOOD...
HOW EMBARRASSING.
YOU'RE TAKING A SHOWER NOW?!
I'LL BE FAST. IT'S FINE.
WE DON'T HAVE TIME!
THEN HURRY UP!
DON'T DAWDLE!
OW!

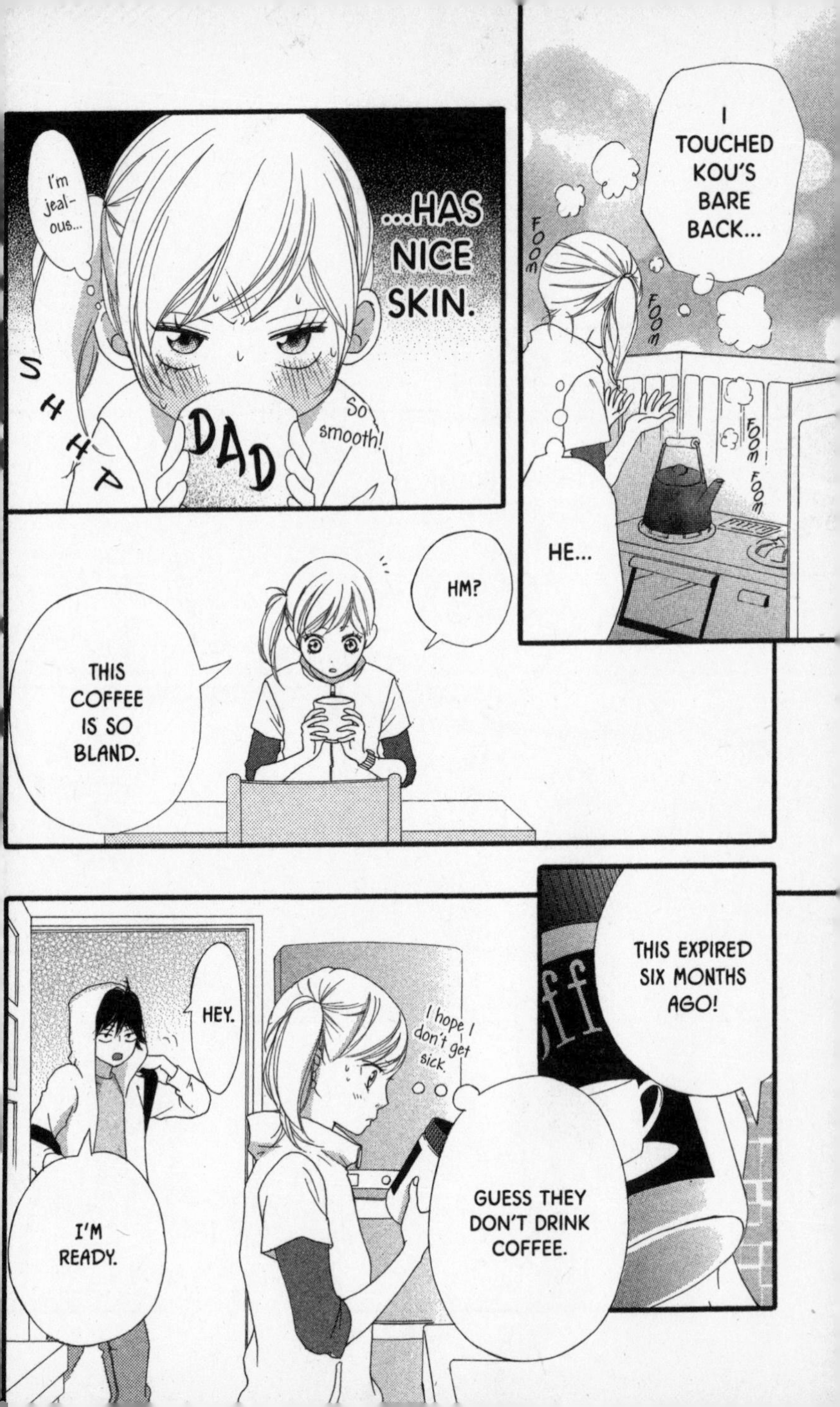
I TOUCHED KOU'S BARE BACK...
FOOM FOOM
FOOM FOOM
HE...
...HAS NICE SKIN.
I'm jeal-ous...
So smooth!
DAD
SHHP
HM?
THIS COFFEE IS SO BLAND.
THIS EXPIRED SIX MONTHS AGO!
GUESS THEY DON'T DRINK COFFEE.
I hope I don't get sick.
HEY.
I'M READY.

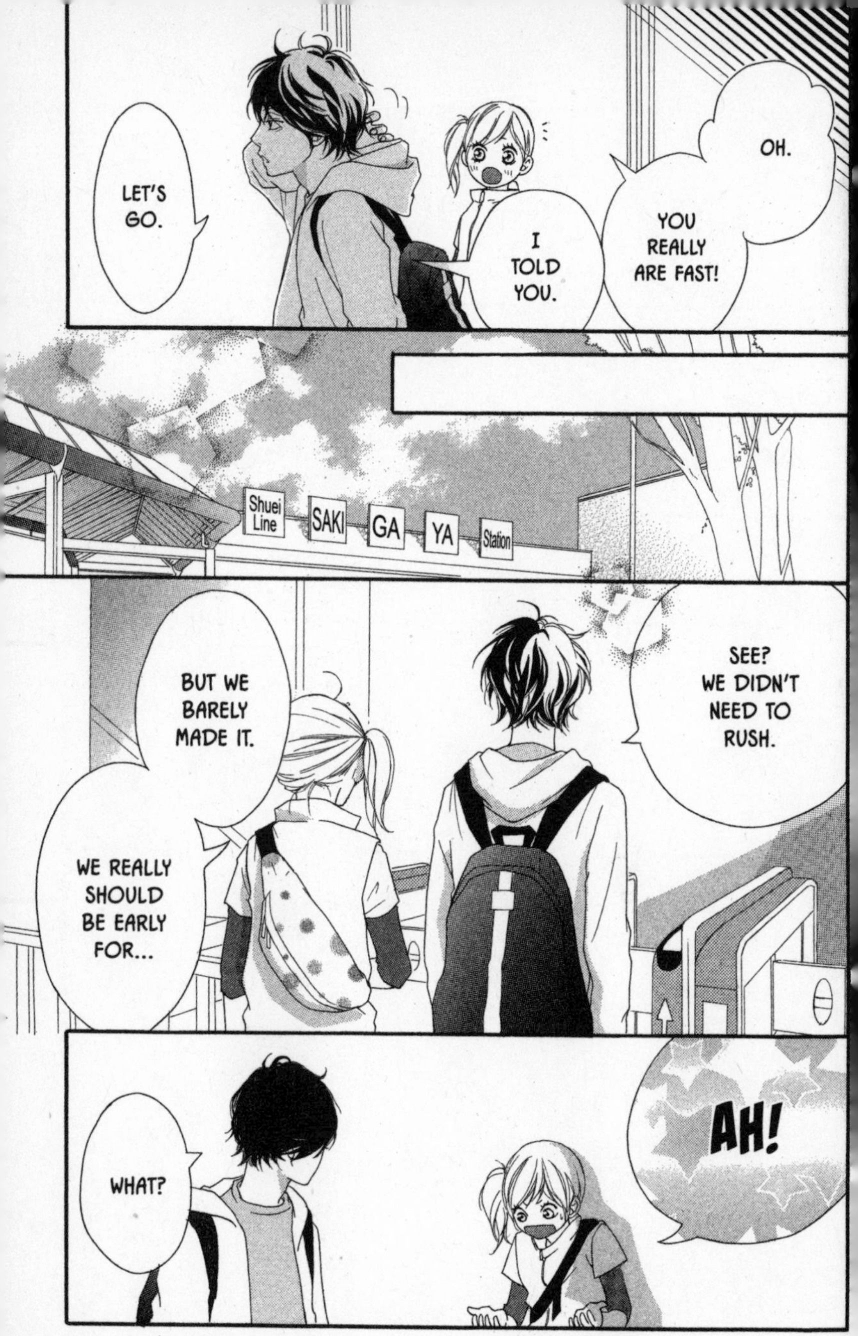
OH.
YOU REALLY ARE FAST!
I TOLD YOU.
LET'S GO.
Shuei Line SAKI GA YA Station
SEE? WE DIDN'T NEED TO RUSH.
BUT WE BARELY MADE IT.
WE REALLY SHOULD BE EARLY FOR...
AH!
WHAT?

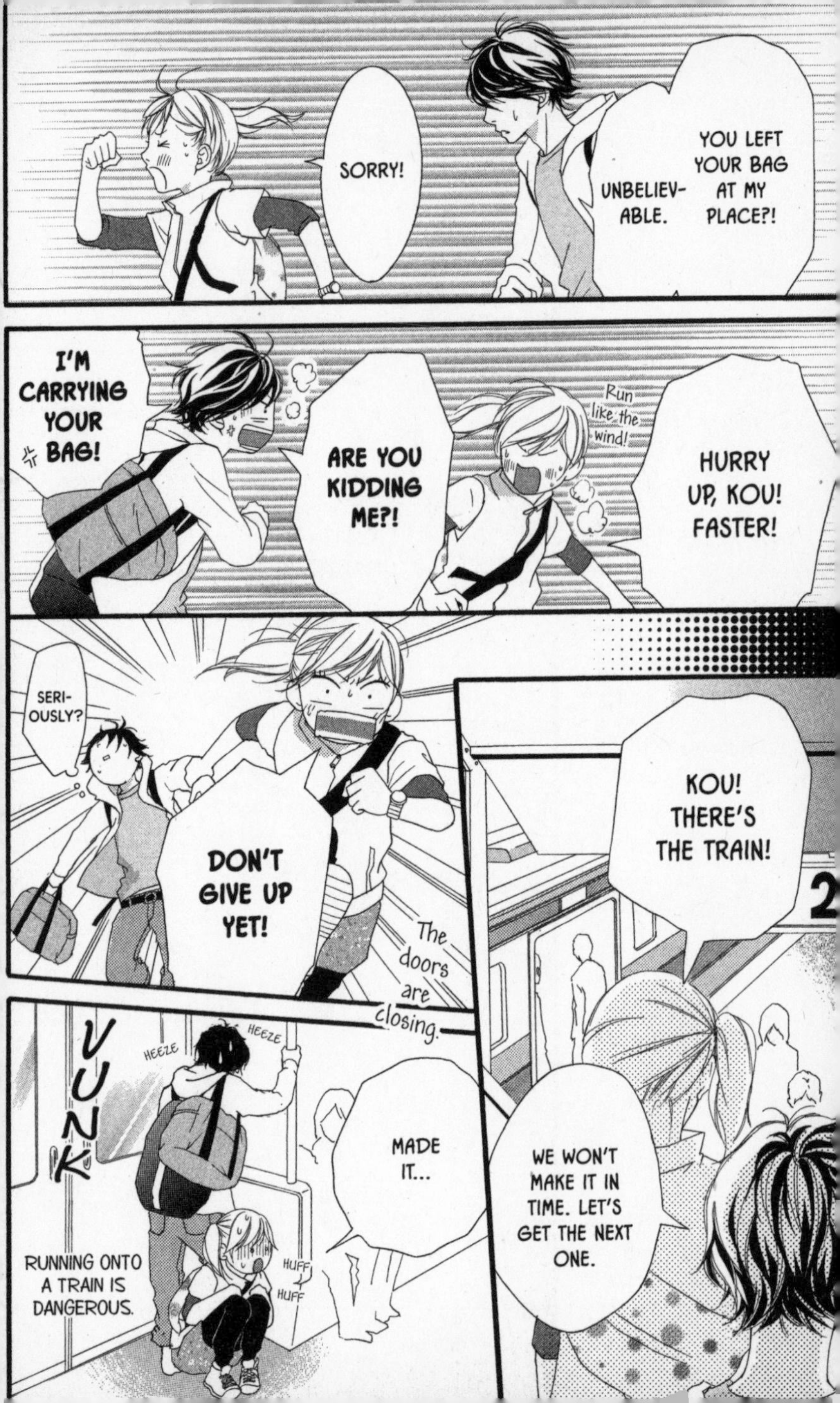
YOU LEFT YOUR BAG AT MY PLACE?!
UNBELIEV-ABLE.
SORRY!
HURRY UP, KOU! FASTER!
Run like the wind!
ARE YOU KIDDING ME?!
I'M CARRYING YOUR BAG!
KOU! THERE'S THE TRAIN!
WE WON'T MAKE IT IN TIME. LET'S GET THE NEXT ONE.
DON'T GIVE UP YET!
The doors are closing.
SERI-OUSLY?
MADE IT...
HEEZE
HEEZE
VUNK
HUFF HUFF
RUNNING ONTO A TRAIN IS DANGEROUS.

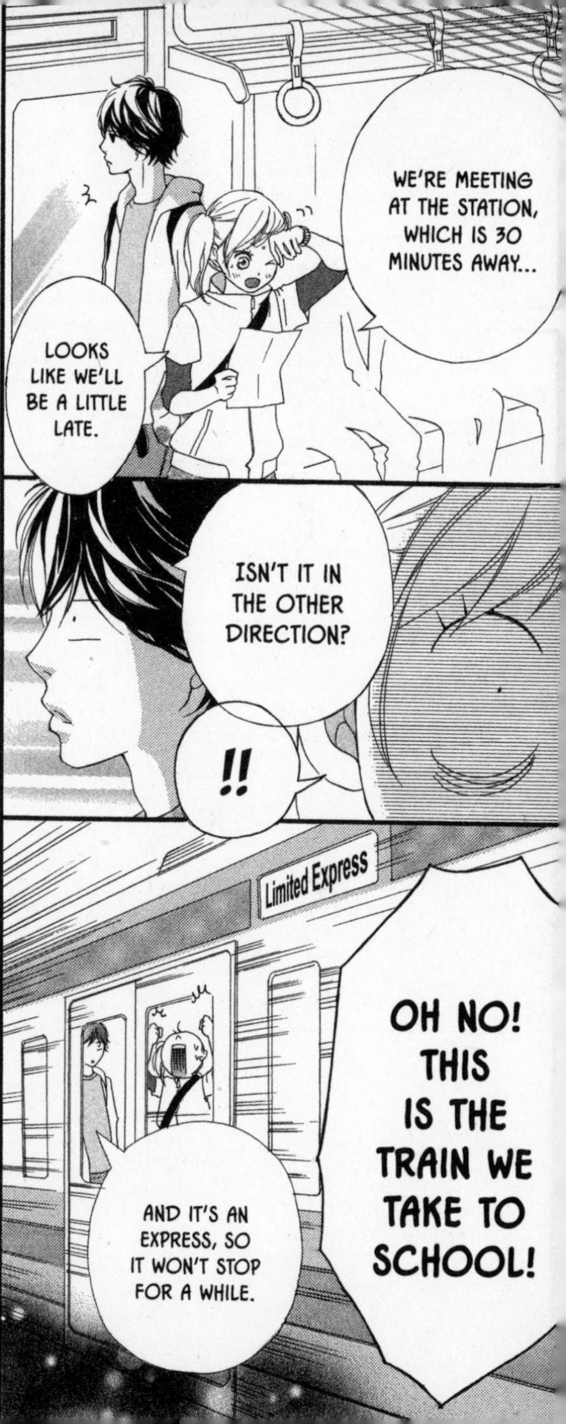
WE'RE MEETING AT THE STATION, WHICH IS 30 MINUTES AWAY...
LOOKS LIKE WE'LL BE A LITTLE LATE.
ISN'T IT IN THE OTHER DIRECTION?
!!
Limited Express
OH NO! THIS IS THE TRAIN WE TAKE TO SCHOOL!
AND IT'S AN EXPRESS, SO IT WON'T STOP FOR A WHILE.

♡ ♡ ♡ K's Love Life ♡ ♡ ♡

This is a story about "K," an acquaintance of mine, who was going to her boy-friend's house for the first time.

Her boyfriend asked her to cook dinner for him that day. This didn't make sense to K because, in her mind, she was the guest and he should be serving her. (Plus I think she was also kind of over him.)

When she showed up at his house, she brought a bunch of canned food, handed it over to him and then dumped him.

I love this story. Part of me thinks that she could've just cooked him a meal, but there's something about K's toughness that I like.

Oh, K... The truth is, she's more than an acquaintance. She's my older sister. Sorry for lying.

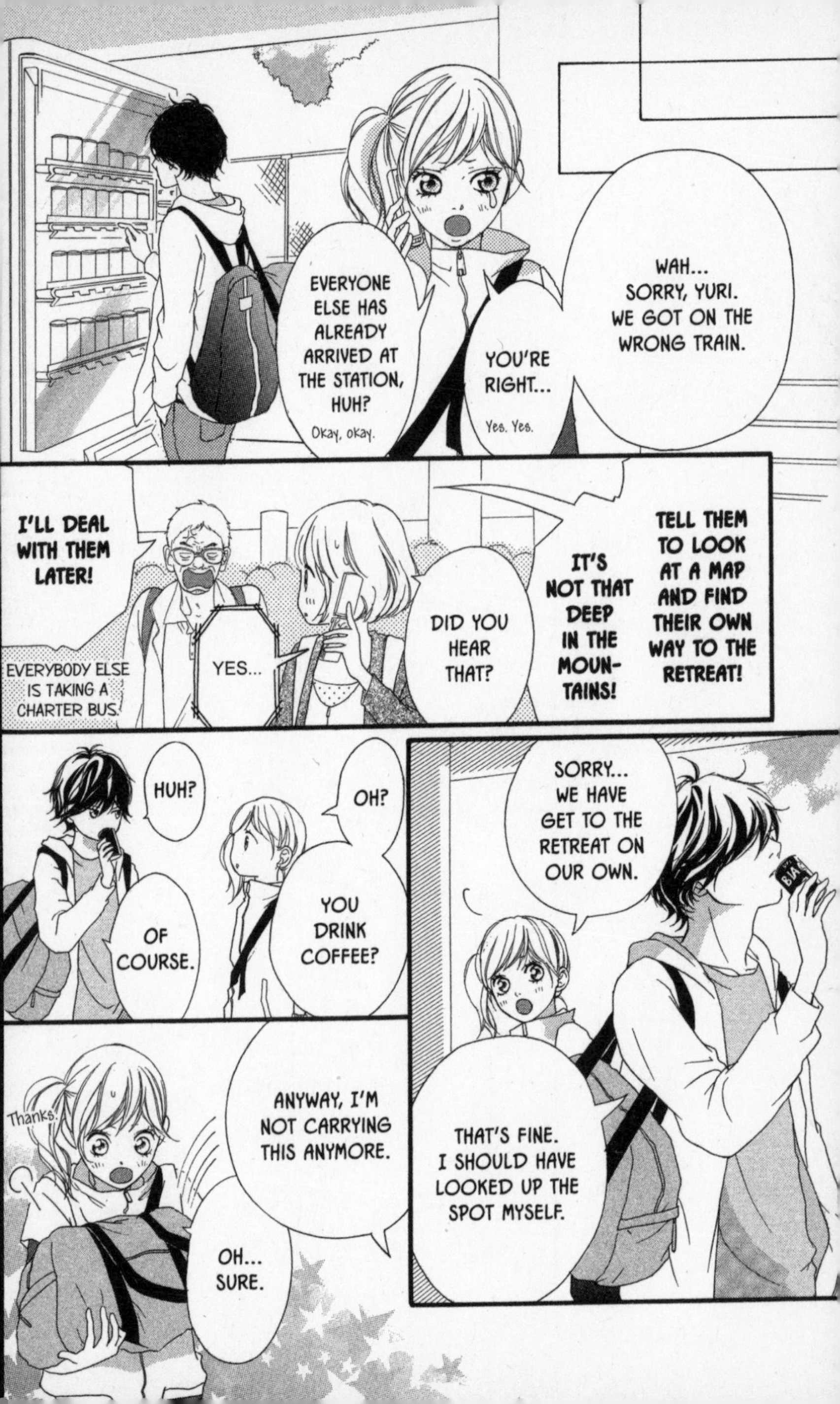
WAH... SORRY, YURI. WE GOT ON THE WRONG TRAIN.
YOU'RE RIGHT...
Yes. Yes.
EVERYONE ELSE HAS ALREADY ARRIVED AT THE STATION, HUH?
Okay, okay.
TELL THEM TO LOOK AT A MAP AND FIND THEIR OWN WAY TO THE RETREAT!
IT'S NOT THAT DEEP IN THE MOUN-TAINS!
DID YOU HEAR THAT?
YES...
I'LL DEAL WITH THEM LATER!
EVERYBODY ELSE IS TAKING A CHARTER BUS.
SORRY... WE HAVE GET TO THE RETREAT ON OUR OWN.
THAT'S FINE. I SHOULD HAVE LOOKED UP THE SPOT MYSELF.
OH?
HUH?
YOU DRINK COFFEE?
OF COURSE.
ANYWAY, I'M NOT CARRYING THIS ANYMORE.
OH... SURE.
Thanks.

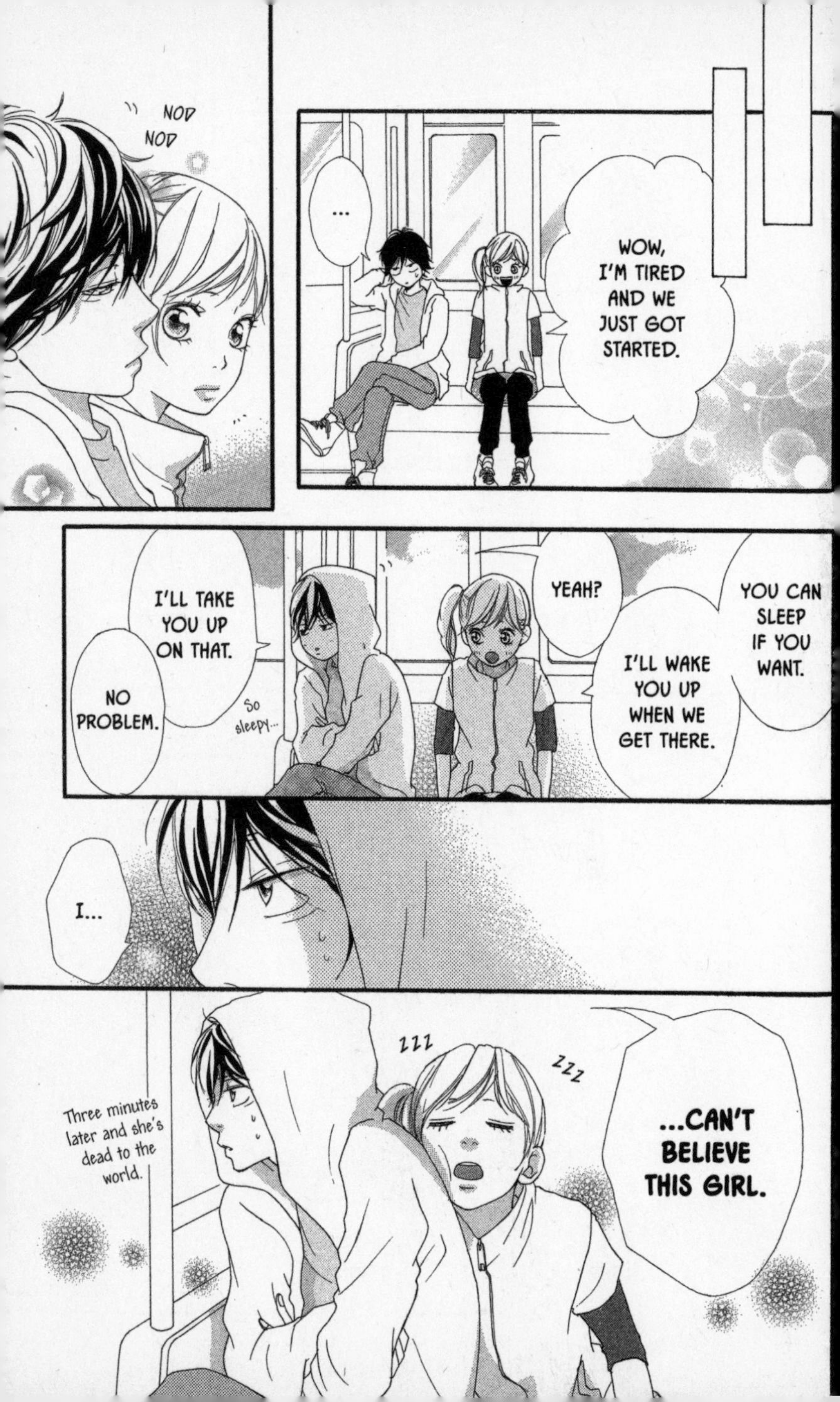
WOW, I'M TIRED AND WE JUST GOT STARTED.
...
NOD NOD
...
YOU CAN SLEEP IF YOU WANT.
YEAH?
I'LL WAKE YOU UP WHEN WE GET THERE.
I'LL TAKE YOU UP ON THAT.
So sleepy...
NO PROBLEM.
I...
...CAN'T BELIEVE THIS GIRL.
ZZZ
ZZZ
Three minutes later and she's dead to the world.

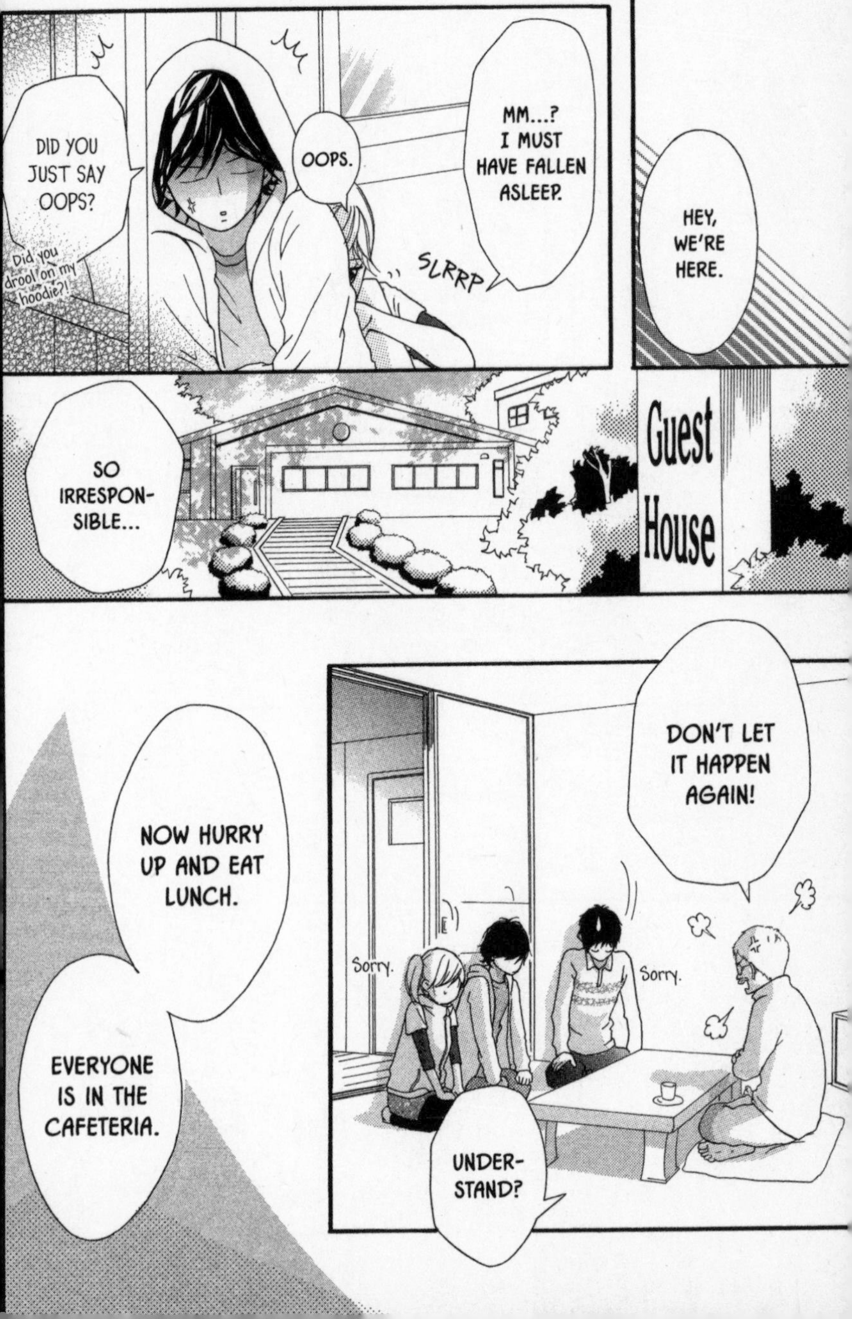
HEY, WE'RE HERE.
MM...? I MUST HAVE FALLEN ASLEEP.
SLRRP
OOPS.
DID YOU JUST SAY OOPS?
Did you drool on my hoodie?!
Guest House
SO IRRESPON-SIBLE...
DON'T LET IT HAPPEN AGAIN!
Sorry.
Sorry.
UNDER-STAND?
NOW HURRY UP AND EAT LUNCH.
EVERYONE IS IN THE CAFETERIA.

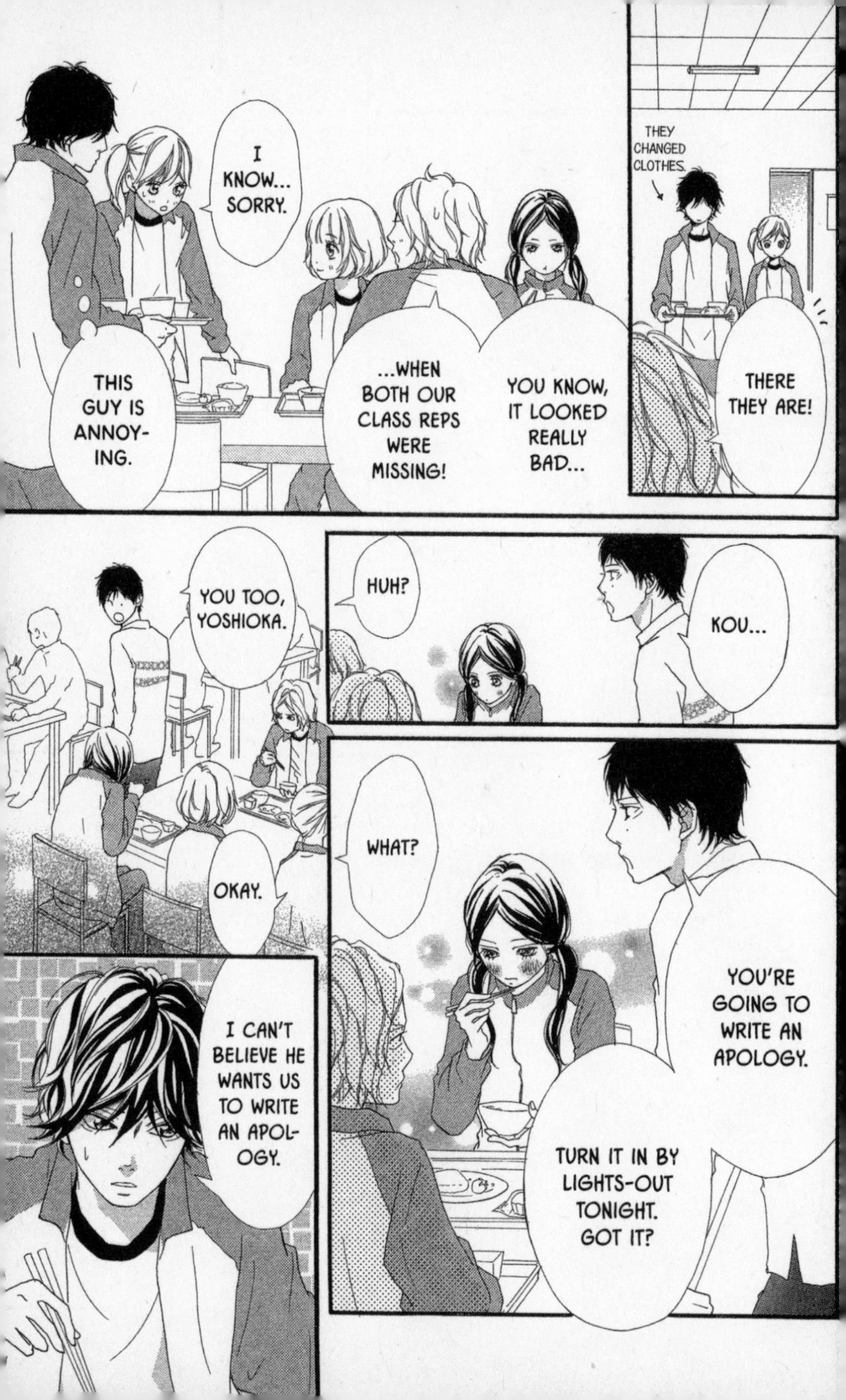
THEY CHANGED CLOTHES.
THERE THEY ARE!
YOU KNOW, IT LOOKED REALLY BAD...
...WHEN BOTH OUR CLASS REPS WERE MISSING!
I KNOW... SORRY.
THIS GUY IS ANNOYING.
KOU...
HUH?
YOU'RE GOING TO WRITE AN APOLOGY.
TURN IT IN BY LIGHTS-OUT TONIGHT. GOT IT?
WHAT?
YOU TOO, YOSHIOKA.
OKAY.
I CAN'T BELIEVE HE WANTS US TO WRITE AN APOLOGY.

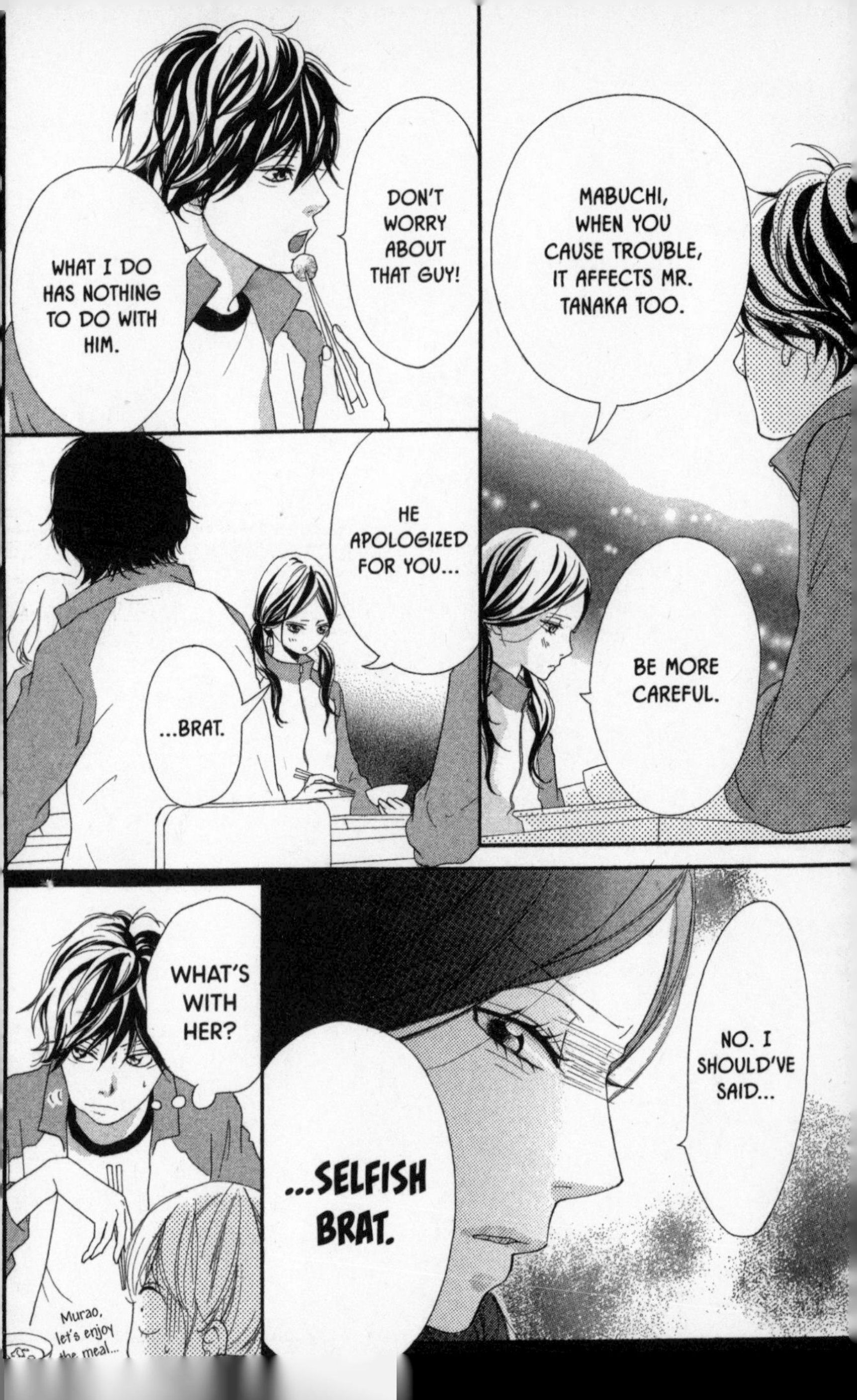
MABUCHI, WHEN YOU CAUSE TROUBLE, IT AFFECTS MR. TANAKA TOO.
BE MORE CAREFUL.
DON'T WORRY ABOUT THAT GUY!
WHAT I DO HAS NOTHING TO DO WITH HIM.
HE APOLOGIZED FOR YOU...
...BRAT.
NO. I SHOULD'VE SAID...
...SELFISH BRAT.
WHAT'S WITH HER?
Murao, let's enjoy the meal...

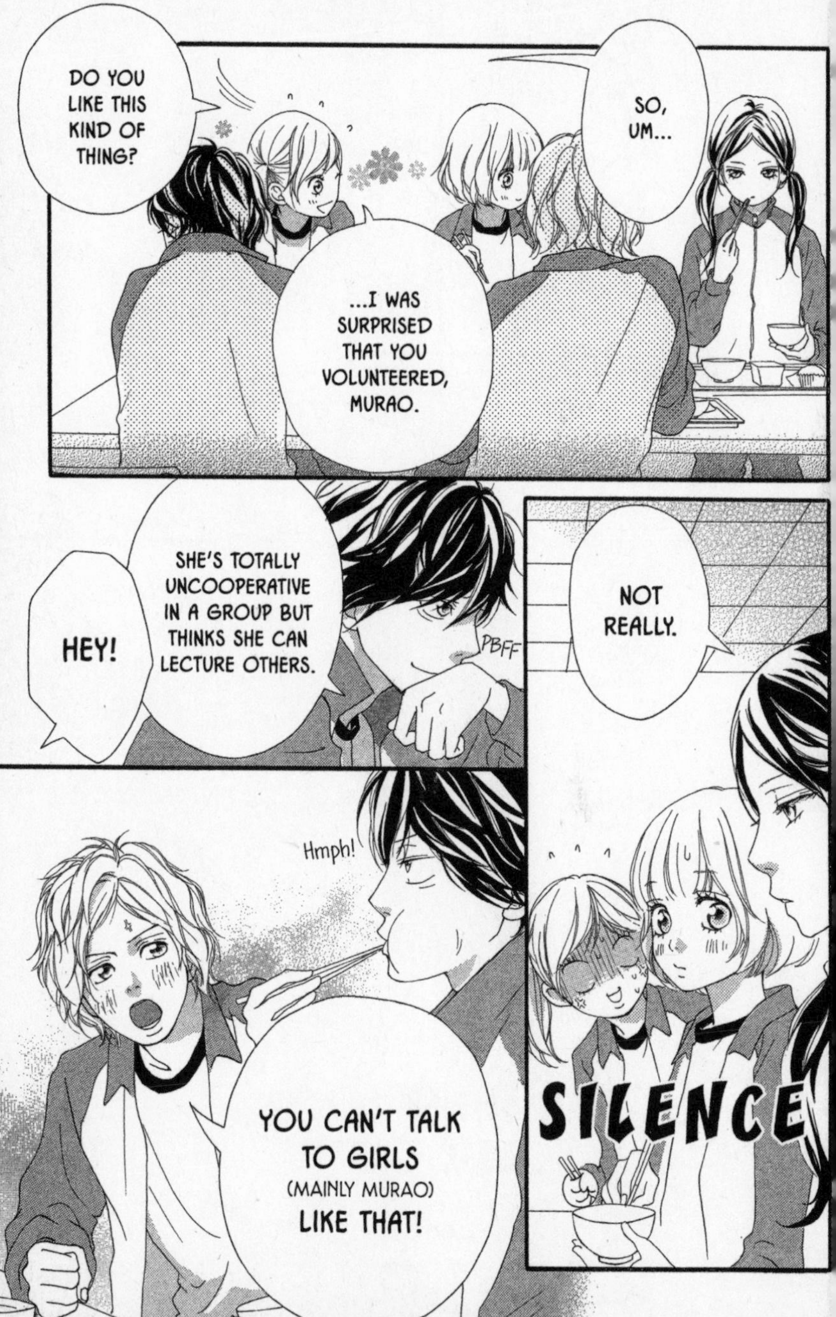

SO, UM...
...I WAS SURPRISED THAT YOU VOLUNTEERED, MURAO.
DO YOU LIKE THIS KIND OF THING?
NOT REALLY.
SILENCE
SHE'S TOTALLY UNCOOPERATIVE IN A GROUP BUT THINKS SHE CAN LECTURE OTHERS.
PBFF
HEY!
Hmph!
YOU CAN'T TALK TO GIRLS (MAINLY MURAO) LIKE THAT!

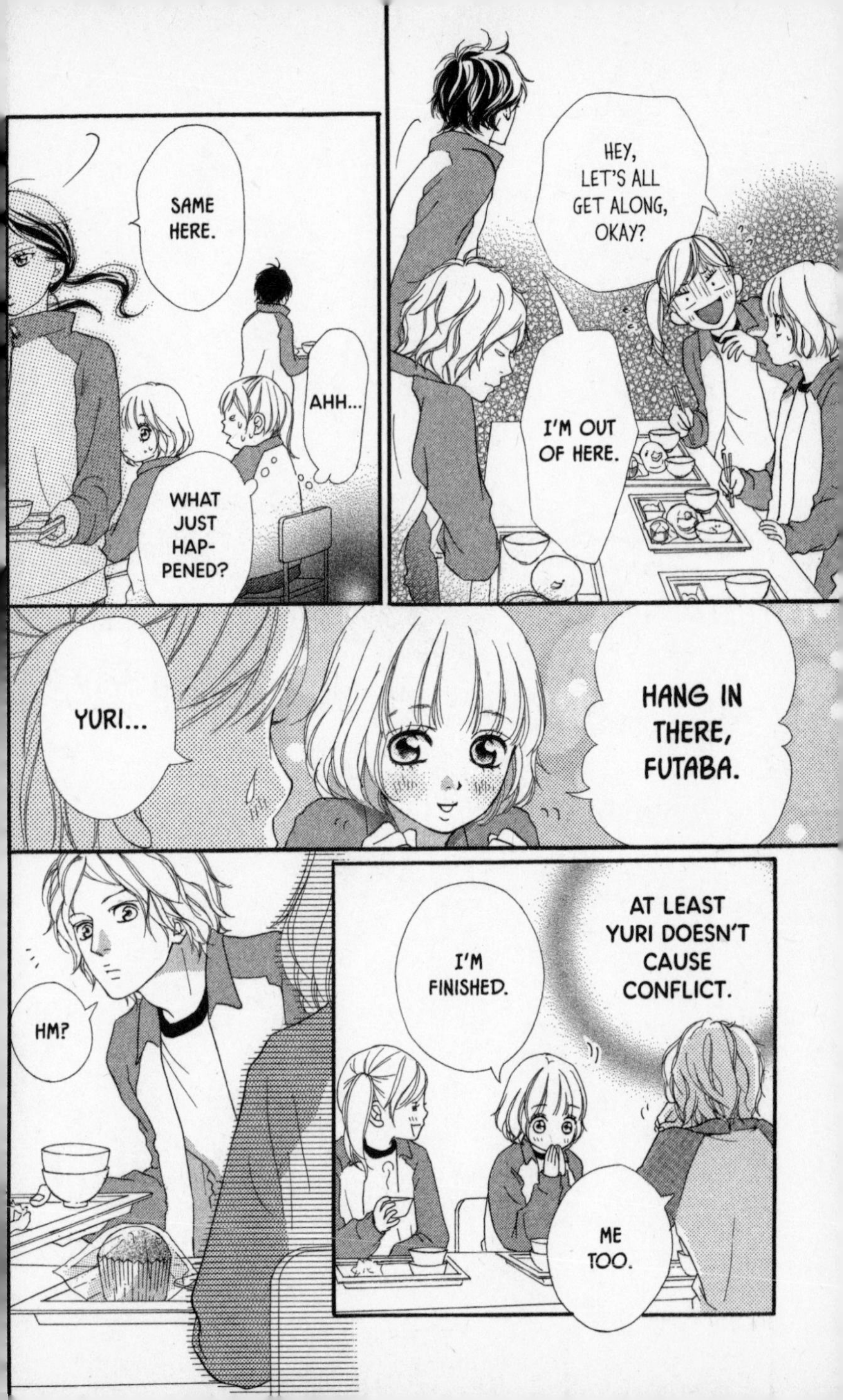
HEY, LET'S ALL GET ALONG, OKAY?
I'M OUT OF HERE.
SAME HERE.
AHH...
WHAT JUST HAP-PENED?
HANG IN THERE, FUTABA.
YURI...
AT LEAST YURI DOESN'T CAUSE CONFLICT.
I'M FINISHED.
ME TOO.
HM?

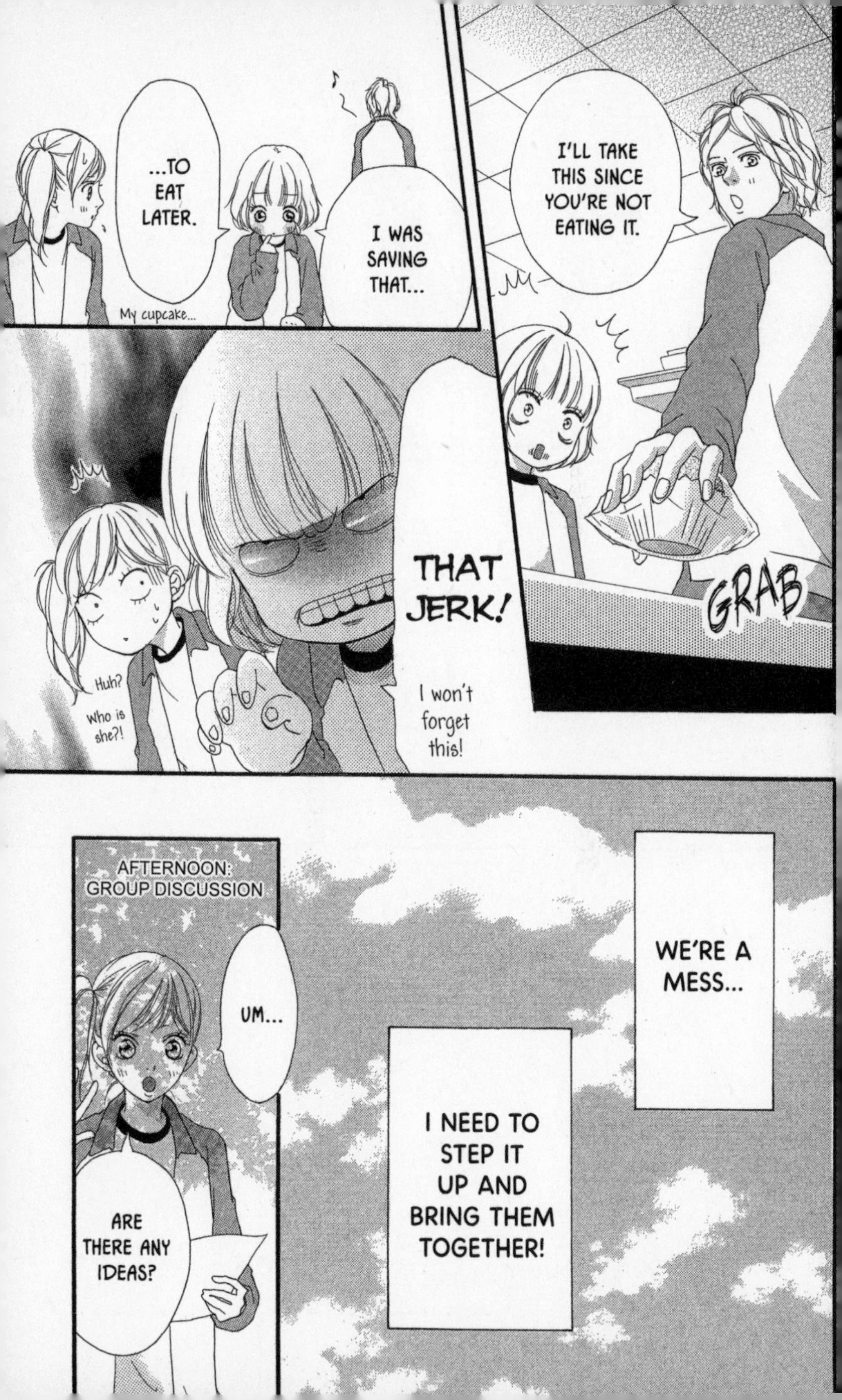
I'LL TAKE THIS SINCE YOU'RE NOT EATING IT.
GRAB
I WAS SAVING THAT...
...TO EAT LATER.
My cupcake...
THAT JERK!
I won't forget this!
Huh?
Who is she?!
WE'RE A MESS...
I NEED TO STEP IT UP AND BRING THEM TOGETHER!
AFTERNOON: GROUP DISCUSSION
UM...
ARE THERE ANY IDEAS?

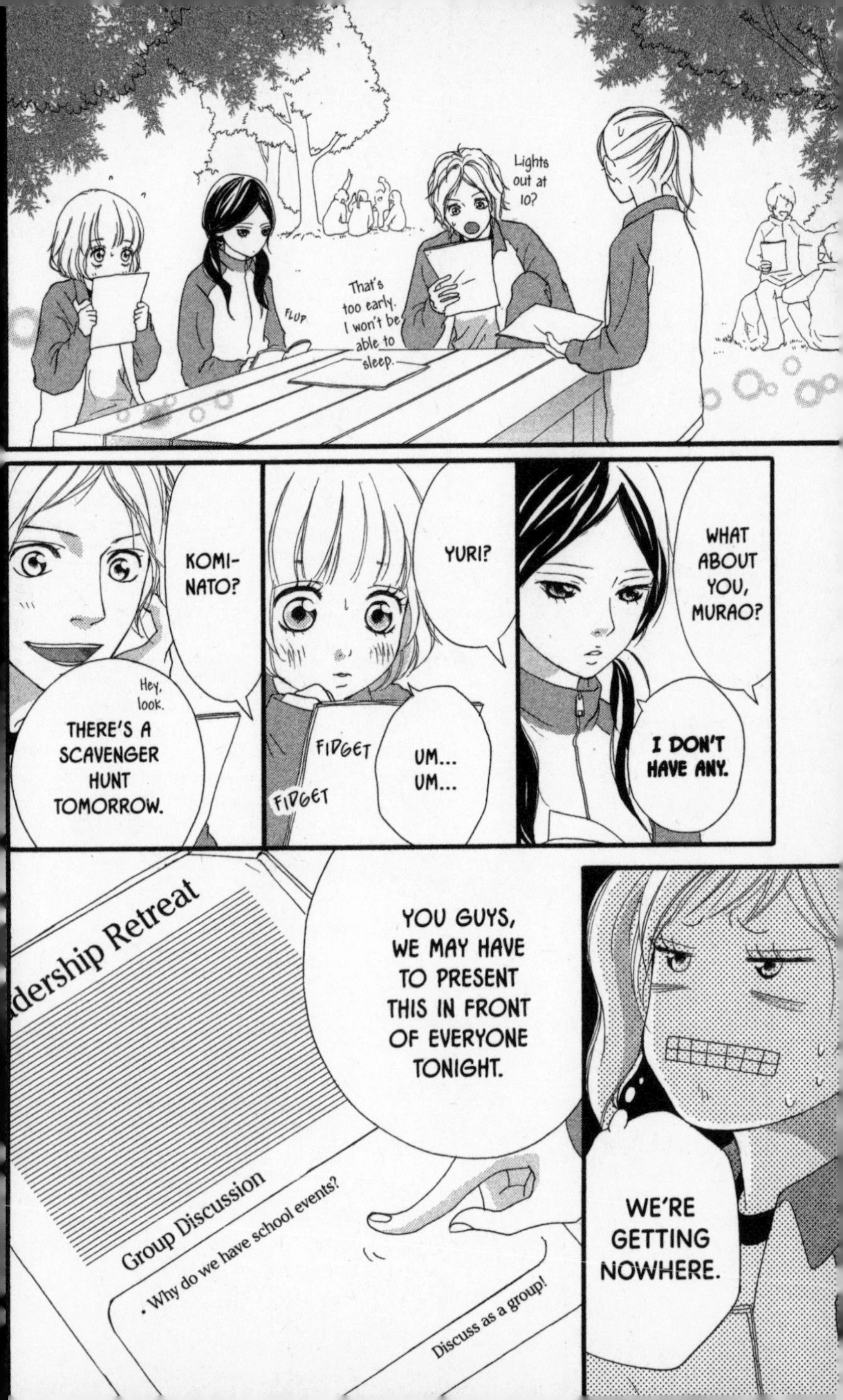
Lights out at 10?
That's too early. I won't be able to sleep.
FLUP
WHAT ABOUT YOU, MURAO?
I DON'T HAVE ANY.
YURI?
UM... UM...
FIDGET
FIDGET
KOMI-NATO?
Hey, look.
THERE'S A SCAVENGER HUNT TOMORROW.
WE'RE GETTING NOWHERE.
YOU GUYS, WE MAY HAVE TO PRESENT THIS IN FRONT OF EVERYONE TONIGHT.
dership Retreat
Group Discussion
• Why do we have school events?
Discuss as a group!

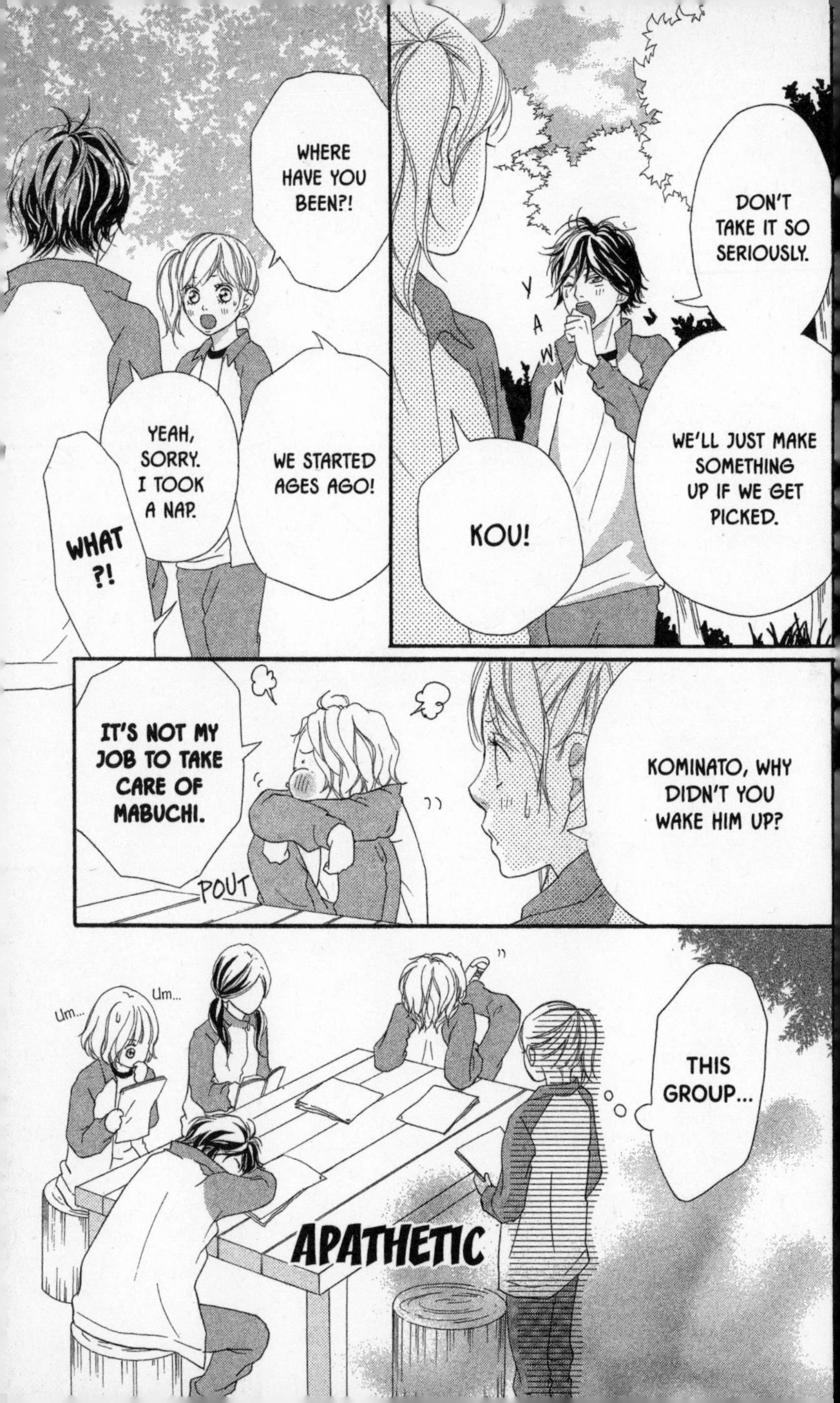
DON'T TAKE IT SO SERIOUSLY.
YAWN
WE'LL JUST MAKE SOMETHING UP IF WE GET PICKED.
KOU!
WHERE HAVE YOU BEEN?!
WE STARTED AGES AGO!
YEAH, SORRY. I TOOK A NAP.
WHAT?!
KOMINATO, WHY DIDN'T YOU WAKE HIM UP?
IT'S NOT MY JOB TO TAKE CARE OF MABUCHI.
POUT
THIS GROUP...
Um...
Um...
APATHETIC

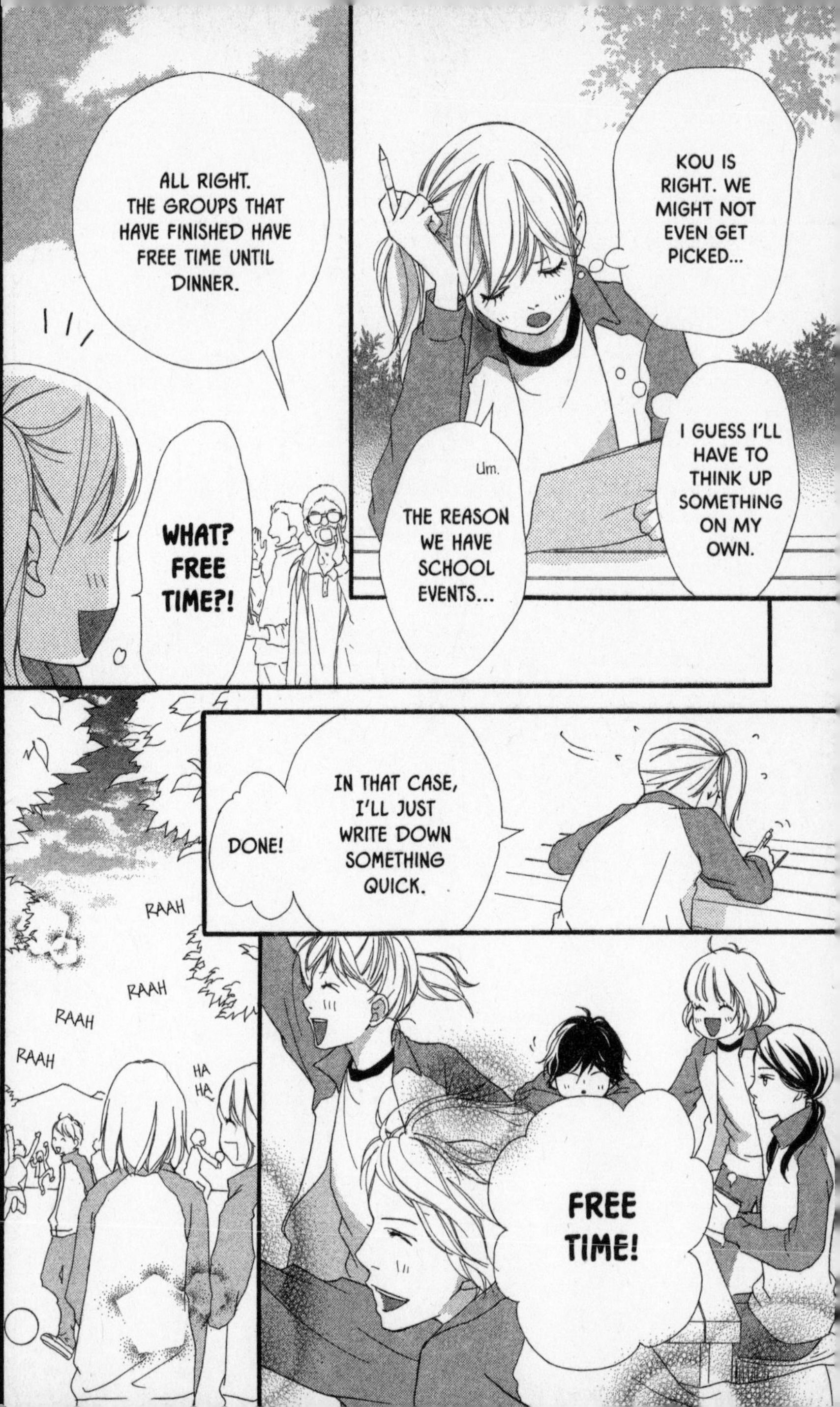
KOU IS RIGHT. WE MIGHT NOT EVEN GET PICKED...
I GUESS I'LL HAVE TO THINK UP SOMETHING ON MY OWN.
Um.
THE REASON WE HAVE SCHOOL EVENTS...
ALL RIGHT. THE GROUPS THAT HAVE FINISHED HAVE FREE TIME UNTIL DINNER.
WHAT? FREE TIME?!
IN THAT CASE, I'LL JUST WRITE DOWN SOMETHING QUICK.
DONE!
FREE TIME!
RAAH
RAAH
RAAH
RAAH
HA HA

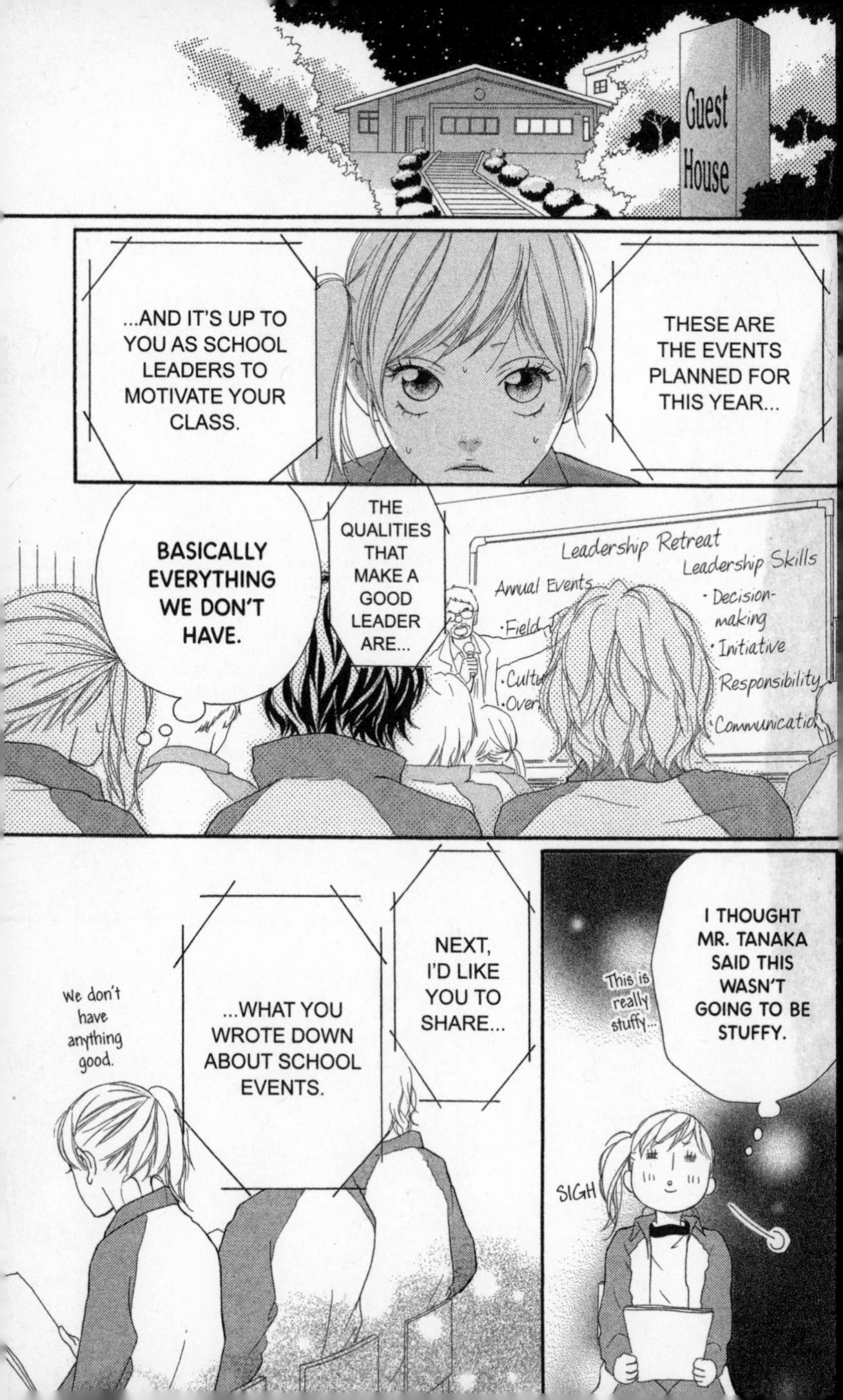

Guest House
THESE ARE THE EVENTS PLANNED FOR THIS YEAR...
...AND IT'S UP TO YOU AS SCHOOL LEADERS TO MOTIVATE YOUR CLASS.
Leadership Retreat
Leadership Skills
· Decision-making
· Initiative
Responsibility
Annual Events
THE QUALITIES THAT MAKE A GOOD LEADER ARE...
BASICALLY EVERYTHING WE DON'T HAVE.
I THOUGHT MR. TANAKA SAID THIS WASN'T GOING TO BE STUFFY.
This is really stuffy...
SIGH
NEXT, I'D LIKE YOU TO SHARE...
...WHAT YOU WROTE DOWN ABOUT SCHOOL EVENTS.
We don't have anything good.

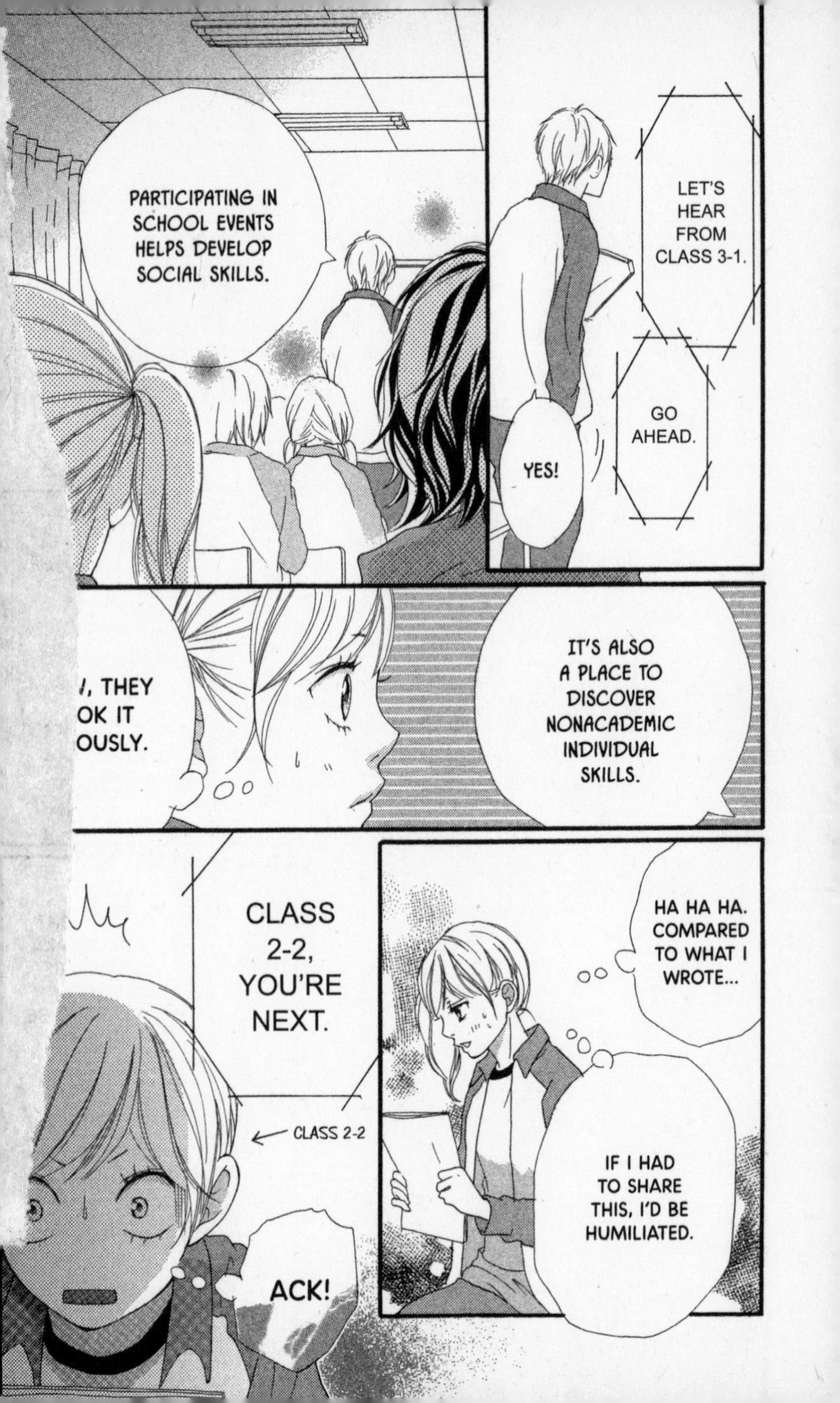
LET'S HEAR FROM CLASS 3-1.
GO AHEAD.
YES!
PARTICIPATING IN SCHOOL EVENTS HELPS DEVELOP SOCIAL SKILLS.
IT'S ALSO A PLACE TO DISCOVER NONACADEMIC INDIVIDUAL SKILLS.
, THEY OK IT OUSLY.
HA HA HA. COMPARED TO WHAT I WROTE...
IF I HAD TO SHARE THIS, I'D BE HUMILIATED.
CLASS 2-2, YOU'RE NEXT.
CLASS 2-2
ACK!

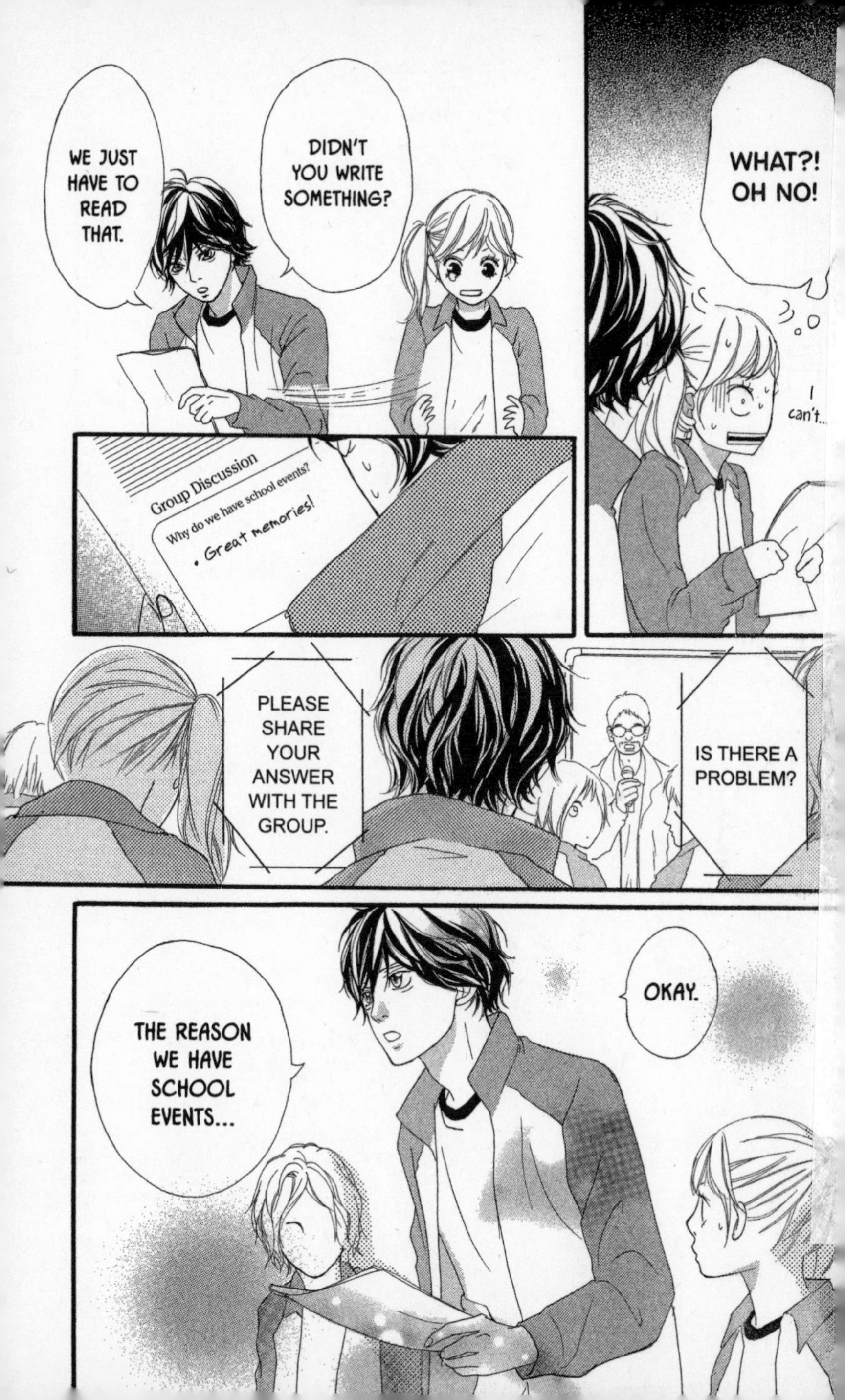
WHAT?! OH NO!
I can't...
DIDN'T YOU WRITE SOMETHING?
WE JUST HAVE TO READ THAT.
Group Discussion
Why do we have school events?
• Great memories!
IS THERE A PROBLEM?
PLEASE SHARE YOUR ANSWER WITH THE GROUP.
OKAY.
THE REASON WE HAVE SCHOOL EVENTS...

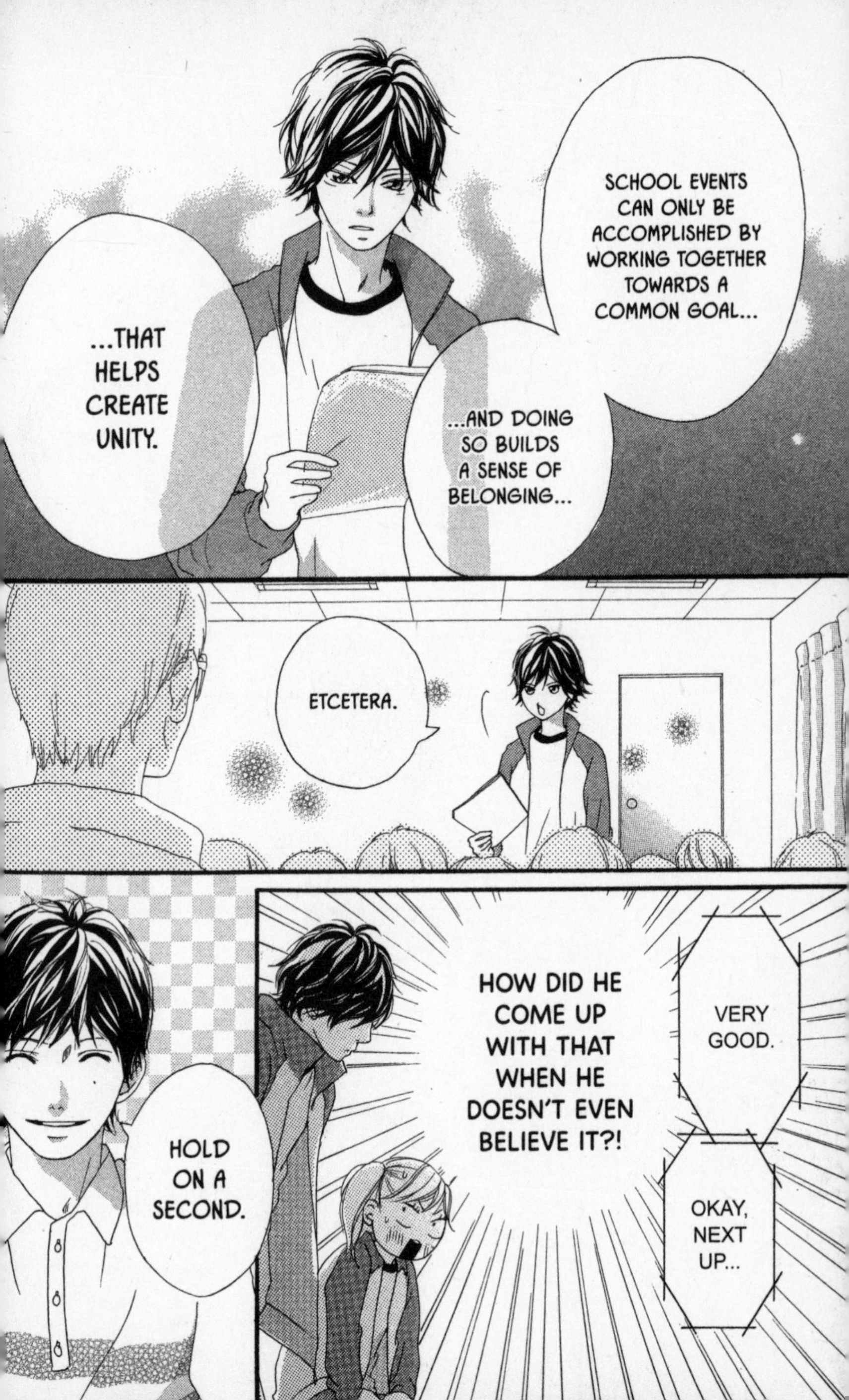
SCHOOL EVENTS CAN ONLY BE ACCOMPLISHED BY WORKING TOGETHER TOWARDS A COMMON GOAL...
...AND DOING SO BUILDS A SENSE OF BELONGING...
...THAT HELPS CREATE UNITY.
ETCETERA.
VERY GOOD.
OKAY, NEXT UP...
HOW DID HE COME UP WITH THAT WHEN HE DOESN'T EVEN BELIEVE IT?!
HOLD ON A SECOND.

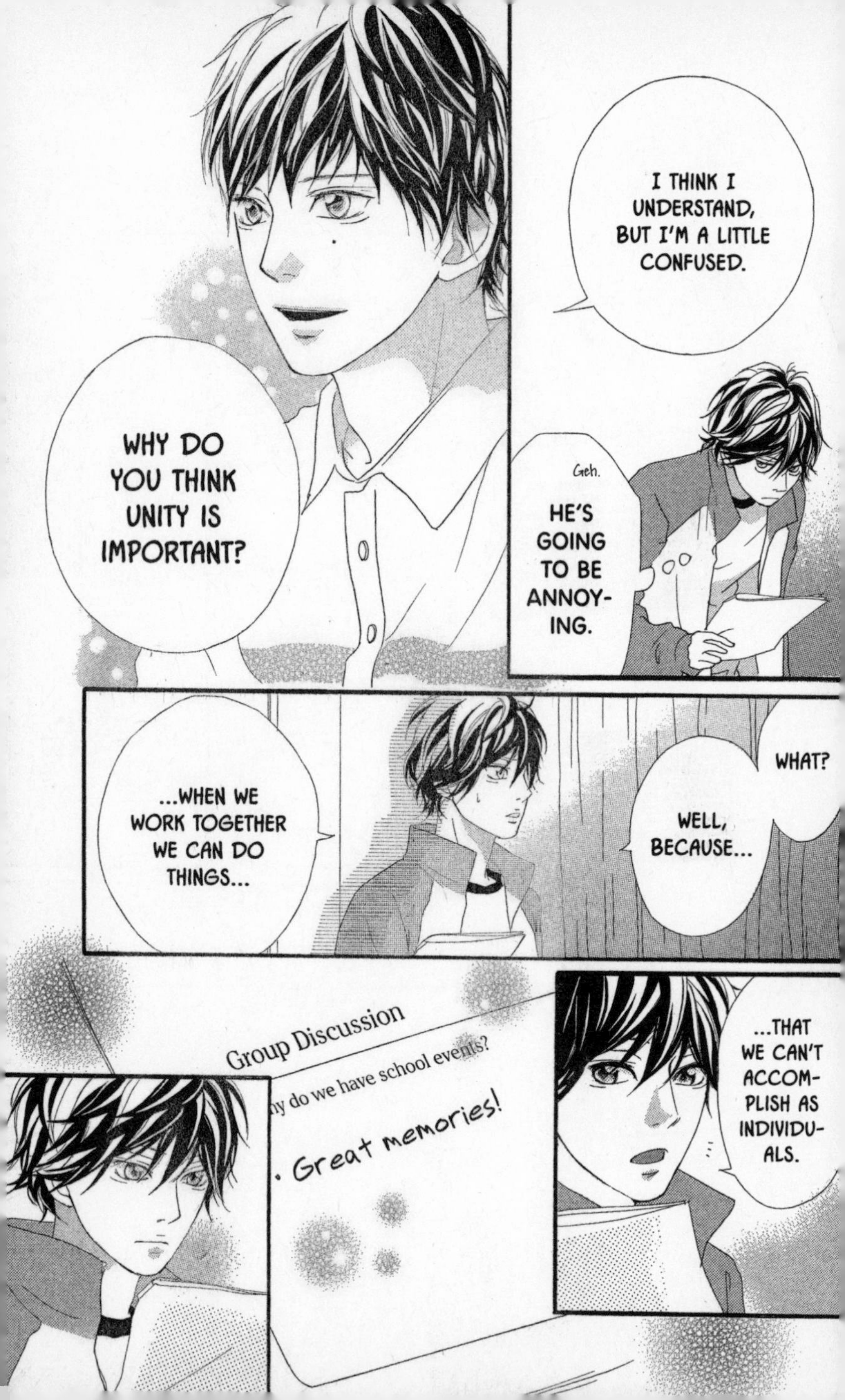
I THINK I UNDERSTAND, BUT I'M A LITTLE CONFUSED.
Geh.
HE'S GOING TO BE ANNOY-ING.
WHY DO YOU THINK UNITY IS IMPORTANT?
WHAT?
WELL, BECAUSE...
...WHEN WE WORK TOGETHER WE CAN DO THINGS...
...THAT WE CAN'T ACCOMPLISH AS INDIVIDU-ALS.
Group Discussion
hy do we have school events?
· Great memories!

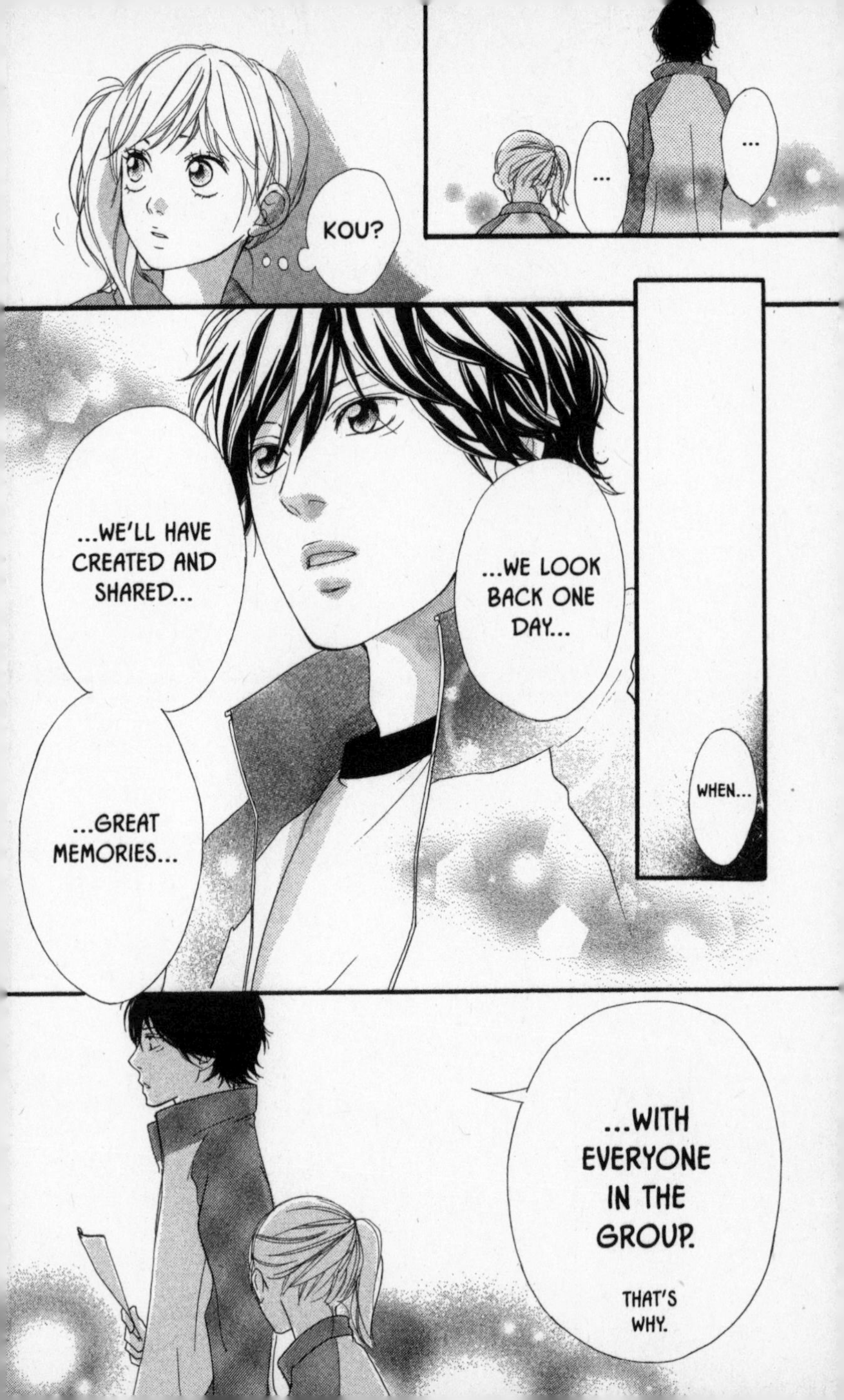
...
...
KOU?
WHEN...
...WE LOOK BACK ONE DAY...
...WE'LL HAVE CREATED AND SHARED...
...GREAT MEMORIES...
...WITH EVERYONE IN THE GROUP.
THAT'S WHY.

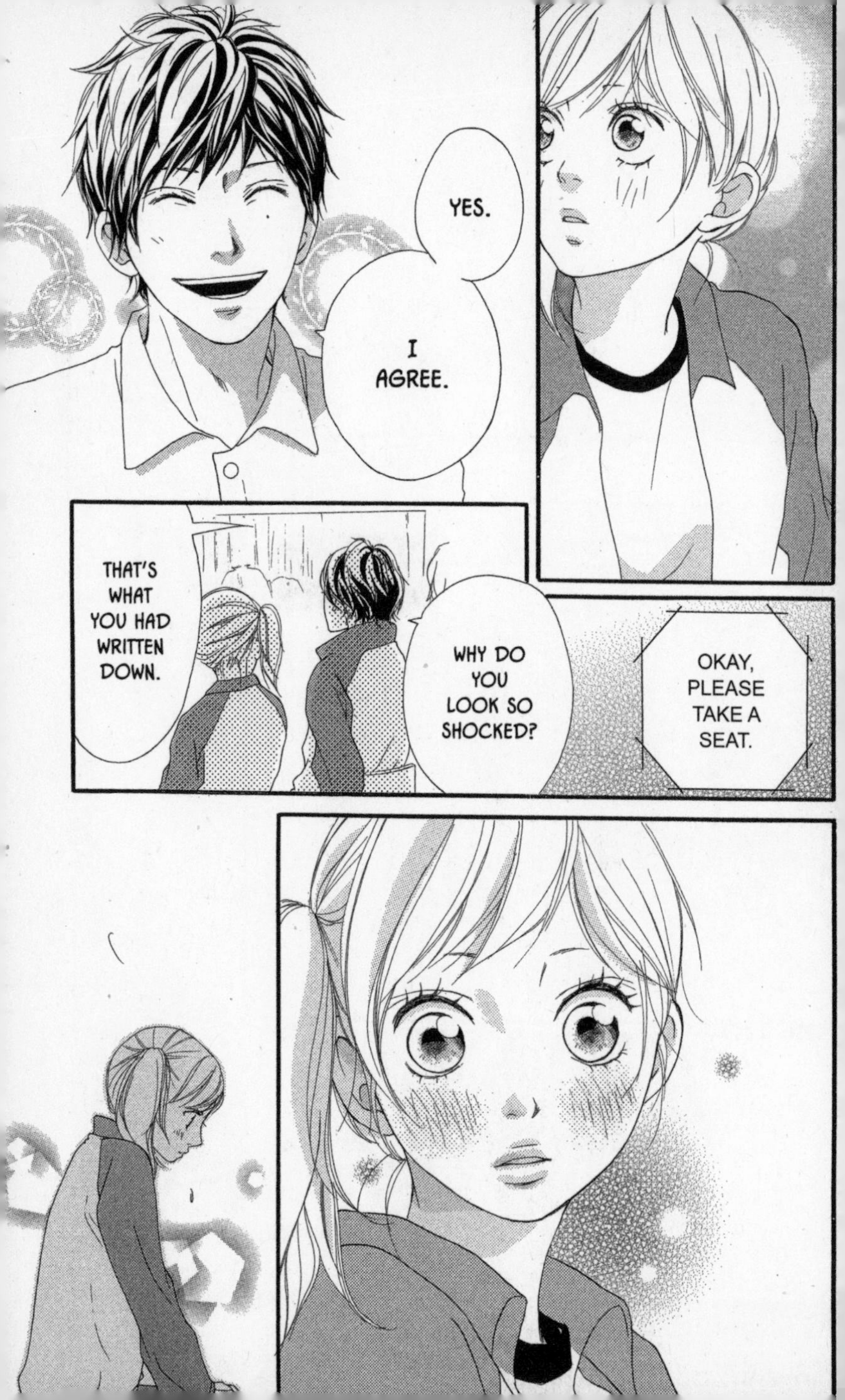
YES.
I AGREE.
THAT'S WHAT YOU HAD WRITTEN DOWN.
WHY DO YOU LOOK SO SHOCKED?
OKAY, PLEASE TAKE A SEAT.

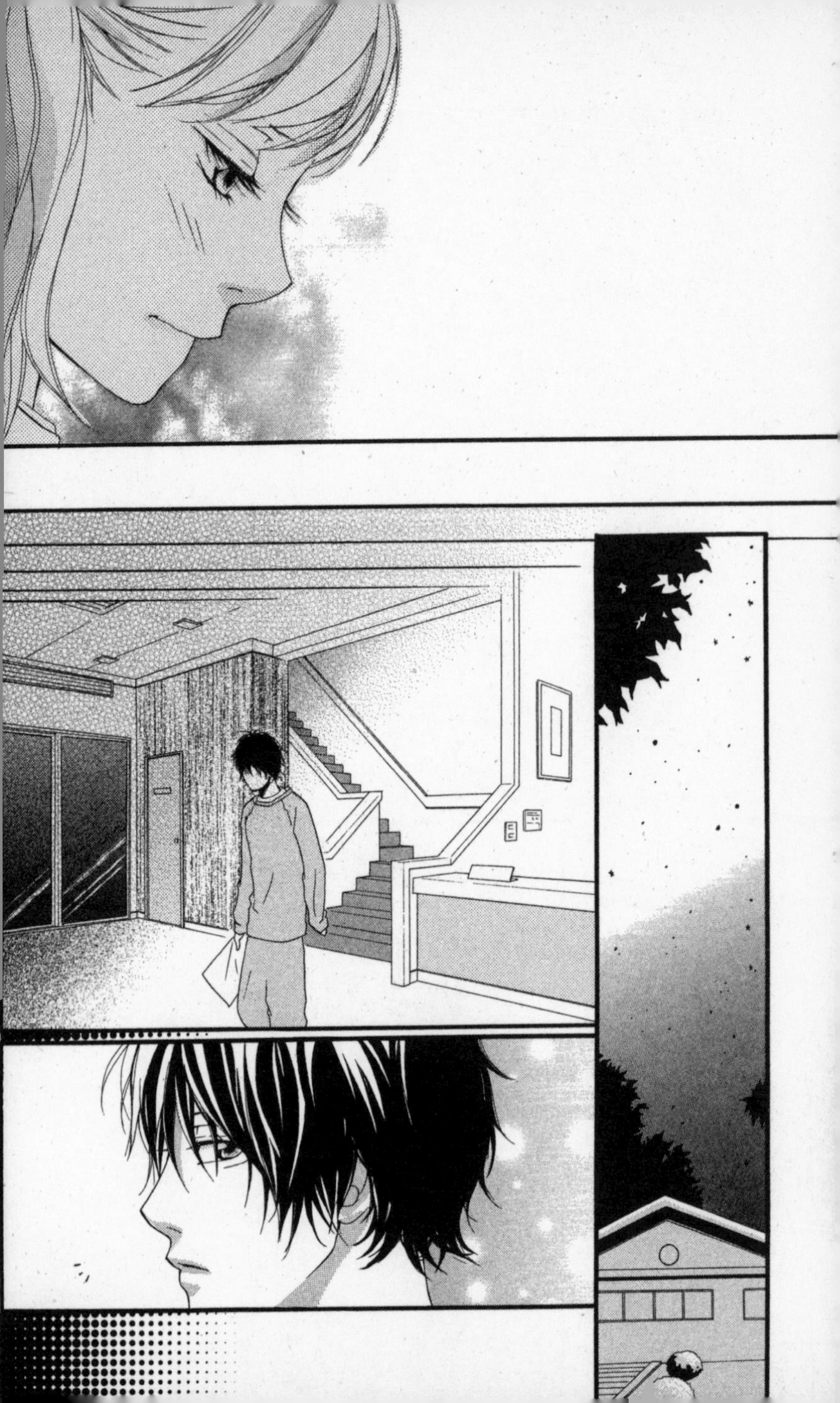

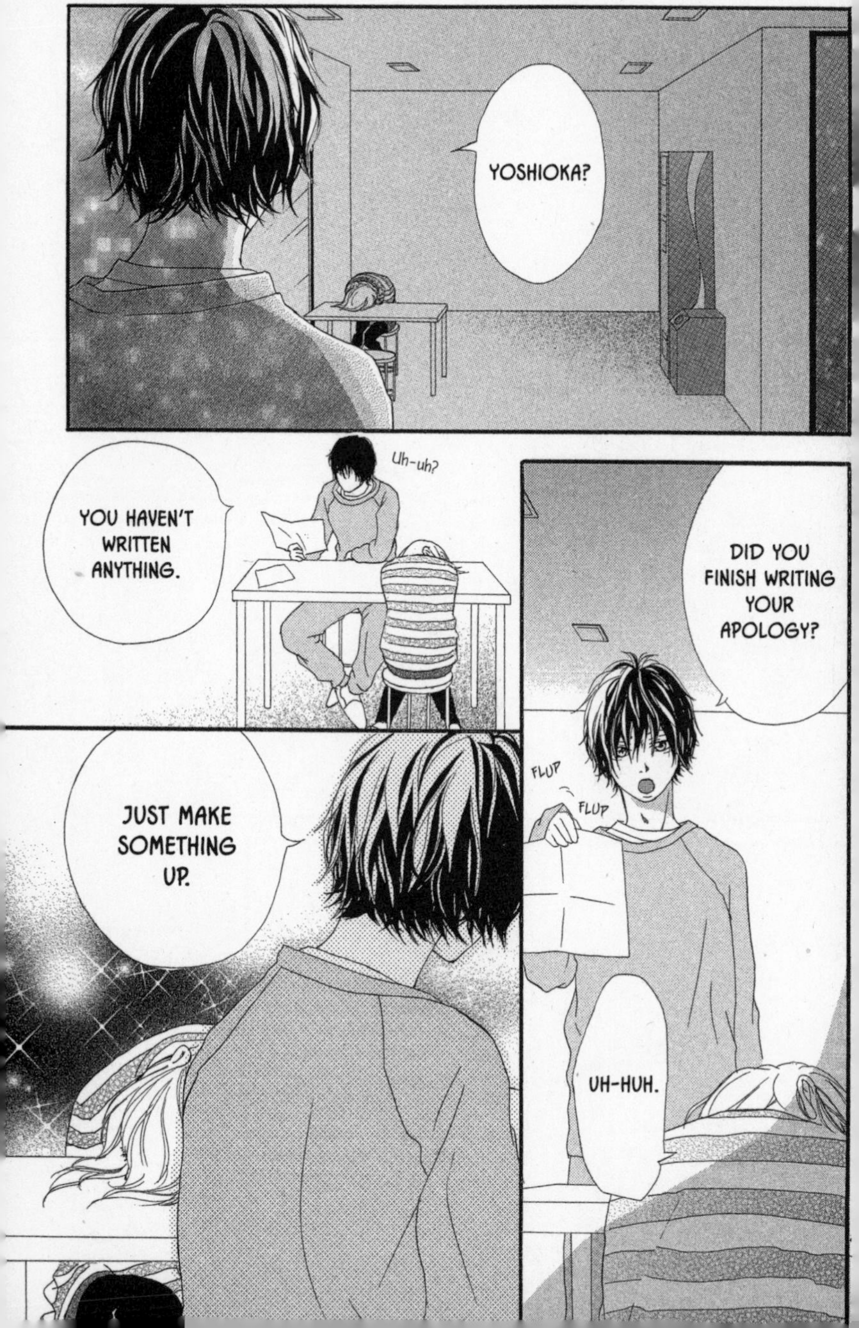
YOSHIOKA?
DID YOU FINISH WRITING YOUR APOLOGY?
FLUP
FLUP
UH-HUH.
Uh-uh?
YOU HAVEN'T WRITTEN ANYTHING.
JUST MAKE SOMETHING UP.

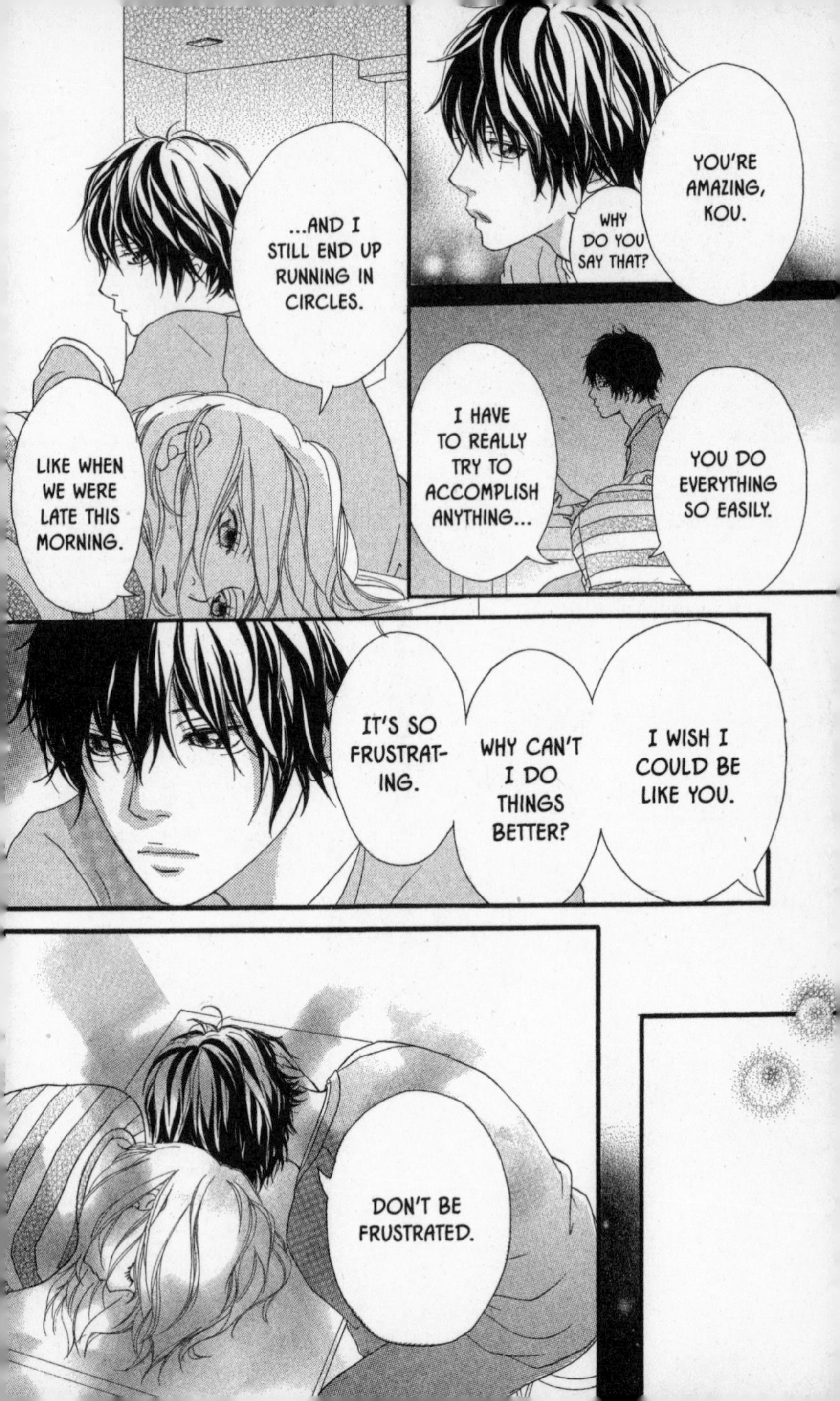
YOU'RE AMAZING, KOU.
WHY DO YOU SAY THAT?
YOU DO EVERYTHING SO EASILY.
I HAVE TO REALLY TRY TO ACCOMPLISH ANYTHING...
...AND I STILL END UP RUNNING IN CIRCLES.
LIKE WHEN WE WERE LATE THIS MORNING.
I WISH I COULD BE LIKE YOU.
WHY CAN'T I DO THINGS BETTER?
IT'S SO FRUSTRAT-ING.
DON'T BE FRUSTRATED.

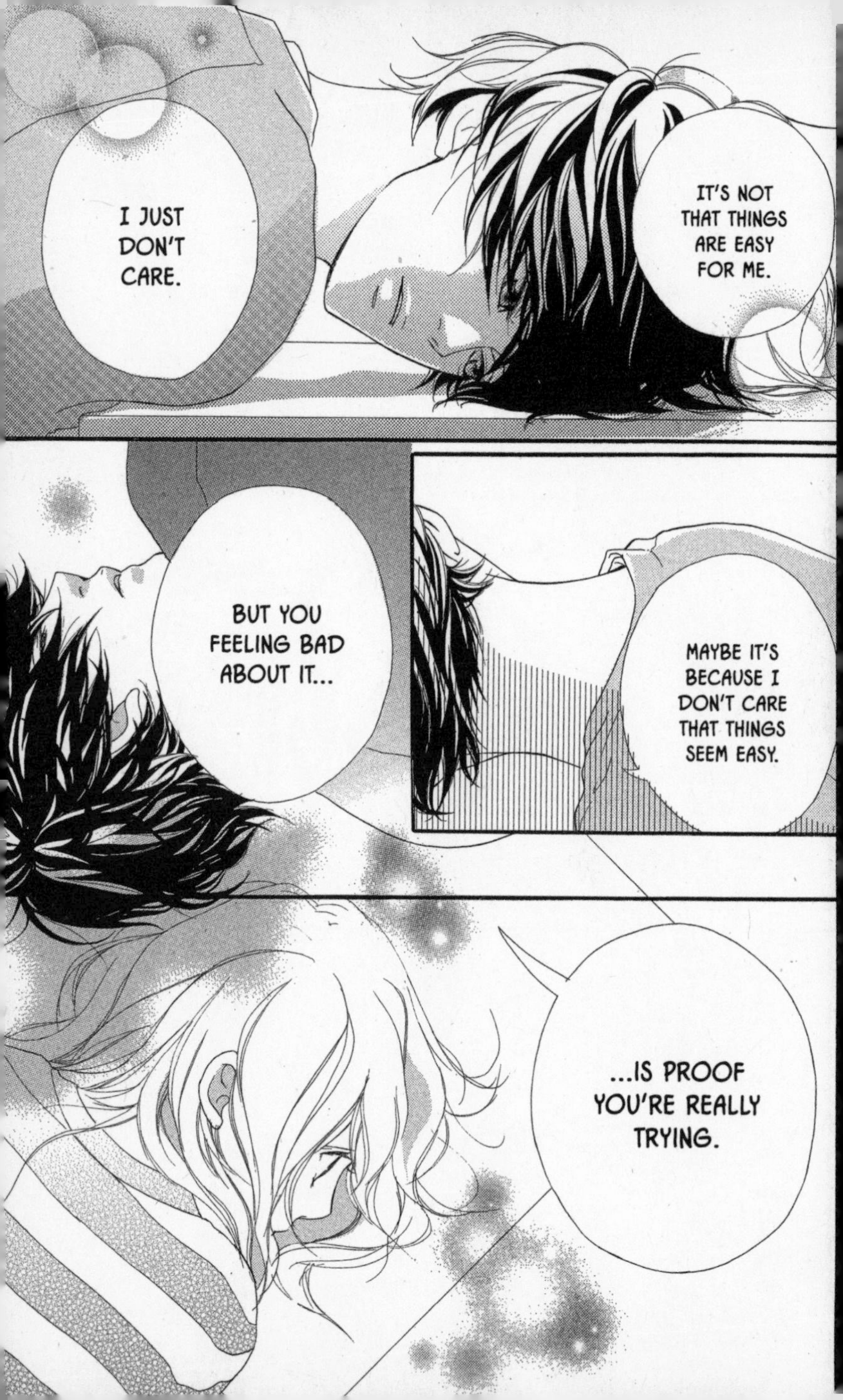
IT'S NOT THAT THINGS ARE EASY FOR ME.
I JUST DON'T CARE.
MAYBE IT'S BECAUSE I DON'T CARE THAT THINGS SEEM EASY.
BUT YOU FEELING BAD ABOUT IT...
...IS PROOF YOU'RE REALLY TRYING.

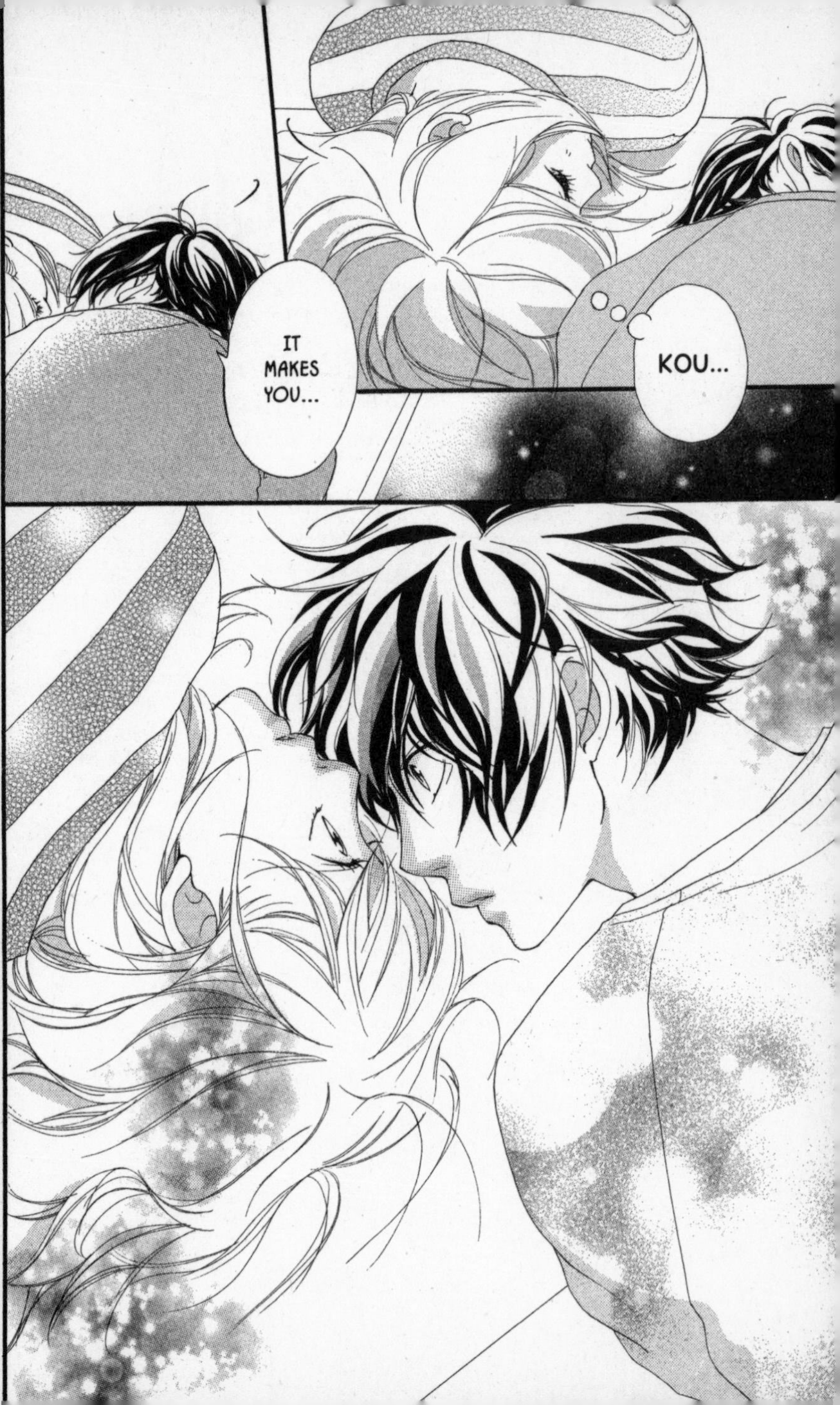
KOU...
IT MAKES YOU...

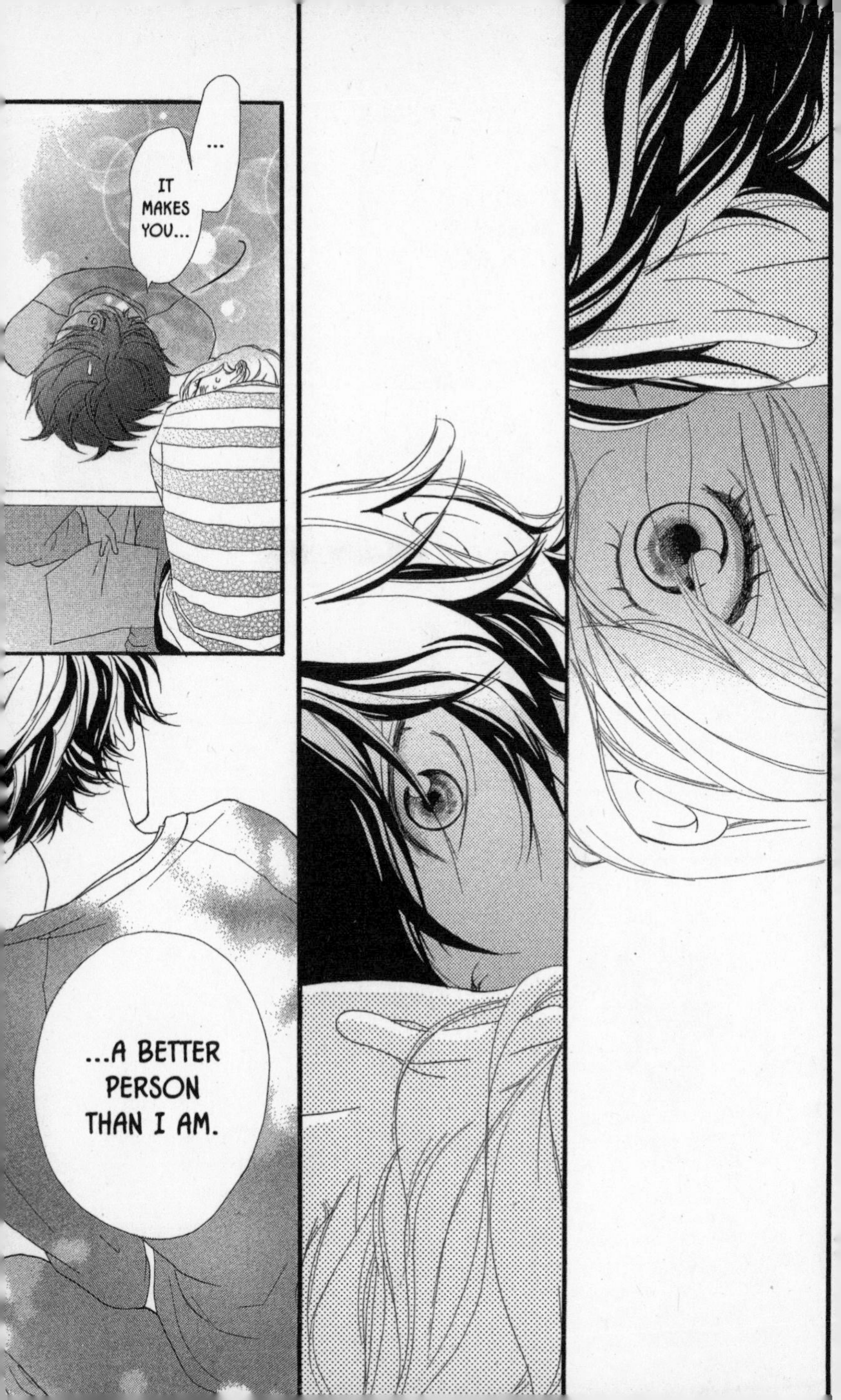
...
IT MAKES YOU...
...A BETTER PERSON THAN I AM.

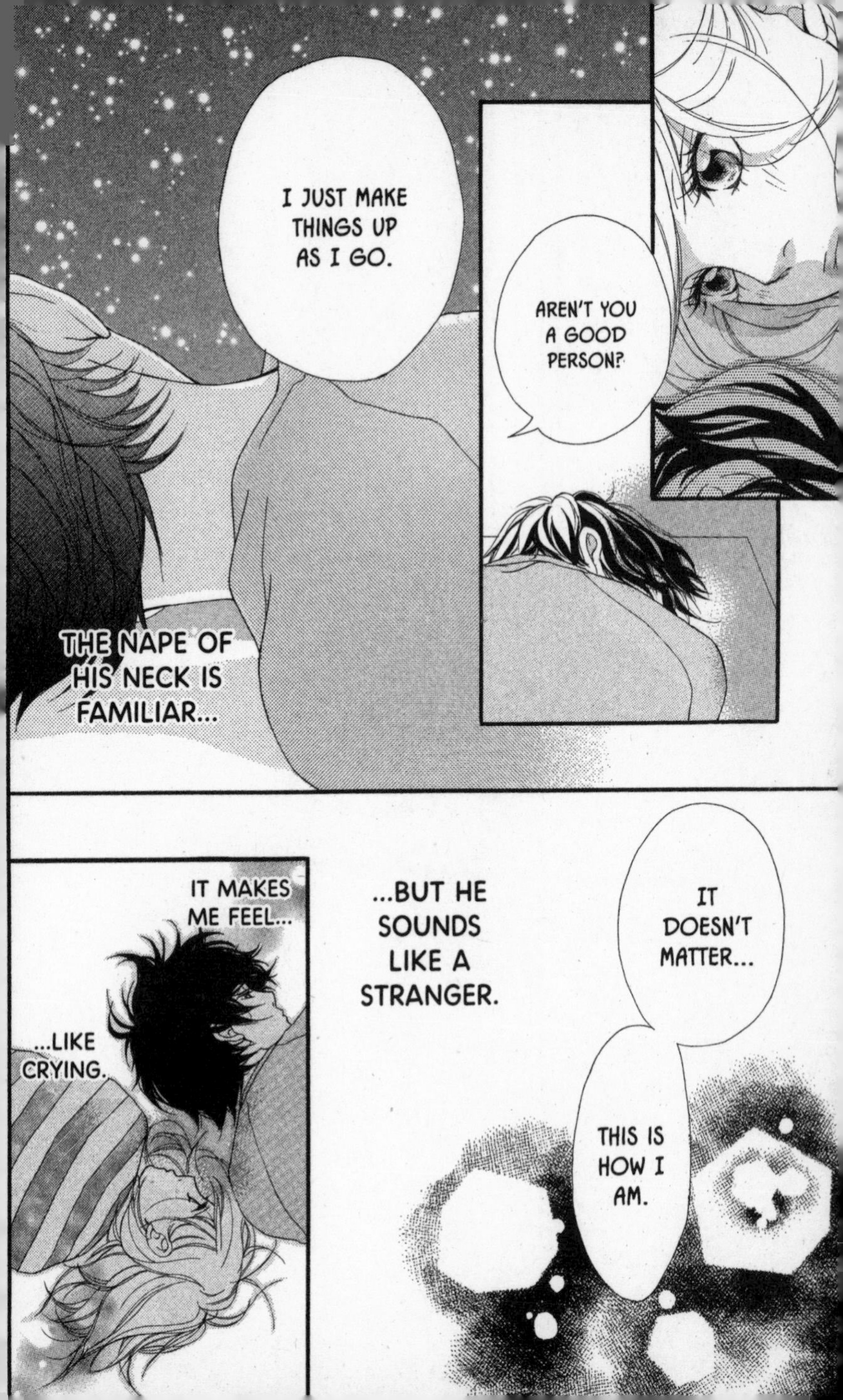
AREN'T YOU A GOOD PERSON?
I JUST MAKE THINGS UP AS I GO.
THE NAPE OF HIS NECK IS FAMILIAR...
IT DOESN'T MATTER...
THIS IS HOW I AM.
...BUT HE SOUNDS LIKE A STRANGER.
IT MAKES ME FEEL...
...LIKE CRYING.

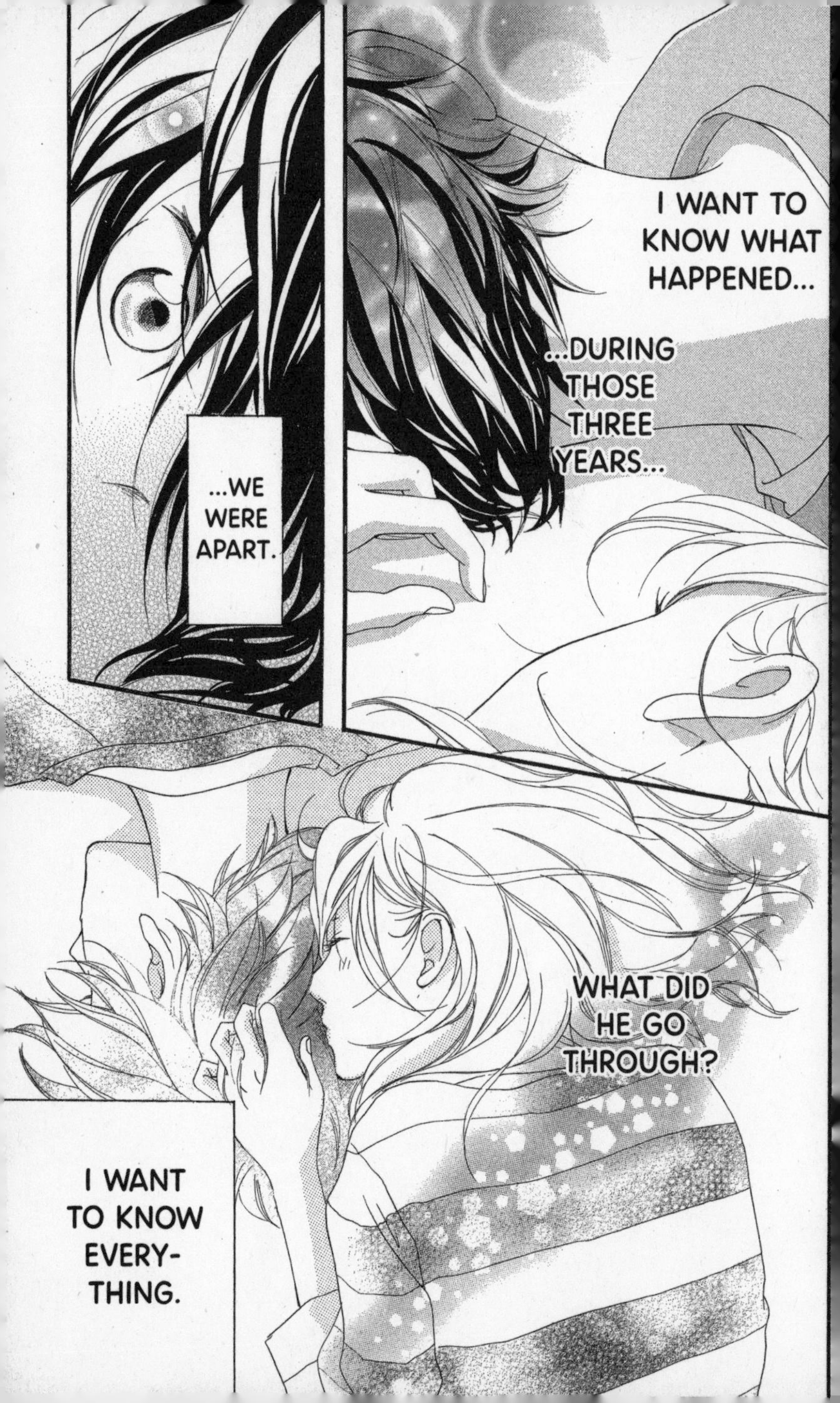
I WANT TO KNOW WHAT HAPPENED...
...DURING THOSE THREE YEARS...
...WE WERE APART.
WHAT DID HE GO THROUGH?
I WANT TO KNOW EVERY-THING.

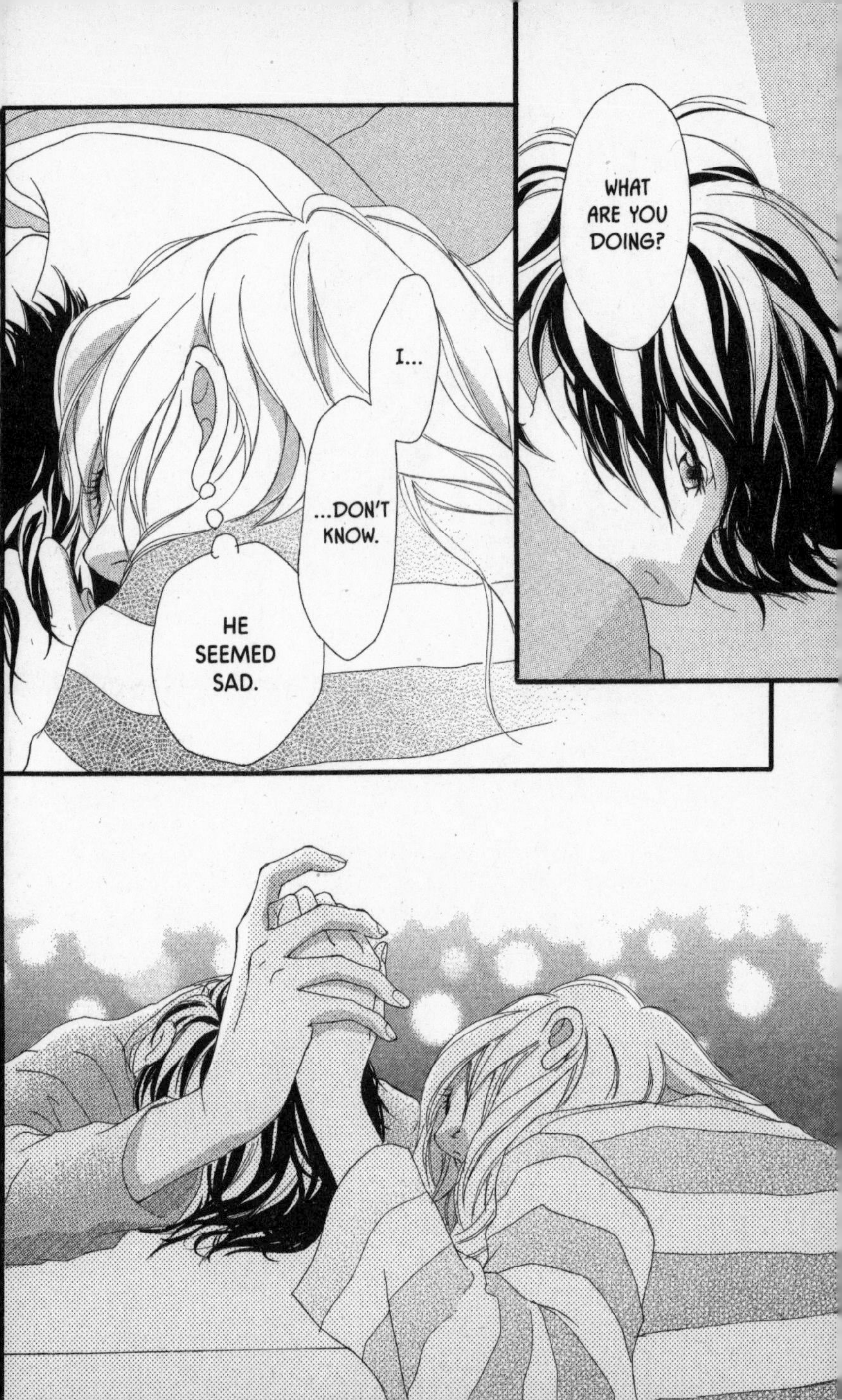
WHAT ARE YOU DOING?
I...
...DON'T KNOW.
HE SEEMED SAD.

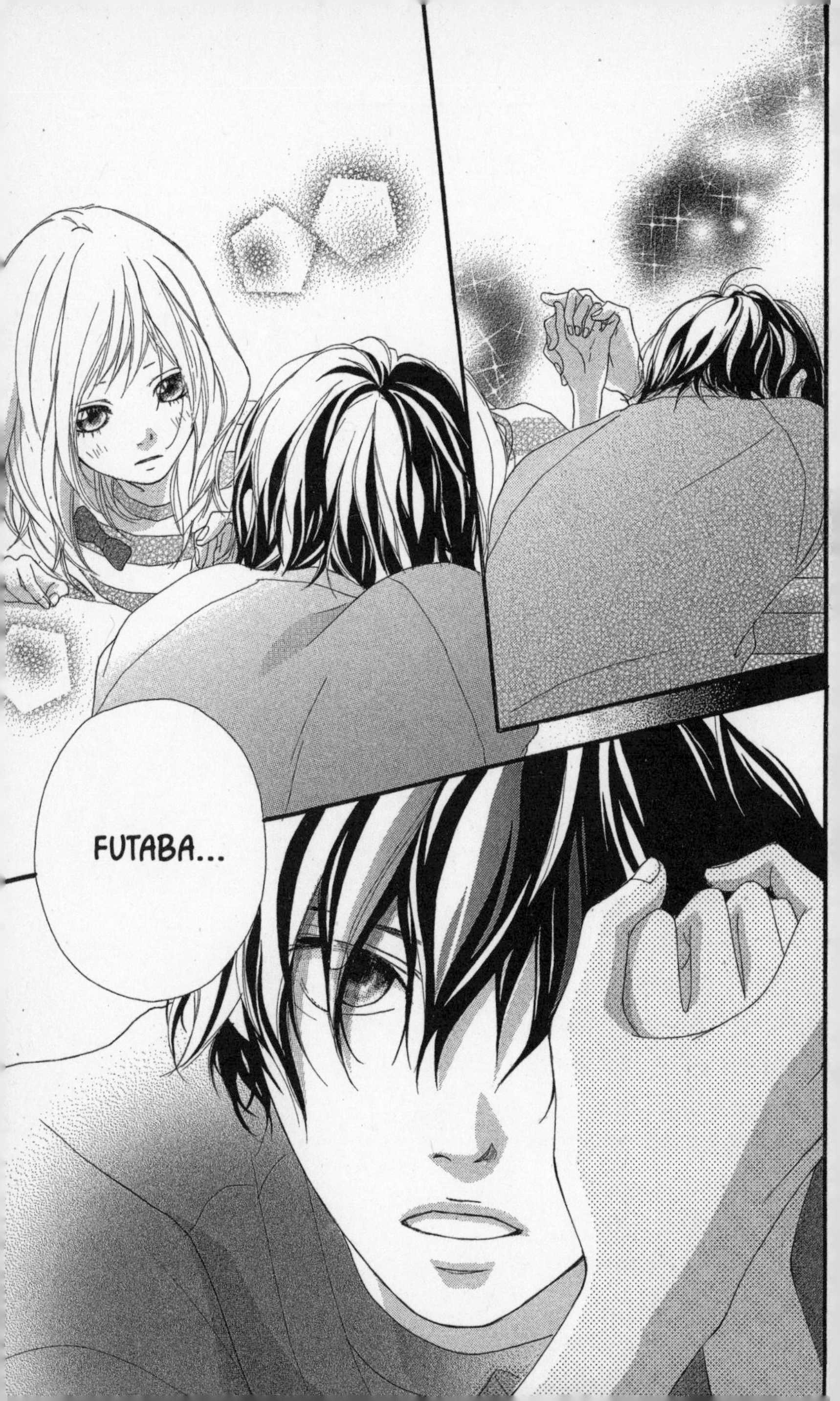
FUTABA...

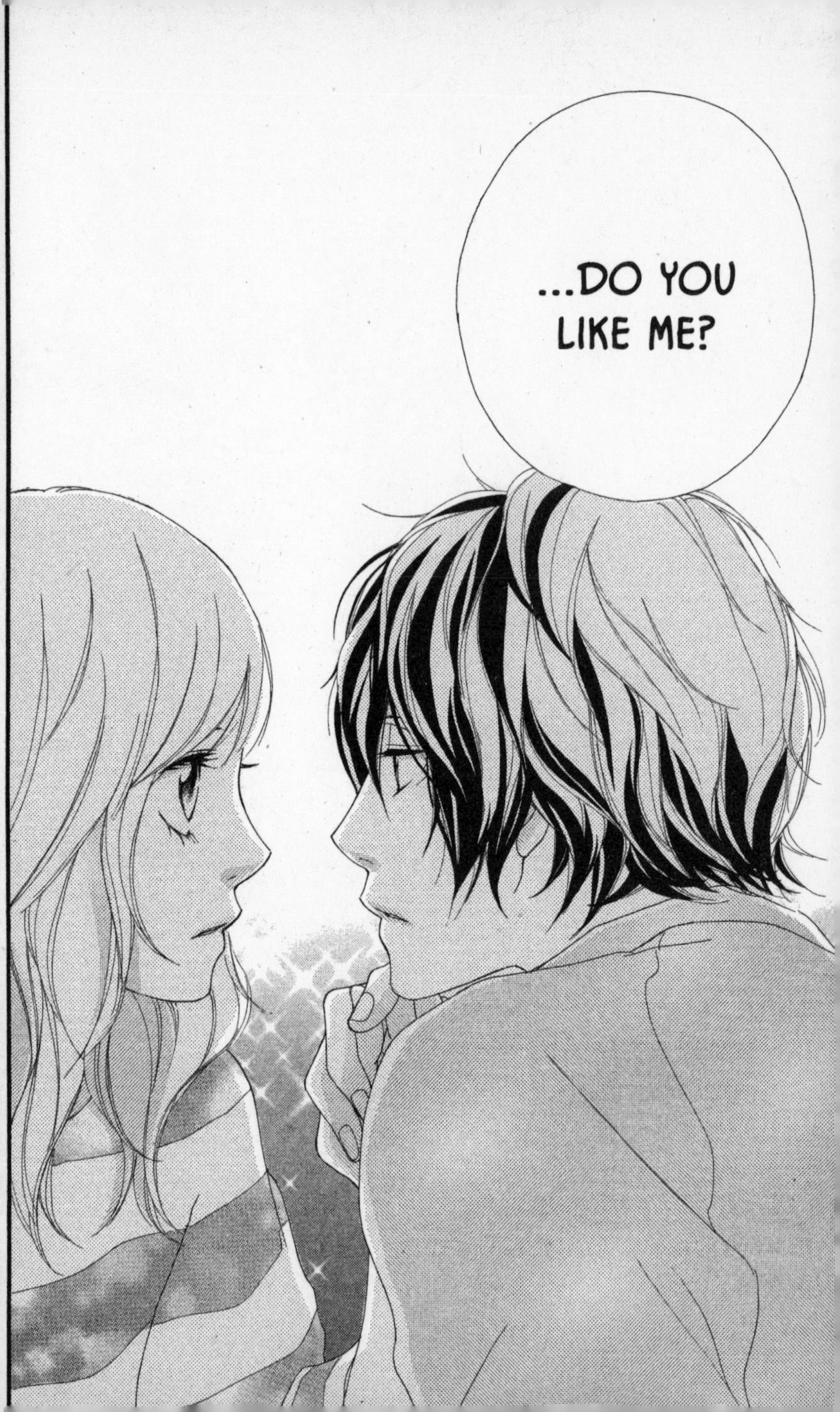
...DO YOU LIKE ME?

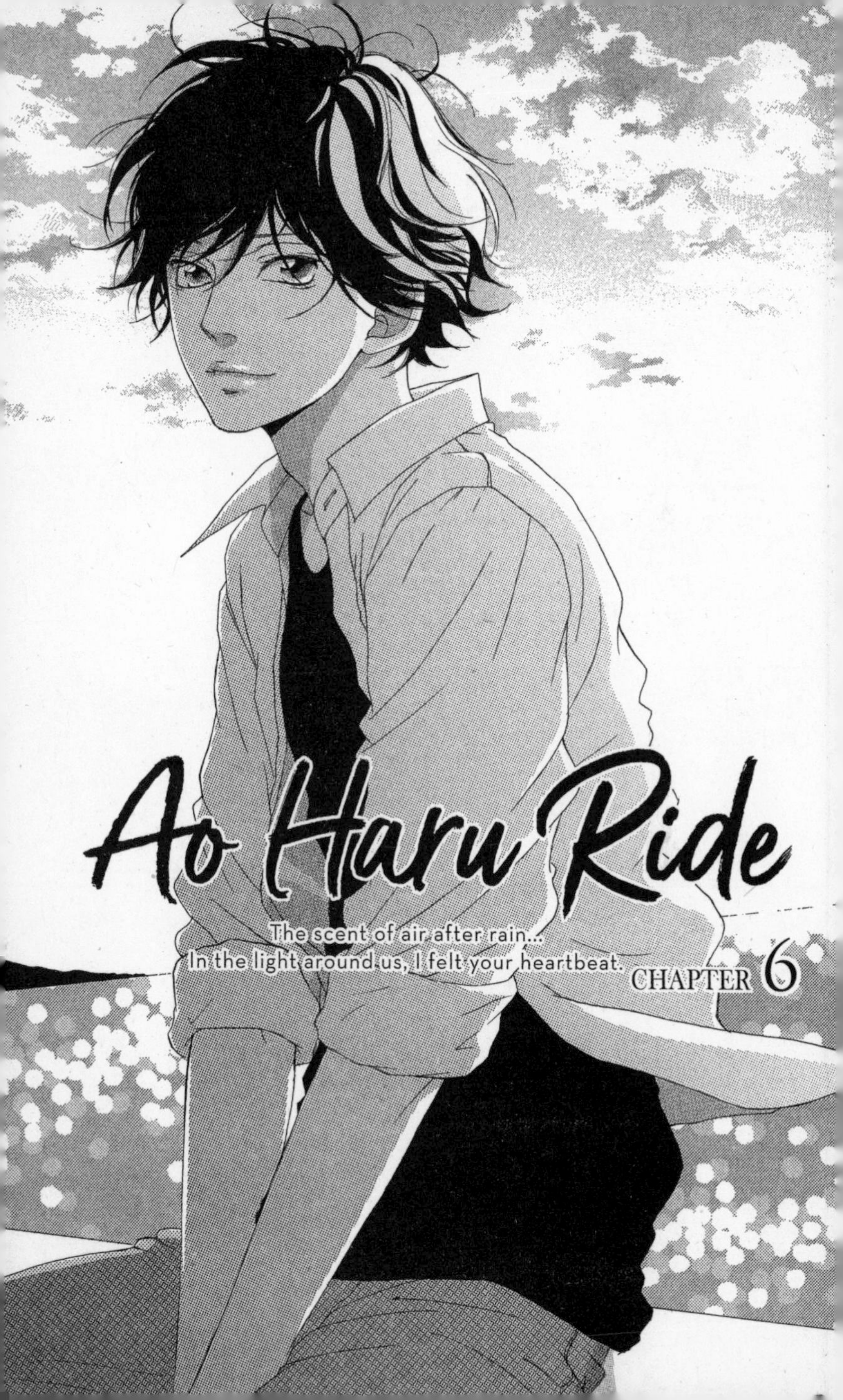
Ao Haru Ride
The scent of air after rain...
In the light around us, I felt your heartbeat.
CHAPTER 6

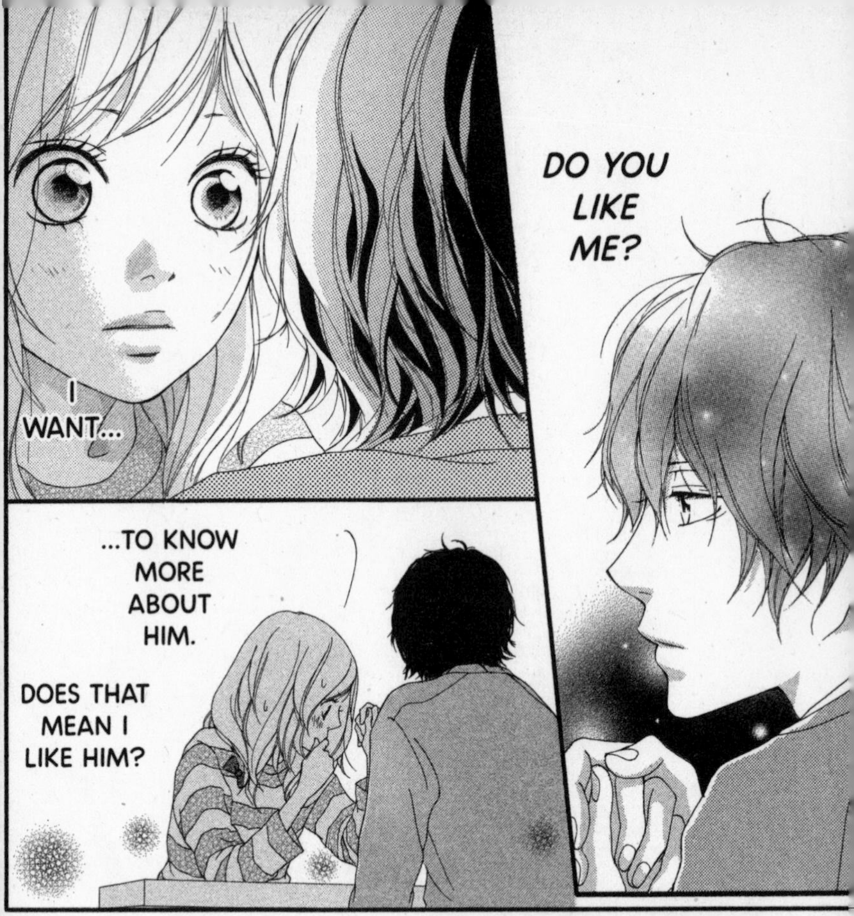
DO YOU LIKE ME?
I WANT...
...TO KNOW MORE ABOUT HIM.
DOES THAT MEAN I LIKE HIM?

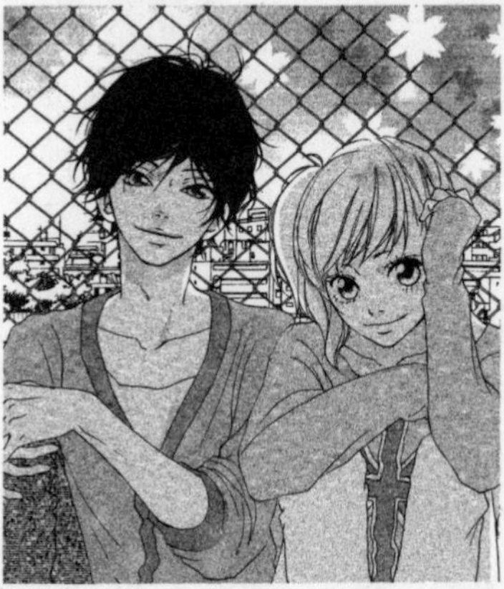

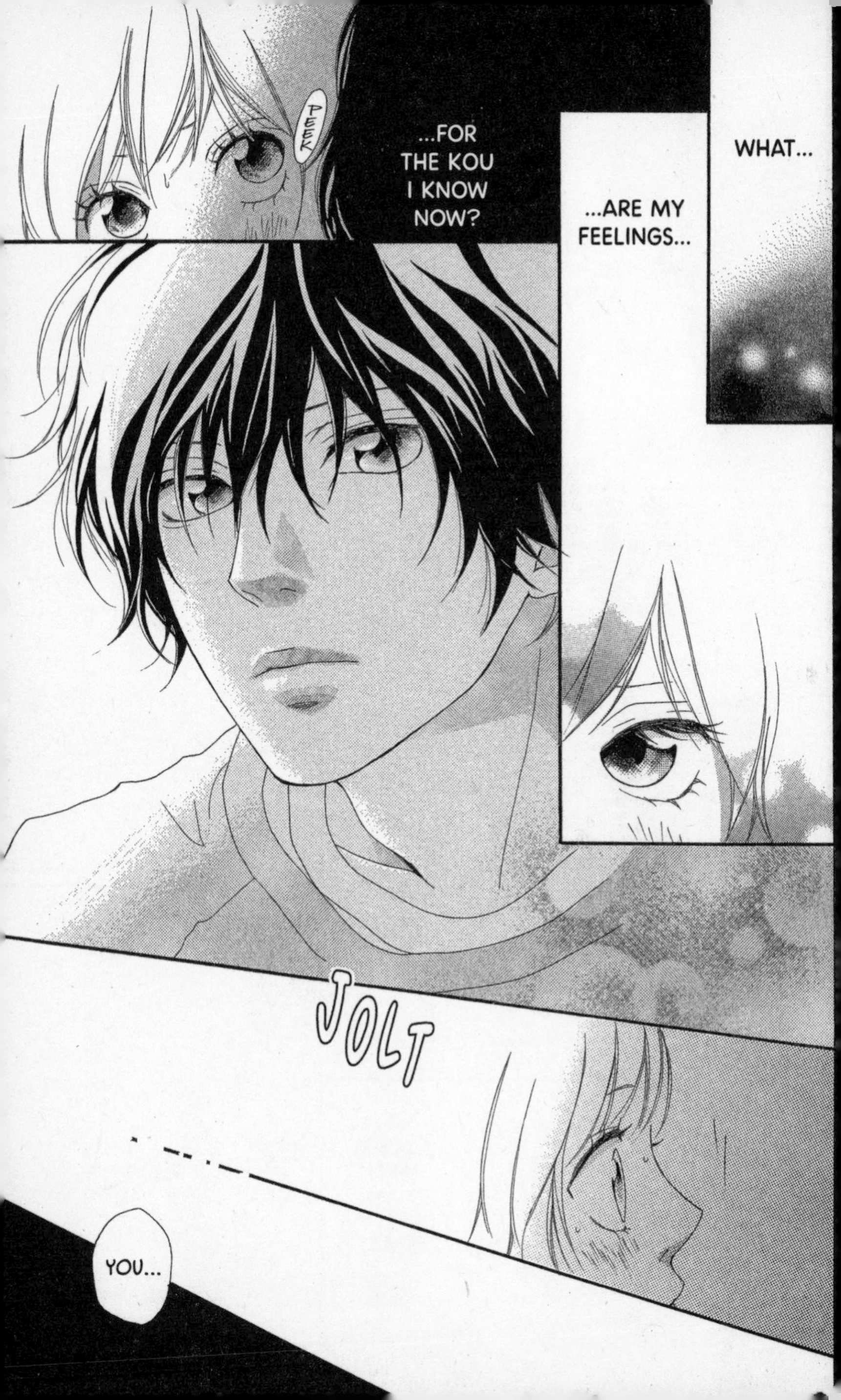
WHAT...
...ARE MY FEELINGS...
...FOR THE KOU I KNOW NOW?
PEEK
JOLT
YOU...

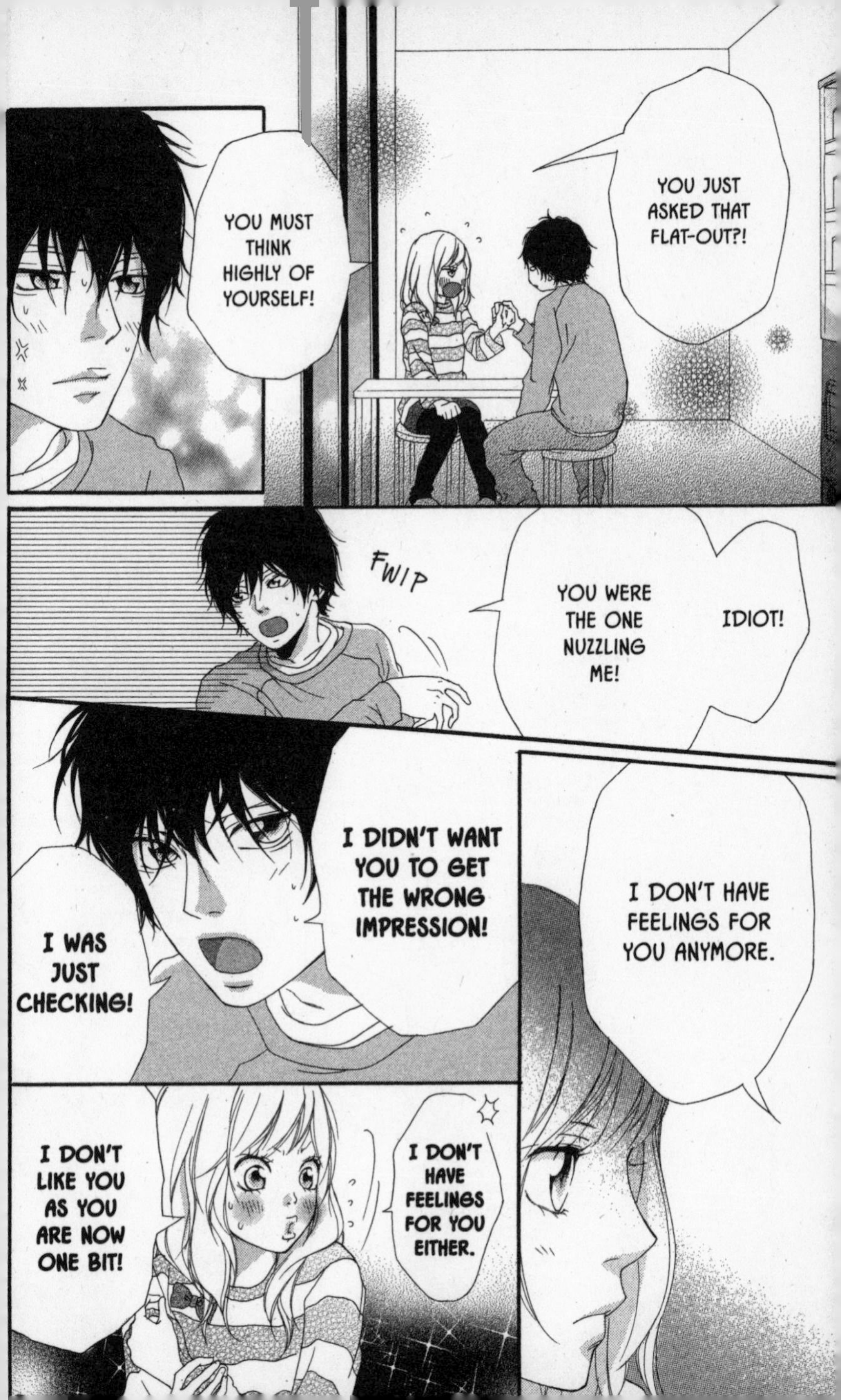
YOU JUST ASKED THAT FLAT-OUT?!
YOU MUST THINK HIGHLY OF YOURSELF!
IDIOT!
YOU WERE THE ONE NUZZLING ME!
FWIP
I DON'T HAVE FEELINGS FOR YOU ANYMORE.
I DIDN'T WANT YOU TO GET THE WRONG IMPRESSION!
I WAS JUST CHECKING!
I DON'T HAVE FEELINGS FOR YOU EITHER.
I DON'T LIKE YOU AS YOU ARE NOW ONE BIT!

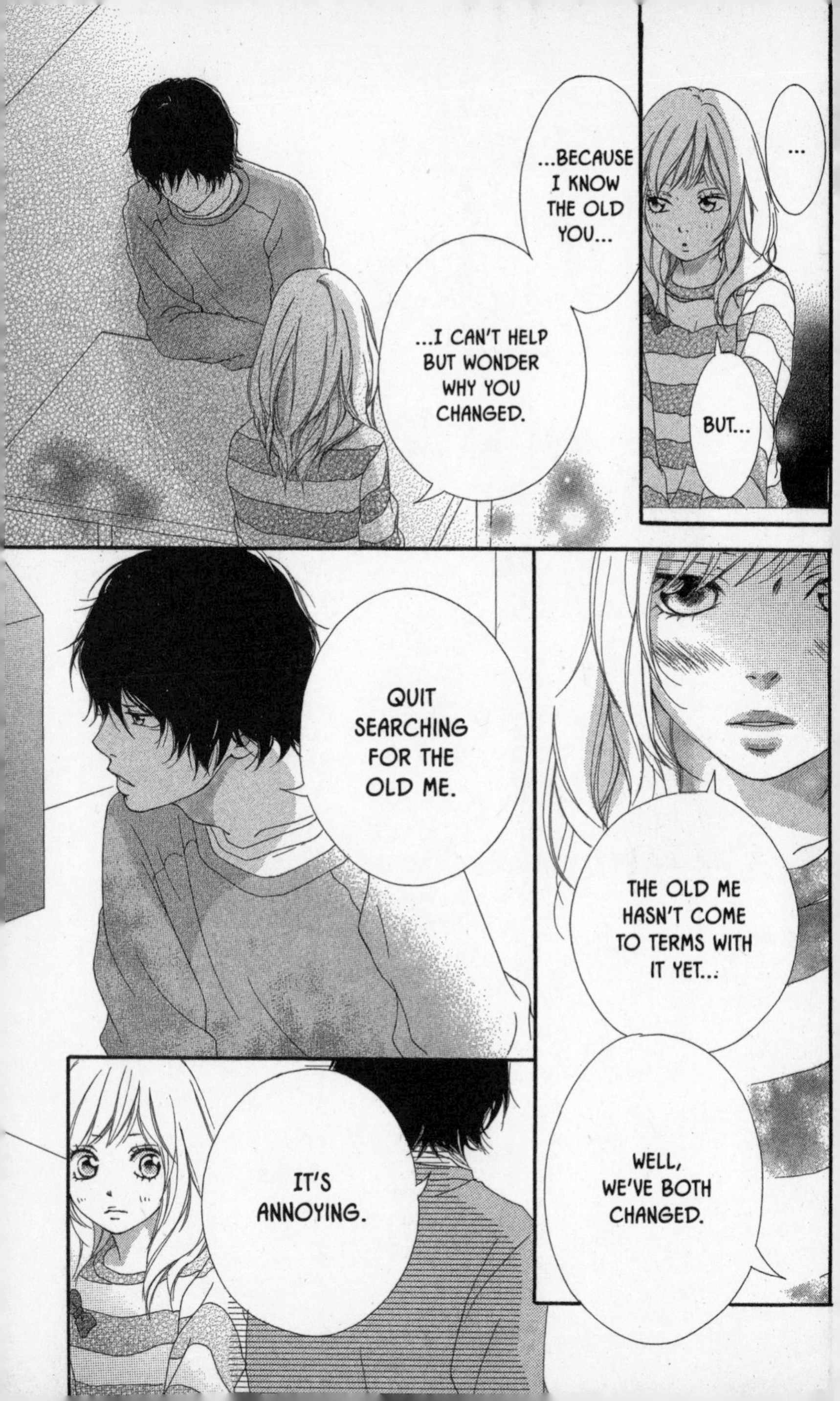
...
BUT...
...BECAUSE I KNOW THE OLD YOU...
...I CAN'T HELP BUT WONDER WHY YOU CHANGED.
THE OLD ME HASN'T COME TO TERMS WITH IT YET...
WELL, WE'VE BOTH CHANGED.
QUIT SEARCHING FOR THE OLD ME.
IT'S ANNOYING.

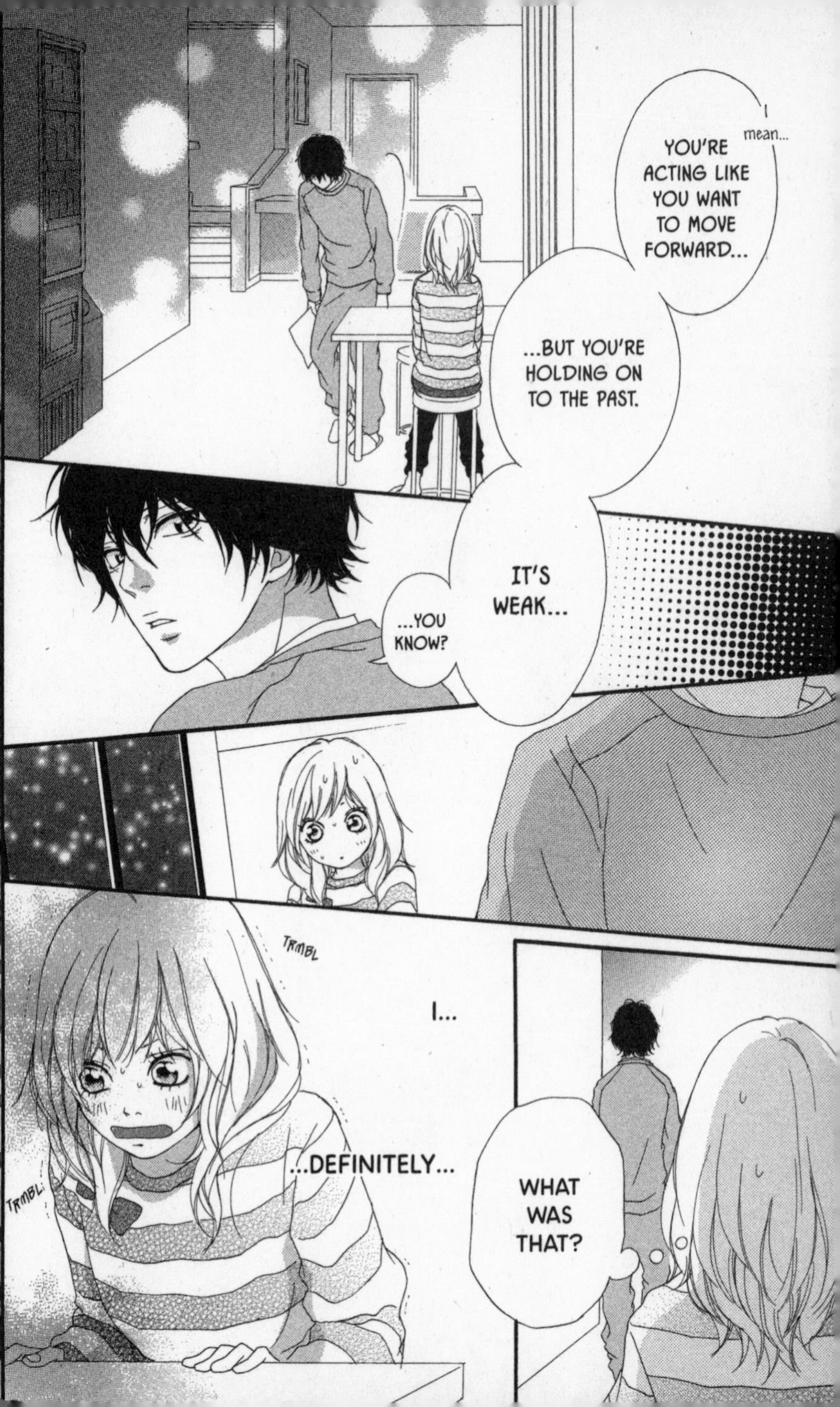
I mean...
YOU'RE ACTING LIKE YOU WANT TO MOVE FORWARD...
...BUT YOU'RE HOLDING ON TO THE PAST.
IT'S WEAK...
...YOU KNOW?
WHAT WAS THAT?
TRMBL
I...
...DEFINITELY...
TRMBL

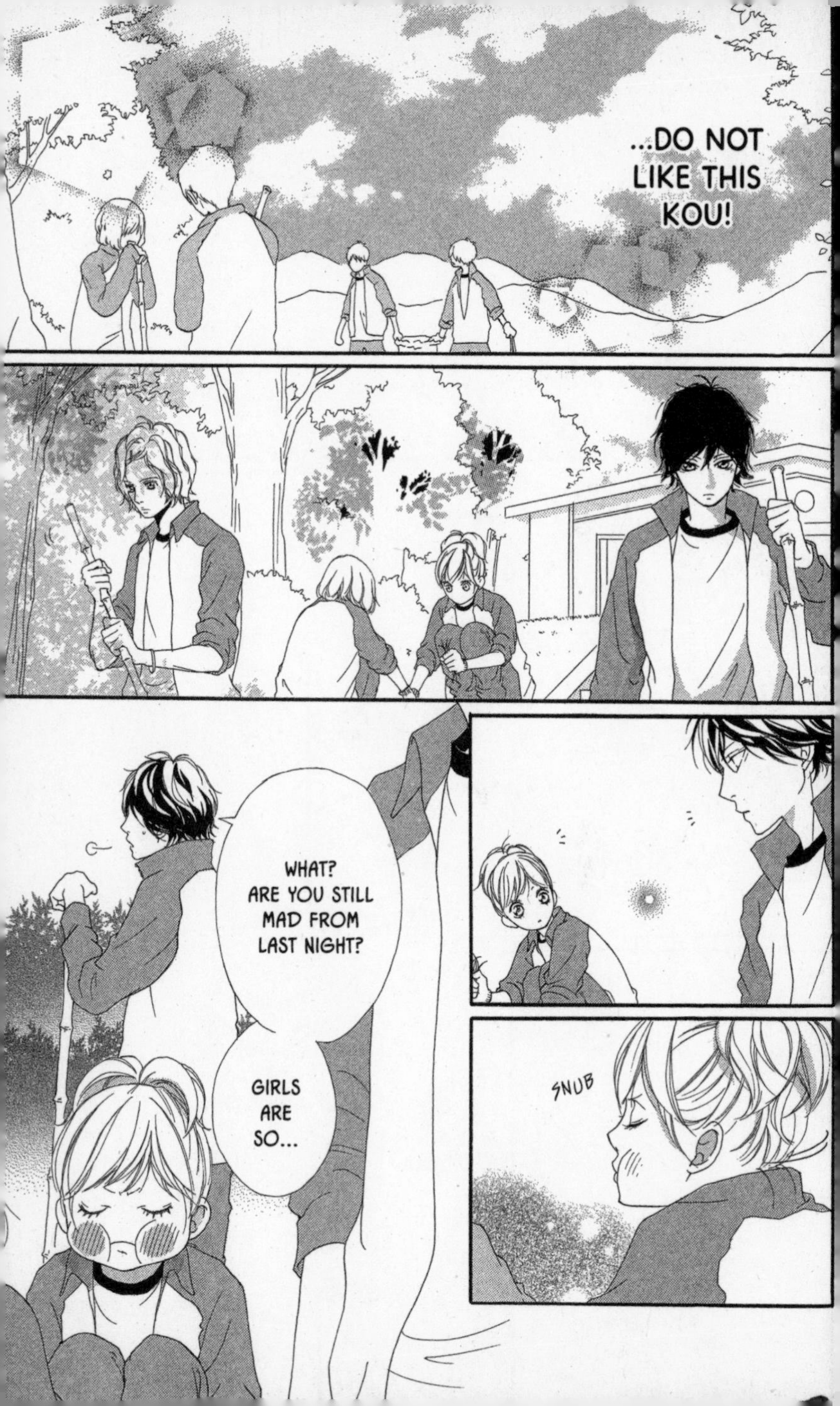
...DO NOT LIKE THIS KOU!
SNUB
WHAT? ARE YOU STILL MAD FROM LAST NIGHT?
GIRLS ARE SO...

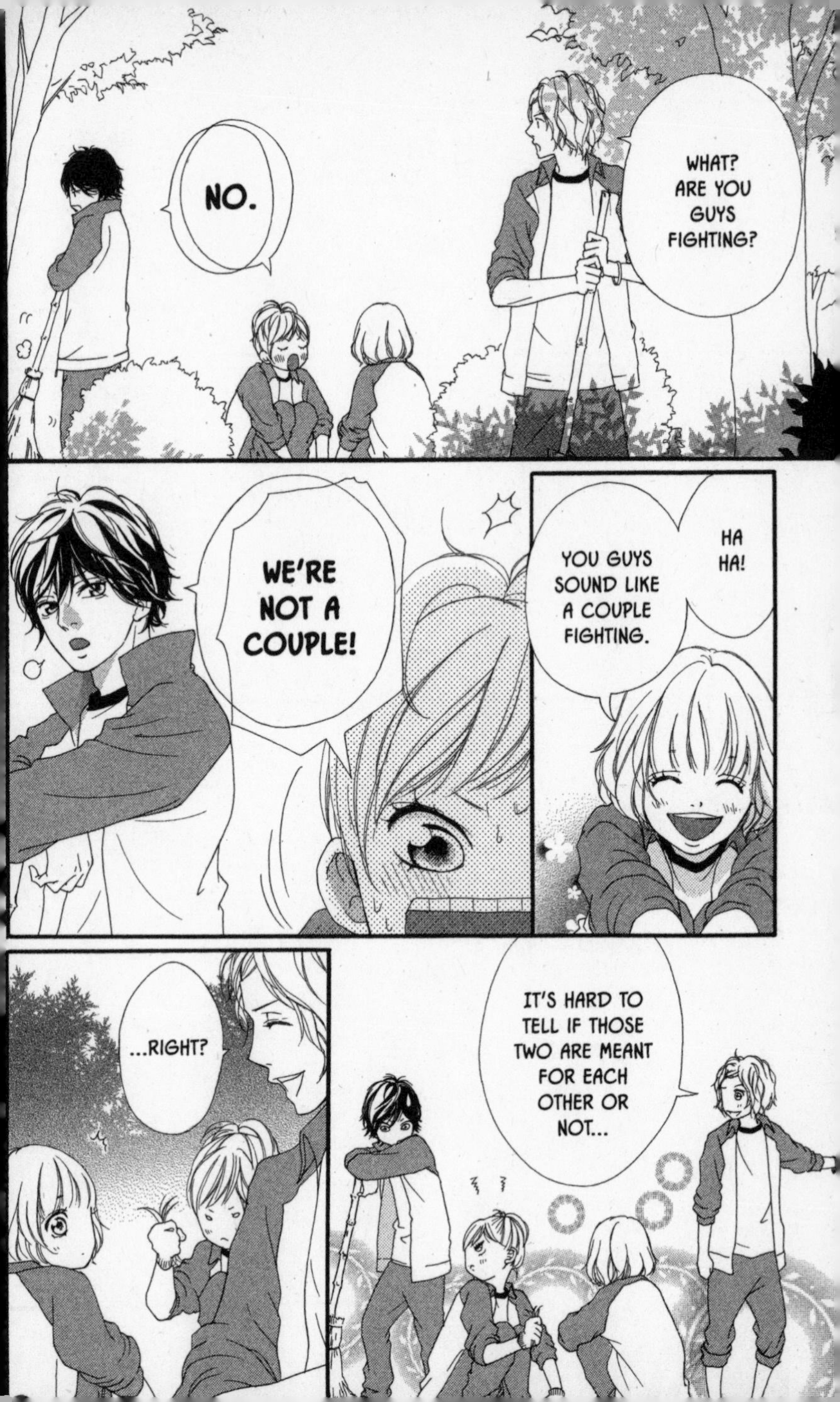
WHAT? ARE YOU GUYS FIGHTING?
NO.
HA HA!
YOU GUYS SOUND LIKE A COUPLE FIGHTING.
WE'RE NOT A COUPLE!
IT'S HARD TO TELL IF THOSE TWO ARE MEANT FOR EACH OTHER OR NOT...
...RIGHT?

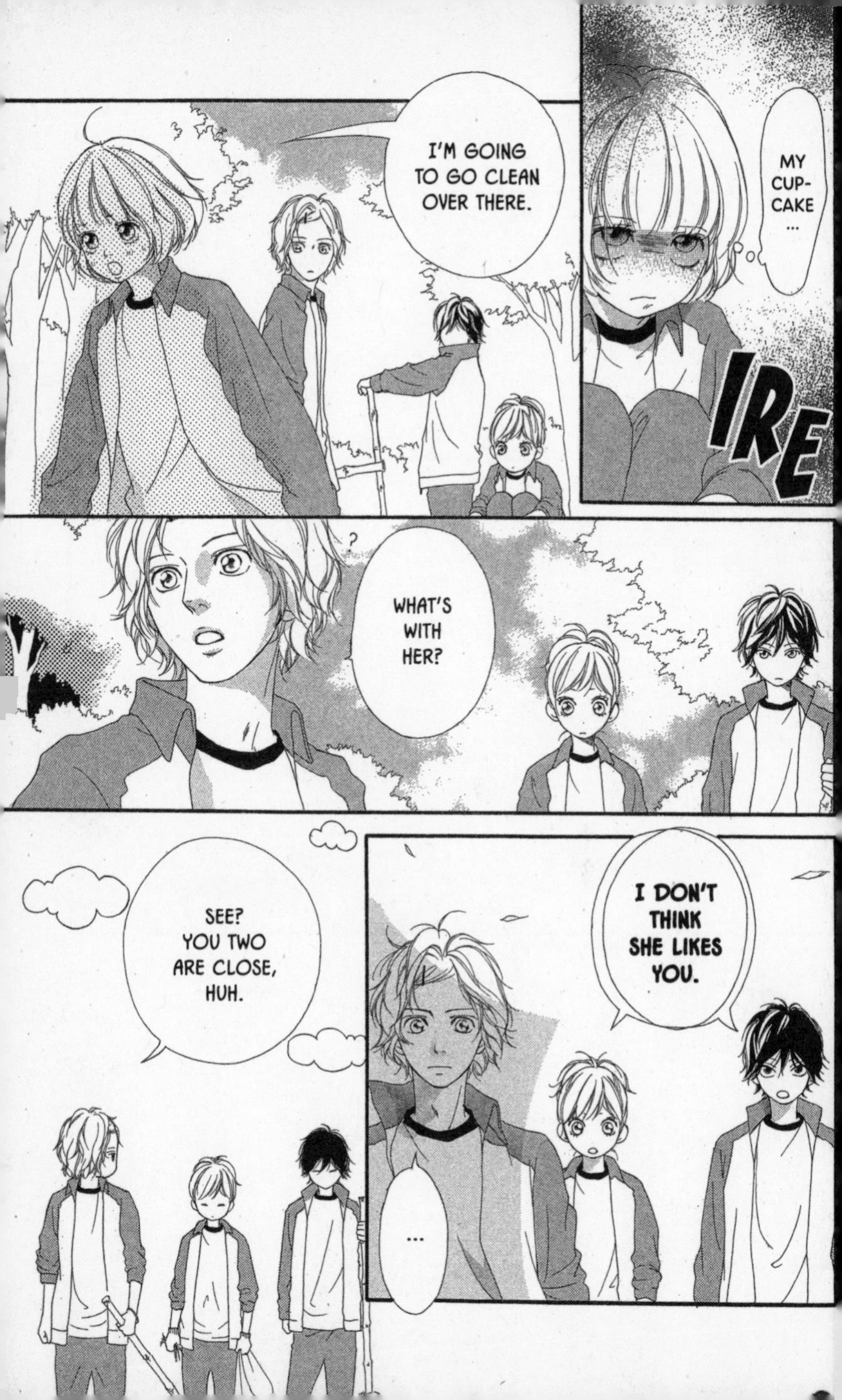
MY CUP-CAKE ...
IRE
I'M GOING TO GO CLEAN OVER THERE.
WHAT'S WITH HER?
I DON'T THINK SHE LIKES YOU.
...
SEE? YOU TWO ARE CLOSE, HUH.

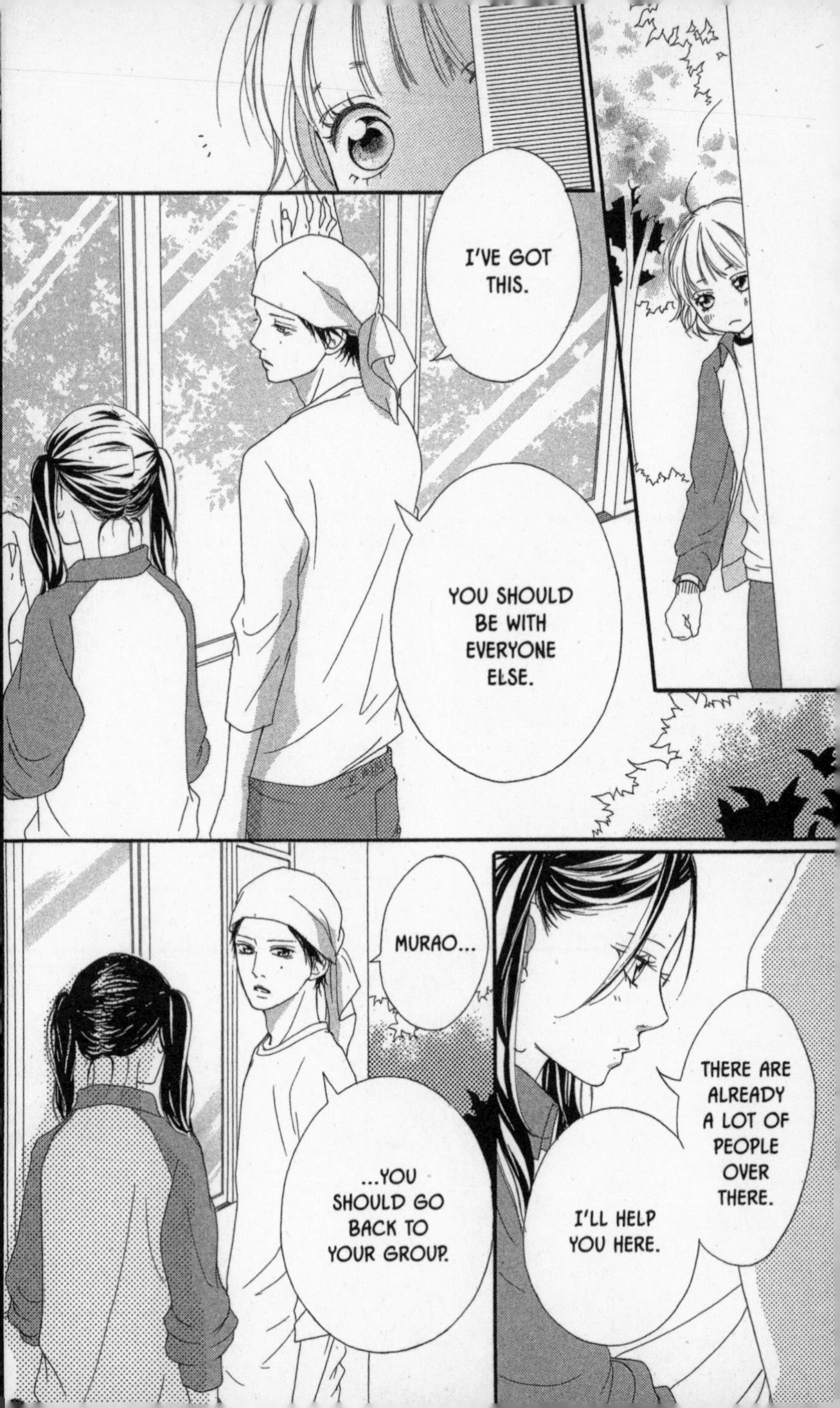
I'VE GOT THIS.
YOU SHOULD BE WITH EVERYONE ELSE.
THERE ARE ALREADY A LOT OF PEOPLE OVER THERE.
I'LL HELP YOU HERE.
MURAO...
...YOU SHOULD GO BACK TO YOUR GROUP.

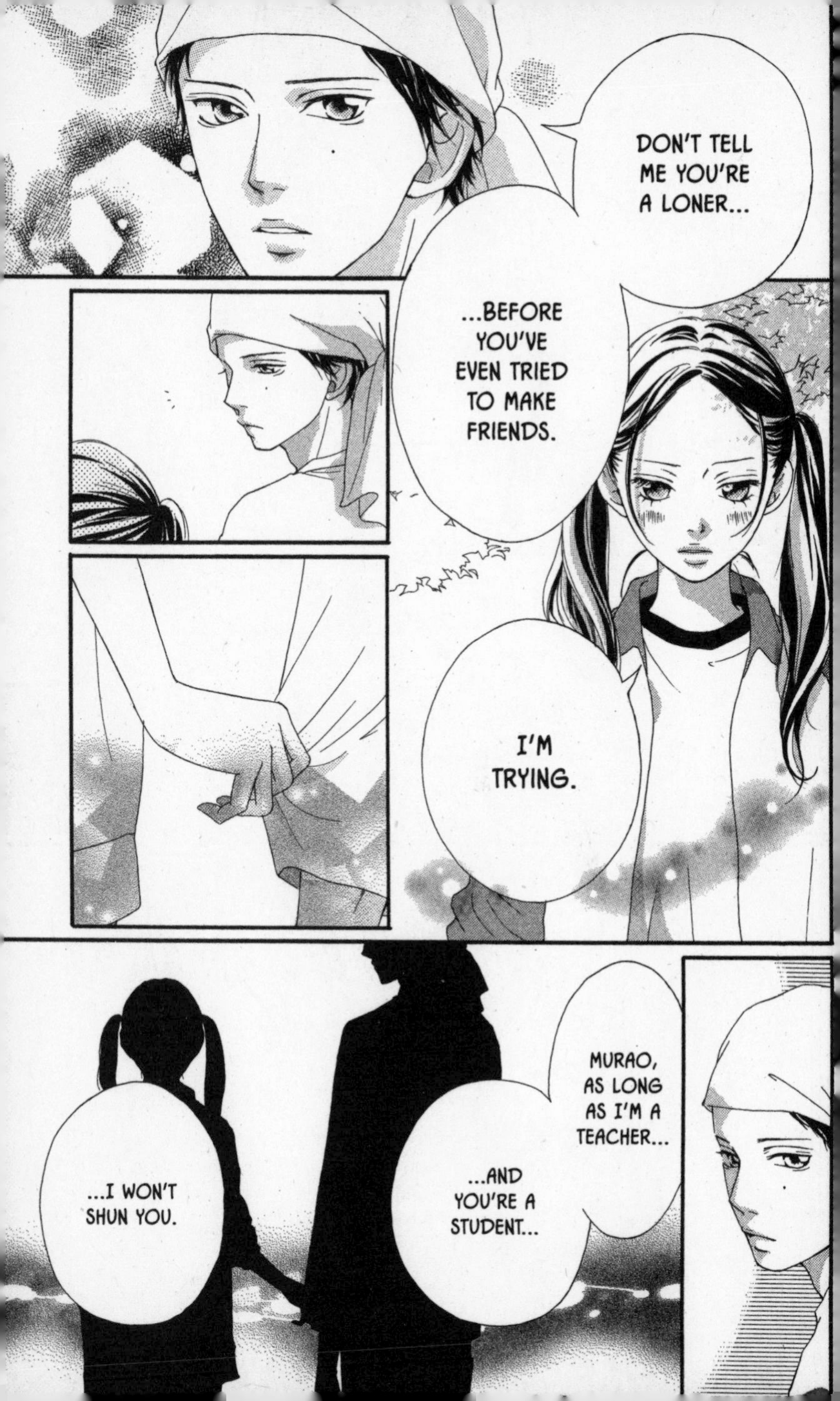
DON'T TELL ME YOU'RE A LONER...
...BEFORE YOU'VE EVEN TRIED TO MAKE FRIENDS.
I'M TRYING.
MURAO, AS LONG AS I'M A TEACHER...
...AND YOU'RE A STUDENT...
...I WON'T SHUN YOU.

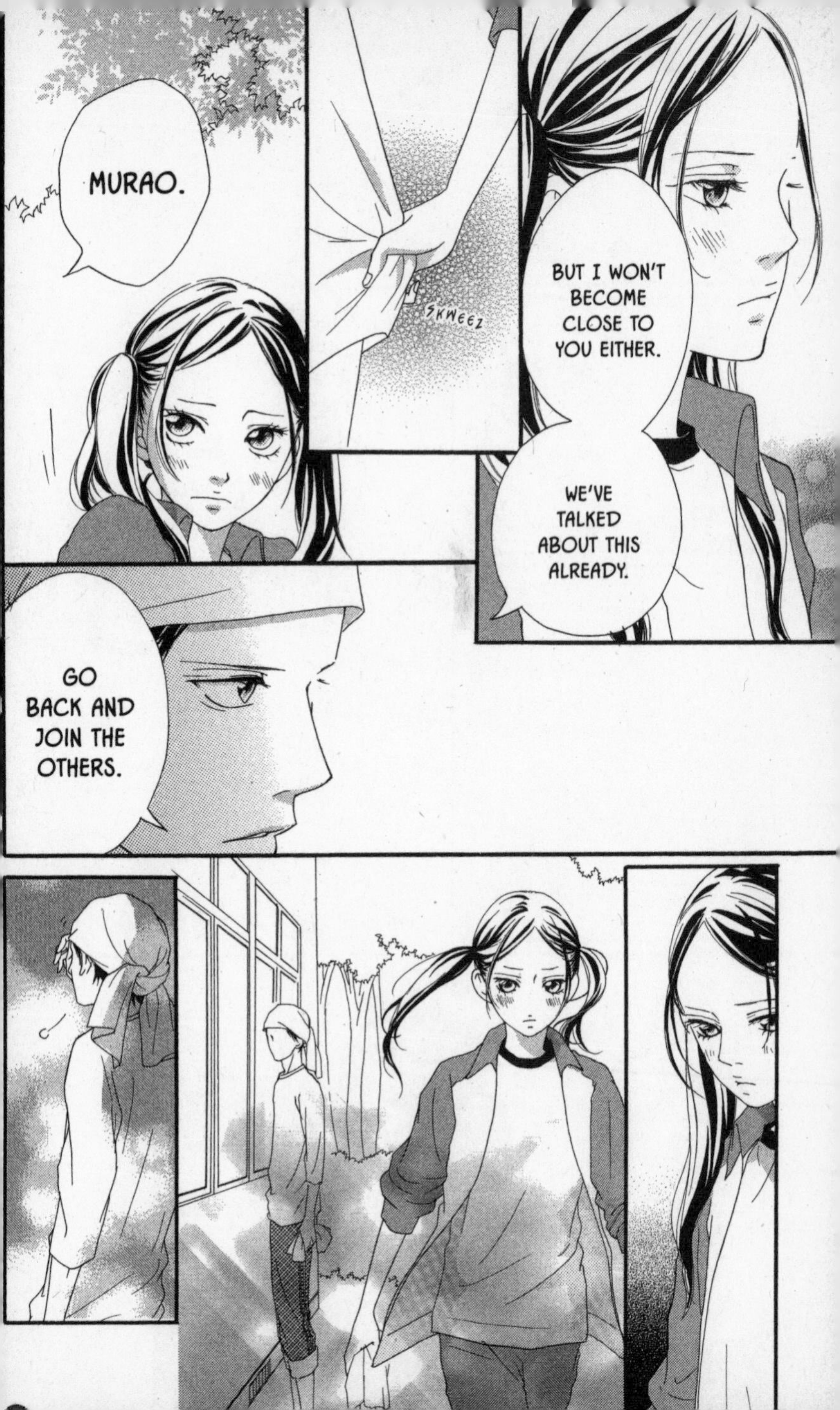
BUT I WON'T BECOME CLOSE TO YOU EITHER.
WE'VE TALKED ABOUT THIS ALREADY.
SKWEEZ
MURAO.
GO BACK AND JOIN THE OTHERS.

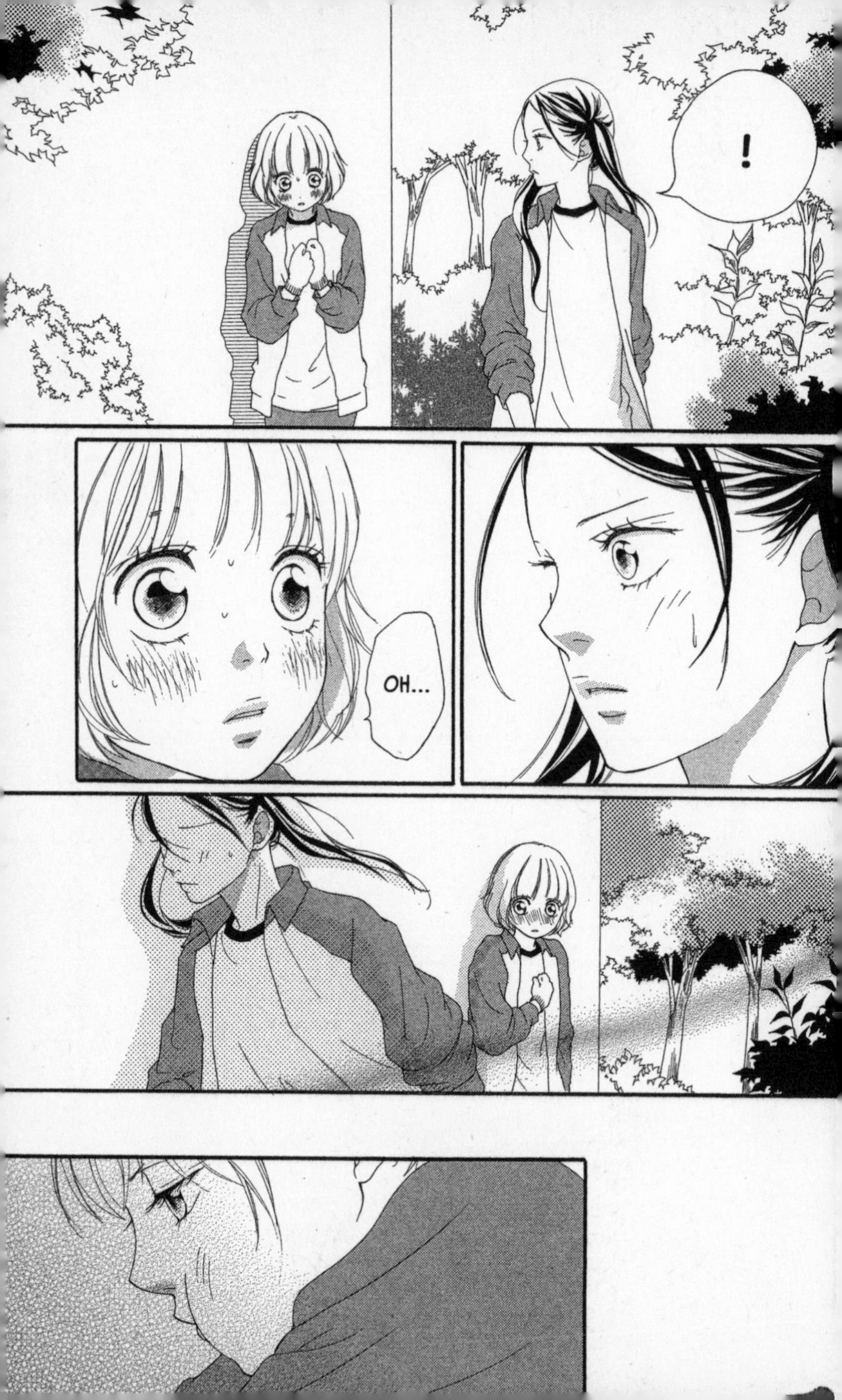
!
OH...

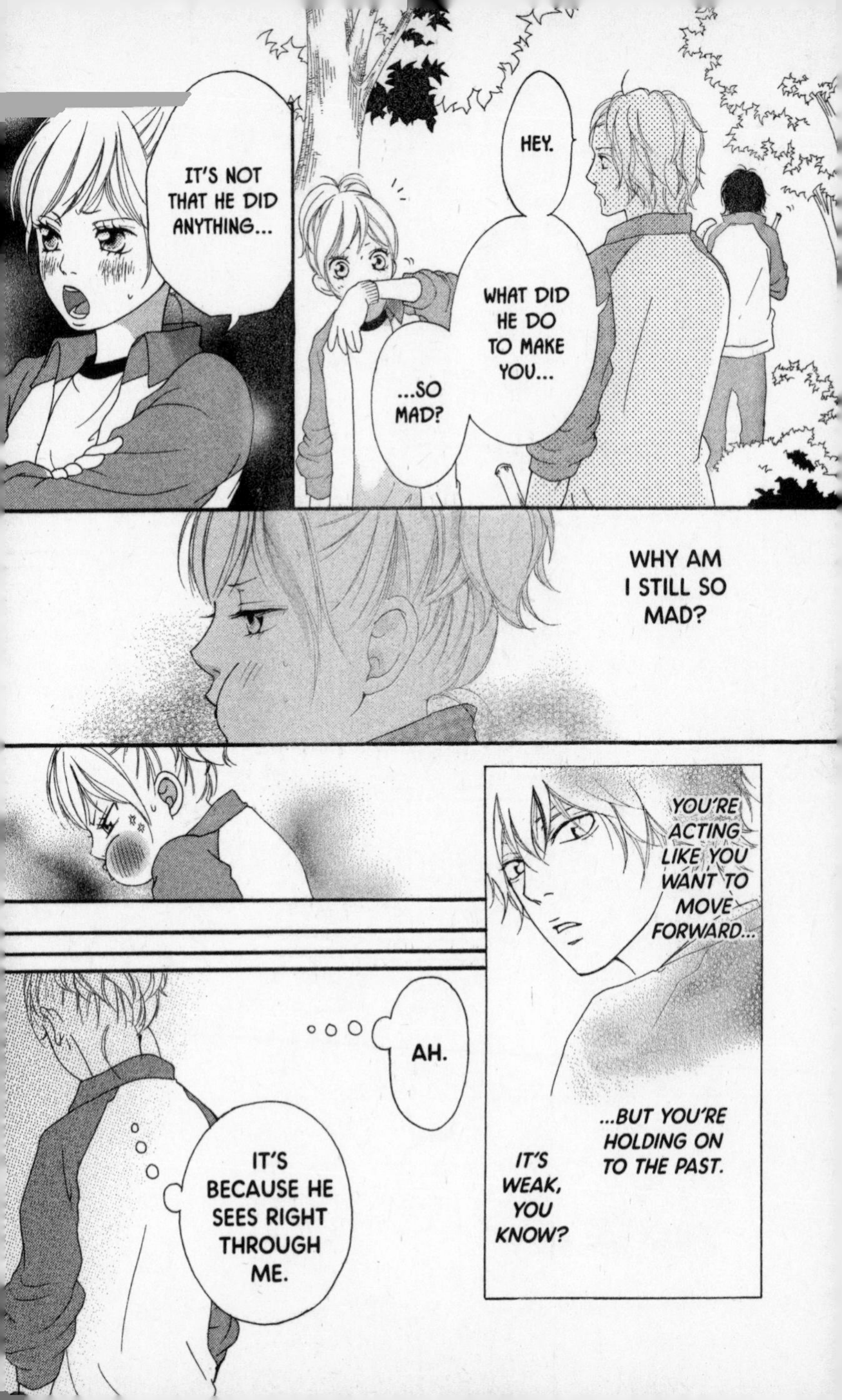
HEY.
WHAT DID HE DO TO MAKE YOU...
...SO MAD?
IT'S NOT THAT HE DID ANYTHING...
WHY AM I STILL SO MAD?
YOU'RE ACTING LIKE YOU WANT TO MOVE FORWARD...
...BUT YOU'RE HOLDING ON TO THE PAST.
IT'S WEAK, YOU KNOW?
AH.
IT'S BECAUSE HE SEES RIGHT THROUGH ME.

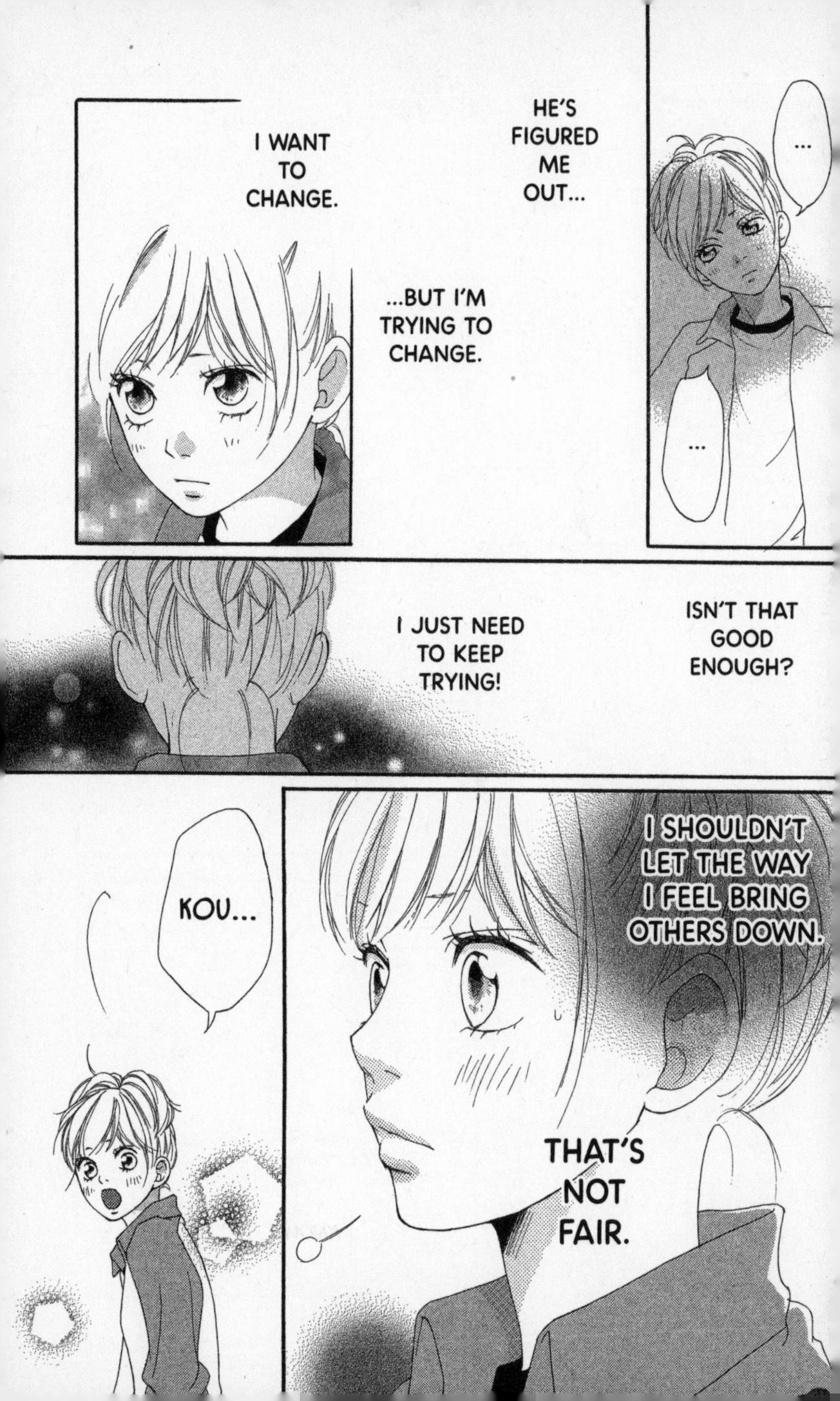
...
...
HE'S FIGURED ME OUT...
I WANT TO CHANGE.
...BUT I'M TRYING TO CHANGE.
ISN'T THAT GOOD ENOUGH?
I JUST NEED TO KEEP TRYING!
I SHOULDN'T LET THE WAY I FEEL BRING OTHERS DOWN.
THAT'S NOT FAIR.
KOU...

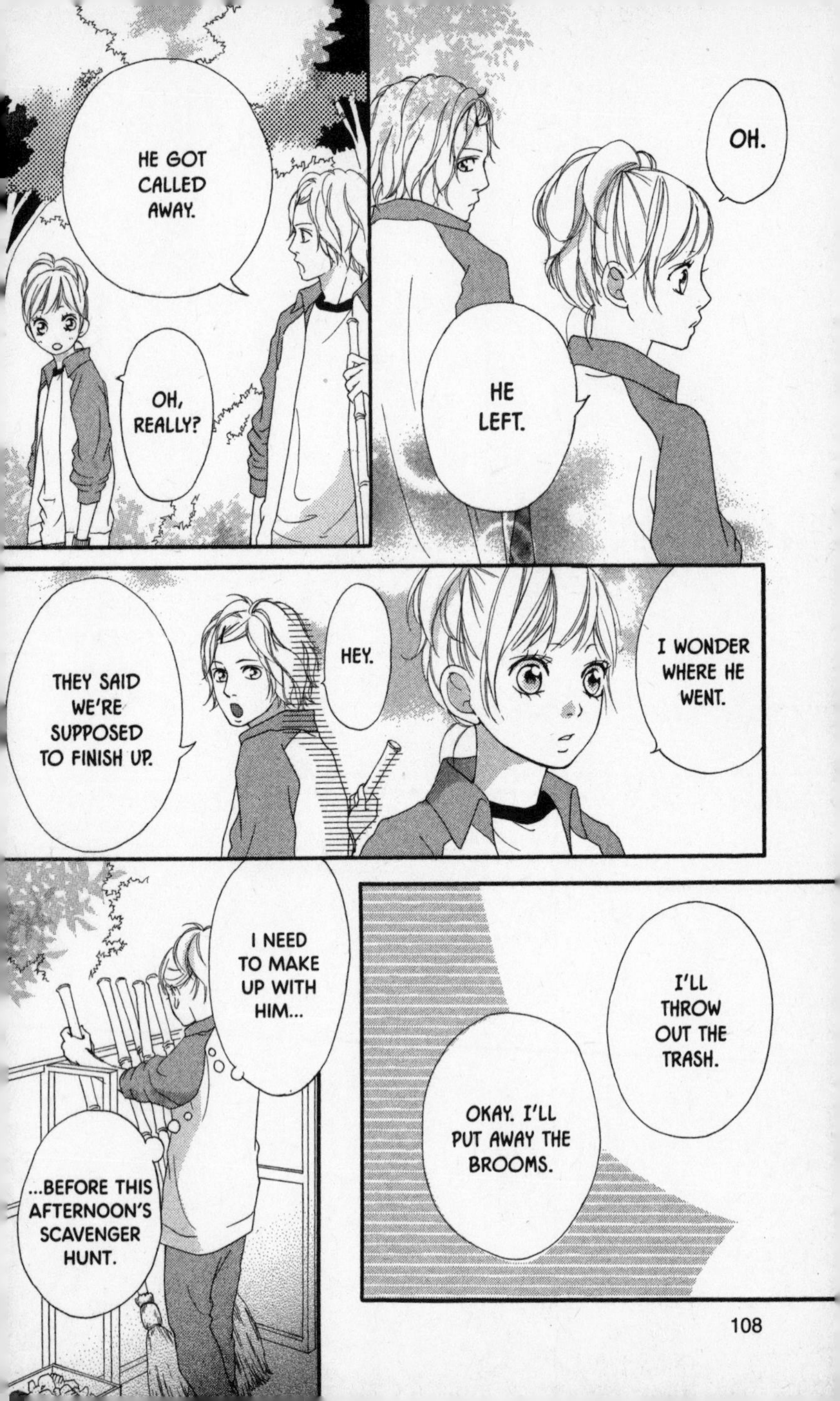
OH.
HE LEFT.
HE GOT CALLED AWAY.
OH, REALLY?
I WONDER WHERE HE WENT.
HEY.
THEY SAID WE'RE SUPPOSED TO FINISH UP.
I'LL THROW OUT THE TRASH.
OKAY. I'LL PUT AWAY THE BROOMS.
I NEED TO MAKE UP WITH HIM...
...BEFORE THIS AFTERNOON'S SCAVENGER HUNT.

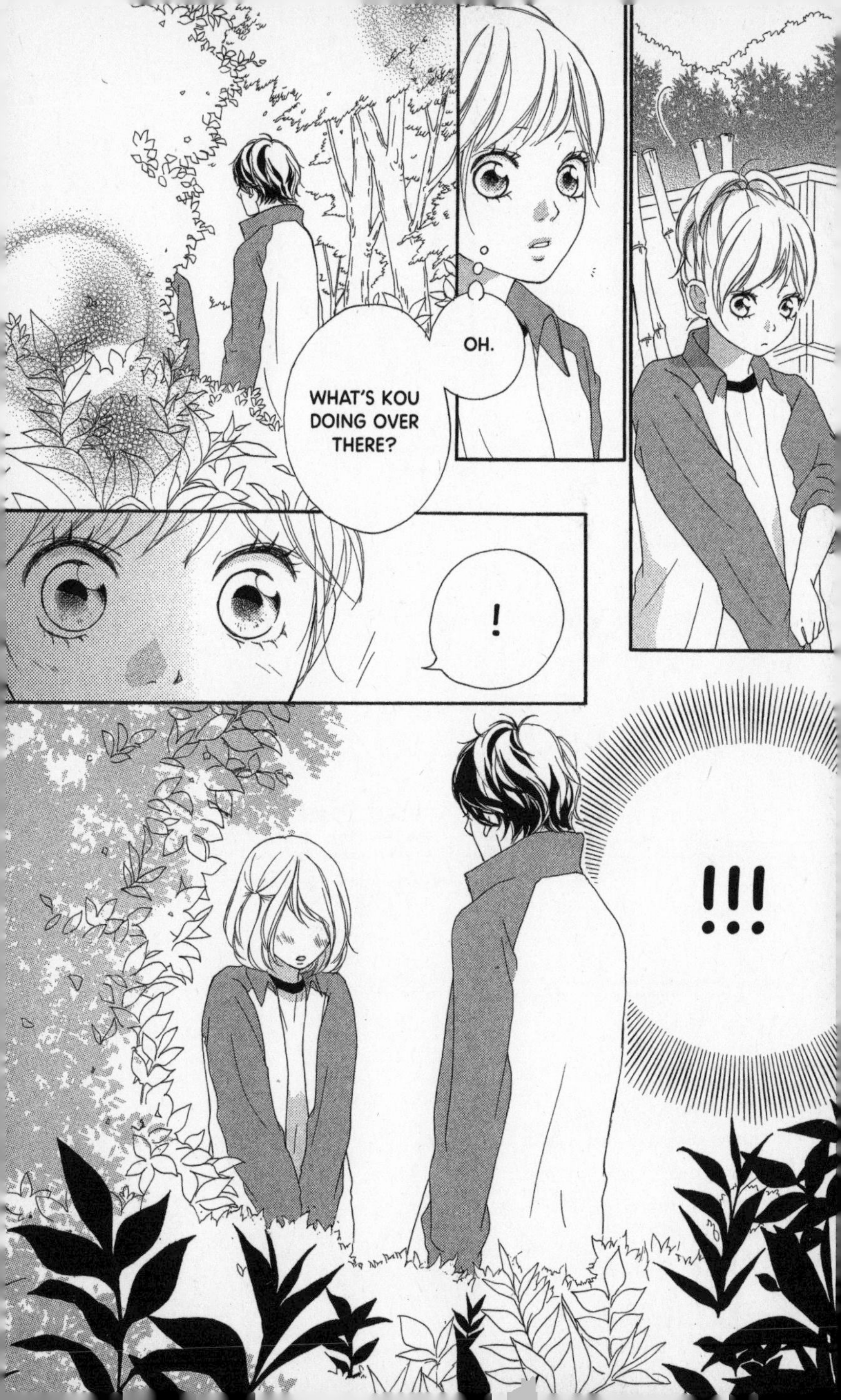
OH.
WHAT'S KOU DOING OVER THERE?
!
!!!

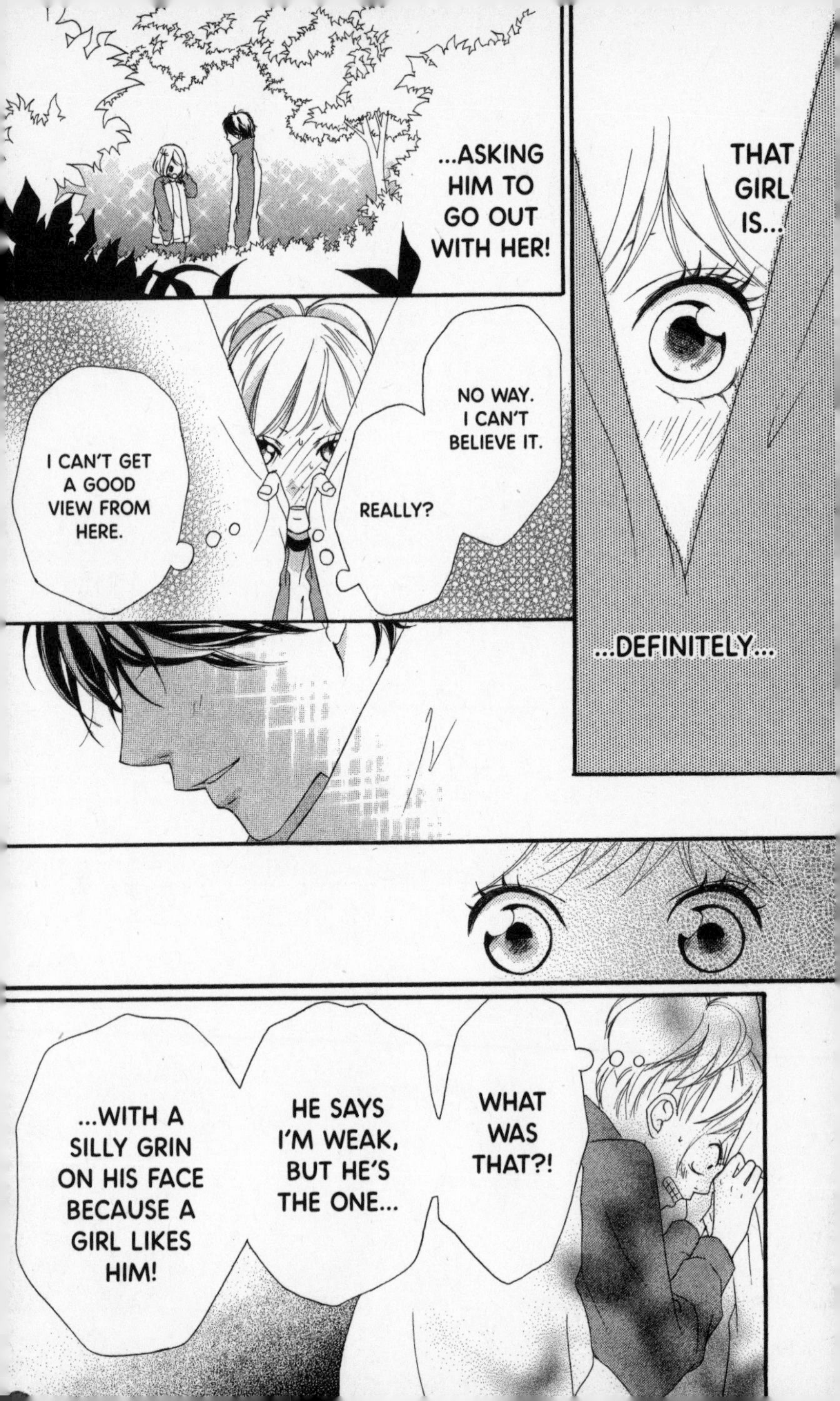
THAT GIRL IS...
...DEFINITELY...
...ASKING HIM TO GO OUT WITH HER!
NO WAY. I CAN'T BELIEVE IT.
REALLY?
I CAN'T GET A GOOD VIEW FROM HERE.
WHAT WAS THAT?!
HE SAYS I'M WEAK, BUT HE'S THE ONE...
...WITH A SILLY GRIN ON HIS FACE BECAUSE A GIRL LIKES HIM!

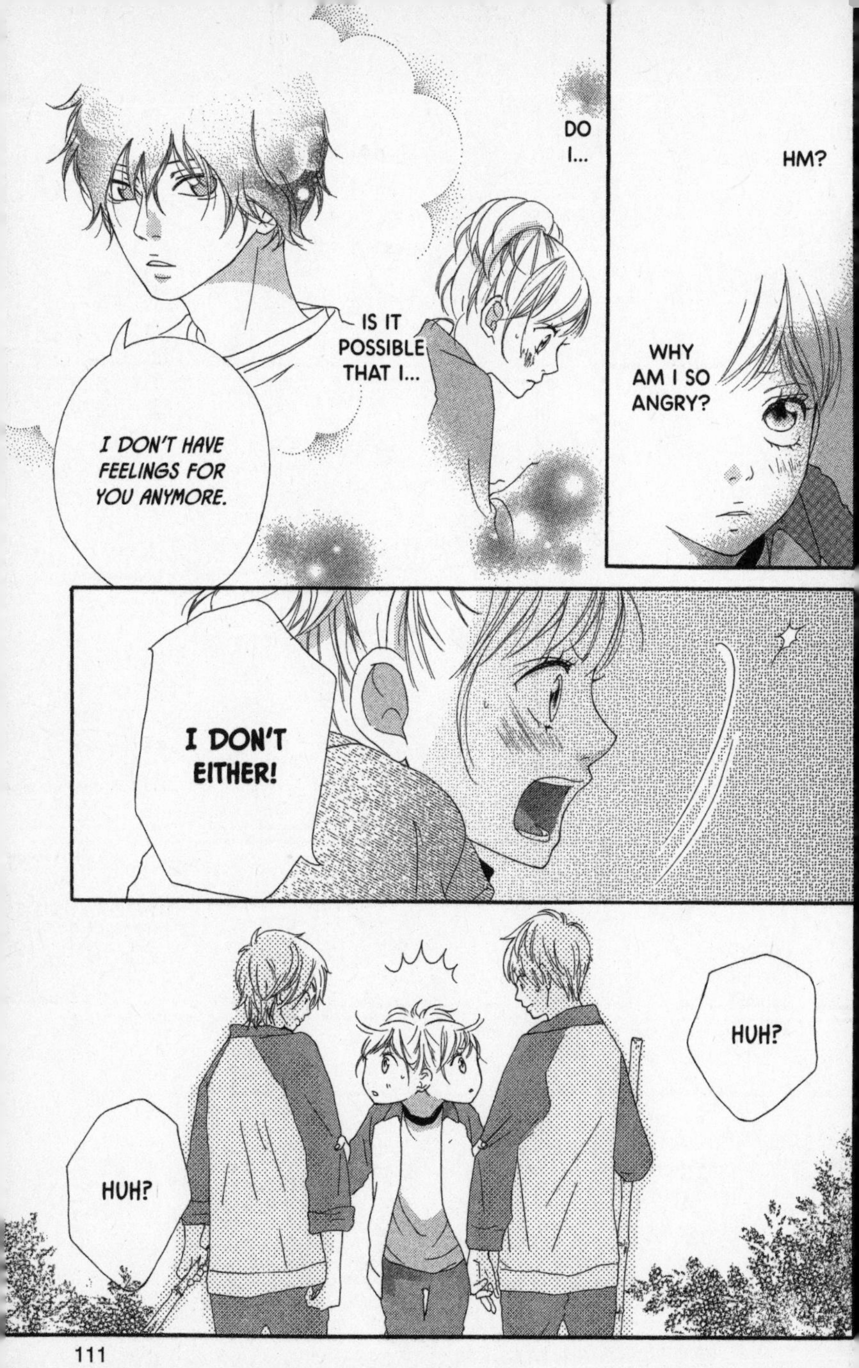
HM?
WHY AM I SO ANGRY?
DO I...
IS IT POSSIBLE THAT I...
I DON'T HAVE FEELINGS FOR YOU ANYMORE.
I DON'T EITHER!
HUH?
HUH?

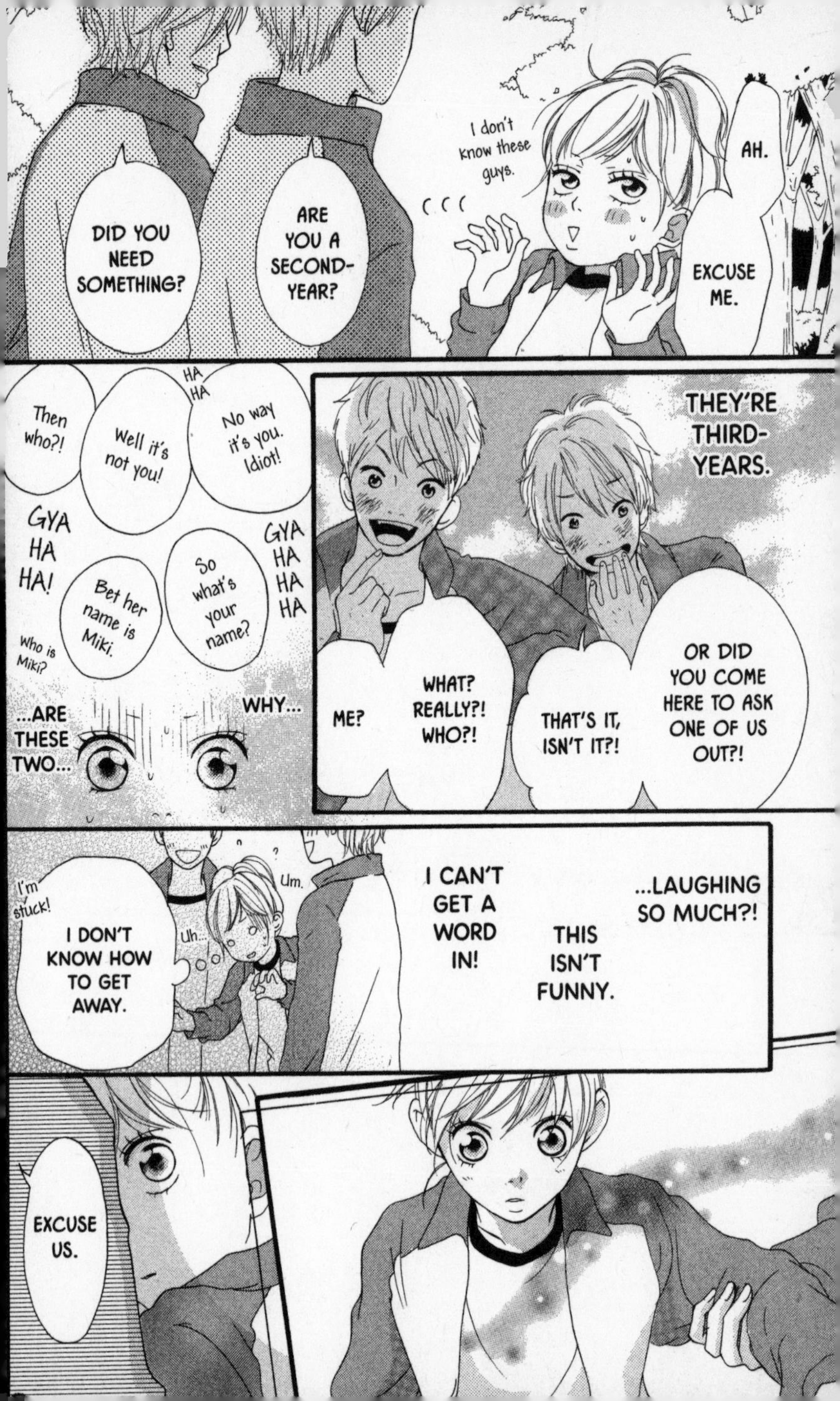
AH.
EXCUSE ME.
I don't know these guys.
ARE YOU A SECOND-YEAR?
DID YOU NEED SOMETHING?
THEY'RE THIRD-YEARS.
OR DID YOU COME HERE TO ASK ONE OF US OUT?!
THAT'S IT, ISN'T IT?!
WHAT? REALLY?! WHO?!
ME?
No way it's you. Idiot!
HA HA
Well it's not you!
Then who?!
GYA HA HA HA
So what's your name?
Bet her name is Miki.
GYA HA HA!
Who is Miki?
WHY...
...ARE THESE TWO...
...LAUGHING SO MUCH?!
THIS ISN'T FUNNY.
I CAN'T GET A WORD IN!
Um.
Uh...
I DON'T KNOW HOW TO GET AWAY.
I'm stuck!
EXCUSE US.

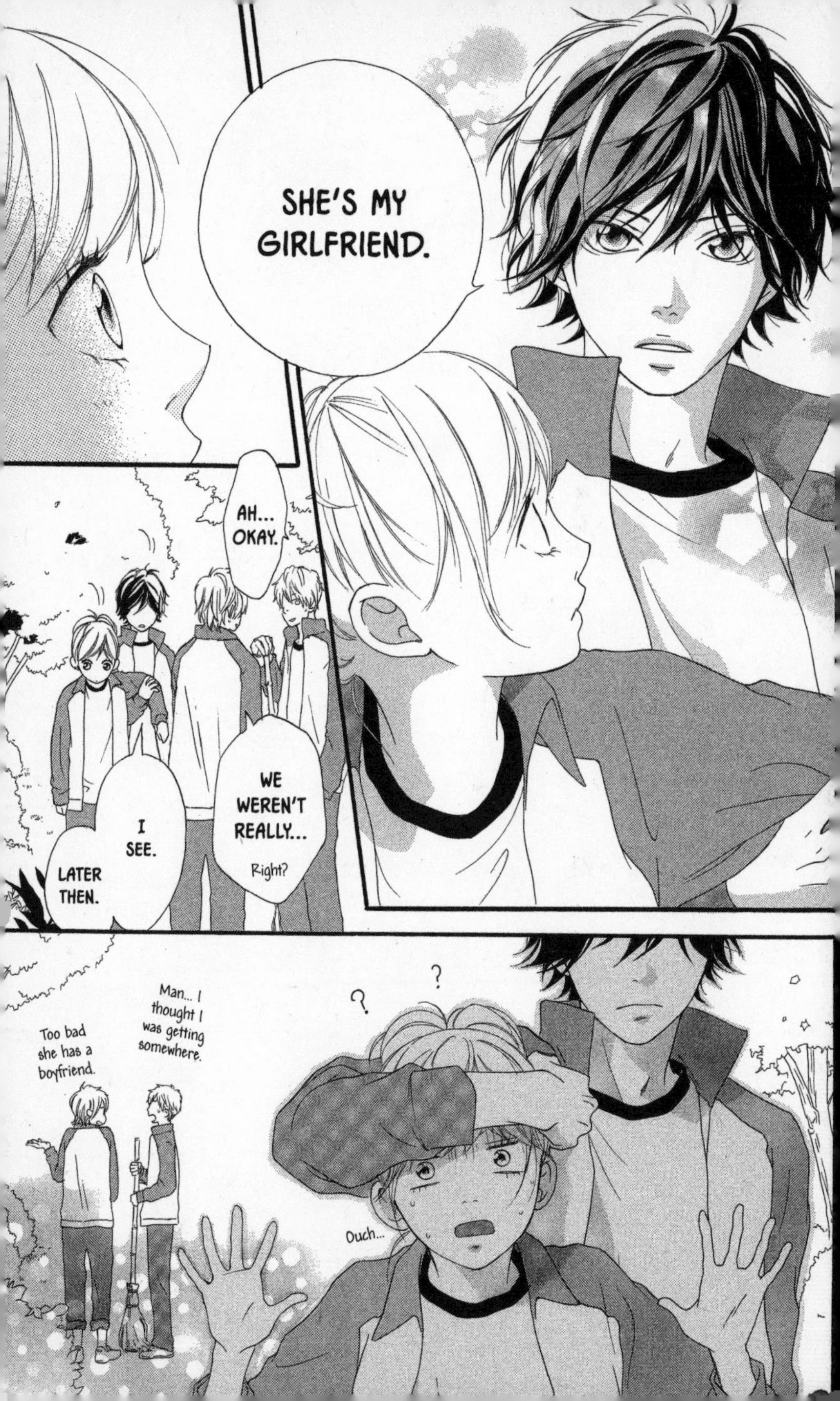
SHE'S MY GIRLFRIEND.
AH... OKAY.
WE WEREN'T REALLY...
Right?
I SEE.
LATER THEN.
?
?
Ouch...
Man... I thought I was getting somewhere.
Too bad she has a boyfriend.

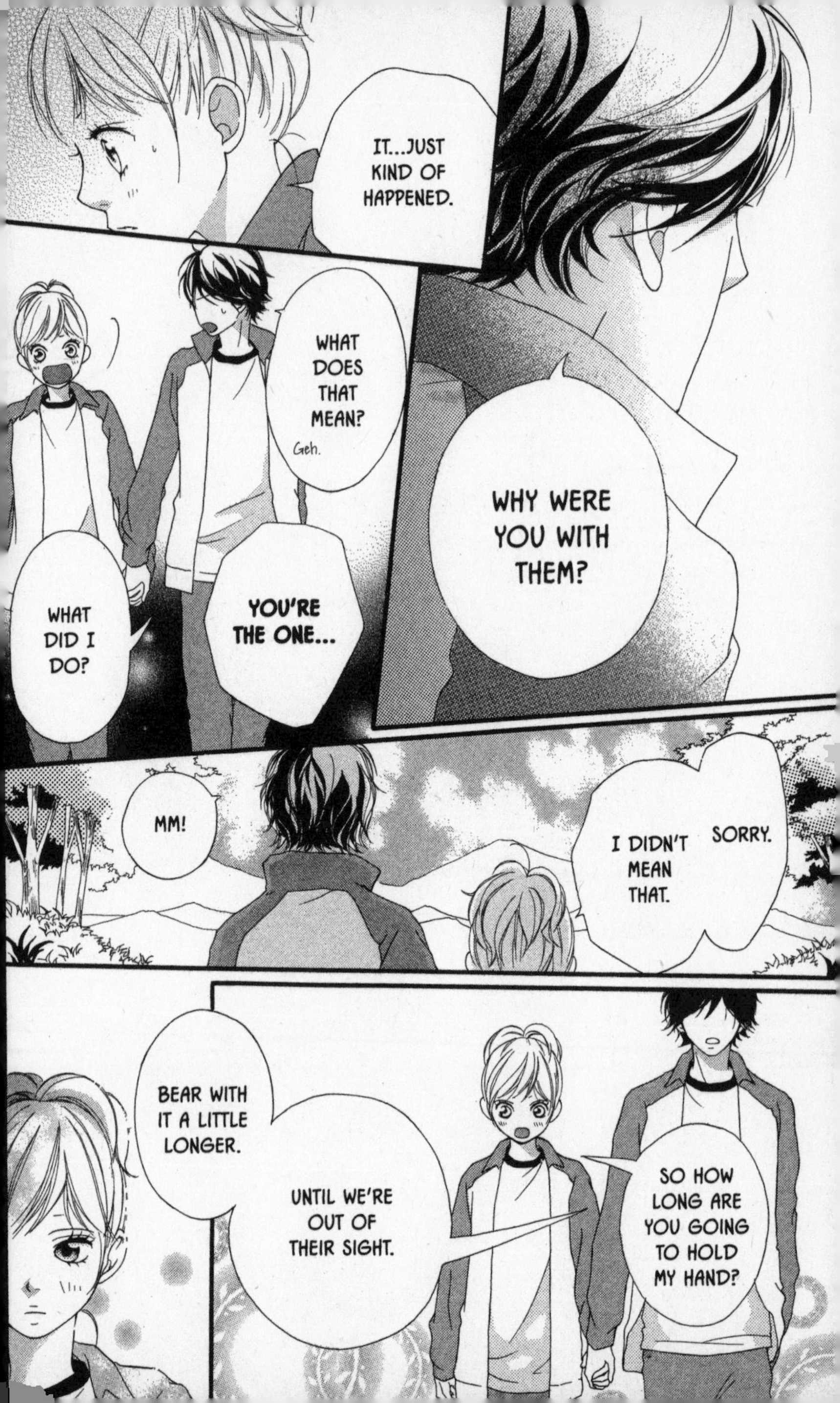
WHY WERE YOU WITH THEM?
IT...JUST KIND OF HAPPENED.
WHAT DOES THAT MEAN?
Geh.
YOU'RE THE ONE...
WHAT DID I DO?
SORRY.
I DIDN'T MEAN THAT.
MM!
SO HOW LONG ARE YOU GOING TO HOLD MY HAND?
BEAR WITH IT A LITTLE LONGER.
UNTIL WE'RE OUT OF THEIR SIGHT.

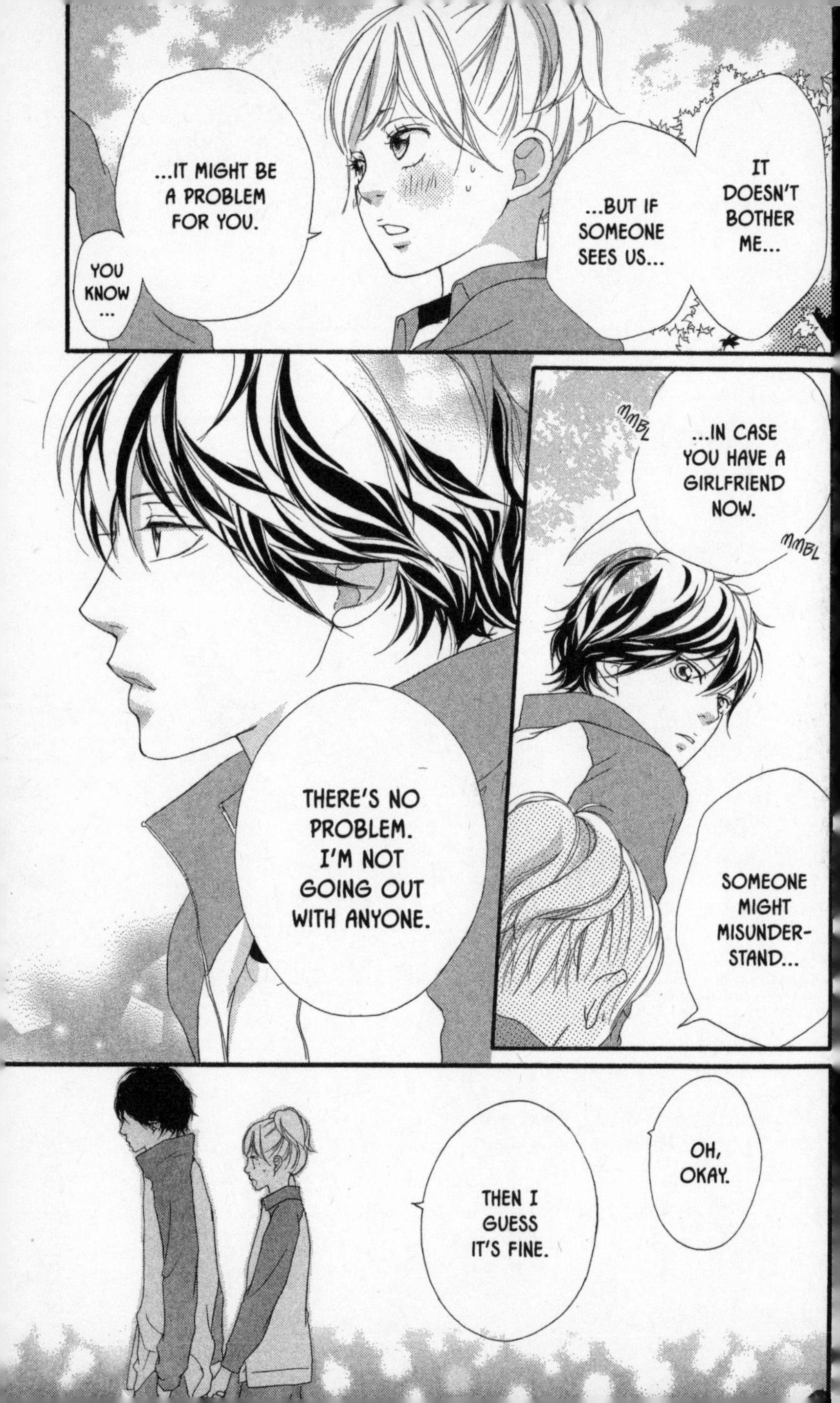
IT DOESN'T BOTHER ME...
...BUT IF SOMEONE SEES US...
...IT MIGHT BE A PROBLEM FOR YOU.
YOU KNOW ...
MMBL
...IN CASE YOU HAVE A GIRLFRIEND NOW.
MMBL
SOMEONE MIGHT MISUNDER-STAND...
THERE'S NO PROBLEM. I'M NOT GOING OUT WITH ANYONE.
OH, OKAY.
THEN I GUESS IT'S FINE.

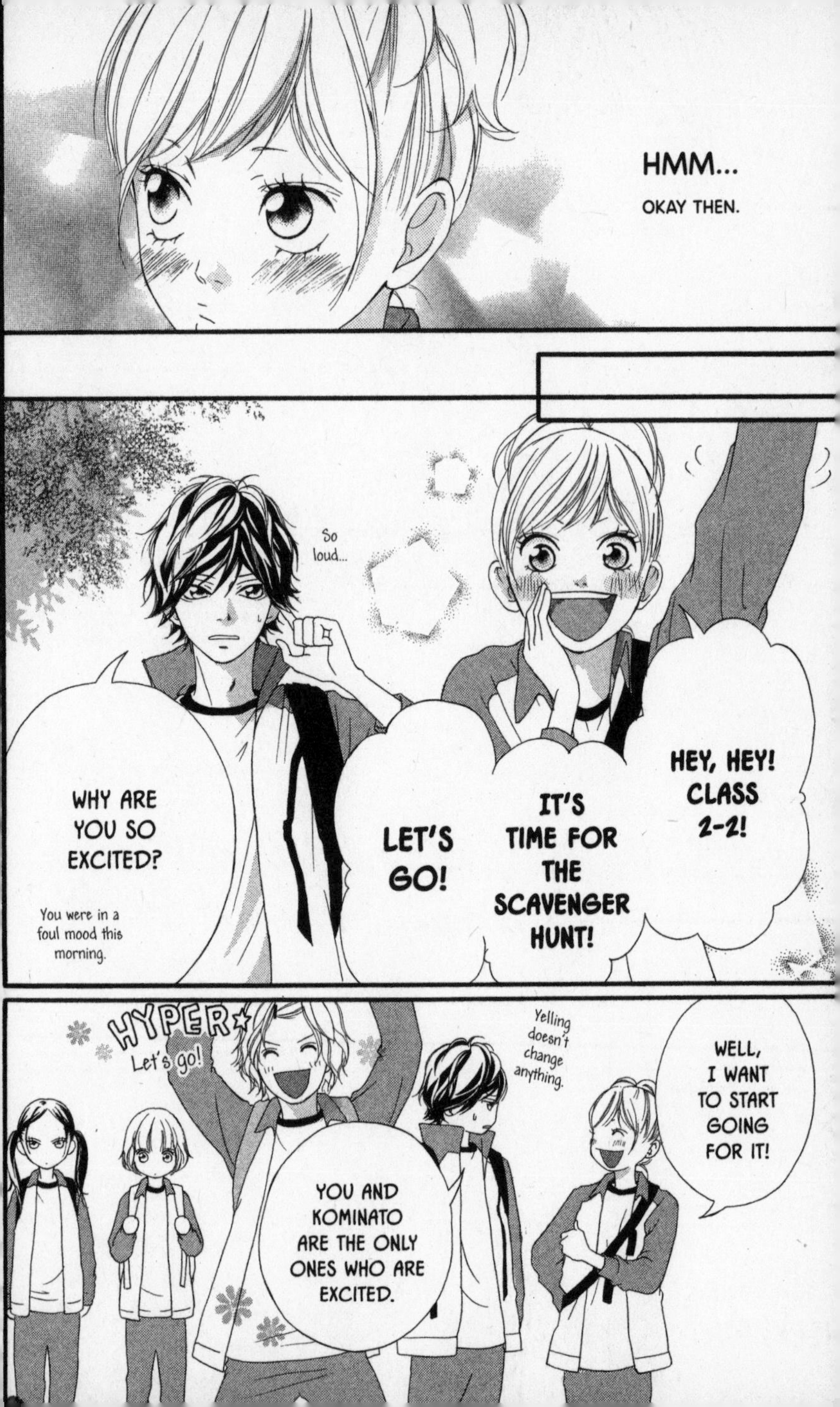
HMM...
OKAY THEN.
HEY, HEY! CLASS 2-2!
IT'S TIME FOR THE SCAVENGER HUNT!
LET'S GO!
So loud...
WHY ARE YOU SO EXCITED?
You were in a foul mood this morning.
WELL, I WANT TO START GOING FOR IT!
Yelling doesn't change anything.
HYPER☆
Let's go!
YOU AND KOMINATO ARE THE ONLY ONES WHO ARE EXCITED.

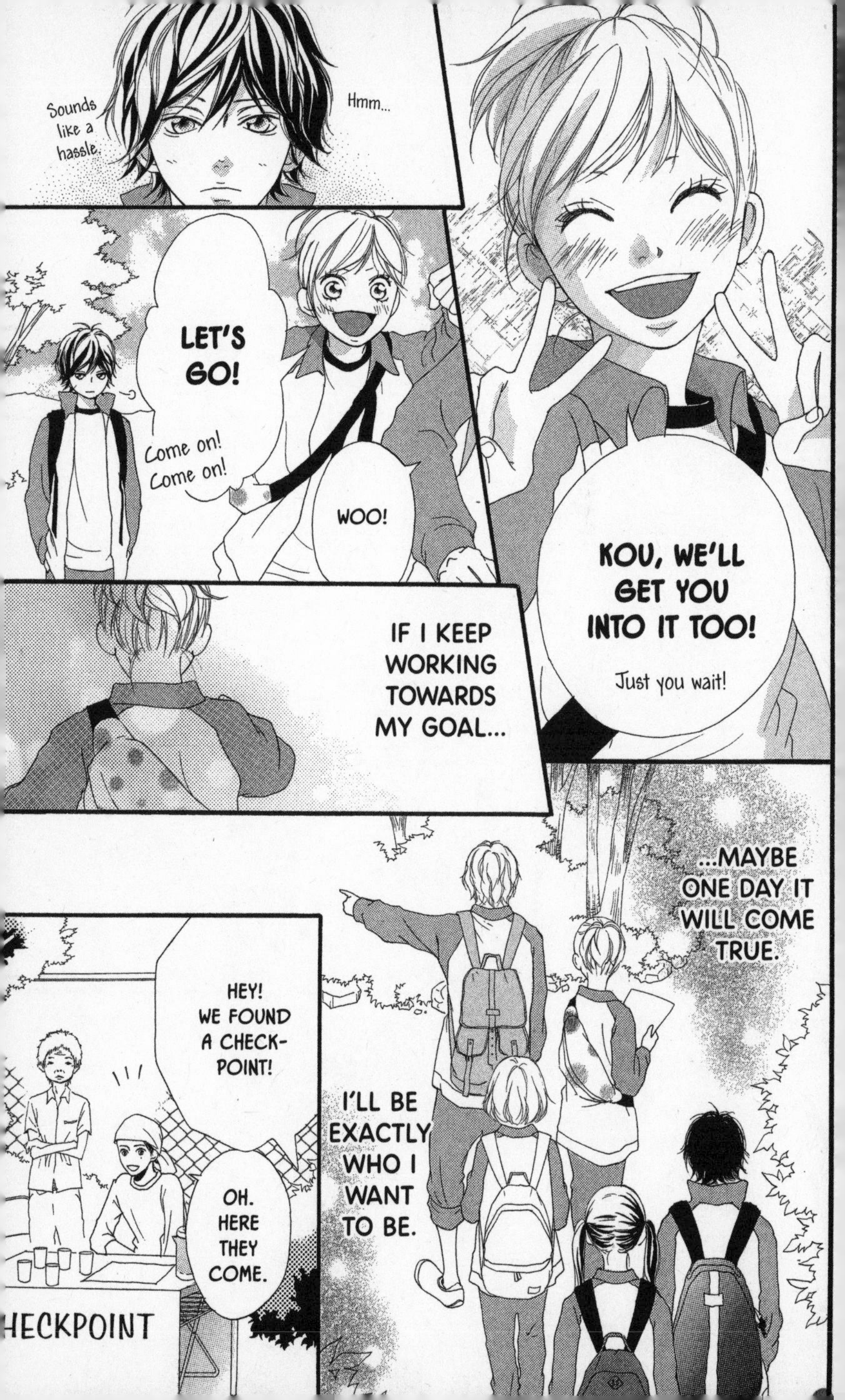
KOU, WE'LL GET YOU INTO IT TOO!
Just you wait!
Hmm...
Sounds like a hassle.
LET'S GO!
WOO!
Come on! Come on!
IF I KEEP WORKING TOWARDS MY GOAL...
...MAYBE ONE DAY IT WILL COME TRUE.
I'LL BE EXACTLY WHO I WANT TO BE.
HEY! WE FOUND A CHECK-POINT!
OH. HERE THEY COME.
HECKPOINT

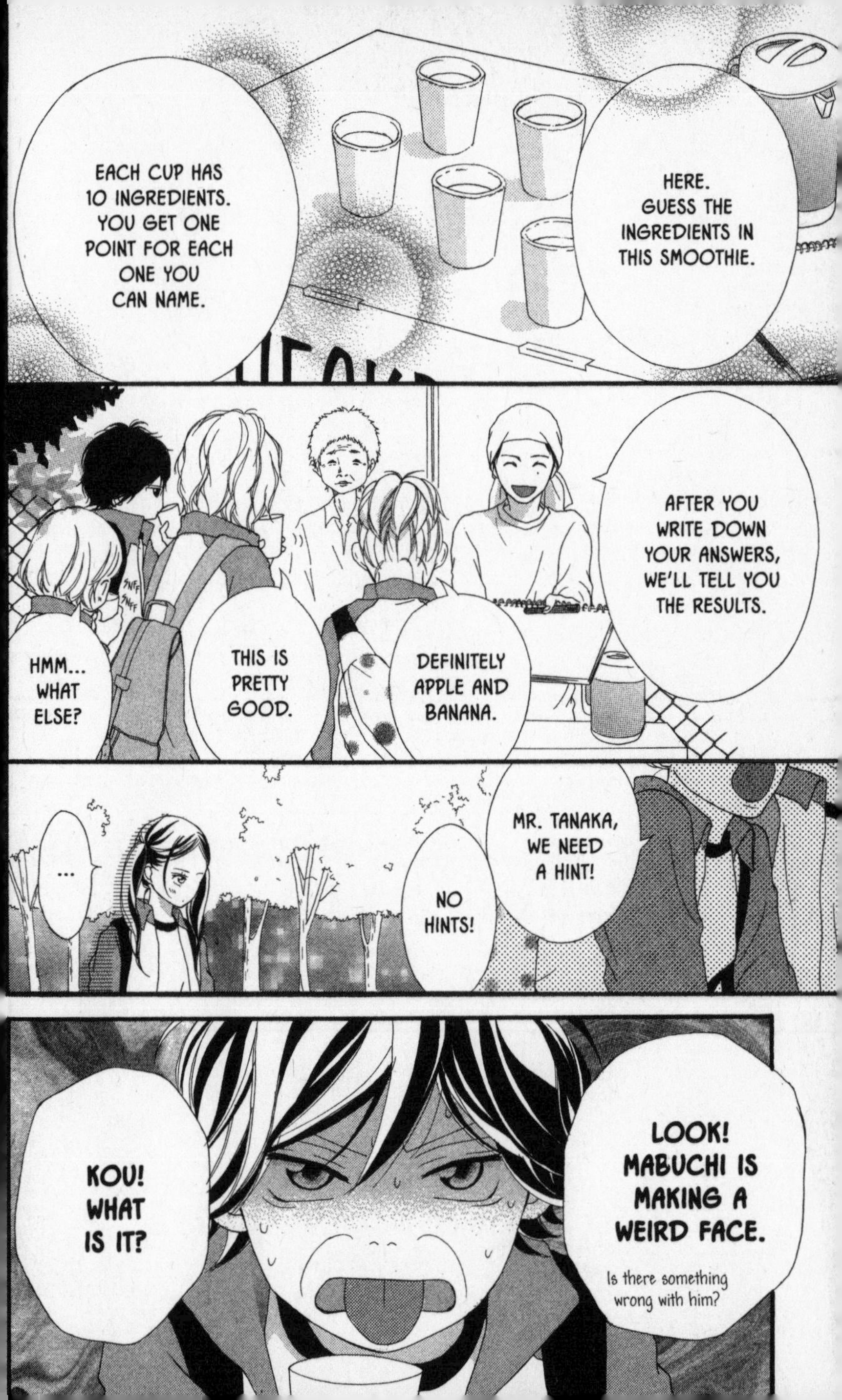
HERE. GUESS THE INGREDIENTS IN THIS SMOOTHIE.
EACH CUP HAS 10 INGREDIENTS. YOU GET ONE POINT FOR EACH ONE YOU CAN NAME.
AFTER YOU WRITE DOWN YOUR ANSWERS, WE'LL TELL YOU THE RESULTS.
DEFINITELY APPLE AND BANANA.
THIS IS PRETTY GOOD.
SNFF SNFF
HMM... WHAT ELSE?
MR. TANAKA, WE NEED A HINT!
NO HINTS!
...
LOOK! MABUCHI IS MAKING A WEIRD FACE.
Is there something wrong with him?
KOU! WHAT IS IT?

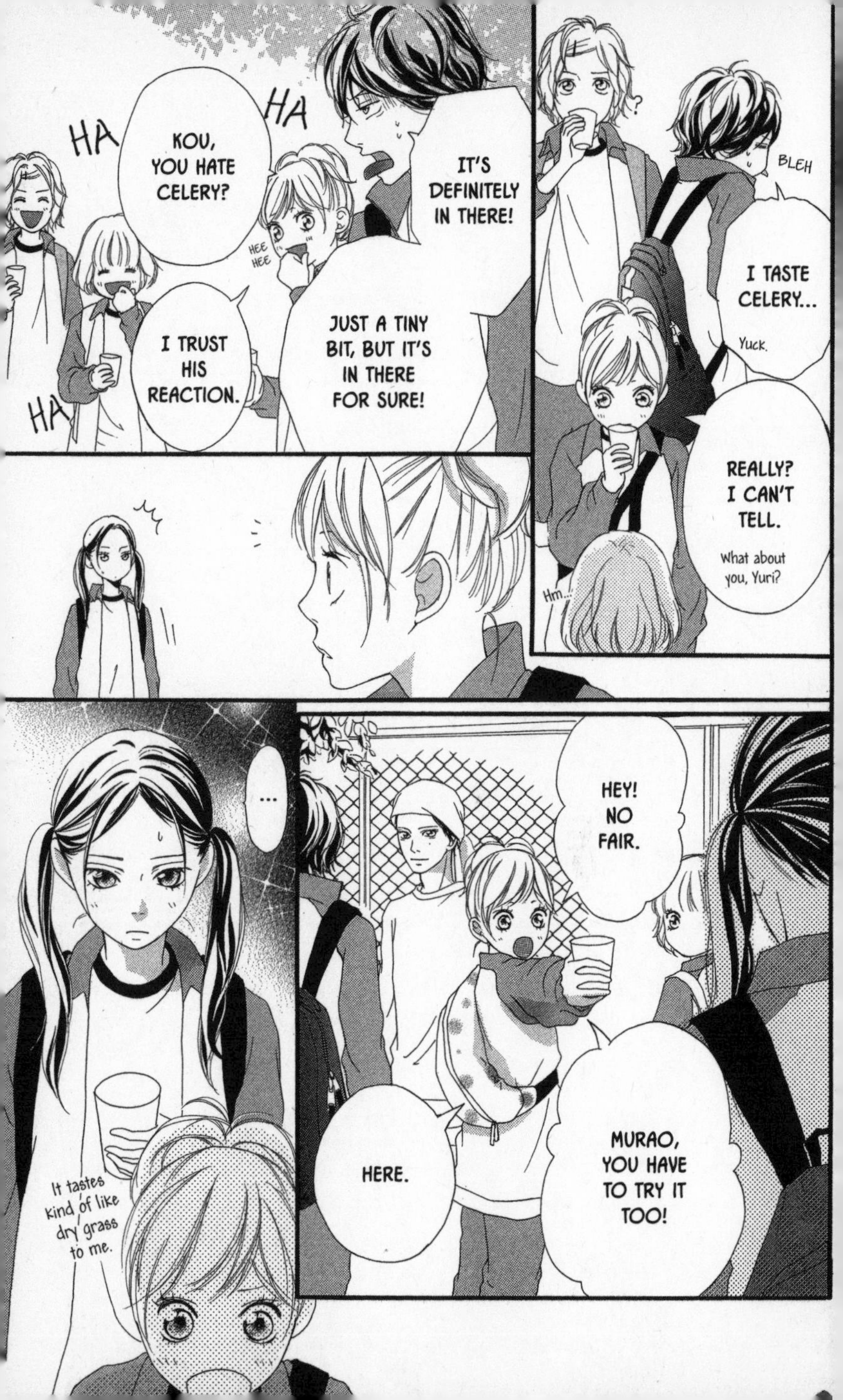
BLEH
I TASTE CELERY...
Yuck.
REALLY? I CAN'T TELL.
What about you, Yuri?
Hm...
IT'S DEFINITELY IN THERE!
HA
KOU, YOU HATE CELERY?
HA
HEE HEE
JUST A TINY BIT, BUT IT'S IN THERE FOR SURE!
I TRUST HIS REACTION.
HA
HEY! NO FAIR.
MURAO, YOU HAVE TO TRY IT TOO!
HERE.
...
It tastes kind of like dry grass to me.

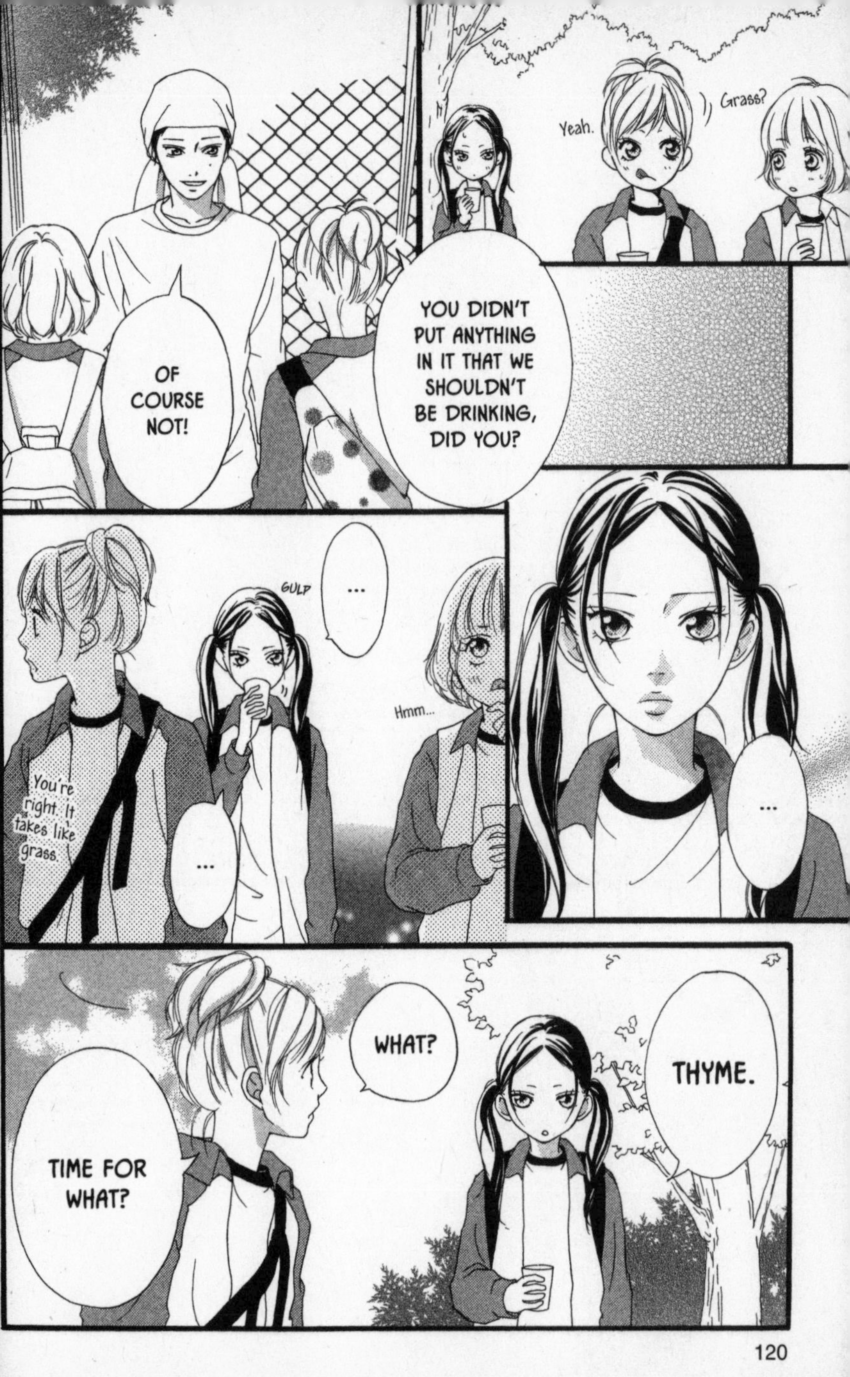

Grass?
Yeah.
YOU DIDN'T PUT ANYTHING IN IT THAT WE SHOULDN'T BE DRINKING, DID YOU?
OF COURSE NOT!
...
...
GULP
Hmm...
You're right. It takes like grass.
...
THYME.
WHAT?
TIME FOR WHAT?

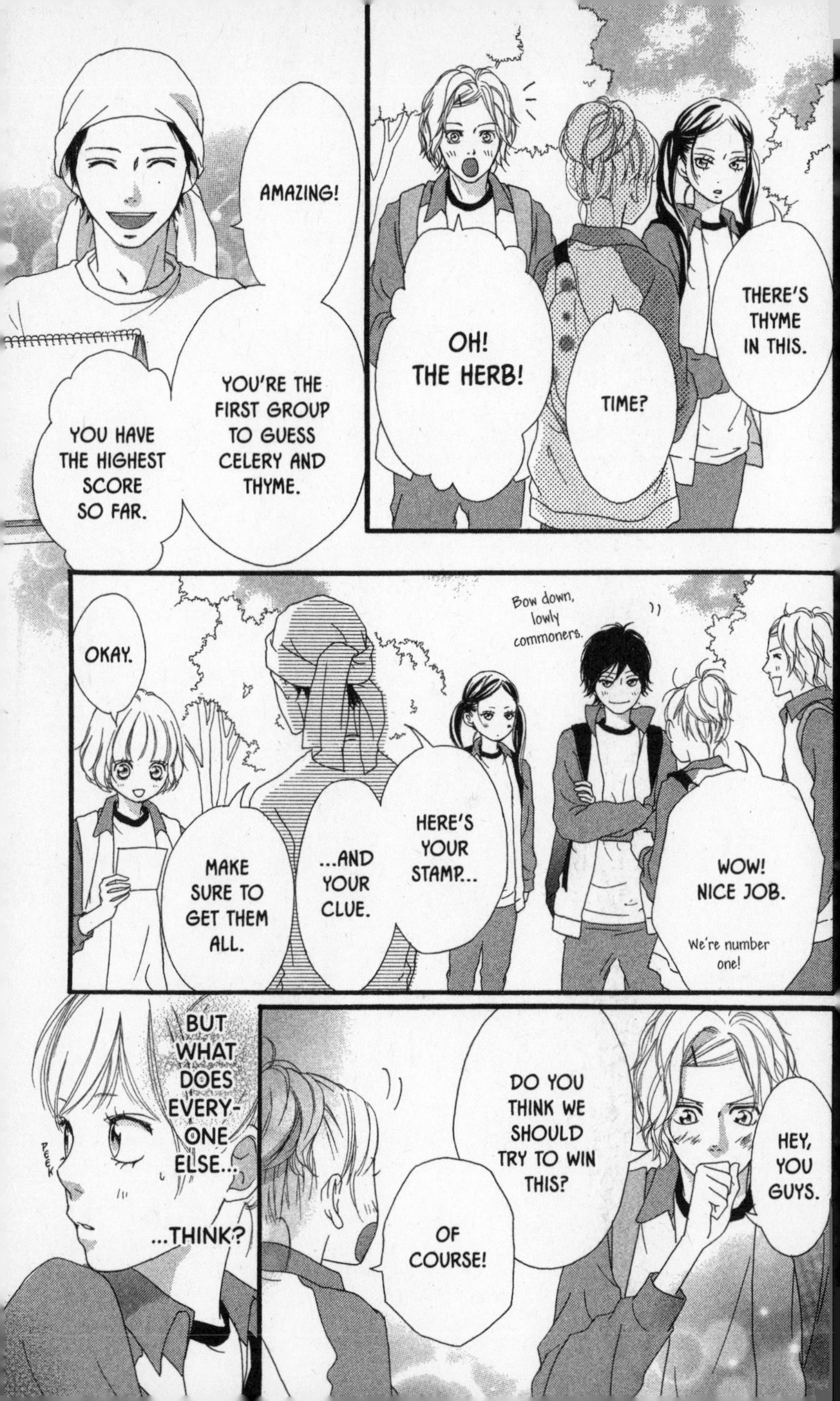
THERE'S THYME IN THIS.
TIME?
OH! THE HERB!
AMAZING!
YOU'RE THE FIRST GROUP TO GUESS CELERY AND THYME.
YOU HAVE THE HIGHEST SCORE SO FAR.
WOW! NICE JOB.
We're number one!
Bow down, lowly commoners.
HERE'S YOUR STAMP...
...AND YOUR CLUE.
MAKE SURE TO GET THEM ALL.
OKAY.
HEY, YOU GUYS.
DO YOU THINK WE SHOULD TRY TO WIN THIS?
OF COURSE!
PEEK
BUT WHAT DOES EVERY-ONE ELSE...
...THINK?

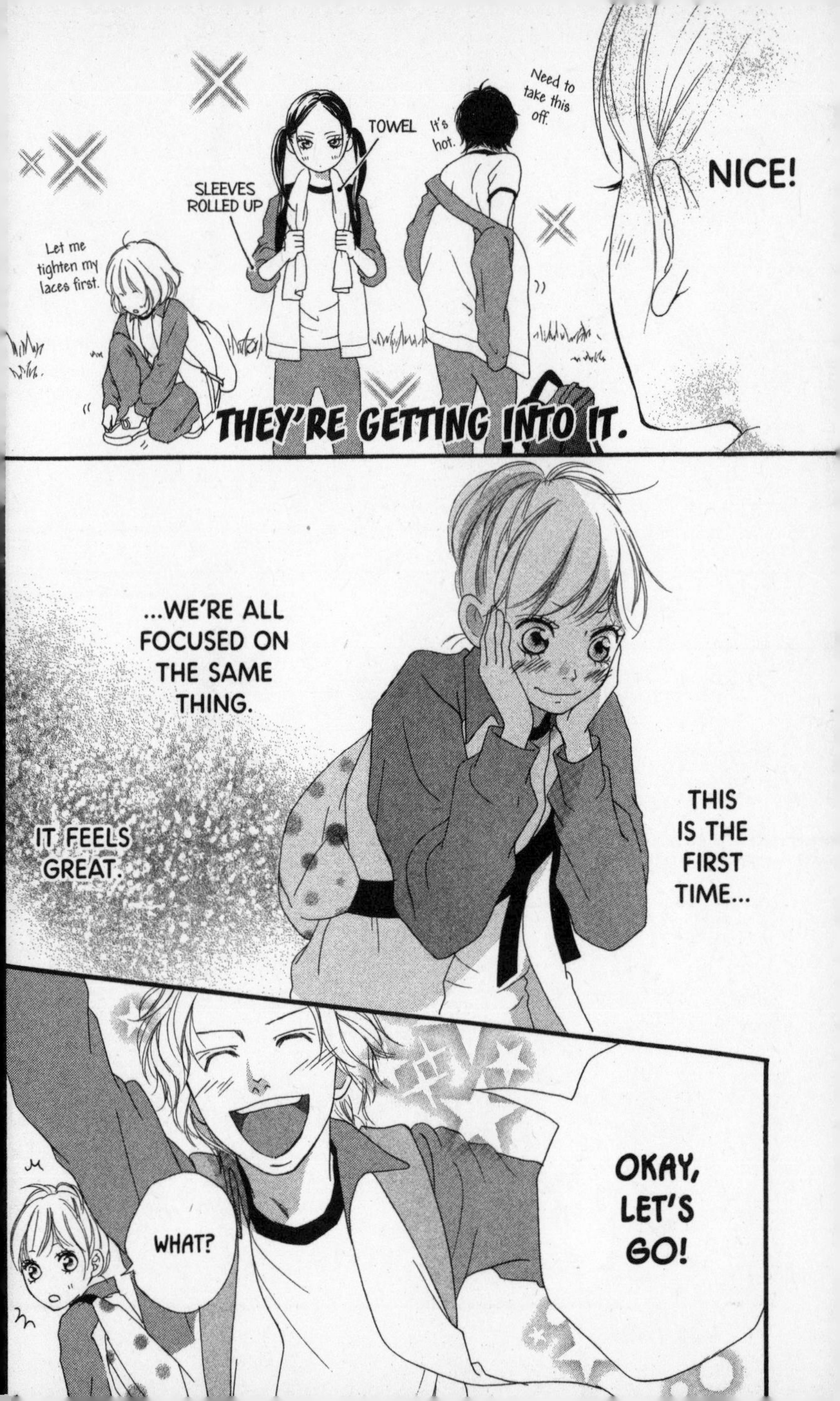
NICE!
Need to take this off.
It's hot.
TOWEL
SLEEVES ROLLED UP
Let me tighten my laces first.
THEY'RE GETTING INTO IT.
THIS IS THE FIRST TIME...
...WE'RE ALL FOCUSED ON THE SAME THING.
IT FEELS GREAT.
OKAY, LET'S GO!
WHAT?

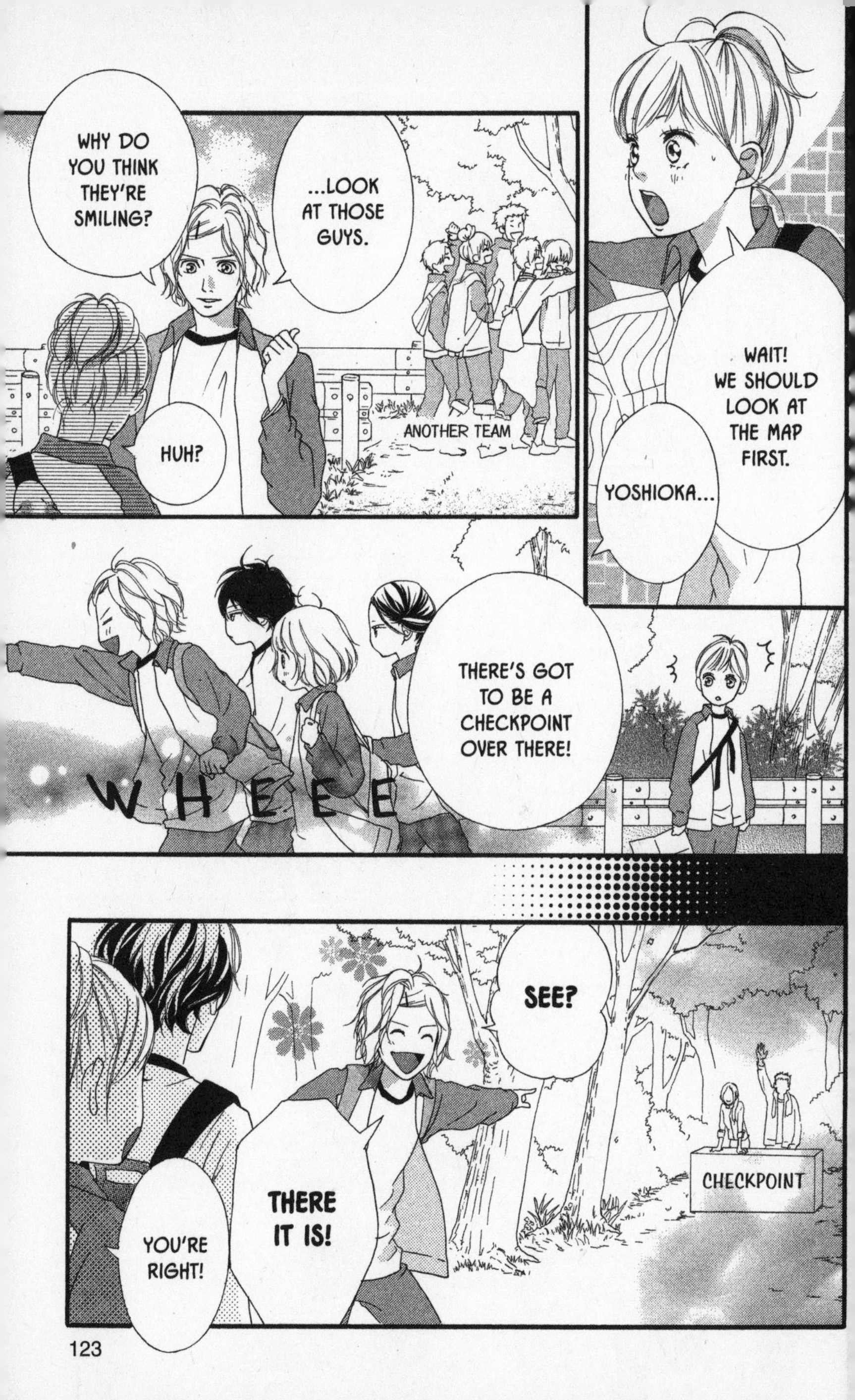
WAIT! WE SHOULD LOOK AT THE MAP FIRST.
YOSHIOKA...
...LOOK AT THOSE GUYS.
WHY DO YOU THINK THEY'RE SMILING?
ANOTHER TEAM
HUH?
THERE'S GOT TO BE A CHECKPOINT OVER THERE!
WHEEE
SEE?
CHECKPOINT
THERE IT IS!
YOU'RE RIGHT!

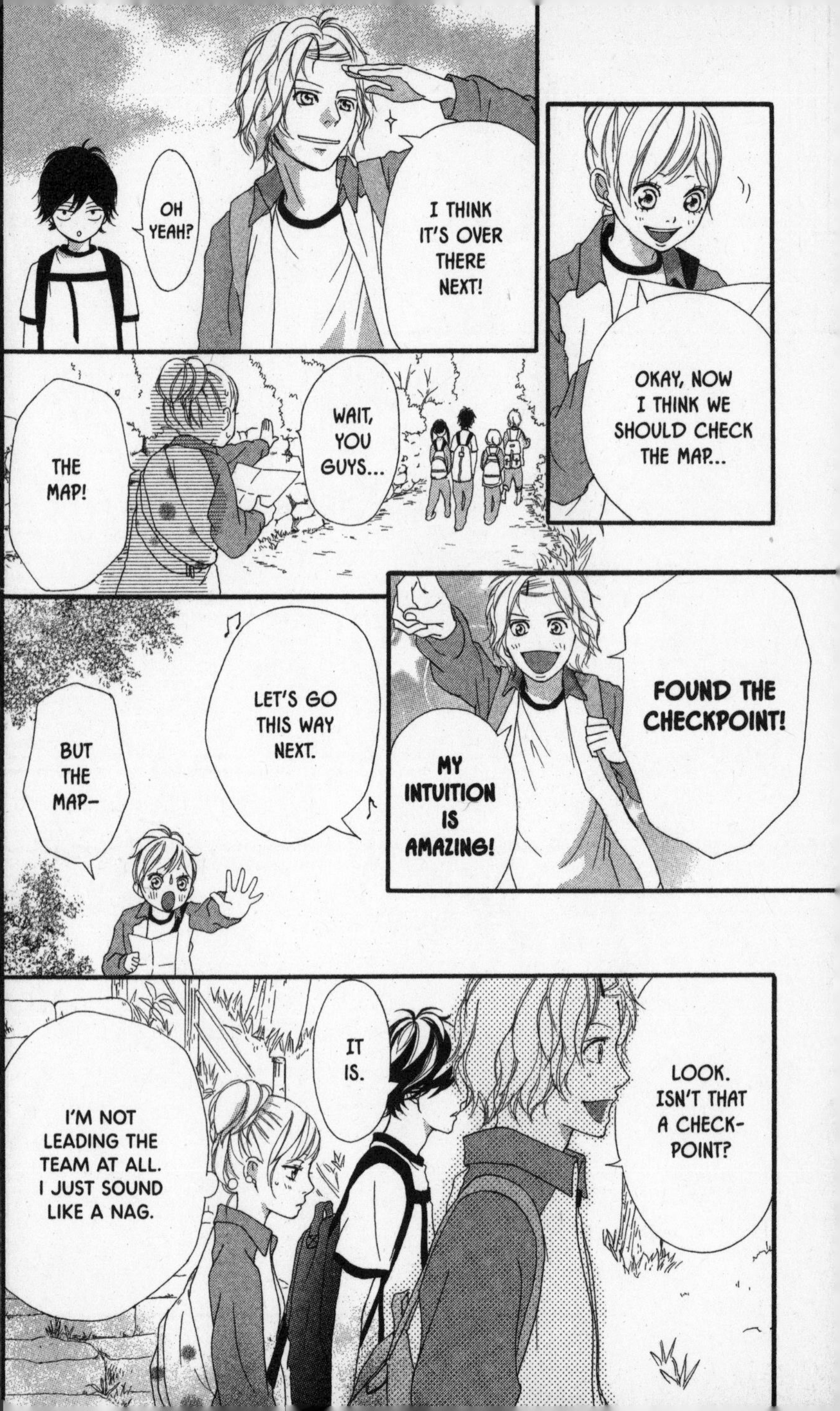
I THINK IT'S OVER THERE NEXT!
OH YEAH?
OKAY, NOW I THINK WE SHOULD CHECK THE MAP...
WAIT, YOU GUYS...
THE MAP!
FOUND THE CHECKPOINT!
MY INTUITION IS AMAZING!
LET'S GO THIS WAY NEXT.
BUT THE MAP—
LOOK. ISN'T THAT A CHECK-POINT?
IT IS.
I'M NOT LEADING THE TEAM AT ALL. I JUST SOUND LIKE A NAG.

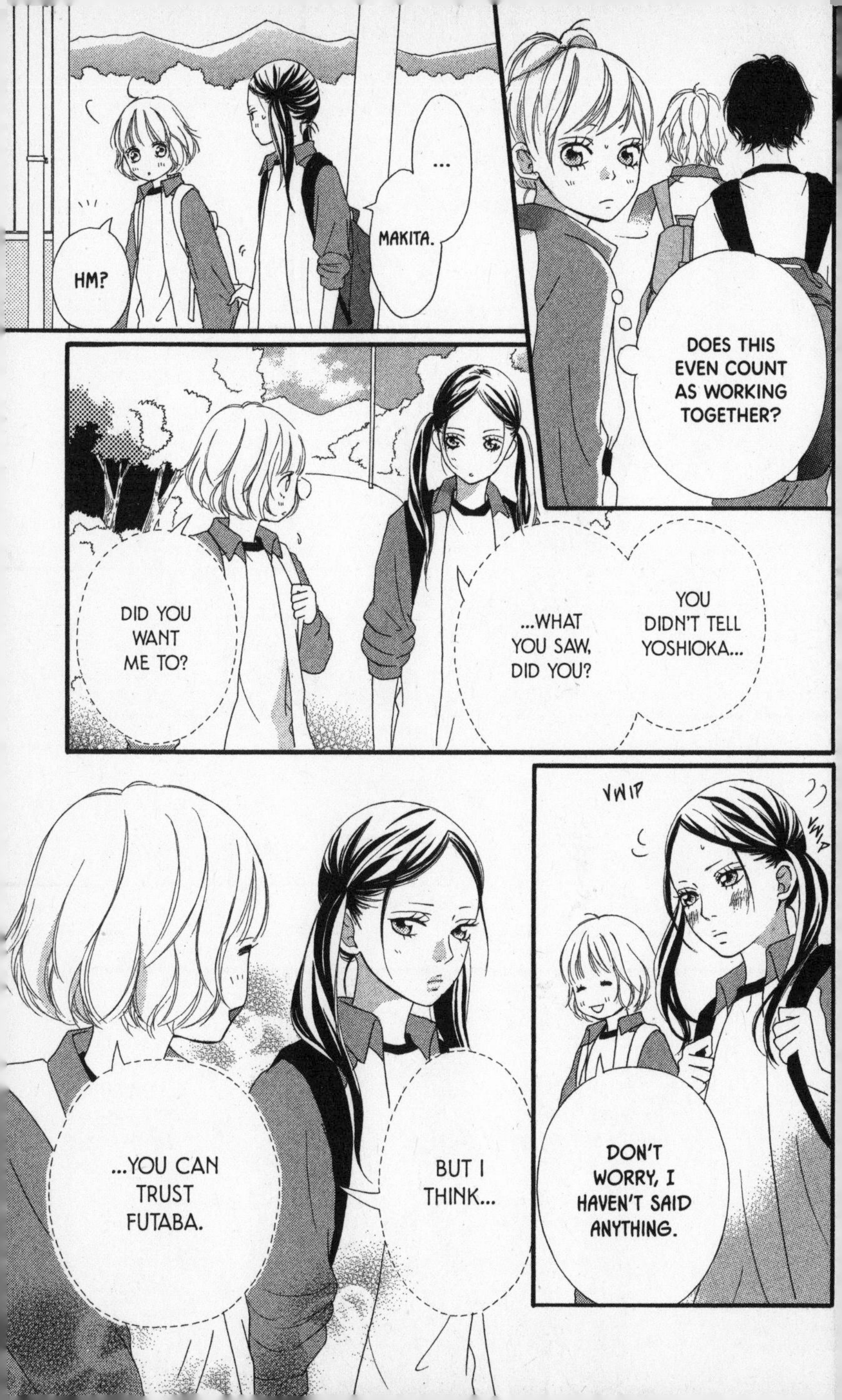
DOES THIS EVEN COUNT AS WORKING TOGETHER?
...
MAKITA.
HM?
YOU DIDN'T TELL YOSHIOKA...
...WHAT YOU SAW, DID YOU?
DID YOU WANT ME TO?
VWIP
VWIP
DON'T WORRY, I HAVEN'T SAID ANYTHING.
BUT I THINK...
...YOU CAN TRUST FUTABA.

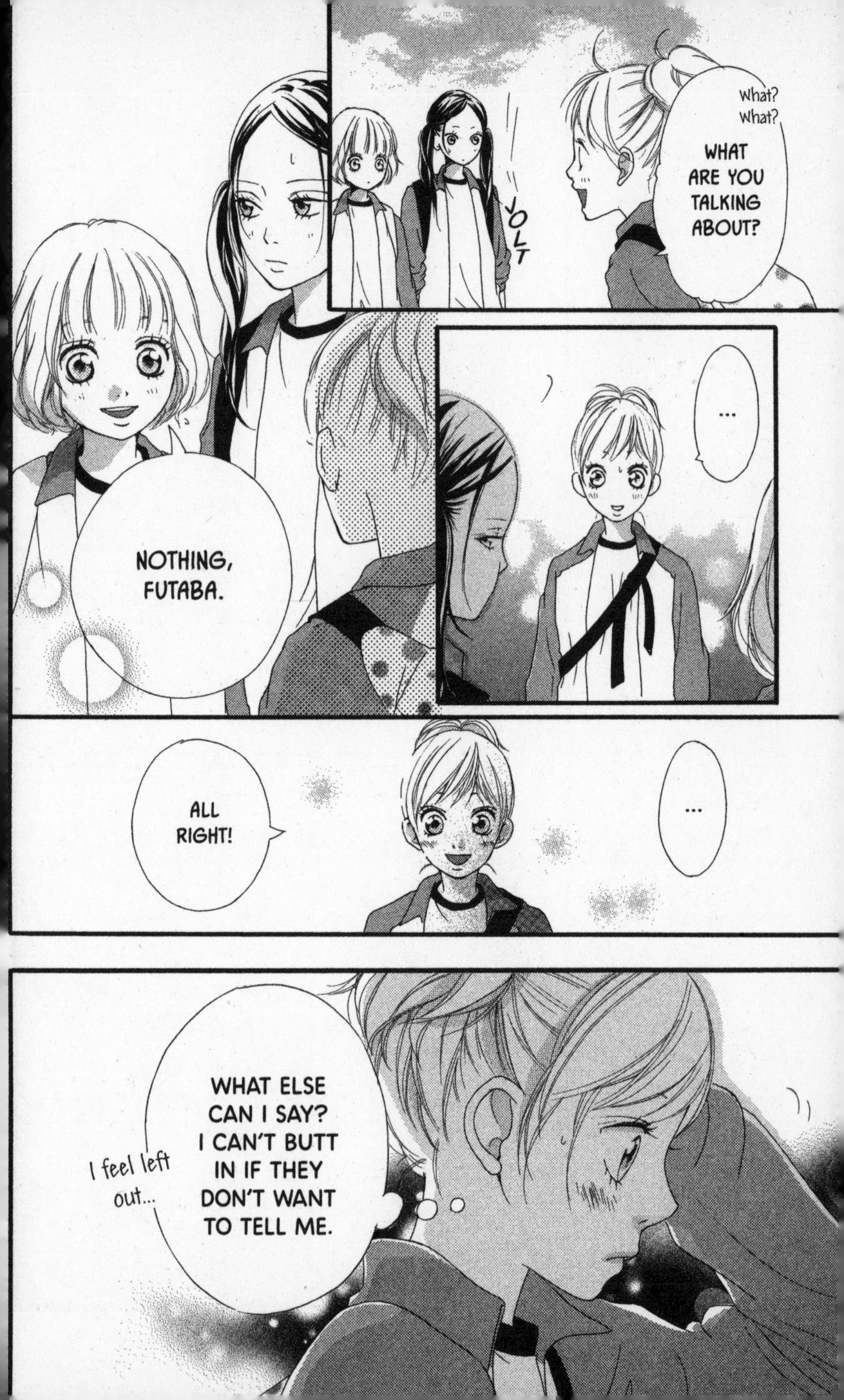
What? What?
WHAT ARE YOU TALKING ABOUT?
VOLT
...
NOTHING, FUTABA.
...
ALL RIGHT!
WHAT ELSE CAN I SAY? I CAN'T BUTT IN IF THEY DON'T WANT TO TELL ME.
I feel left out...

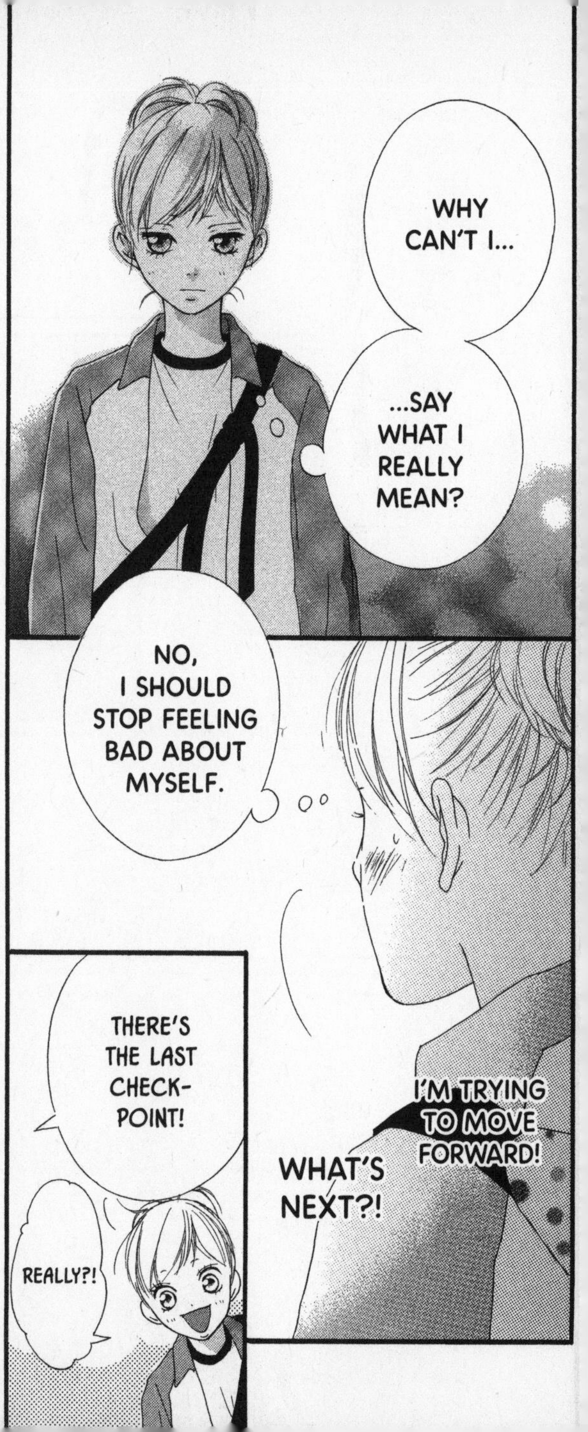
WHY CAN'T I...
...SAY WHAT I REALLY MEAN?
NO, I SHOULD STOP FEELING BAD ABOUT MYSELF.
I'M TRYING TO MOVE FORWARD!
WHAT'S NEXT?!
THERE'S THE LAST CHECK-POINT!
REALLY?!

Ramune

This little guy shows
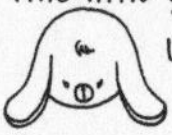
up here and there in the story. His name is Ramune. ♡ (My editor named him, and I think it's the cutest name!)

In the story he's a white lop-eared bunny and the mascot for a fabric softener brand (much like another well-known mascot). There is a lot of Ramune merchandise available. There's also a brown bunny named Brownie. (I named him.)

The reason you don't see Ramune too frequently in the story is because I keep forgetting to draw him in, but I think I'll give Yuri a Ramune back-pack sometime soon. ☆ I have to since we created one as a prize for magazine readers! Congratulations to everyone who received one. ♡

I hope everybody likes Ramune as much as I do.

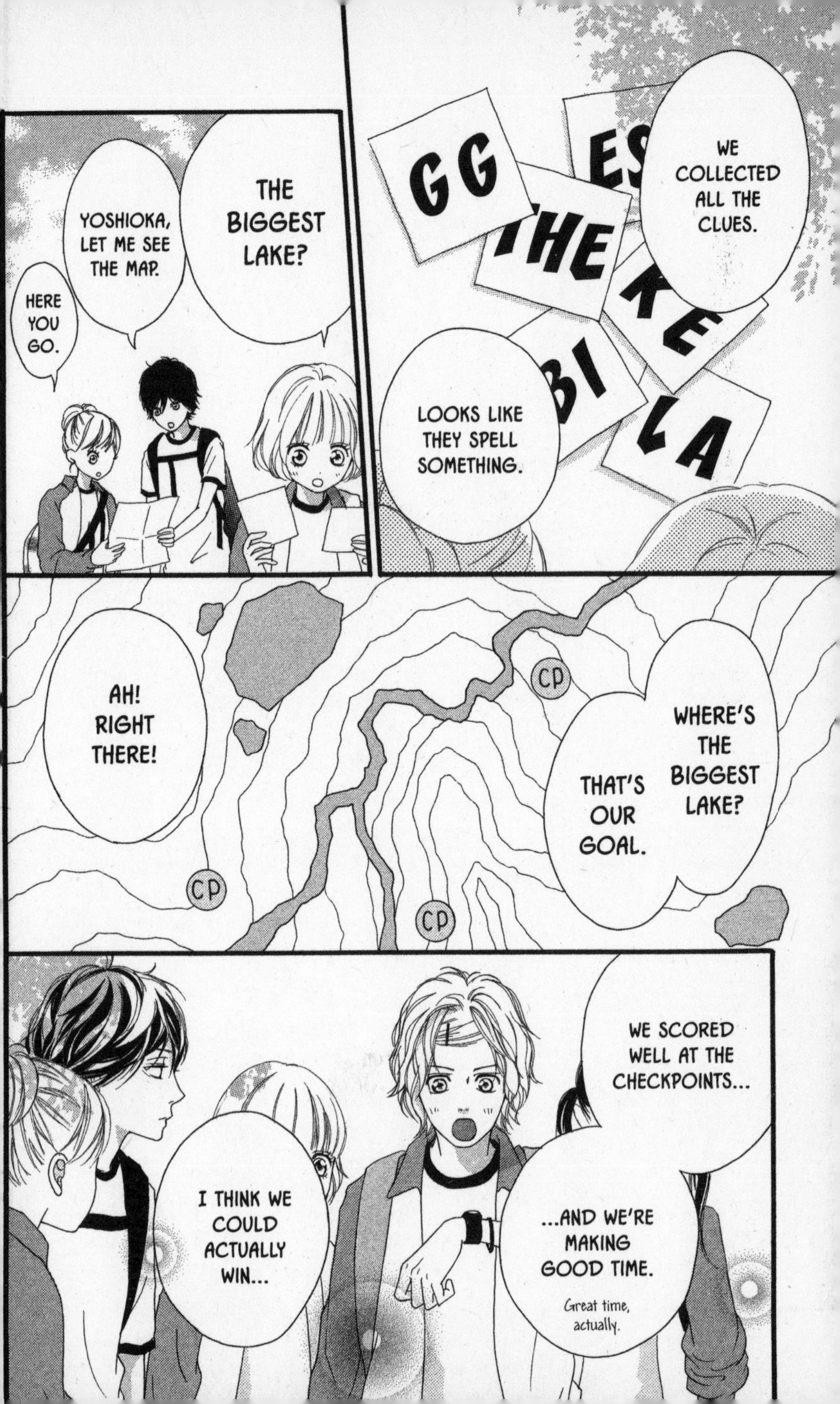
WE COLLECTED ALL THE CLUES.
GG
ES
THE
KE
BI
LA
LOOKS LIKE THEY SPELL SOMETHING.
THE BIGGEST LAKE?
YOSHIOKA, LET ME SEE THE MAP.
HERE YOU GO.
WHERE'S THE BIGGEST LAKE?
THAT'S OUR GOAL.
CP
CP
CP
AH! RIGHT THERE!
WE SCORED WELL AT THE CHECKPOINTS...
...AND WE'RE MAKING GOOD TIME.
Great time, actually.
I THINK WE COULD ACTUALLY WIN...

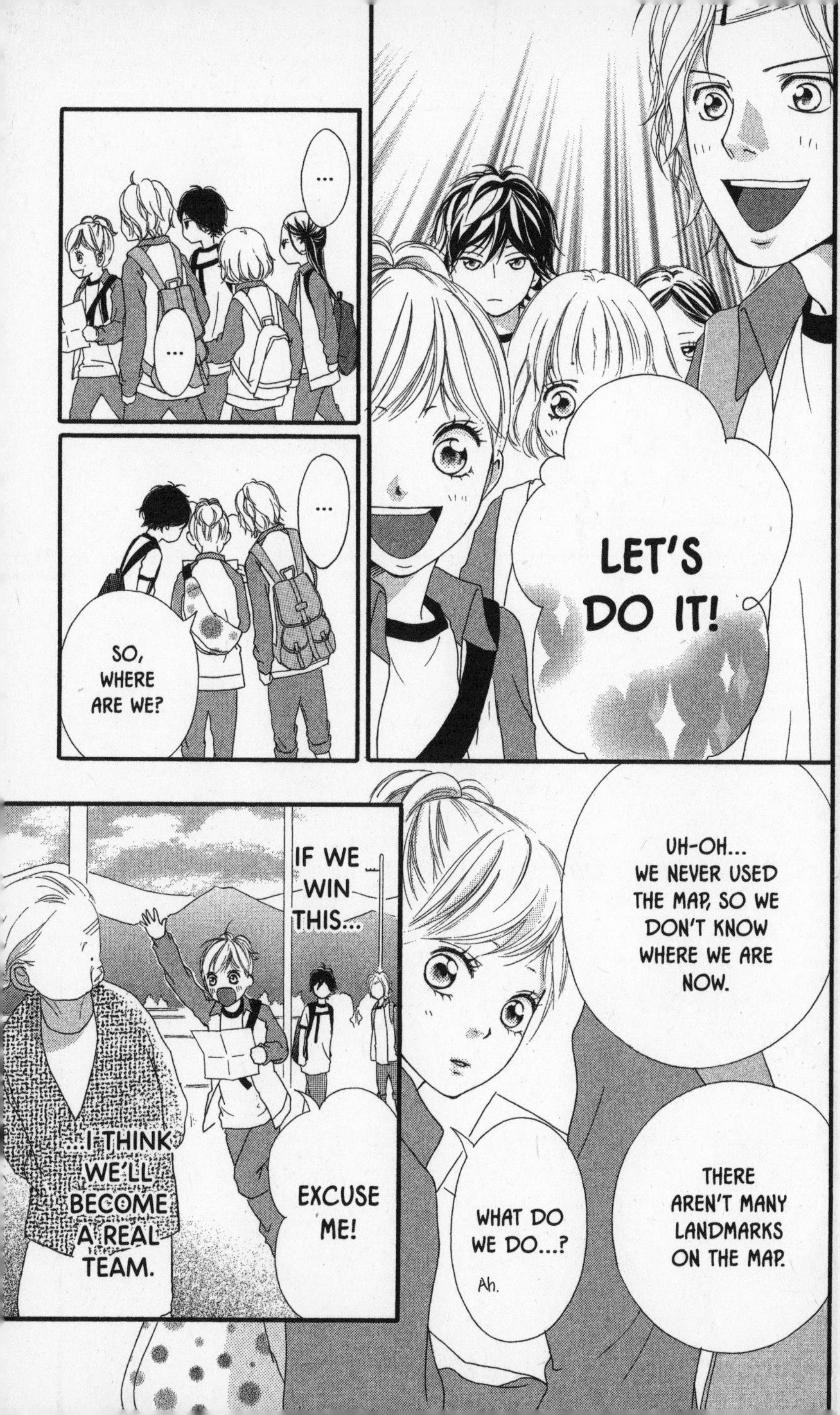
LET'S DO IT!
...
...
...
SO, WHERE ARE WE?
UH-OH... WE NEVER USED THE MAP, SO WE DON'T KNOW WHERE WE ARE NOW.
THERE AREN'T MANY LANDMARKS ON THE MAP.
WHAT DO WE DO...?
Ah.
IF WE WIN THIS...
EXCUSE ME!
...I THINK WE'LL BECOME A REAL TEAM.

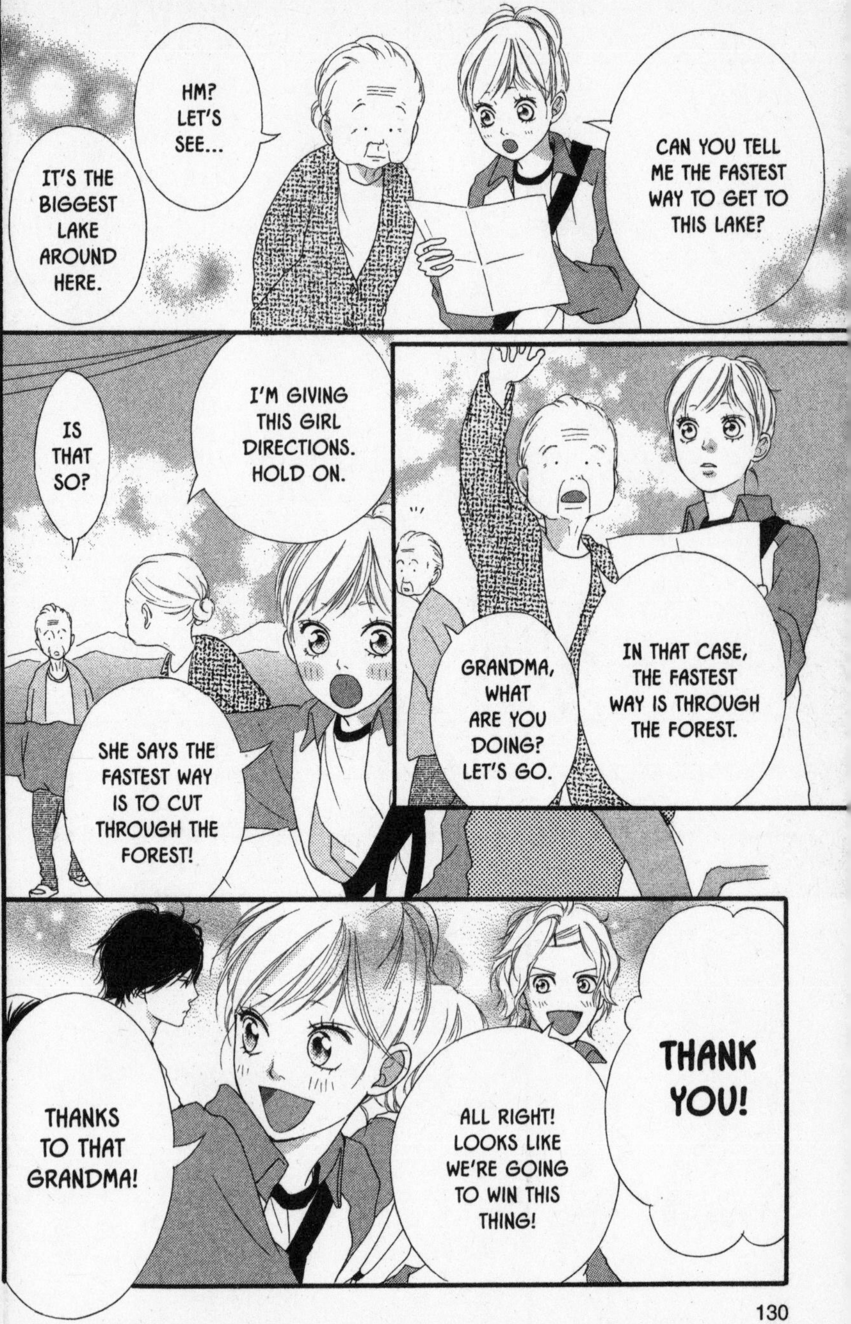

CAN YOU TELL ME THE FASTEST WAY TO GET TO THIS LAKE?
HM? LET'S SEE...
IT'S THE BIGGEST LAKE AROUND HERE.
IN THAT CASE, THE FASTEST WAY IS THROUGH THE FOREST.
GRANDMA, WHAT ARE YOU DOING? LET'S GO.
I'M GIVING THIS GIRL DIRECTIONS. HOLD ON.
IS THAT SO?
SHE SAYS THE FASTEST WAY IS TO CUT THROUGH THE FOREST!
THANK YOU!
ALL RIGHT! LOOKS LIKE WE'RE GOING TO WIN THIS THING!
THANKS TO THAT GRANDMA!

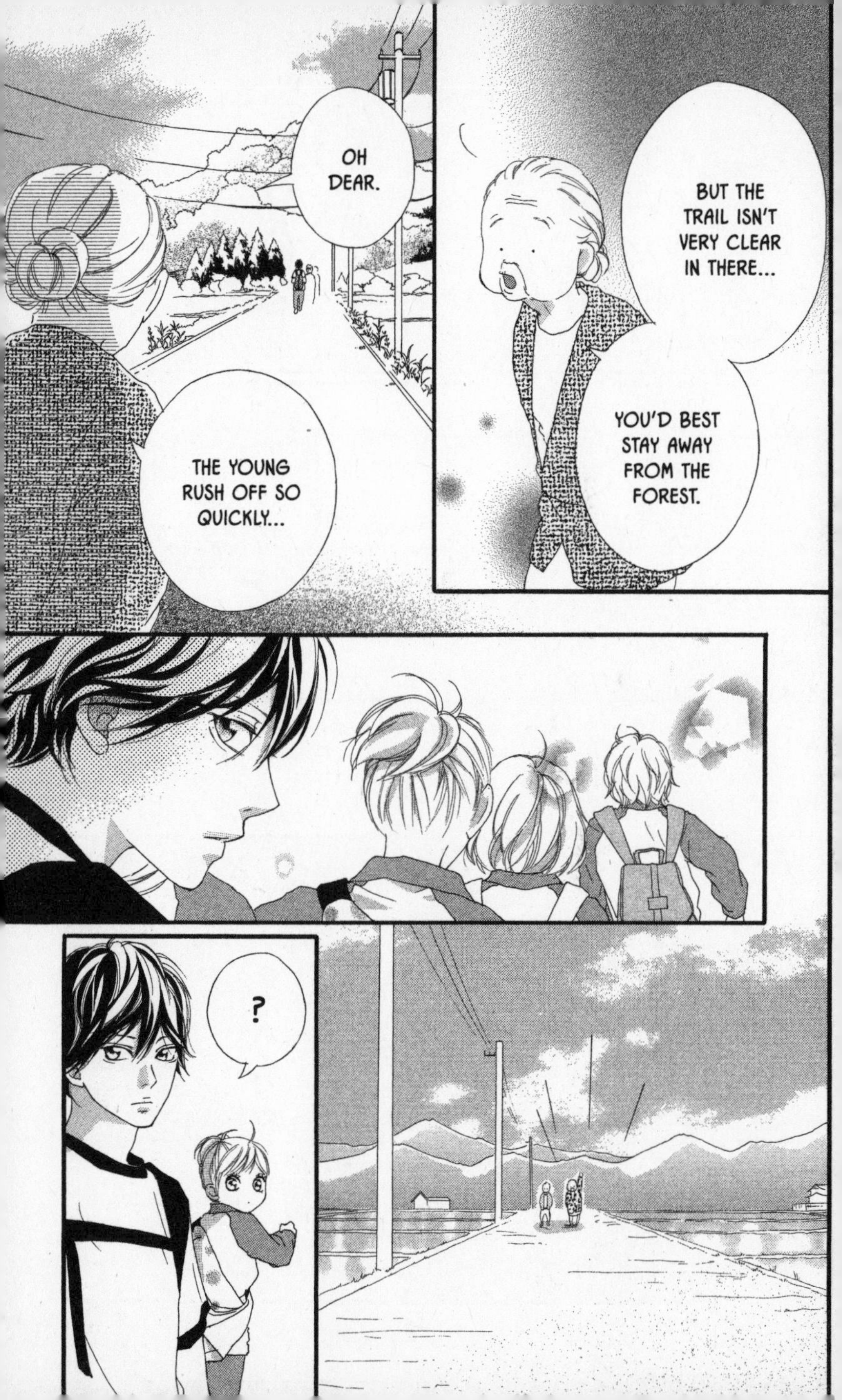
BUT THE TRAIL ISN'T VERY CLEAR IN THERE...
YOU'D BEST STAY AWAY FROM THE FOREST.
OH DEAR.
THE YOUNG RUSH OFF SO QUICKLY...
?

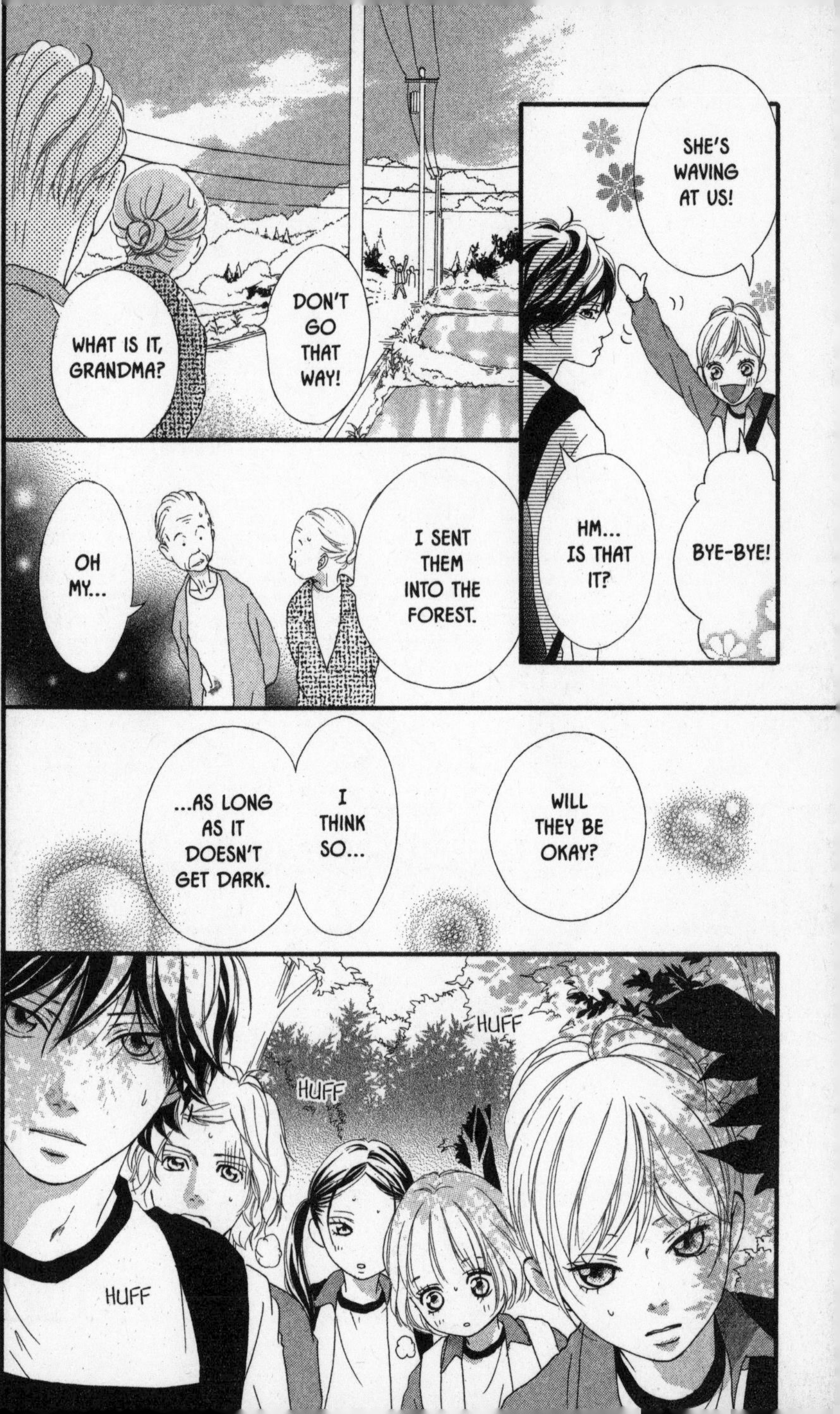
SHE'S WAVING AT US!
BYE-BYE!
HM... IS THAT IT?
DON'T GO THAT WAY!
WHAT IS IT, GRANDMA?
I SENT THEM INTO THE FOREST.
OH MY...
WILL THEY BE OKAY?
I THINK SO...
...AS LONG AS IT DOESN'T GET DARK.
HUFF
HUFF
HUFF

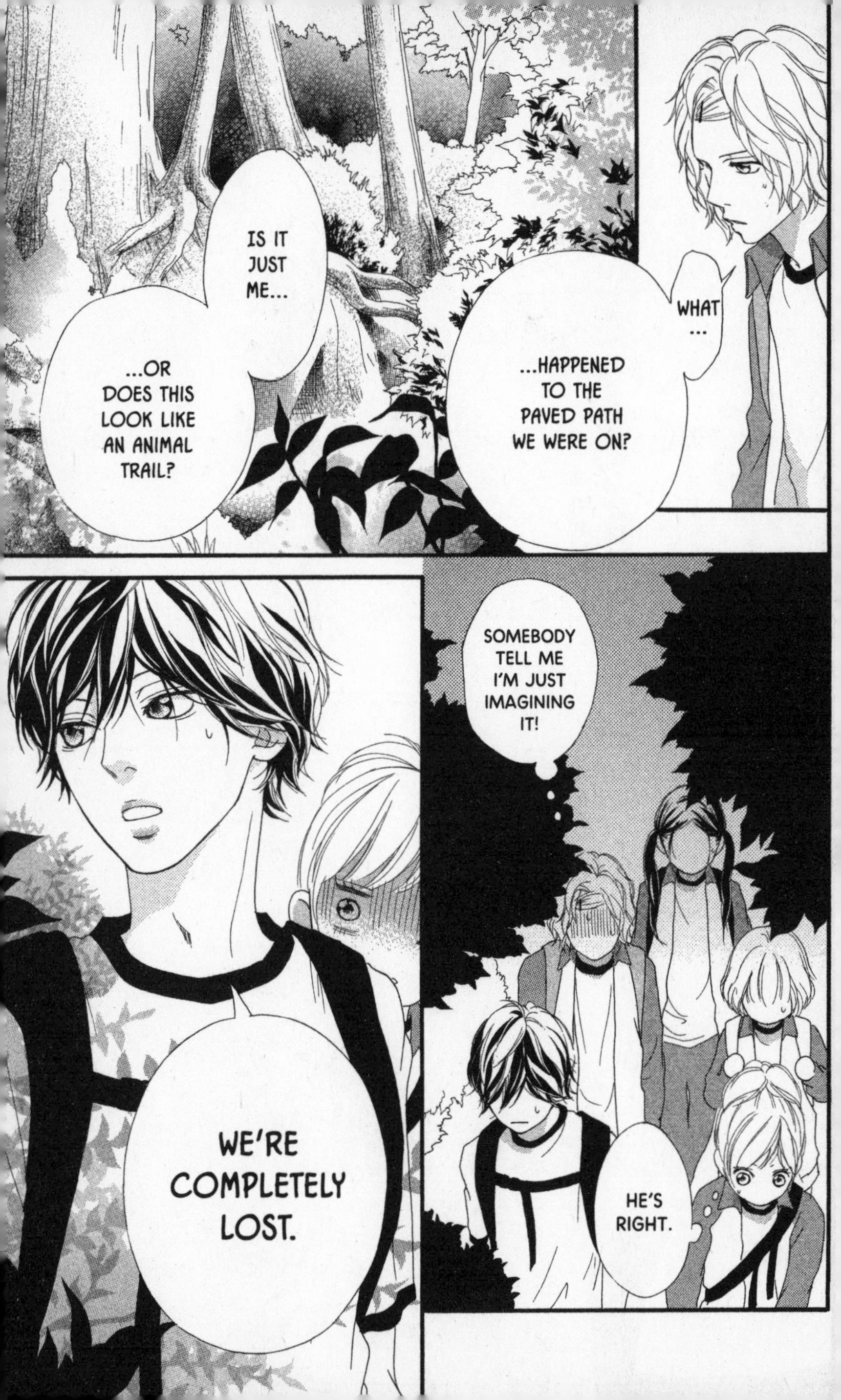
WHAT...
...HAPPENED TO THE PAVED PATH WE WERE ON?
IS IT JUST ME...
...OR DOES THIS LOOK LIKE AN ANIMAL TRAIL?
SOMEBODY TELL ME I'M JUST IMAGINING IT!
HE'S RIGHT.
WE'RE COMPLETELY LOST.

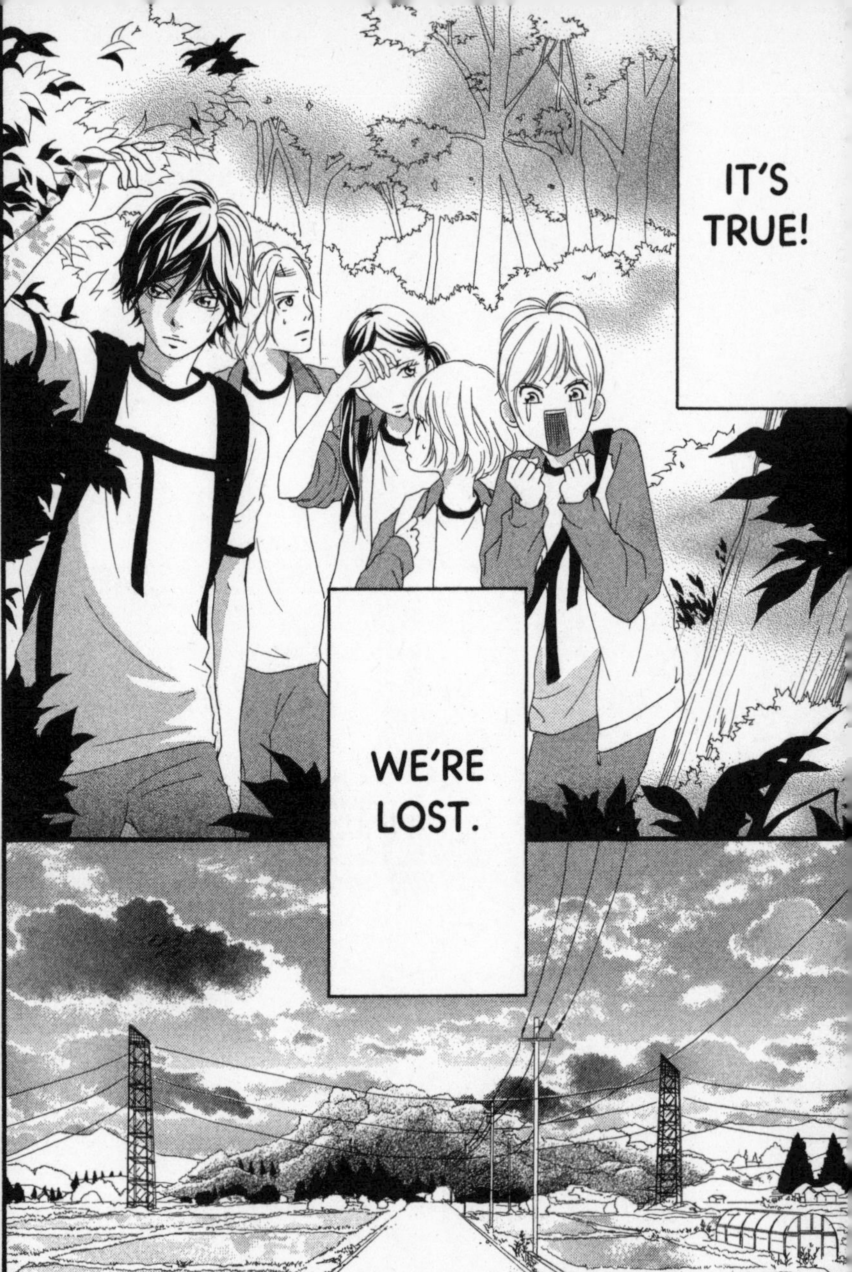
IT'S TRUE!
WE'RE LOST.

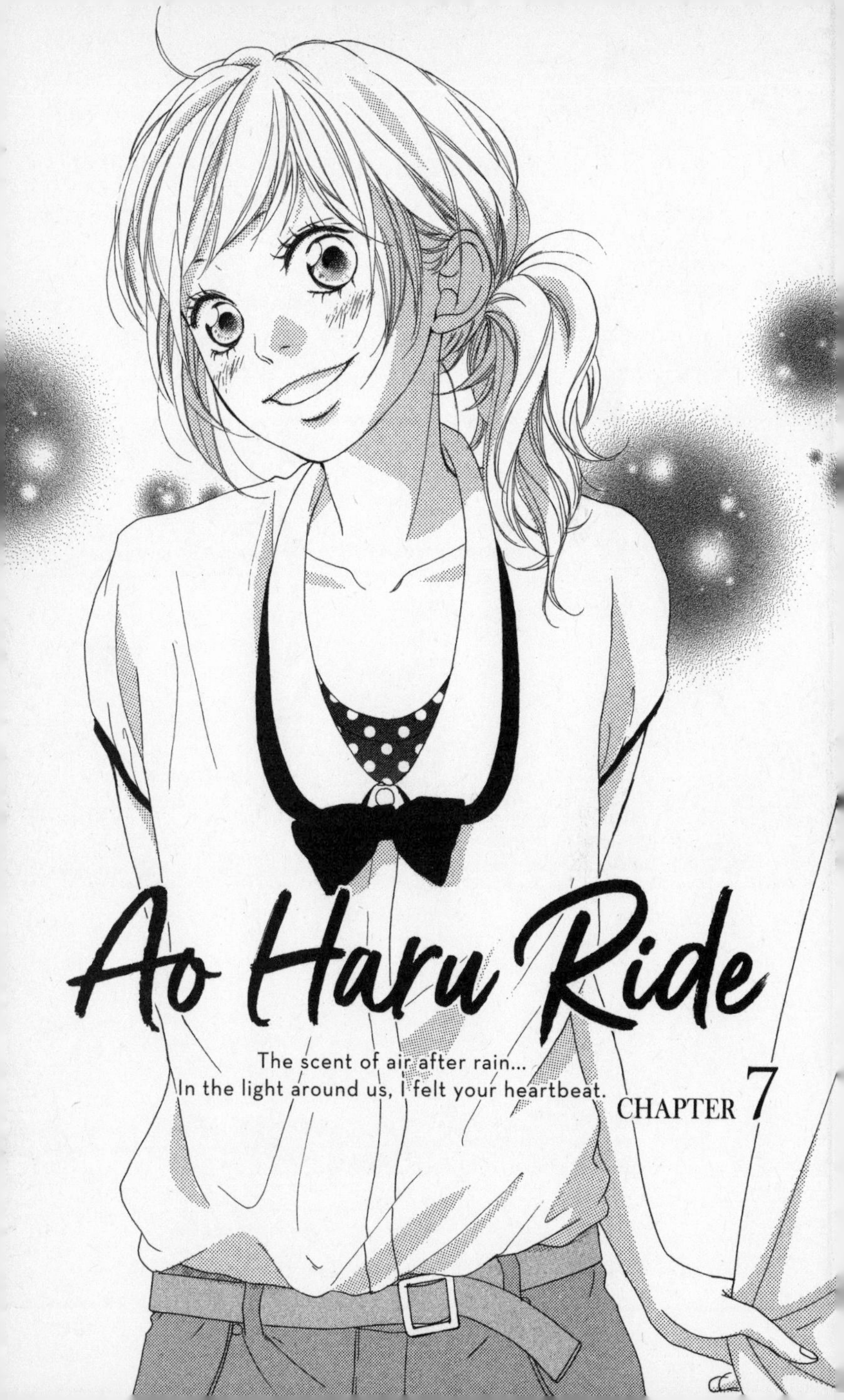
Ao Haru Ride
The scent of air after rain...
In the light around us, I felt your heartbeat.
CHAPTER 7

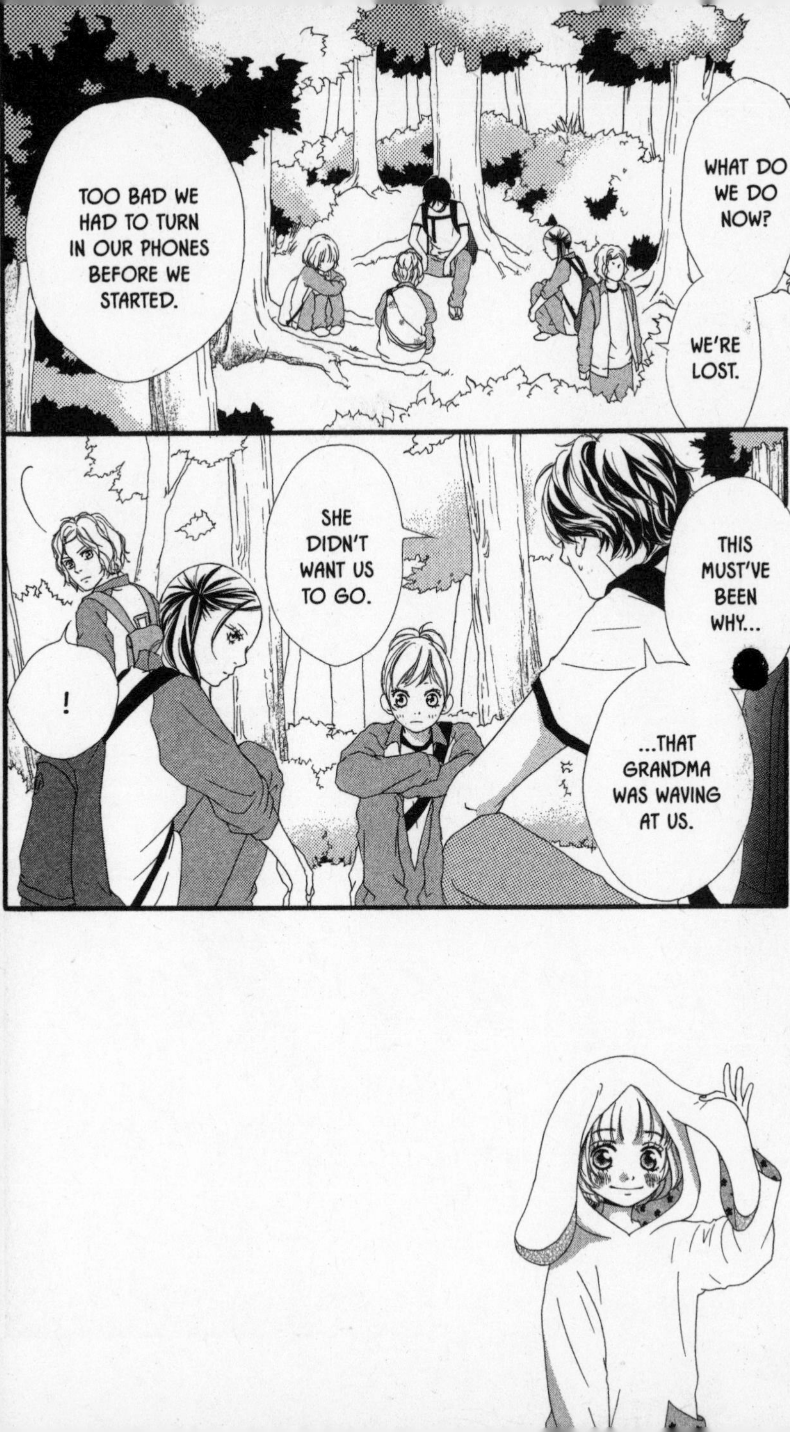
WHAT DO WE DO NOW?
WE'RE LOST.
TOO BAD WE HAD TO TURN IN OUR PHONES BEFORE WE STARTED.
THIS MUST'VE BEEN WHY...
...THAT GRANDMA WAS WAVING AT US.
SHE DIDN'T WANT US TO GO.
!

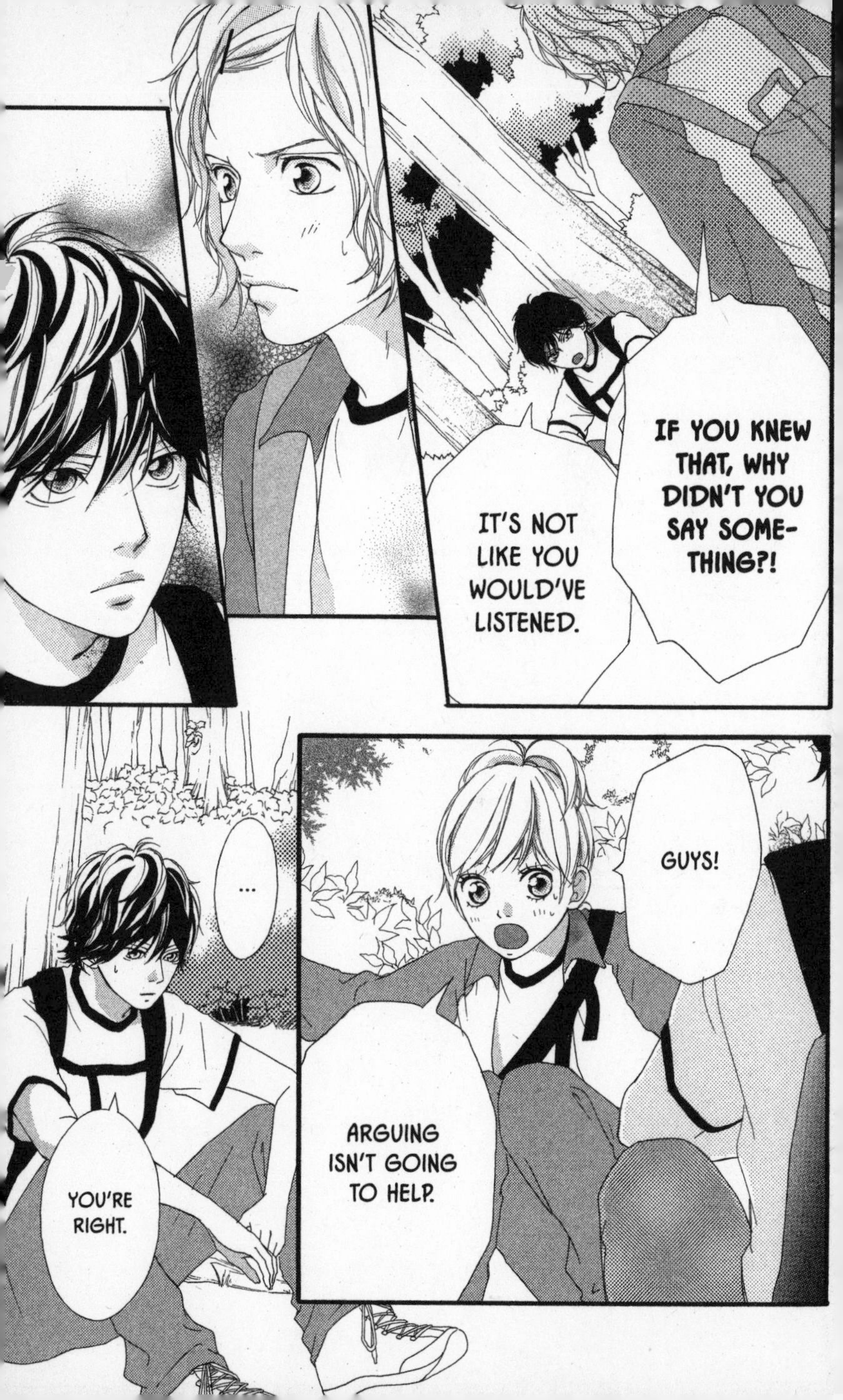
IF YOU KNEW THAT, WHY DIDN'T YOU SAY SOME-THING?!
IT'S NOT LIKE YOU WOULD'VE LISTENED.
GUYS!
ARGUING ISN'T GOING TO HELP.
...
YOU'RE RIGHT.

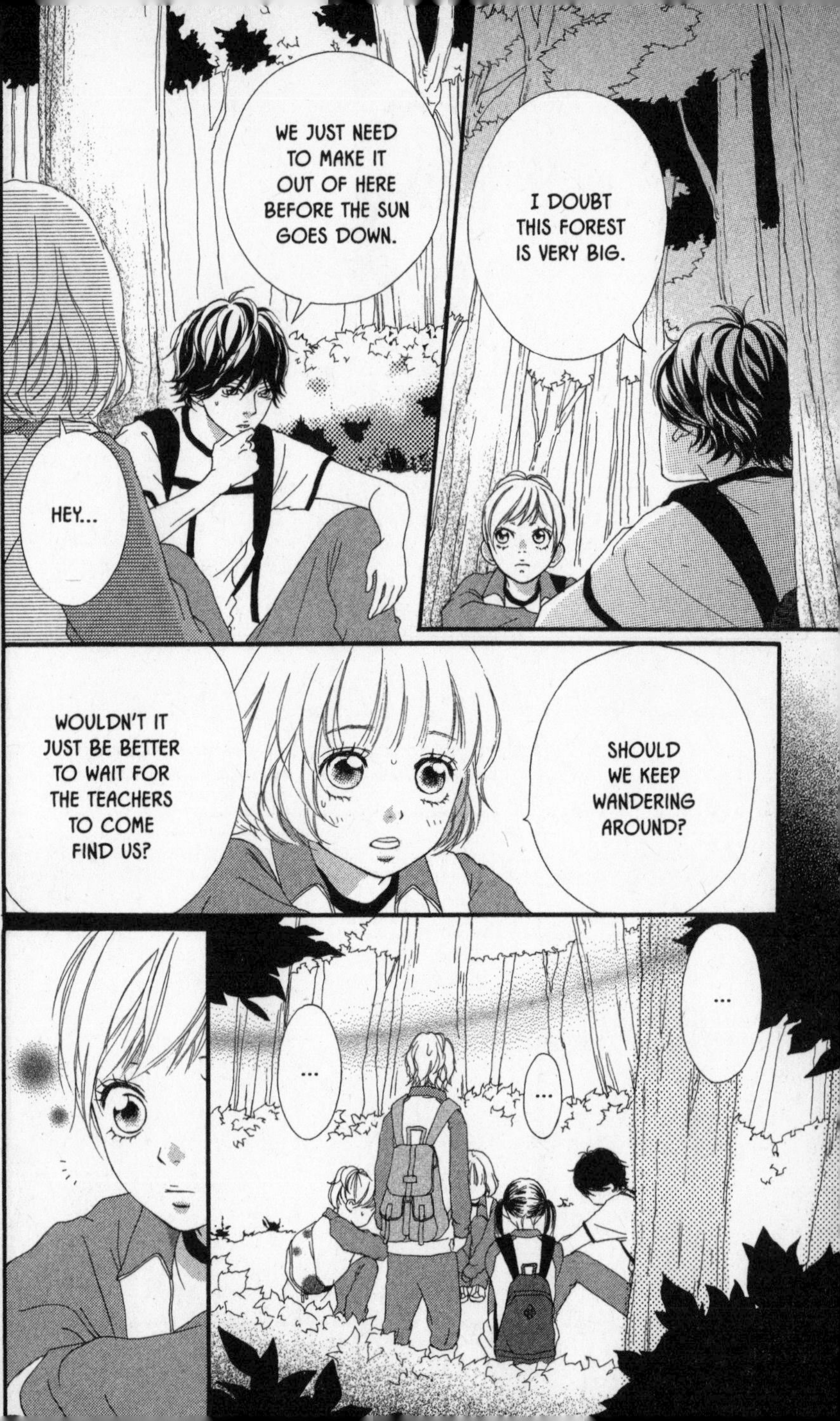
I DOUBT THIS FOREST IS VERY BIG.
WE JUST NEED TO MAKE IT OUT OF HERE BEFORE THE SUN GOES DOWN.
HEY...
SHOULD WE KEEP WANDERING AROUND?
WOULDN'T IT JUST BE BETTER TO WAIT FOR THE TEACHERS TO COME FIND US?
...
...
...

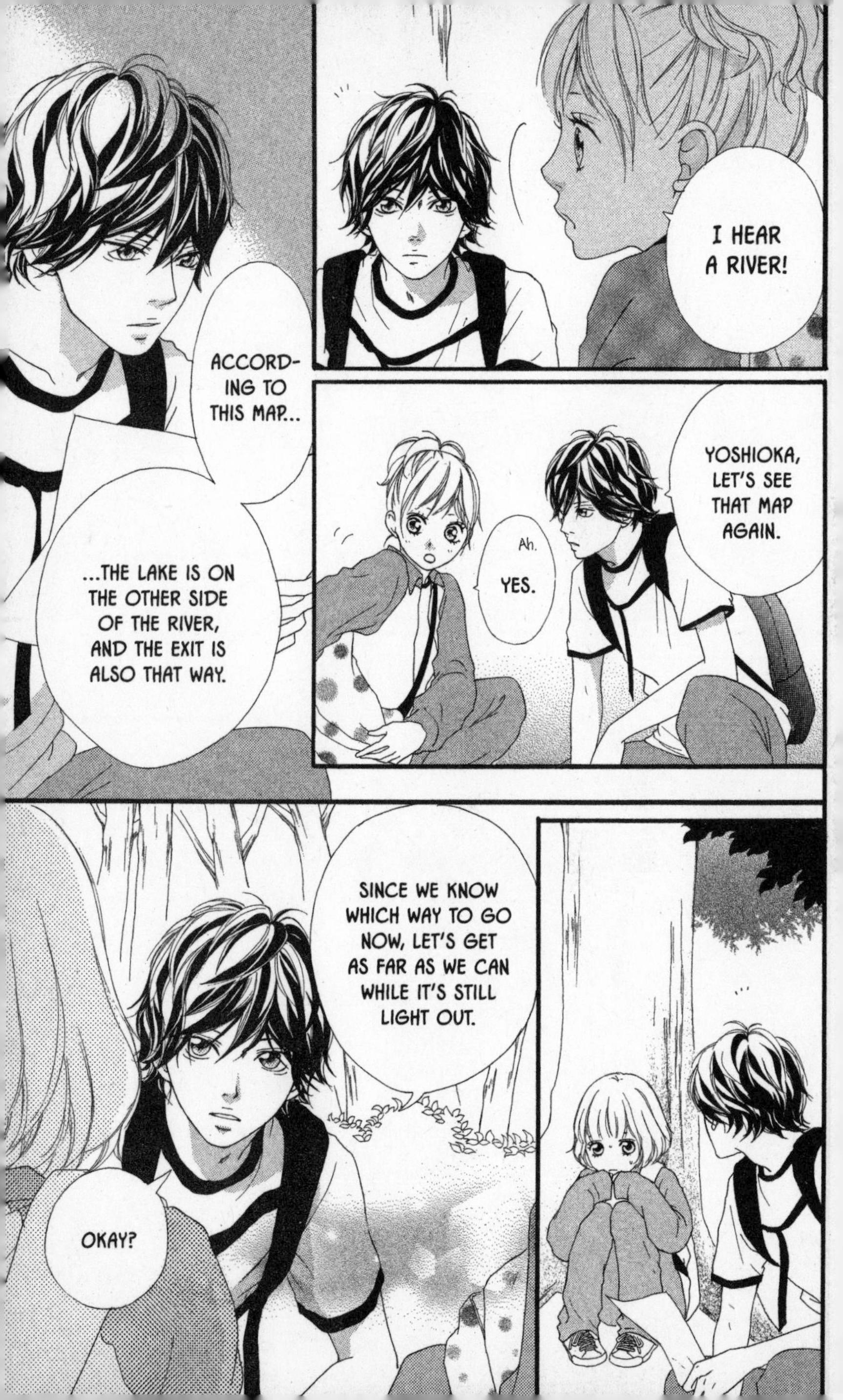
I HEAR A RIVER!
YOSHIOKA, LET'S SEE THAT MAP AGAIN.
Ah.
YES.
ACCORD-ING TO THIS MAP...
...THE LAKE IS ON THE OTHER SIDE OF THE RIVER, AND THE EXIT IS ALSO THAT WAY.
...
SINCE WE KNOW WHICH WAY TO GO NOW, LET'S GET AS FAR AS WE CAN WHILE IT'S STILL LIGHT OUT.
OKAY?

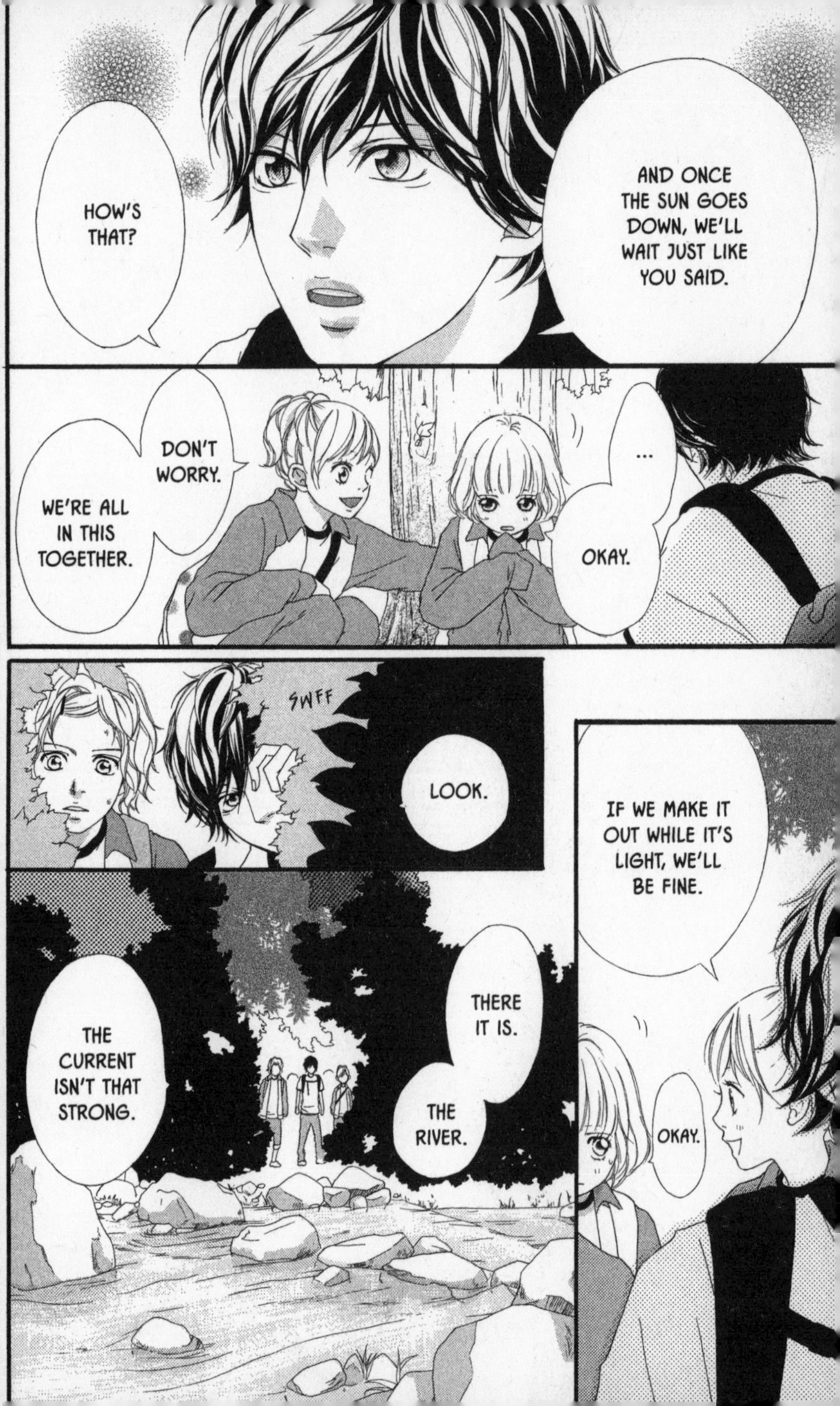
AND ONCE THE SUN GOES DOWN, WE'LL WAIT JUST LIKE YOU SAID.
HOW'S THAT?
...
OKAY.
DON'T WORRY.
WE'RE ALL IN THIS TOGETHER.
IF WE MAKE IT OUT WHILE IT'S LIGHT, WE'LL BE FINE.
OKAY.
SWFF
LOOK.
THERE IT IS.
THE RIVER.
THE CURRENT ISN'T THAT STRONG.

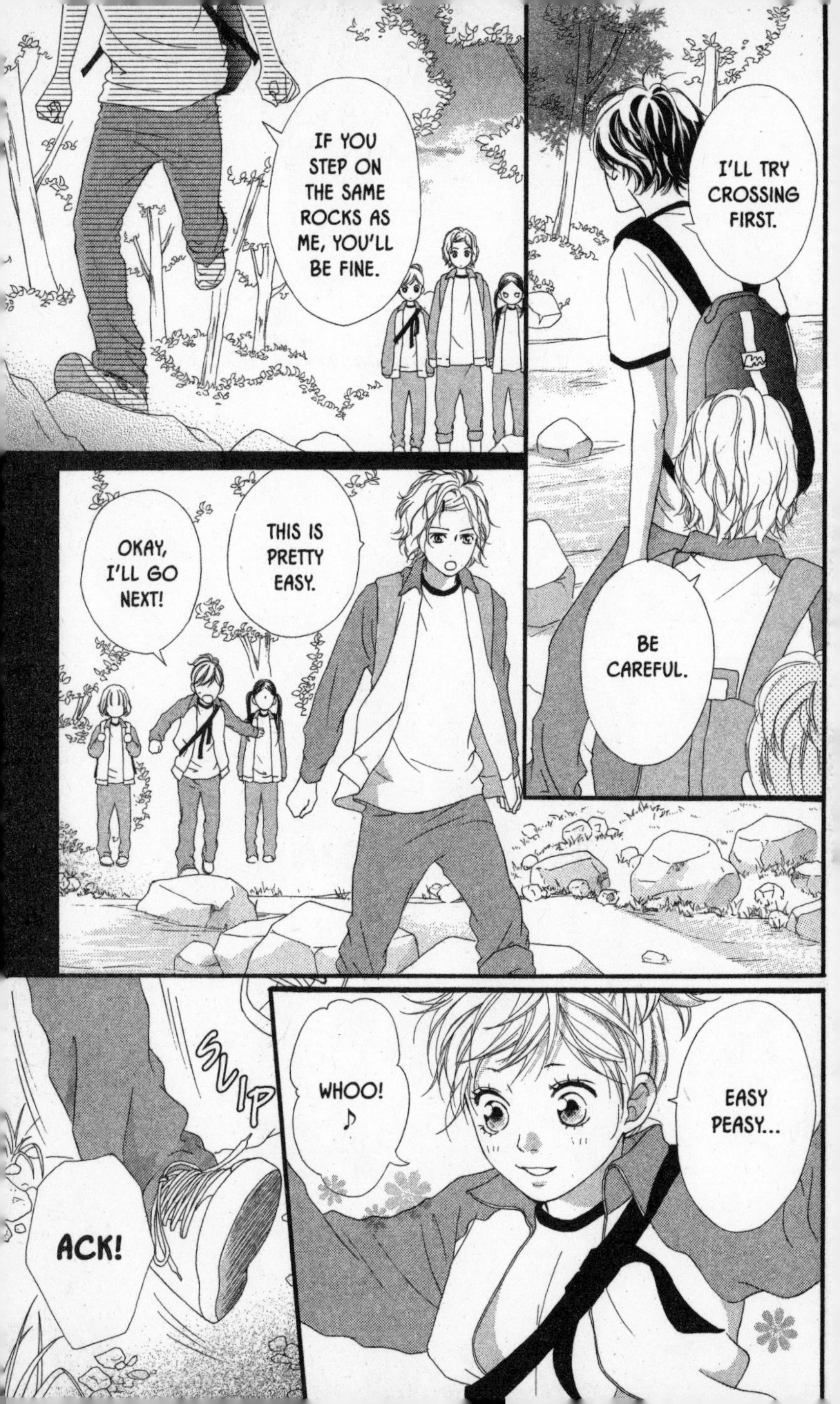
I'LL TRY CROSSING FIRST.
BE CAREFUL.
IF YOU STEP ON THE SAME ROCKS AS ME, YOU'LL BE FINE.
THIS IS PRETTY EASY.
OKAY, I'LL GO NEXT!
EASY PEASY...
WHOO! ♪
SLIP
ACK!

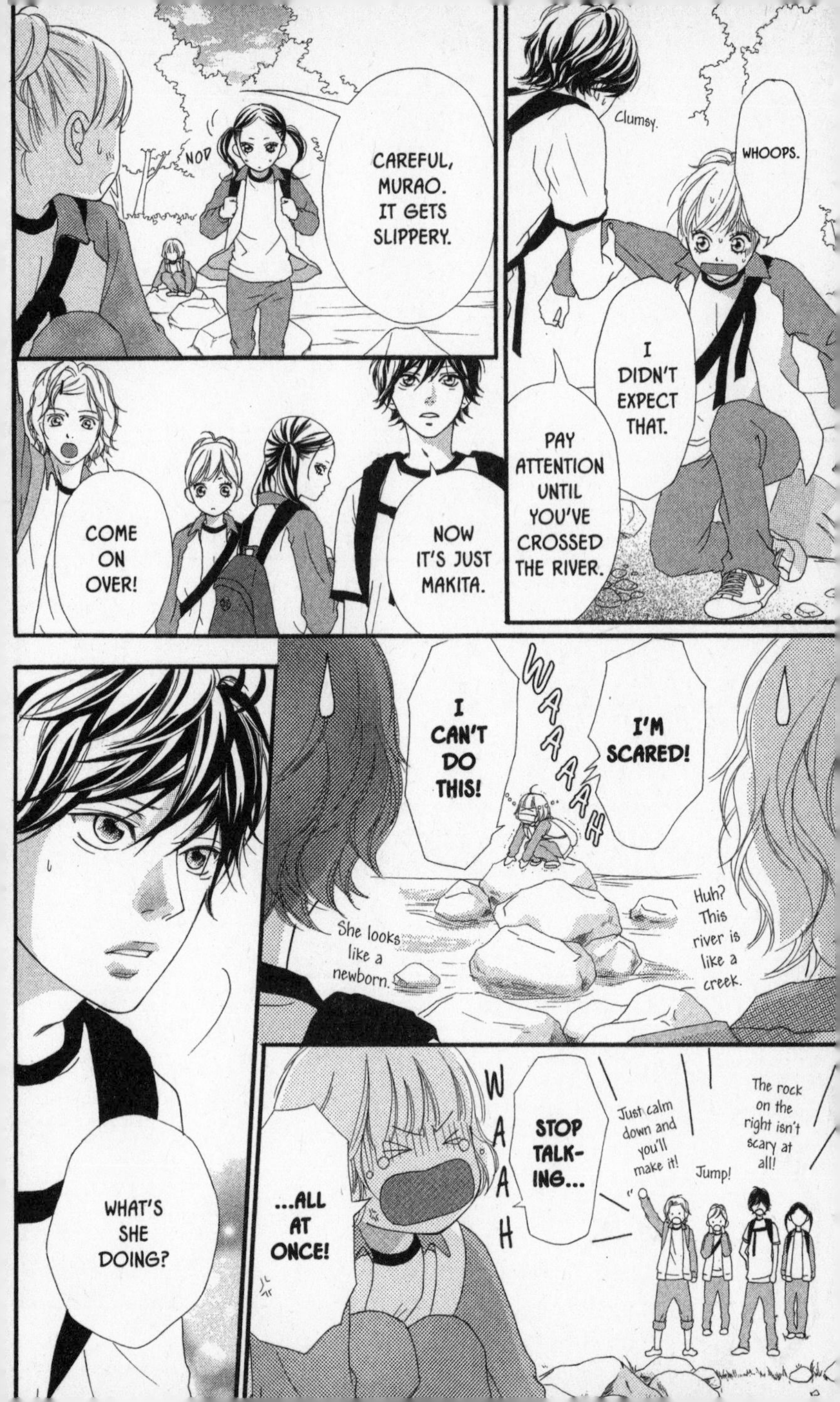
WHOOPS.
Clumsy.
I DIDN'T EXPECT THAT.
PAY ATTENTION UNTIL YOU'VE CROSSED THE RIVER.
CAREFUL, MURAO. IT GETS SLIPPERY.
NOD
NOW IT'S JUST MAKITA.
COME ON OVER!
I'M SCARED!
WAAAAAH
I CAN'T DO THIS!
Huh? This river is like a creek.
She looks like a newborn.
The rock on the right isn't scary at all!
Jump!
Just calm down and you'll make it!
STOP TALKING...
WAAAH
...ALL AT ONCE!
WHAT'S SHE DOING?

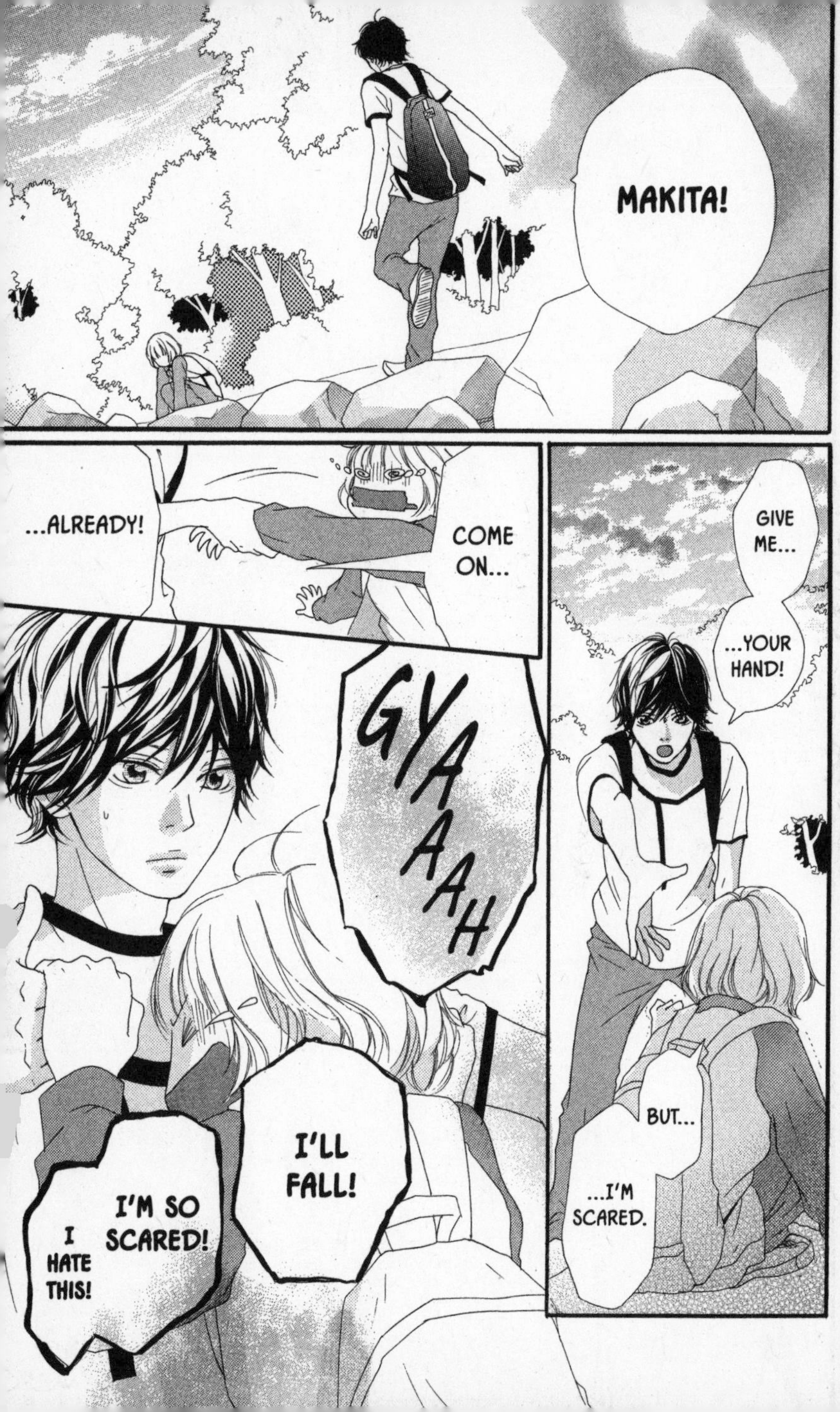
MAKITA!
GIVE ME...
...YOUR HAND!
BUT...
...I'M SCARED.
COME ON...
...ALREADY!
GYAAAH
I'LL FALL!
I'M SO SCARED!
I HATE THIS!

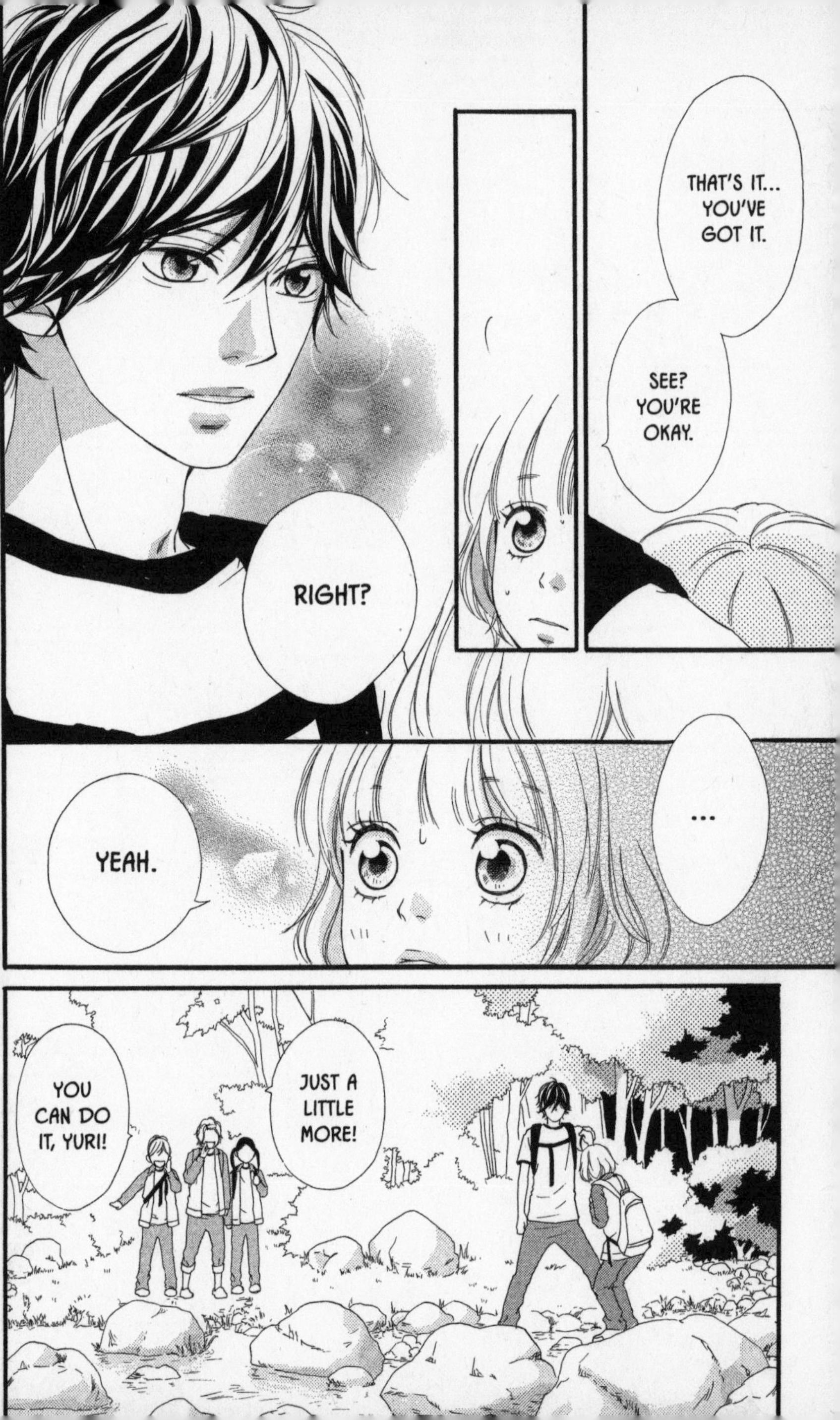
THAT'S IT... YOU'VE GOT IT.
SEE? YOU'RE OKAY.
RIGHT?
...
YEAH.
JUST A LITTLE MORE!
YOU CAN DO IT, YURI!

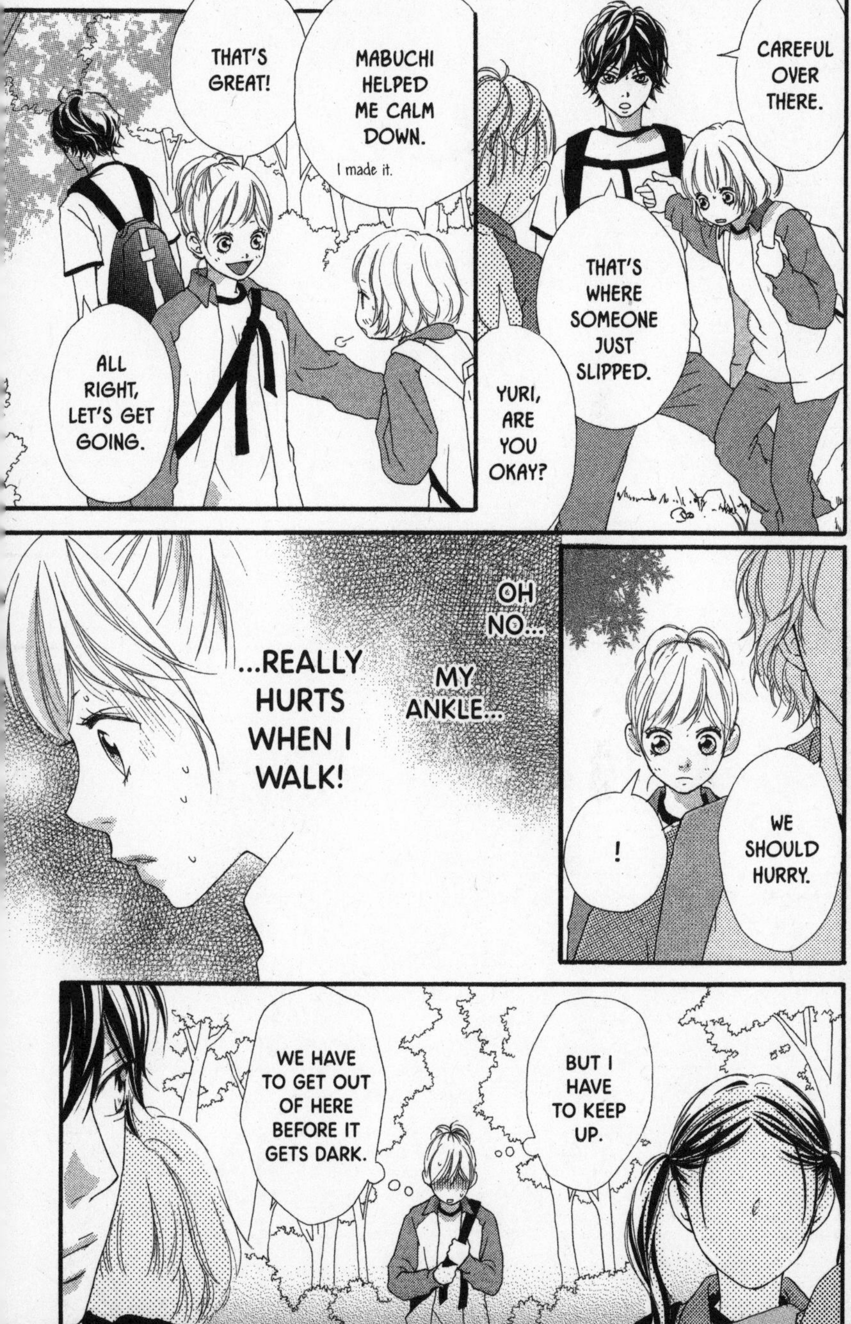
CAREFUL OVER THERE.
THAT'S WHERE SOMEONE JUST SLIPPED.
YURI, ARE YOU OKAY?
MABUCHI HELPED ME CALM DOWN.
I made it.
THAT'S GREAT!
ALL RIGHT, LET'S GET GOING.
WE SHOULD HURRY.
!
OH NO...
MY ANKLE...
...REALLY HURTS WHEN I WALK!
BUT I HAVE TO KEEP UP.
WE HAVE TO GET OUT OF HERE BEFORE IT GETS DARK.

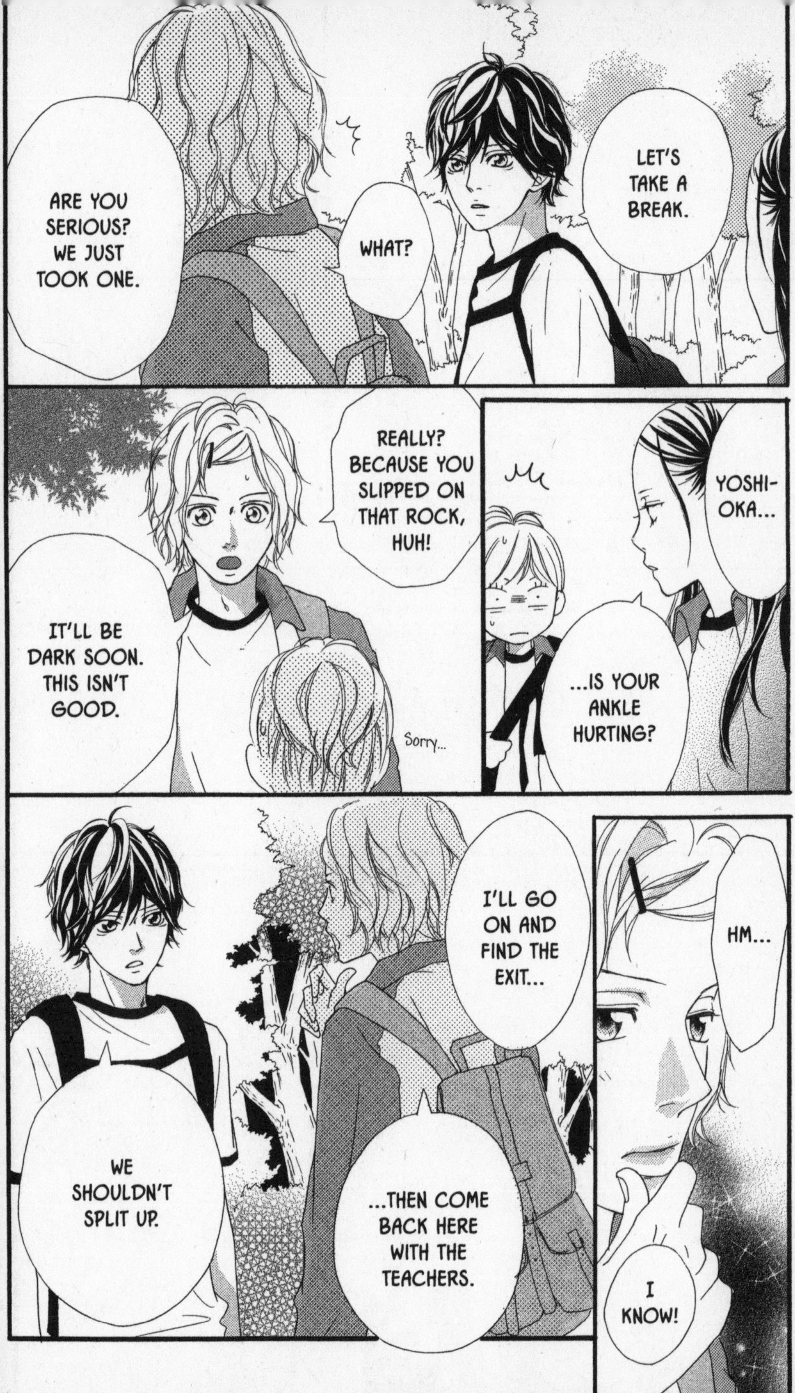
LET'S TAKE A BREAK.
WHAT?
ARE YOU SERIOUS? WE JUST TOOK ONE.
YOSHI-OKA...
...IS YOUR ANKLE HURTING?
REALLY? BECAUSE YOU SLIPPED ON THAT ROCK, HUH!
Sorry...
IT'LL BE DARK SOON. THIS ISN'T GOOD.
HM...
I KNOW!
I'LL GO ON AND FIND THE EXIT...
...THEN COME BACK HERE WITH THE TEACHERS.
WE SHOULDN'T SPLIT UP.

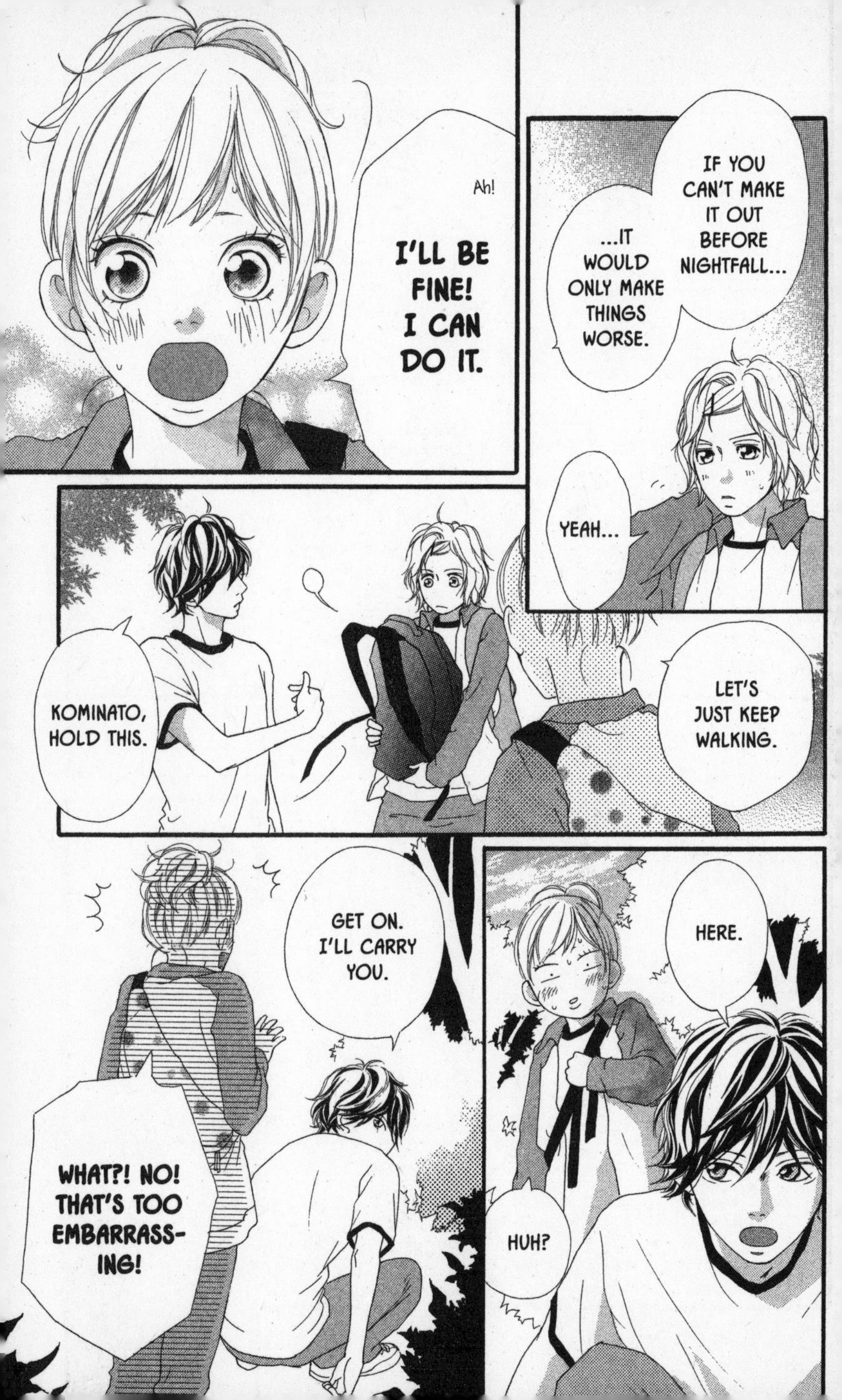
IF YOU CAN'T MAKE IT OUT BEFORE NIGHTFALL...
...IT WOULD ONLY MAKE THINGS WORSE.
YEAH...
Ah!
I'LL BE FINE! I CAN DO IT.
LET'S JUST KEEP WALKING.
KOMINATO, HOLD THIS.
HERE.
HUH?
GET ON. I'LL CARRY YOU.
WHAT?! NO! THAT'S TOO EMBARRASS-ING!

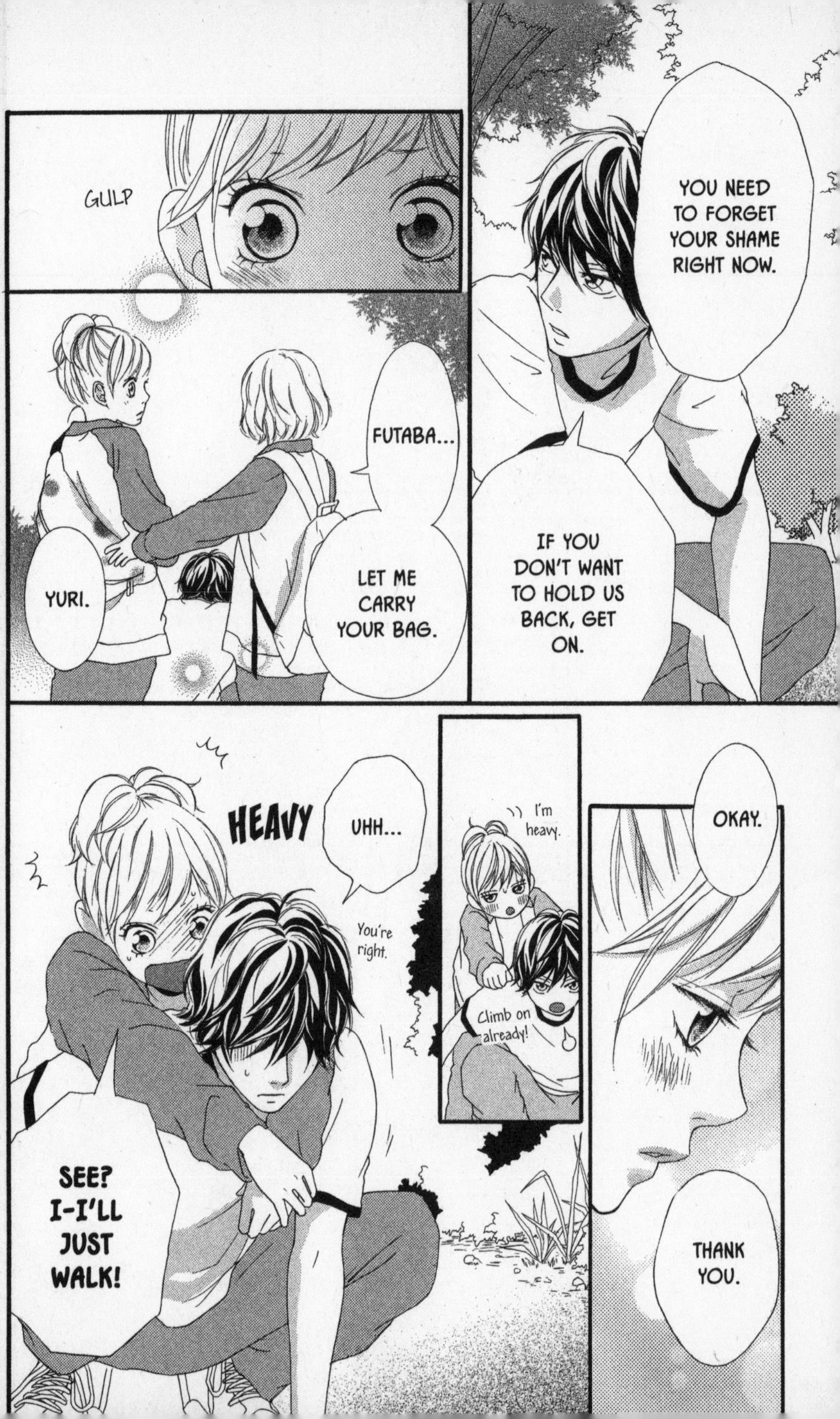
YOU NEED TO FORGET YOUR SHAME RIGHT NOW.
IF YOU DON'T WANT TO HOLD US BACK, GET ON.
GULP
FUTABA...
LET ME CARRY YOUR BAG.
YURI.
OKAY.
THANK YOU.
I'm heavy.
Climb on already!
UHH...
HEAVY
You're right.
SEE? I-I'LL JUST WALK!

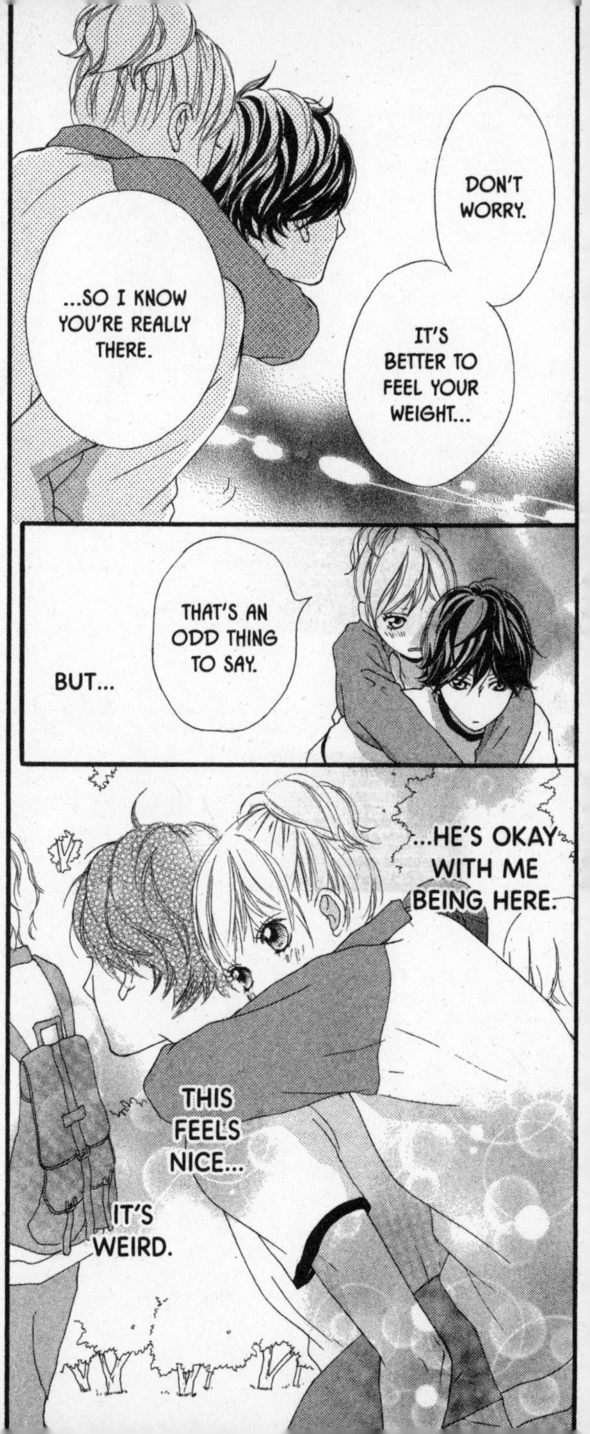
DON'T WORRY.
IT'S BETTER TO FEEL YOUR WEIGHT...
...SO I KNOW YOU'RE REALLY THERE.
THAT'S AN ODD THING TO SAY.
BUT...
...HE'S OKAY WITH ME BEING HERE.
THIS FEELS NICE...
IT'S WEIRD.

♡♡♡♡♡♡♡

In volume 1 I asked you to tell me what you wanted to see in future bonus pages.

No surprise, the overwhelming request was for character profiles, so I'll be introducing the characters one by one starting with this volume.

This time it's Futaba and Kou. The profiles are at the back of the book, so please take a look if you're interested.

There were also questions directed to me, which I will answer starting in the next volume. In the meantime, please feel free to send along any requests that you have!

♡♡♡♡♡♡♡

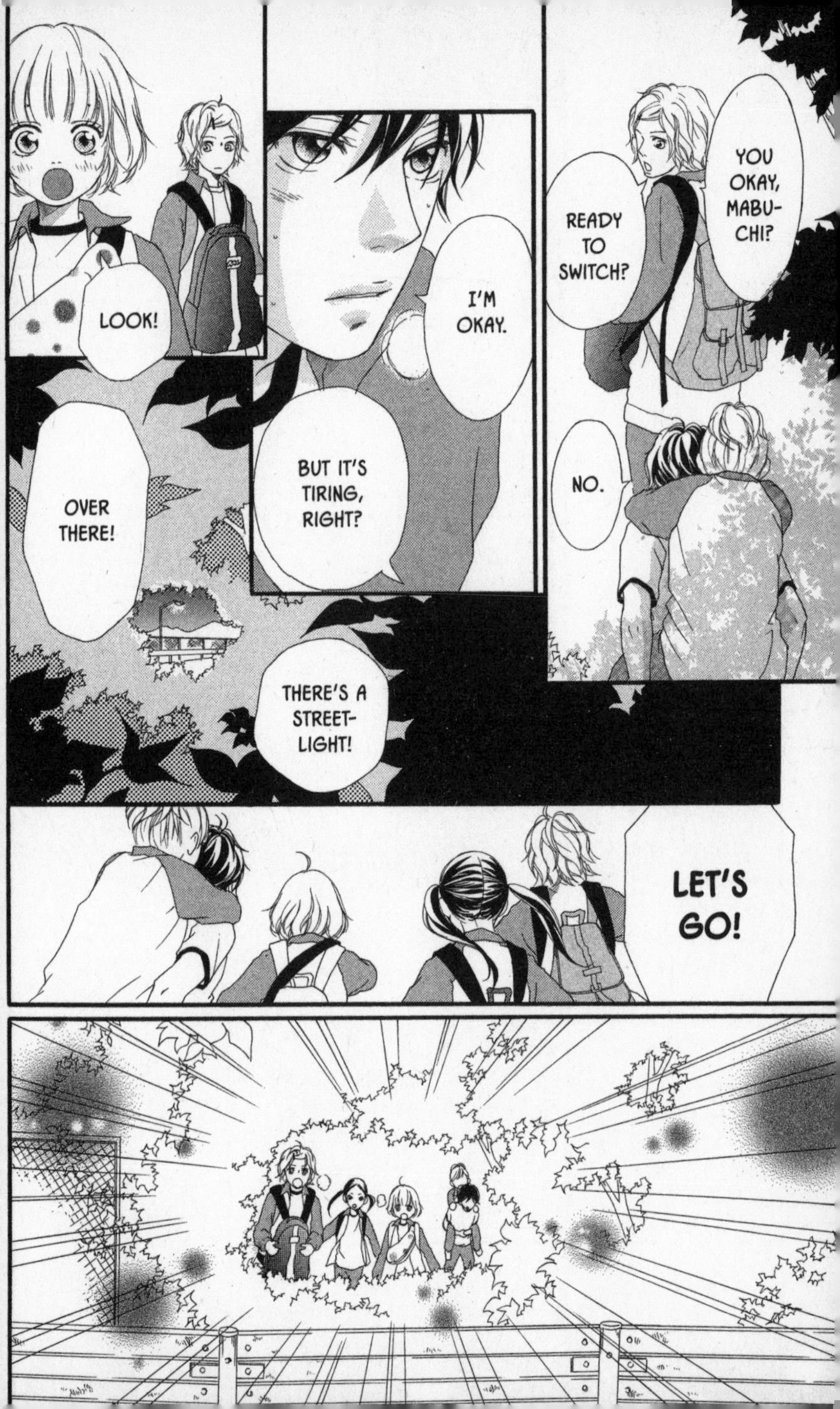
YOU OKAY, MABU-CHI?
READY TO SWITCH?
NO.
I'M OKAY.
BUT IT'S TIRING, RIGHT?
LOOK!
OVER THERE!
THERE'S A STREET-LIGHT!
LET'S GO!

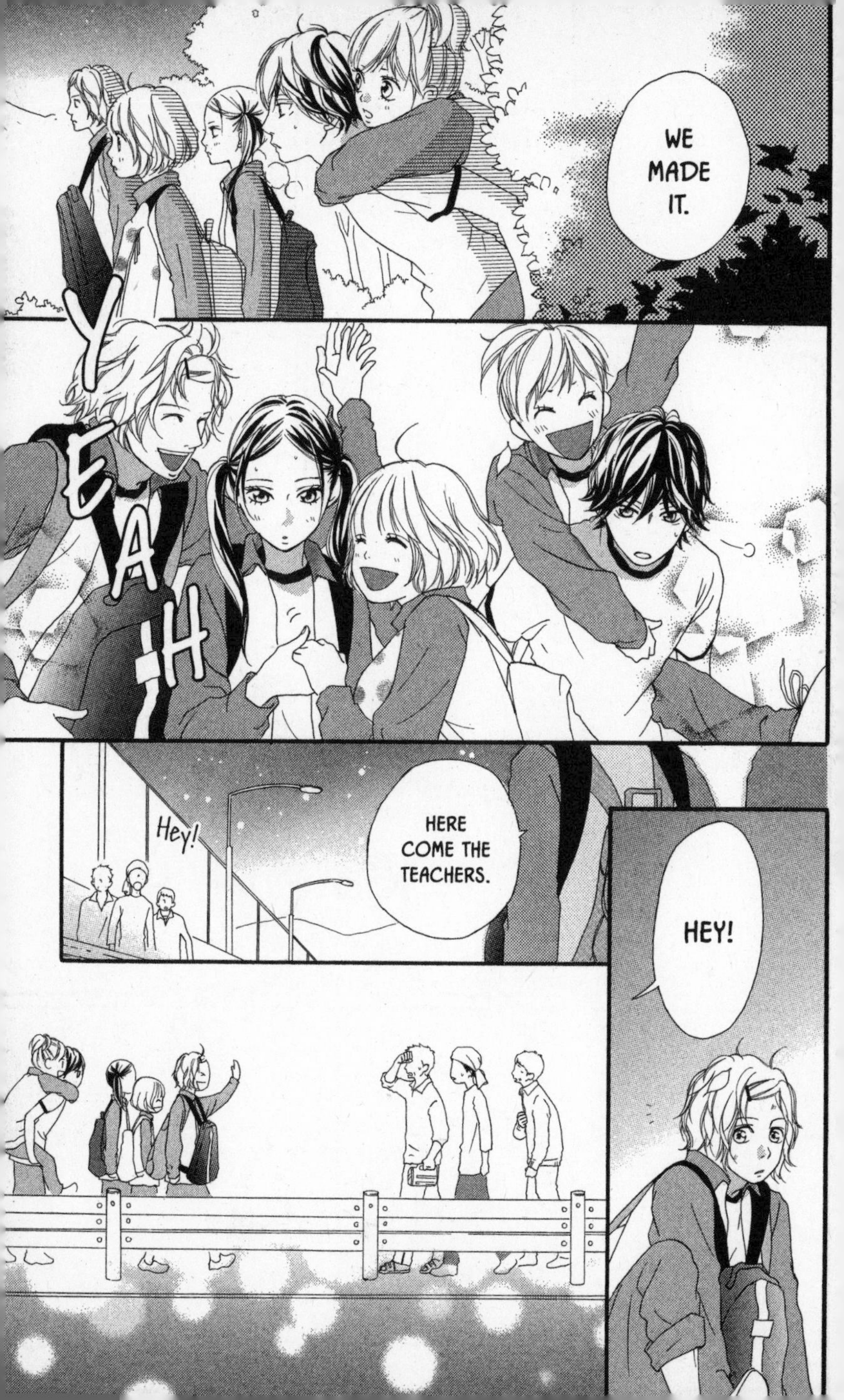
WE MADE IT.
YEAH
HEY!
HERE COME THE TEACHERS.
Hey!

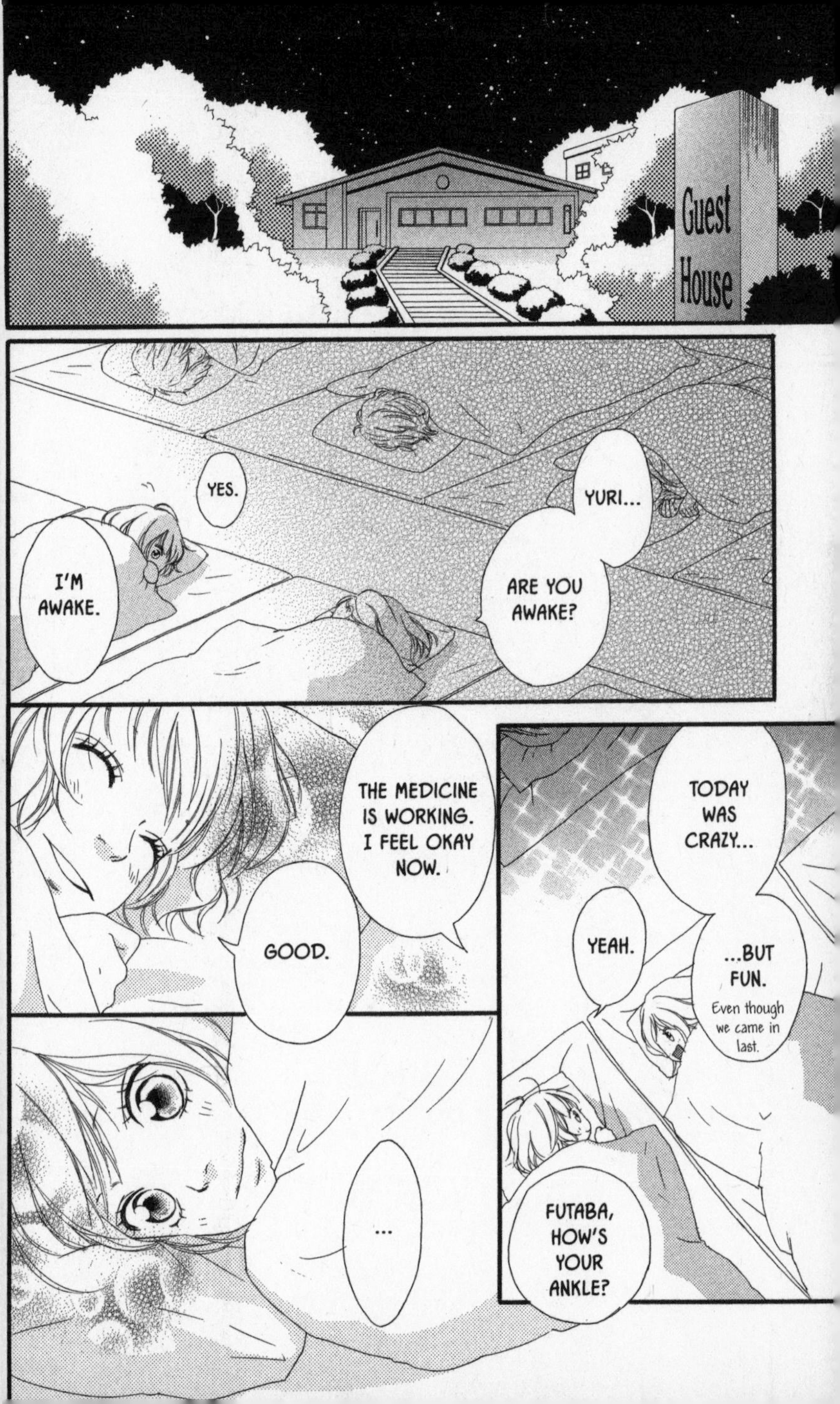
Guest House
YURI...
ARE YOU AWAKE?
YES.
I'M AWAKE.
TODAY WAS CRAZY...
...BUT FUN.
Even though we came in last.
YEAH.
FUTABA, HOW'S YOUR ANKLE?
THE MEDICINE IS WORKING. I FEEL OKAY NOW.
GOOD.
...

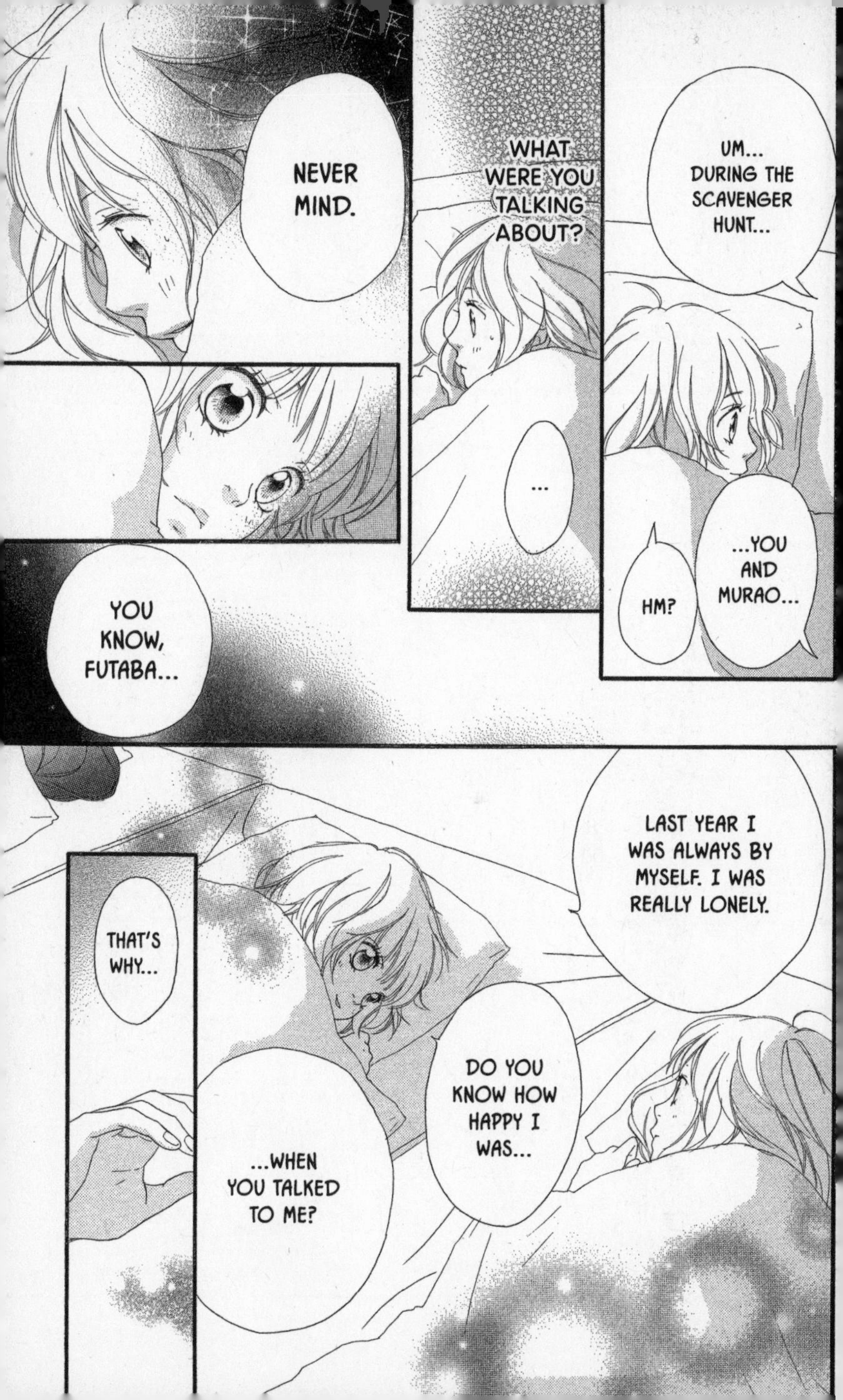
UM... DURING THE SCAVENGER HUNT...
...YOU AND MURAO...
HM?
WHAT WERE YOU TALKING ABOUT?
...
NEVER MIND.
YOU KNOW, FUTABA...
LAST YEAR I WAS ALWAYS BY MYSELF. I WAS REALLY LONELY.
DO YOU KNOW HOW HAPPY I WAS...
...WHEN YOU TALKED TO ME?
THAT'S WHY...

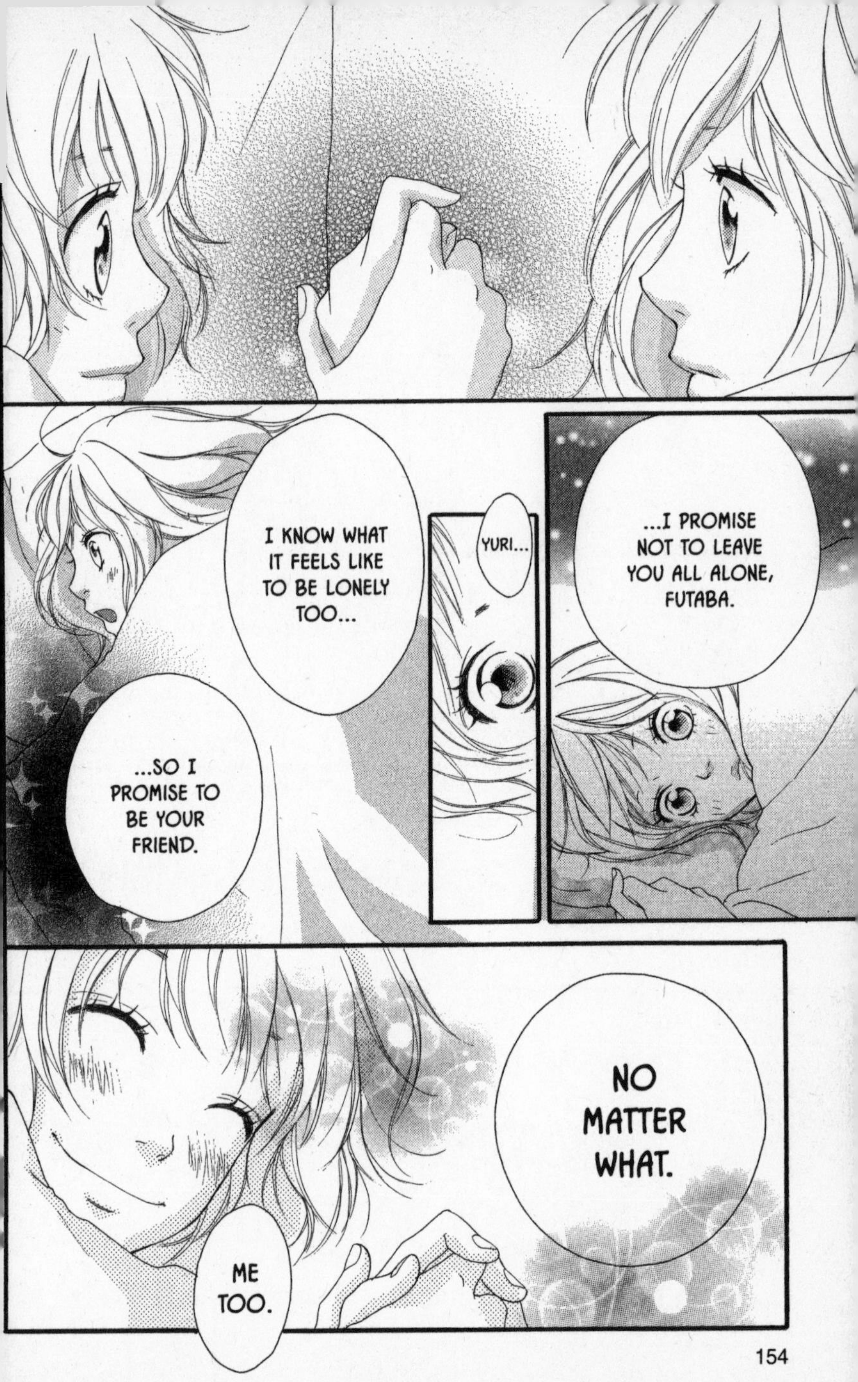
...I PROMISE NOT TO LEAVE YOU ALL ALONE, FUTABA.
YURI...
I KNOW WHAT IT FEELS LIKE TO BE LONELY TOO...
...SO I PROMISE TO BE YOUR FRIEND.
NO MATTER WHAT.
ME TOO.

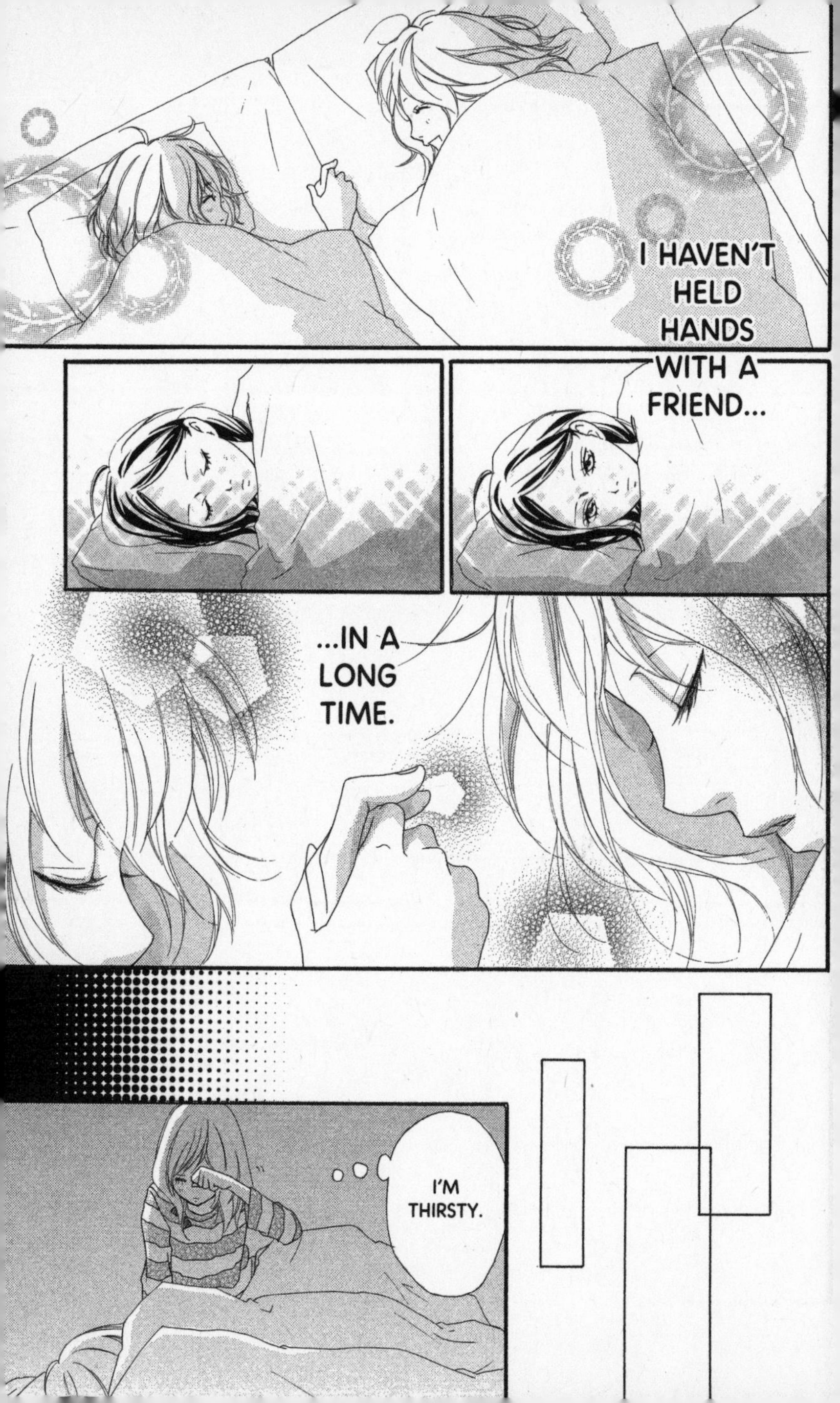
I HAVEN'T HELD HANDS WITH A FRIEND...
...IN A LONG TIME.
I'M THIRSTY.

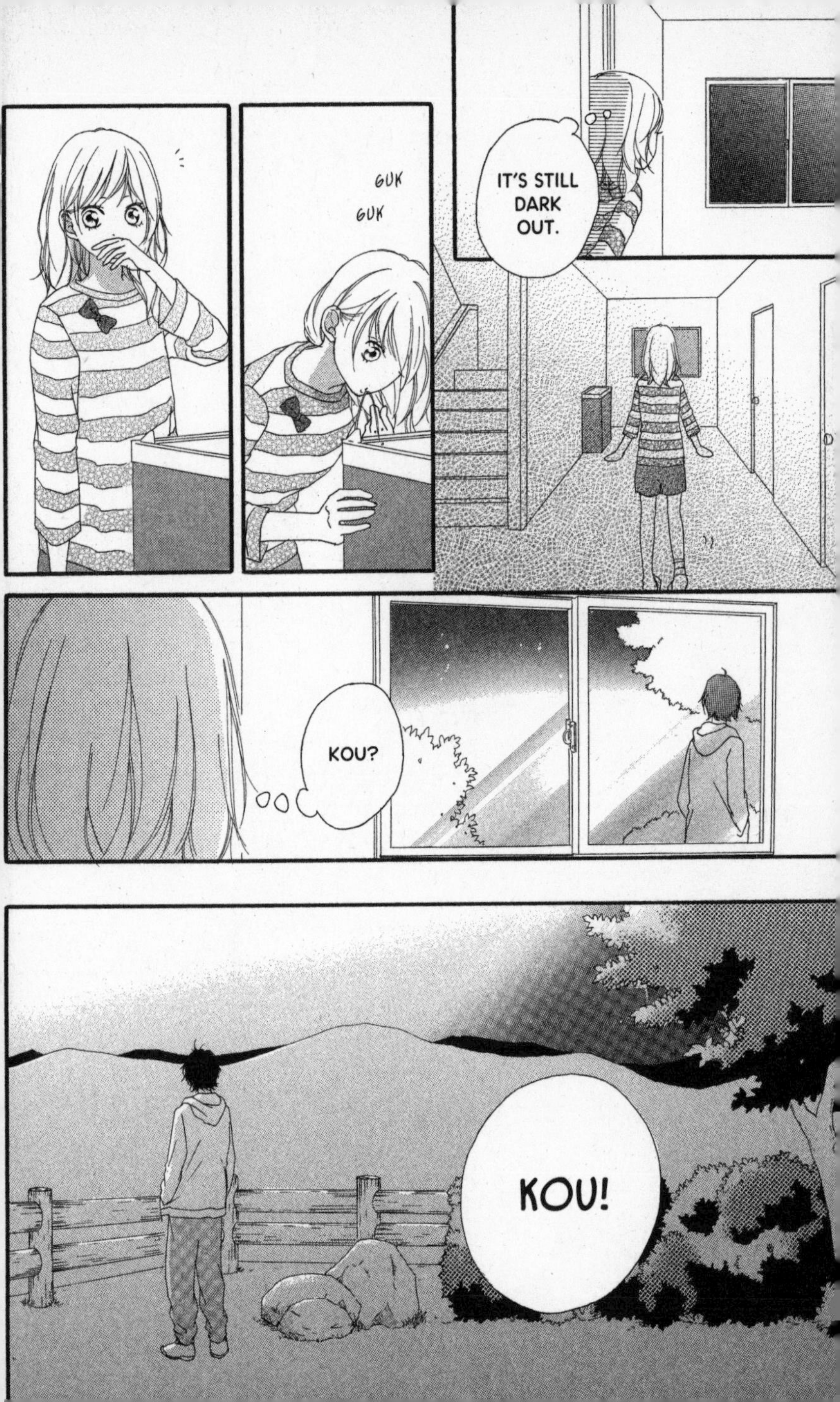
IT'S STILL DARK OUT.
GUK
GUK
KOU?
KOU!

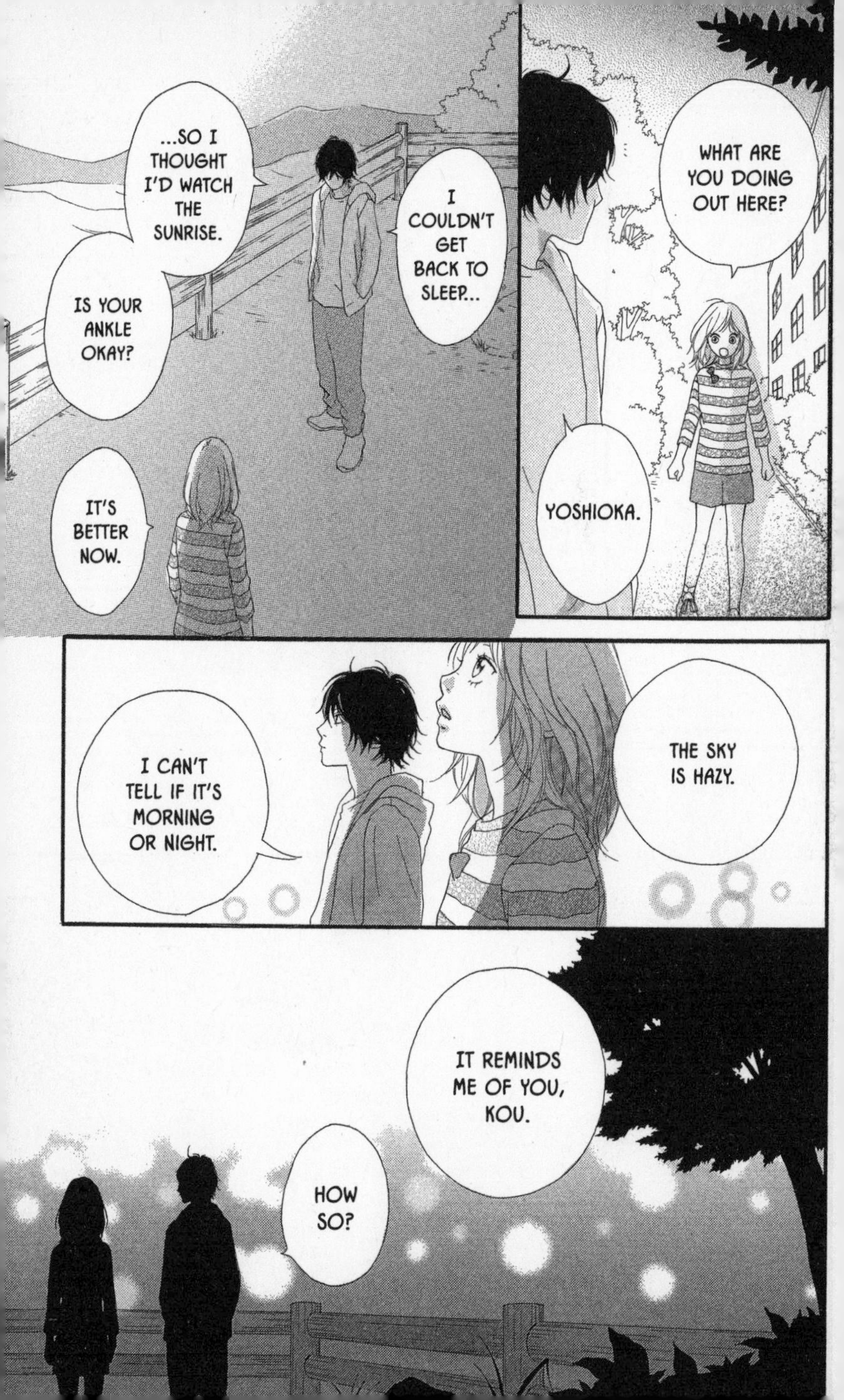
WHAT ARE YOU DOING OUT HERE?
YOSHIOKA.
I COULDN'T GET BACK TO SLEEP...
...SO I THOUGHT I'D WATCH THE SUNRISE.
IS YOUR ANKLE OKAY?
IT'S BETTER NOW.
THE SKY IS HAZY.
I CAN'T TELL IF IT'S MORNING OR NIGHT.
IT REMINDS ME OF YOU, KOU.
HOW SO?

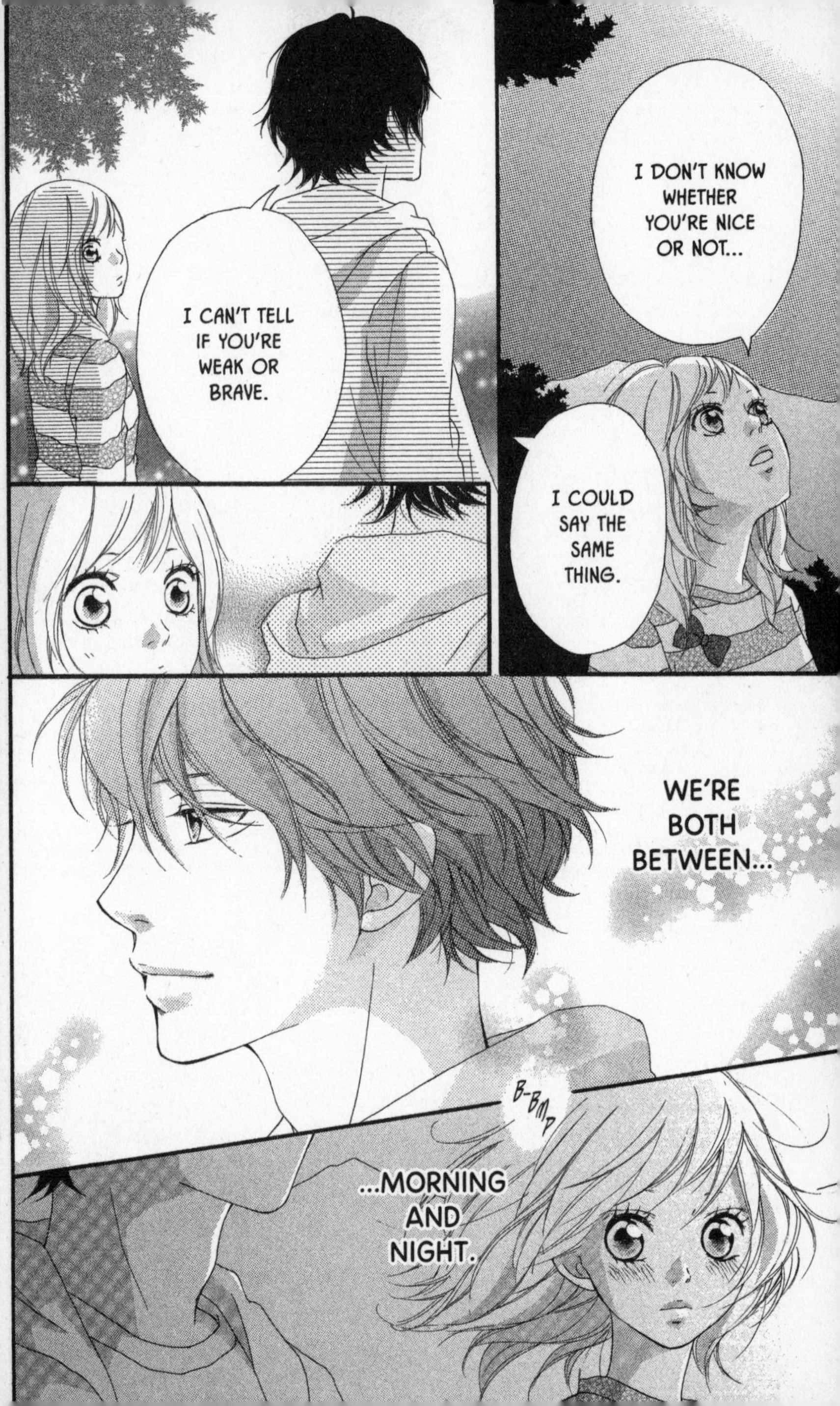
I DON'T KNOW WHETHER YOU'RE NICE OR NOT...
I COULD SAY THE SAME THING.
I CAN'T TELL IF YOU'RE WEAK OR BRAVE.
WE'RE BOTH BETWEEN...
B-BMP
...MORNING AND NIGHT.

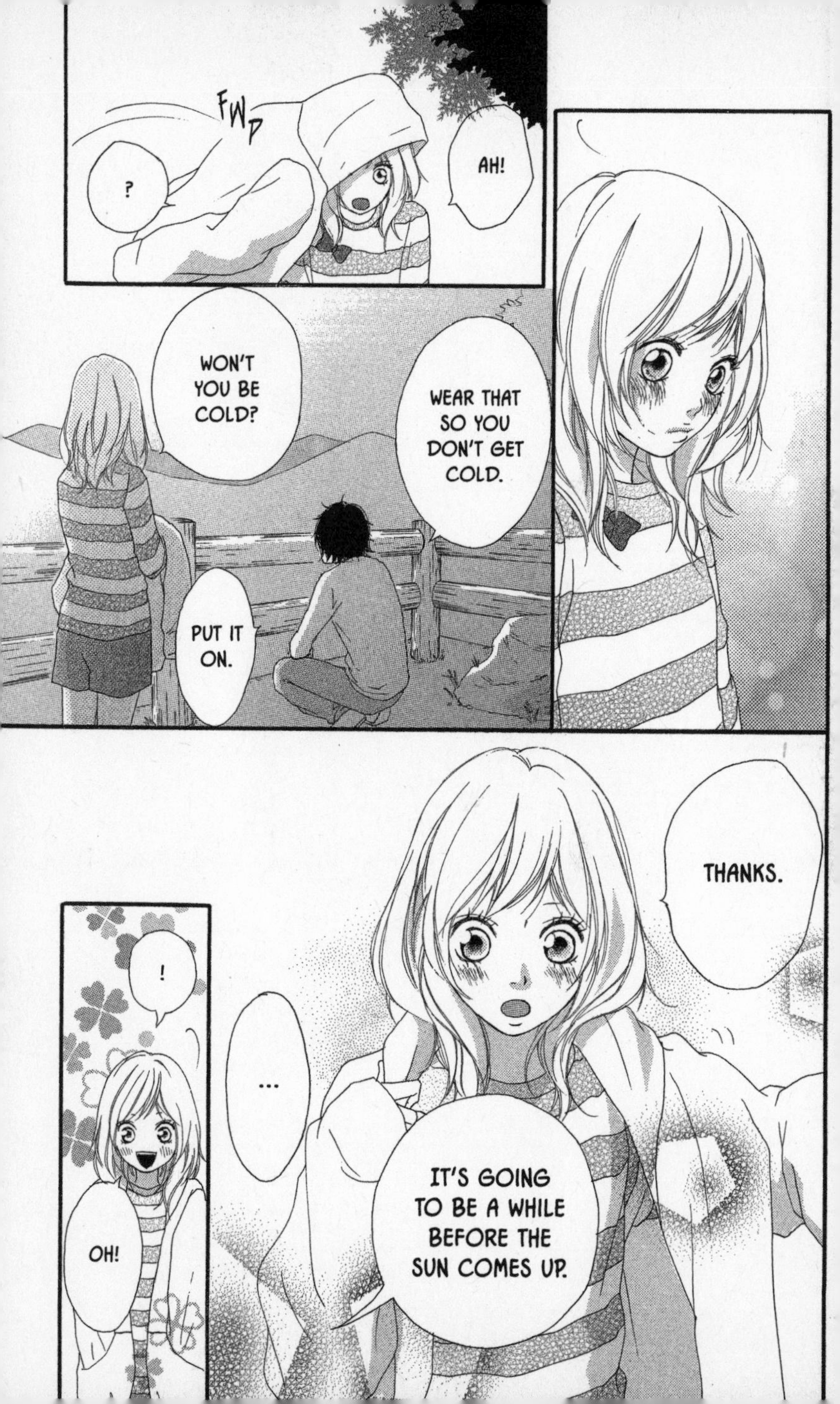
FWP
AH!
?
WEAR THAT SO YOU DON'T GET COLD.
WON'T YOU BE COLD?
PUT IT ON.
THANKS.
...
IT'S GOING TO BE A WHILE BEFORE THE SUN COMES UP.
!
OH!

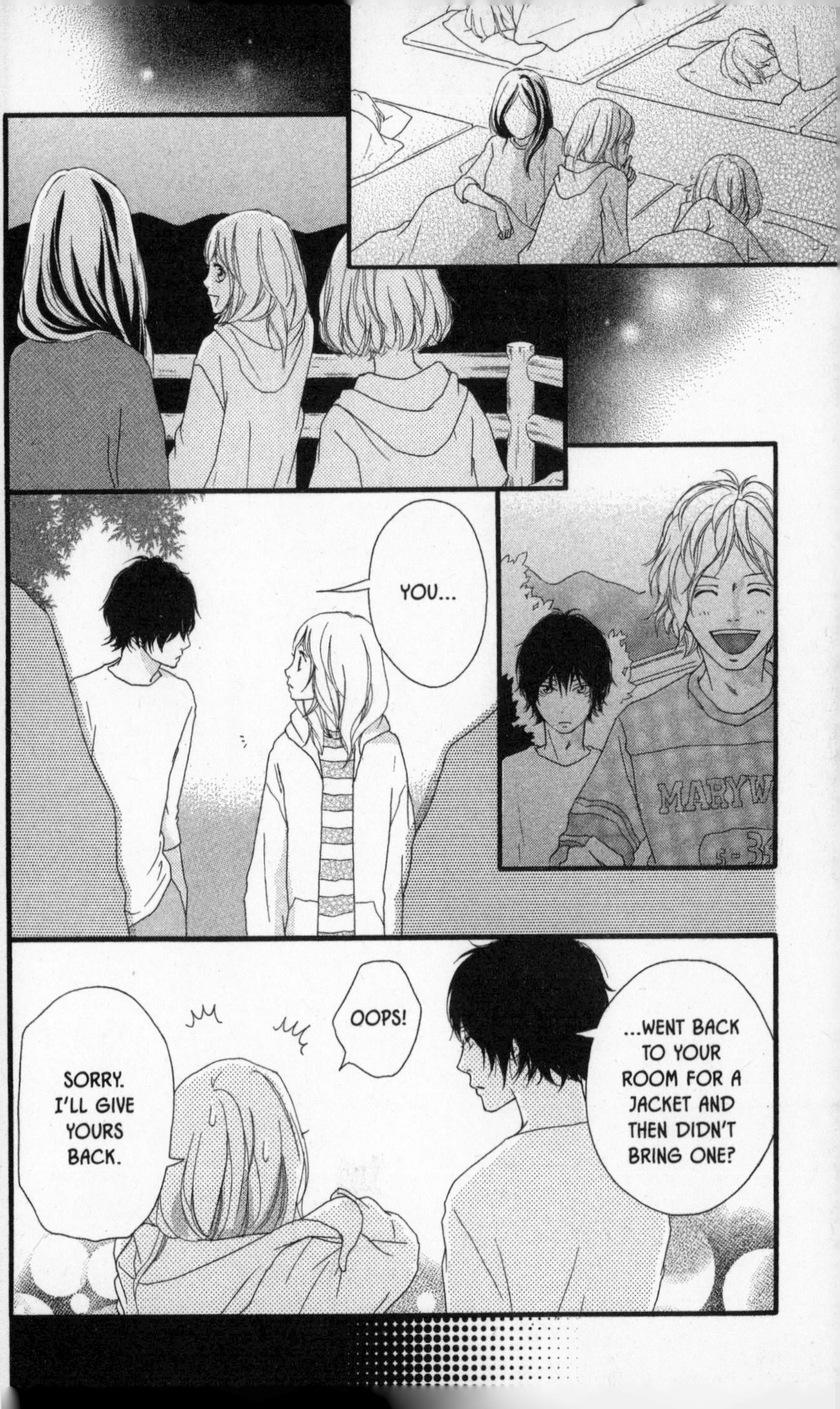
YOU...
...WENT BACK TO YOUR ROOM FOR A JACKET AND THEN DIDN'T BRING ONE?
OOPS!
SORRY. I'LL GIVE YOURS BACK.

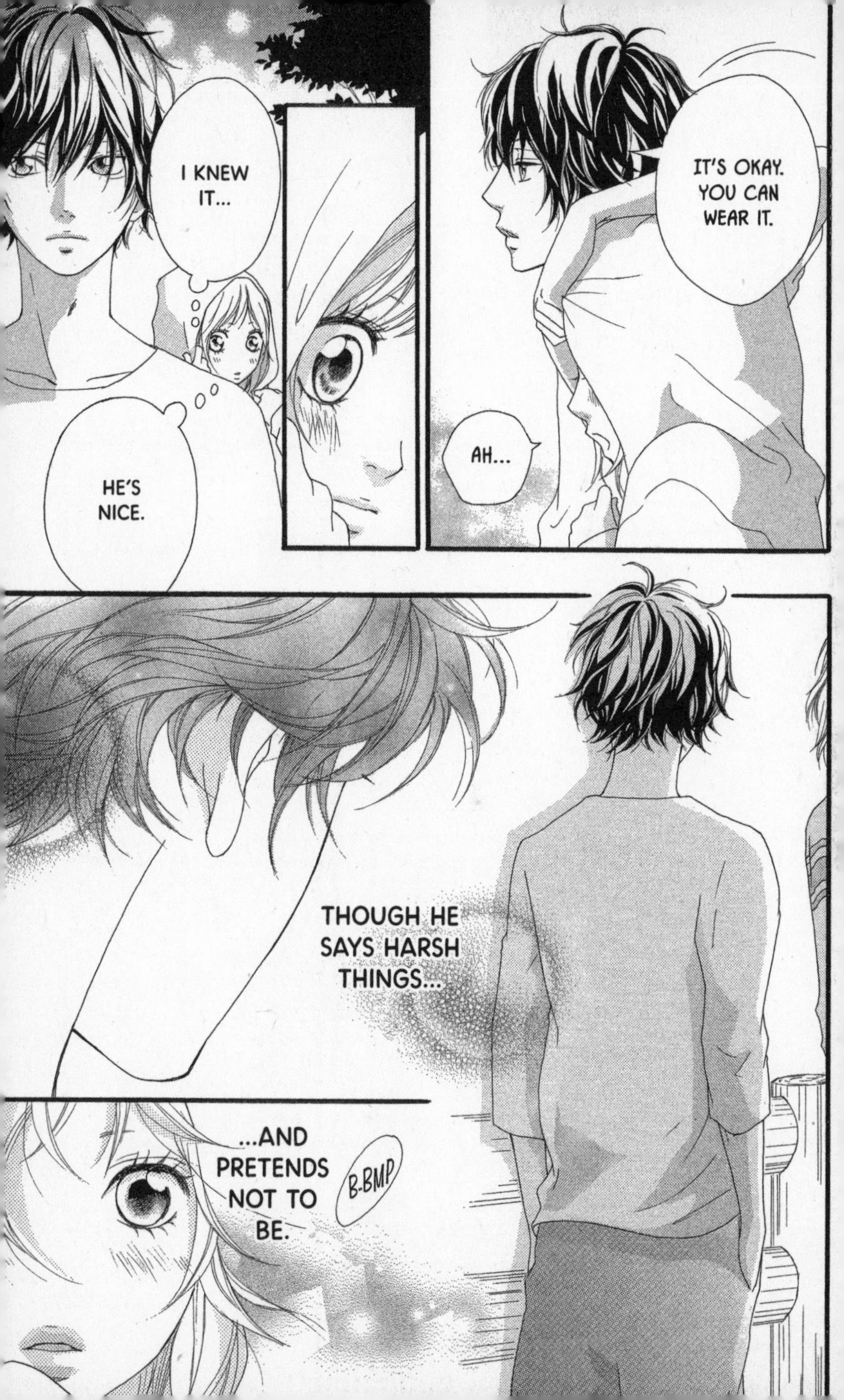
IT'S OKAY. YOU CAN WEAR IT.
AH...
I KNEW IT...
HE'S NICE.
THOUGH HE SAYS HARSH THINGS...
...AND PRETENDS NOT TO BE.
B-BMP

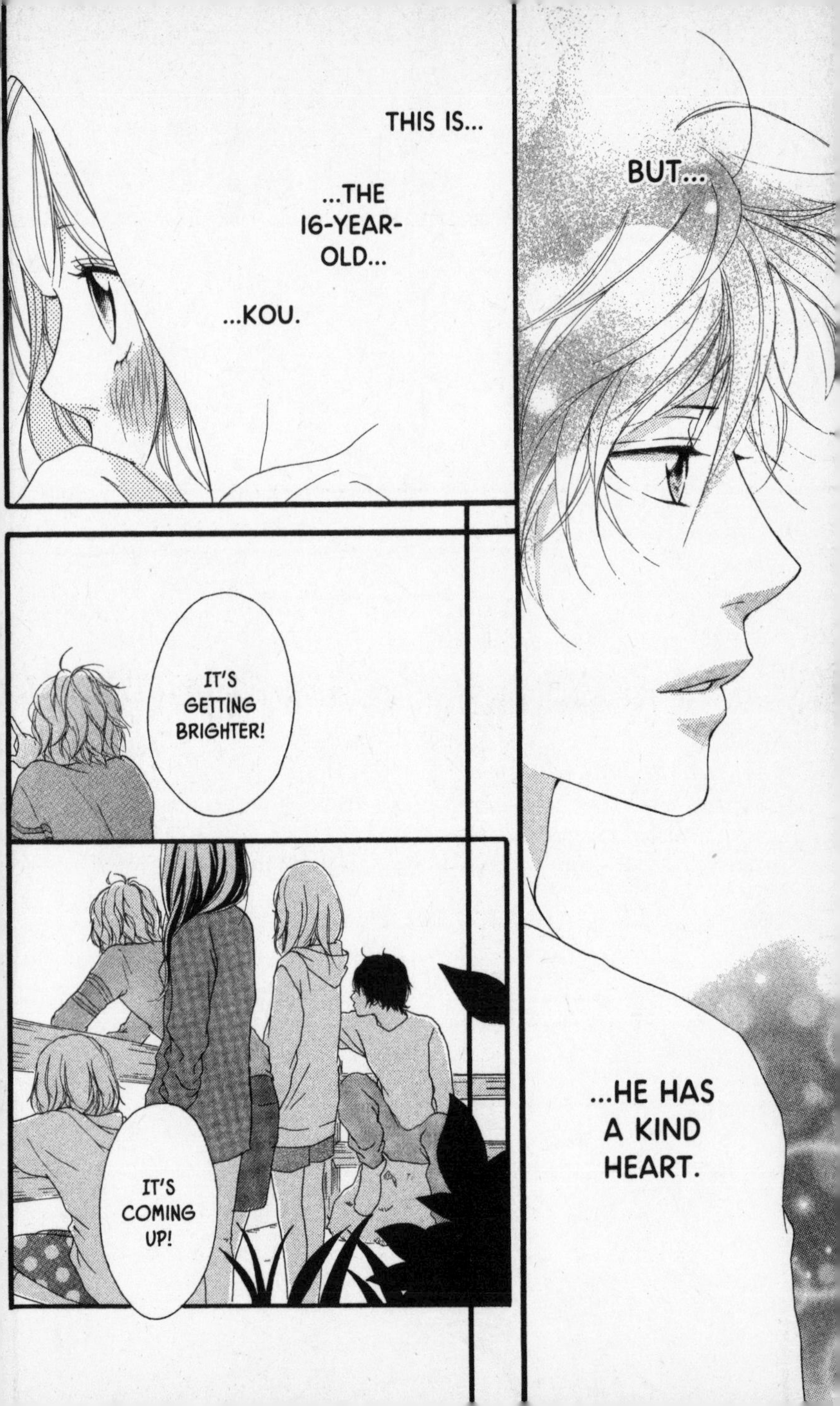
BUT...
...HE HAS A KIND HEART.
THIS IS...
...THE 16-YEAR-OLD...
...KOU.
IT'S GETTING BRIGHTER!
IT'S COMING UP!

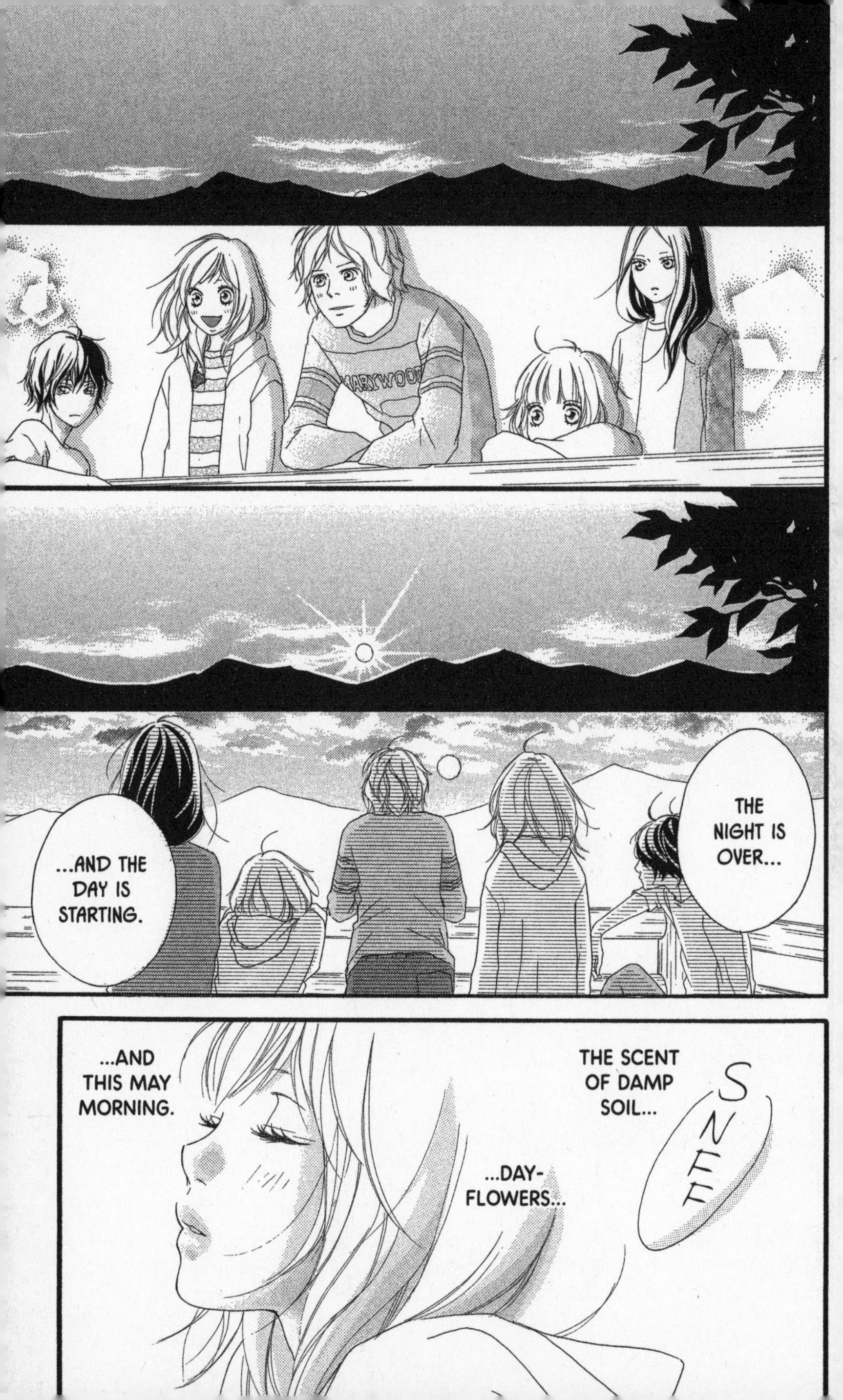
THE NIGHT IS OVER...
...AND THE DAY IS STARTING.
SNFF
THE SCENT OF DAMP SOIL...
...DAY-FLOWERS...
...AND THIS MAY MORNING.

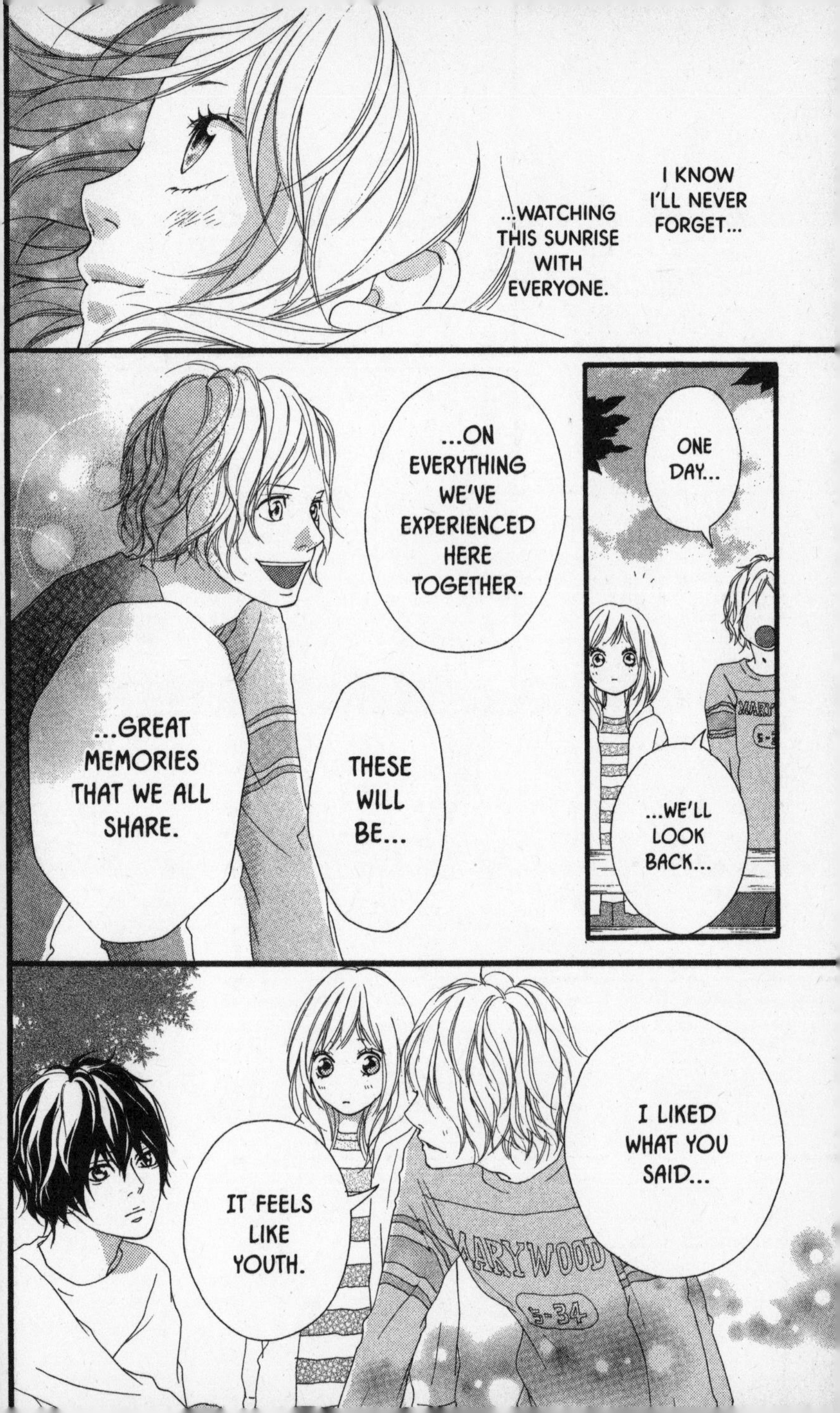
I KNOW I'LL NEVER FORGET...
...WATCHING THIS SUNRISE WITH EVERYONE.
ONE DAY...
...WE'LL LOOK BACK...
...ON EVERYTHING WE'VE EXPERIENCED HERE TOGETHER.
THESE WILL BE...
...GREAT MEMORIES THAT WE ALL SHARE.
I LIKED WHAT YOU SAID...
IT FEELS LIKE YOUTH.

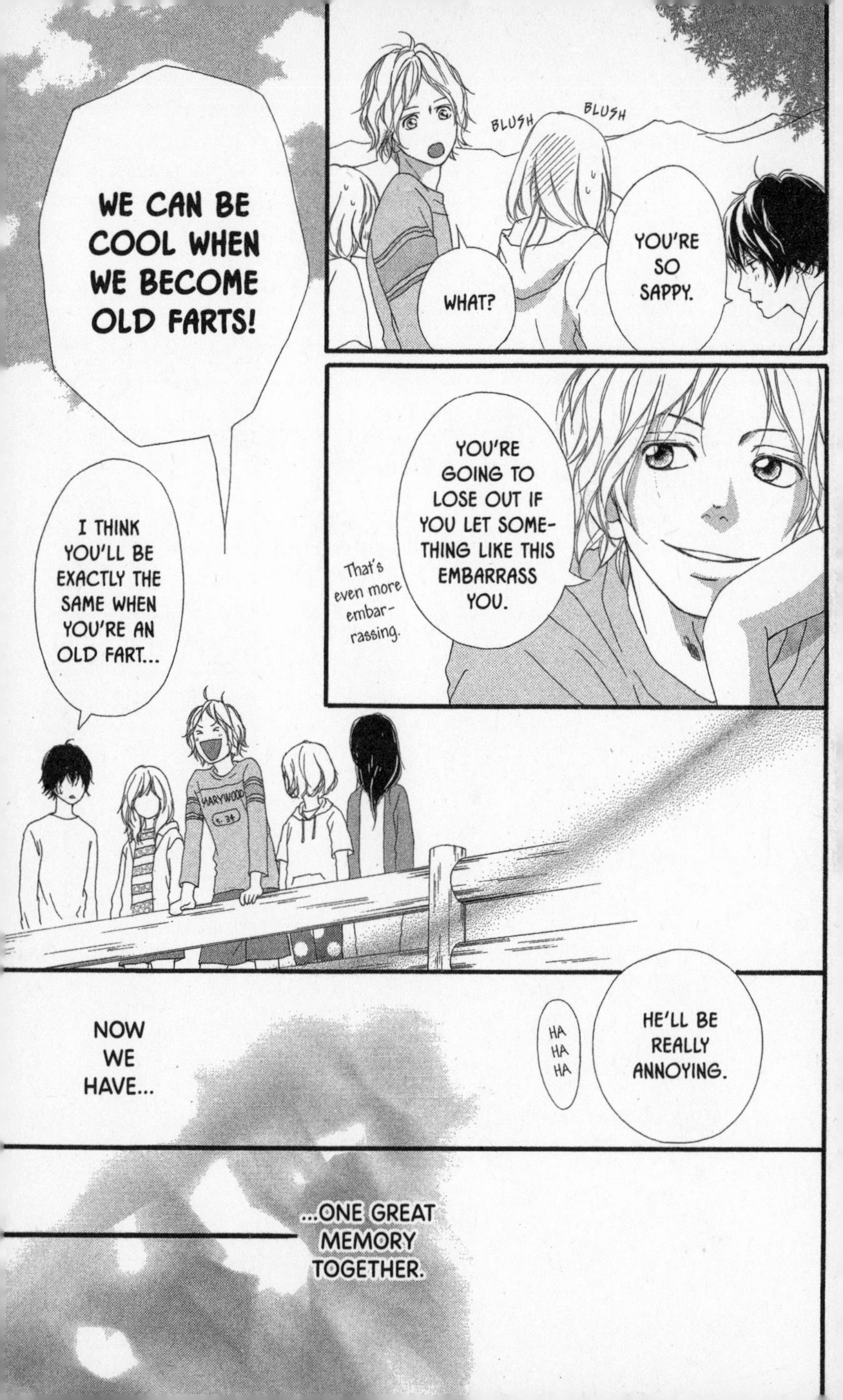
BLUSH
BLUSH
YOU'RE SO SAPPY.
WHAT?
YOU'RE GOING TO LOSE OUT IF YOU LET SOMETHING LIKE THIS EMBARRASS YOU.
That's even more embarrassing.
WE CAN BE COOL WHEN WE BECOME OLD FARTS!
I THINK YOU'LL BE EXACTLY THE SAME WHEN YOU'RE AN OLD FART...
MARYWOOD
HE'LL BE REALLY ANNOYING.
HA HA HA
NOW WE HAVE...
...ONE GREAT MEMORY TOGETHER.

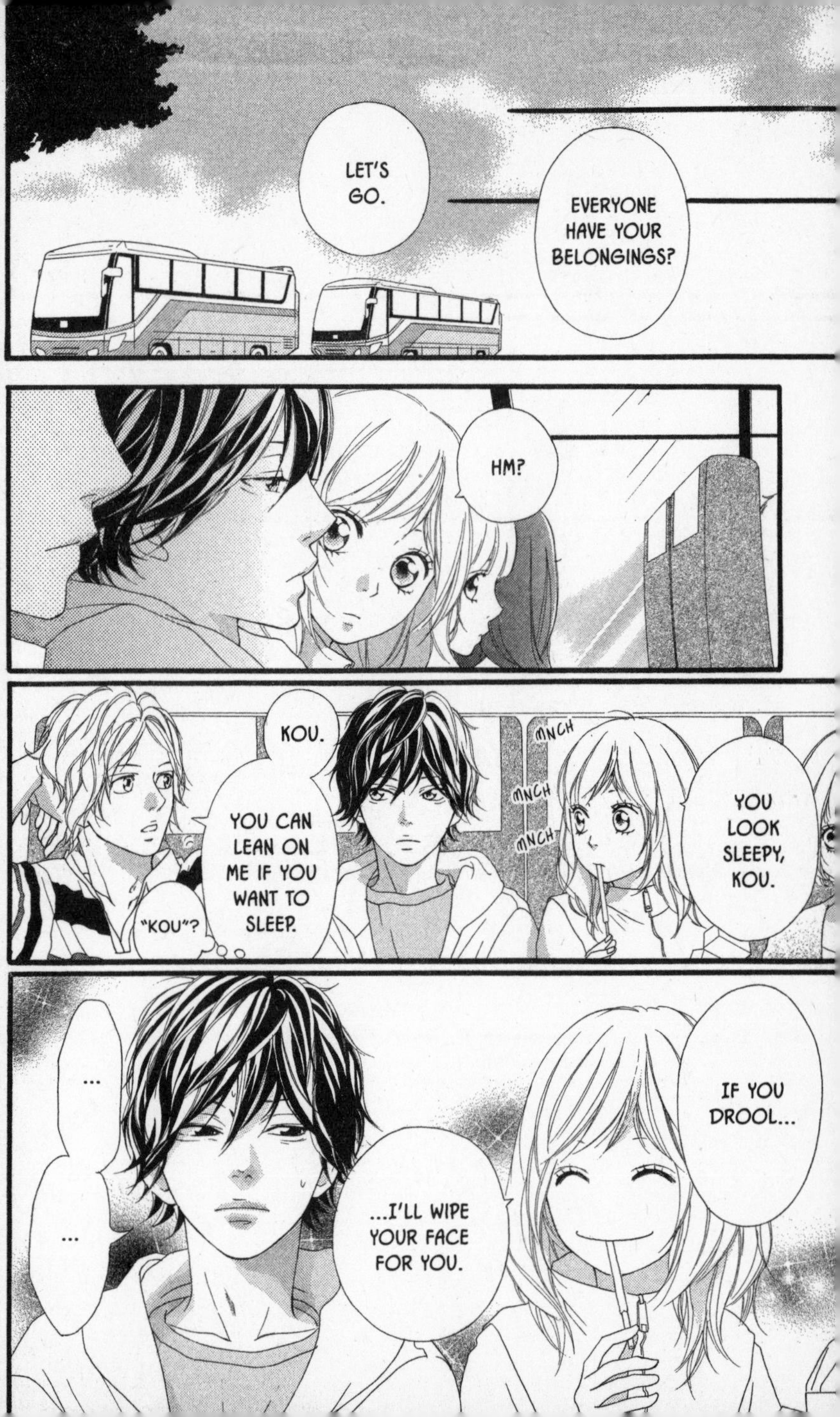
EVERYONE HAVE YOUR BELONGINGS?
LET'S GO.
HM?
YOU LOOK SLEEPY, KOU.
MNCH
MNCH
MNCH
KOU.
YOU CAN LEAN ON ME IF YOU WANT TO SLEEP.
"KOU"?
IF YOU DROOL...
...I'LL WIPE YOUR FACE FOR YOU.
...
...

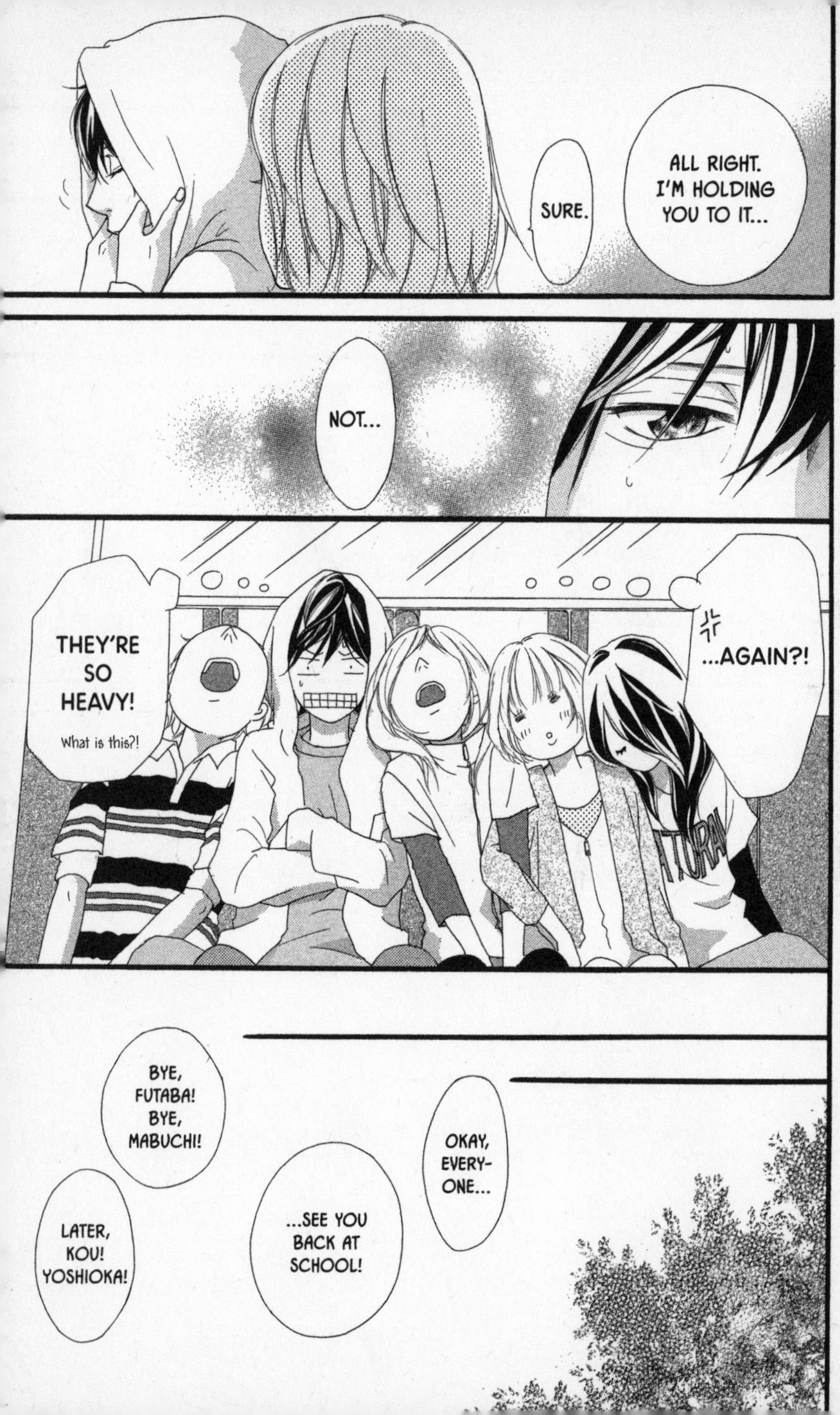
ALL RIGHT. I'M HOLDING YOU TO IT...
SURE.
NOT...
...AGAIN?!
THEY'RE SO HEAVY!
What is this?!
OKAY, EVERYONE...
...SEE YOU BACK AT SCHOOL!
BYE, FUTABA! BYE, MABUCHI!
LATER, KOU! YOSHIOKA!

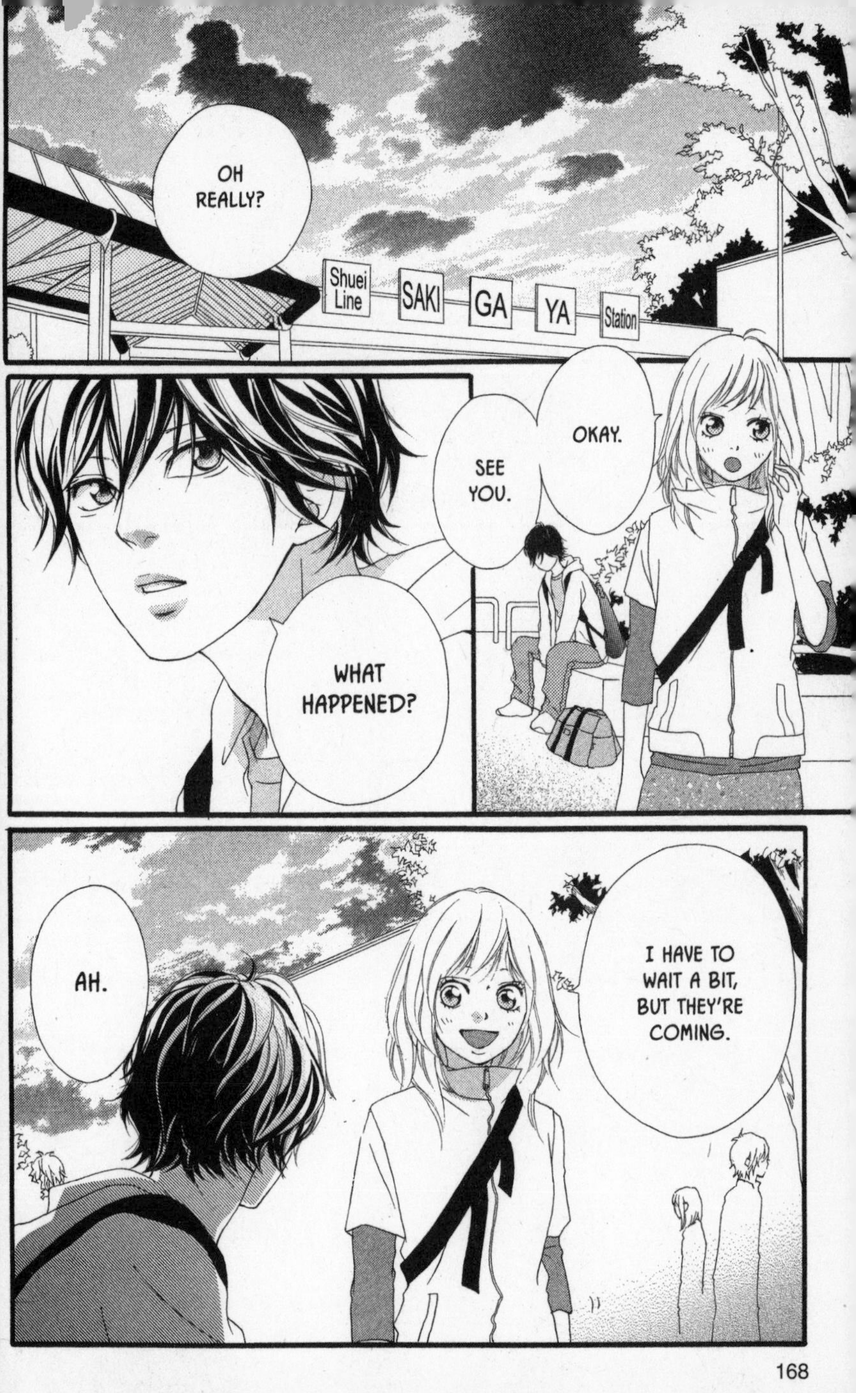
OH REALLY?
Shuei Line
SAKI
GA
YA
Station
OKAY.
SEE YOU.
WHAT HAPPENED?
I HAVE TO WAIT A BIT, BUT THEY'RE COMING.
AH.

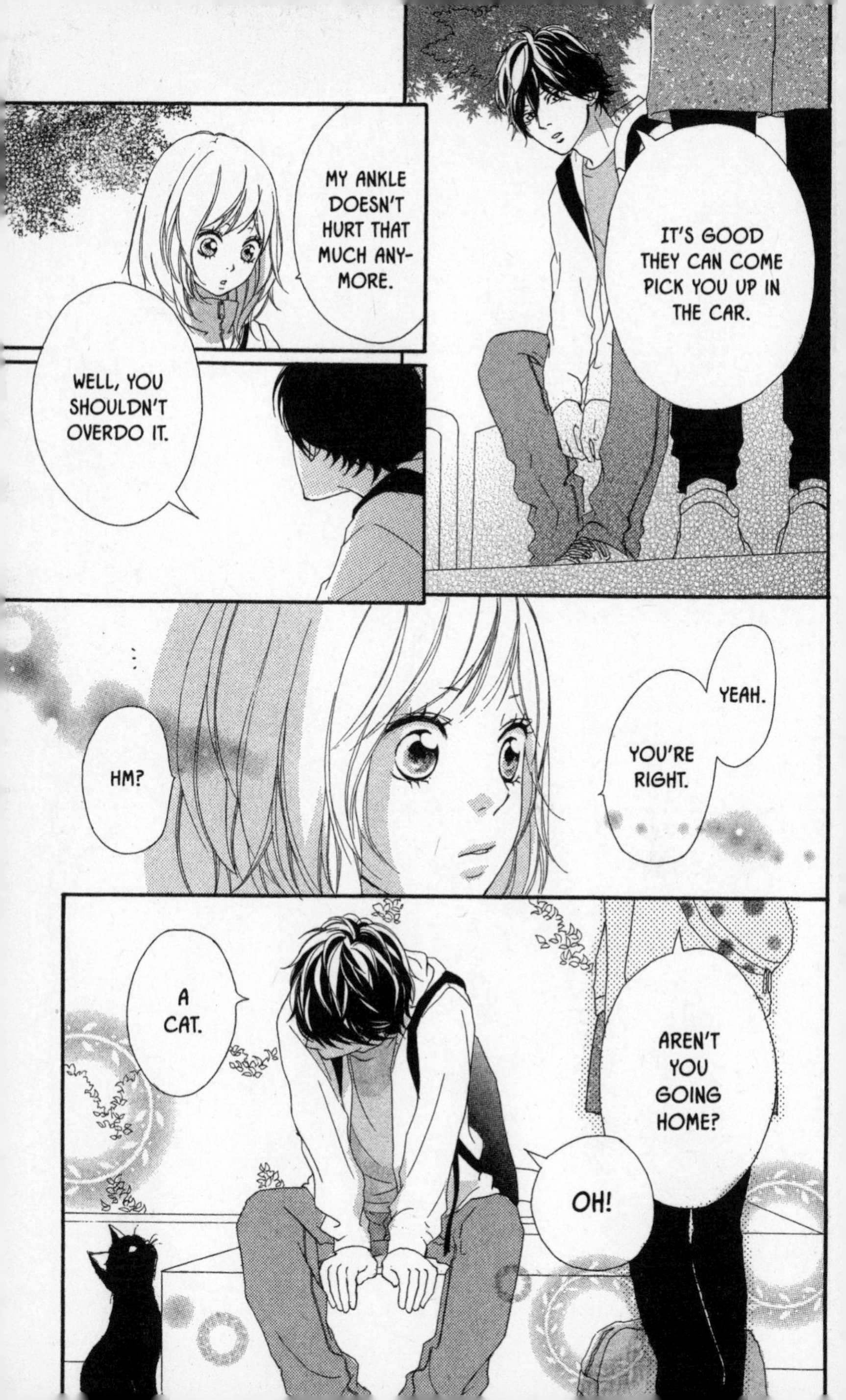
IT'S GOOD THEY CAN COME PICK YOU UP IN THE CAR.
MY ANKLE DOESN'T HURT THAT MUCH ANY-MORE.
WELL, YOU SHOULDN'T OVERDO IT.
YEAH.
YOU'RE RIGHT.
...
HM?
AREN'T YOU GOING HOME?
OH!
A CAT.

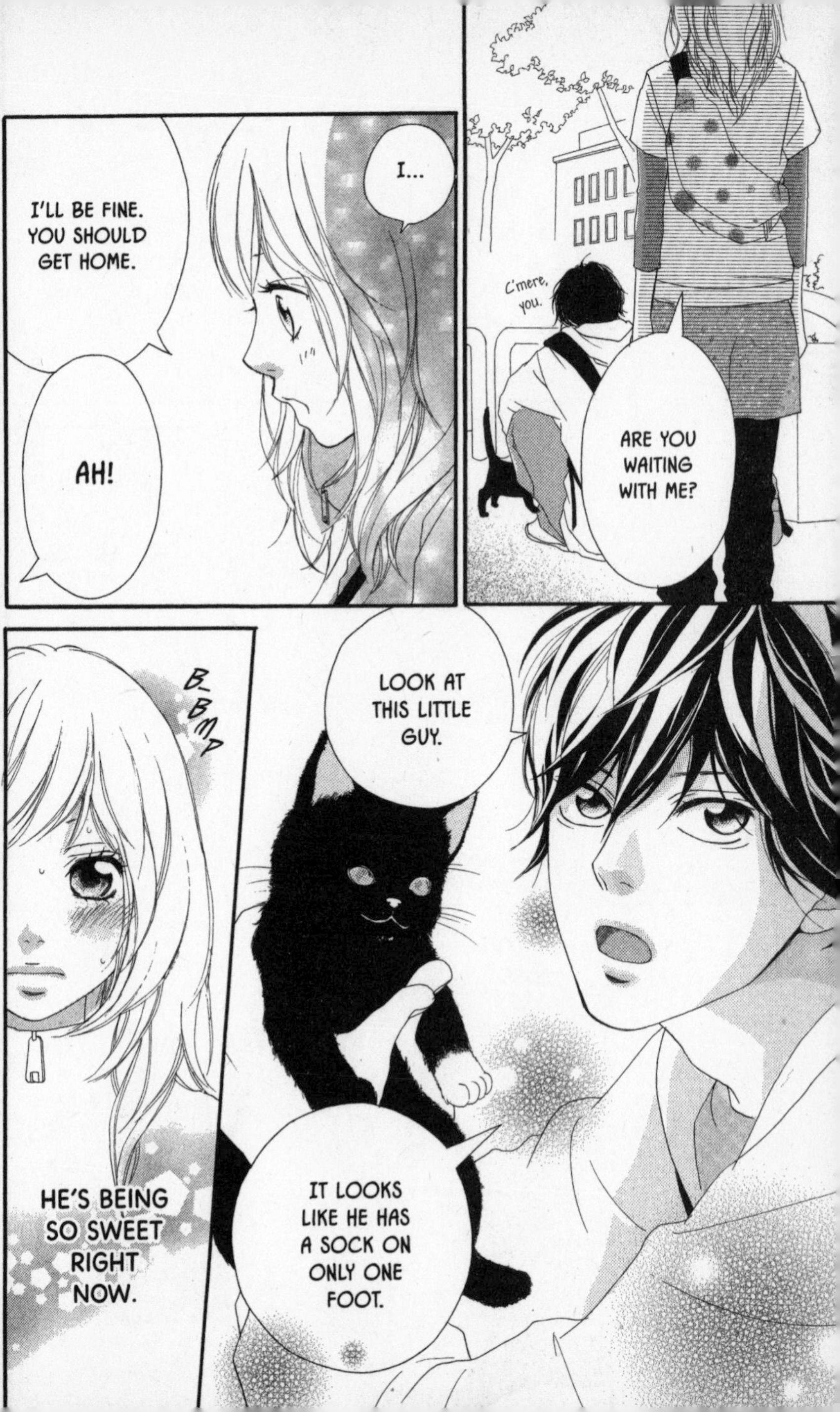
ARE YOU WAITING WITH ME?
C'mere, you.
I...
I'LL BE FINE. YOU SHOULD GET HOME.
AH!
LOOK AT THIS LITTLE GUY.
IT LOOKS LIKE HE HAS A SOCK ON ONLY ONE FOOT.
B-BMP
HE'S BEING SO SWEET RIGHT NOW.

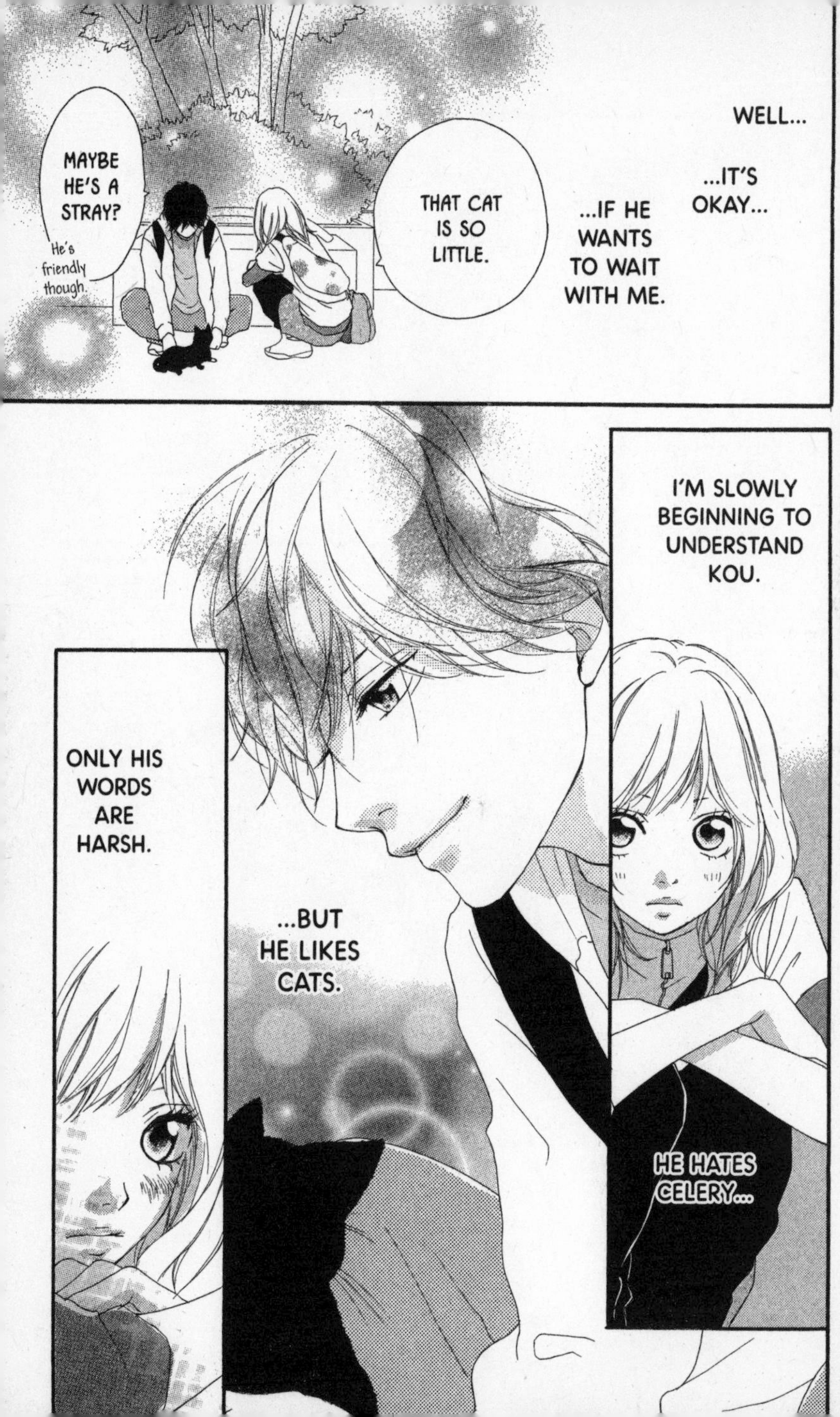
WELL...
...IT'S OKAY...
...IF HE WANTS TO WAIT WITH ME.
THAT CAT IS SO LITTLE.
MAYBE HE'S A STRAY?
He's friendly though.
I'M SLOWLY BEGINNING TO UNDERSTAND KOU.
ONLY HIS WORDS ARE HARSH.
HE HATES CELERY...
...BUT HE LIKES CATS.

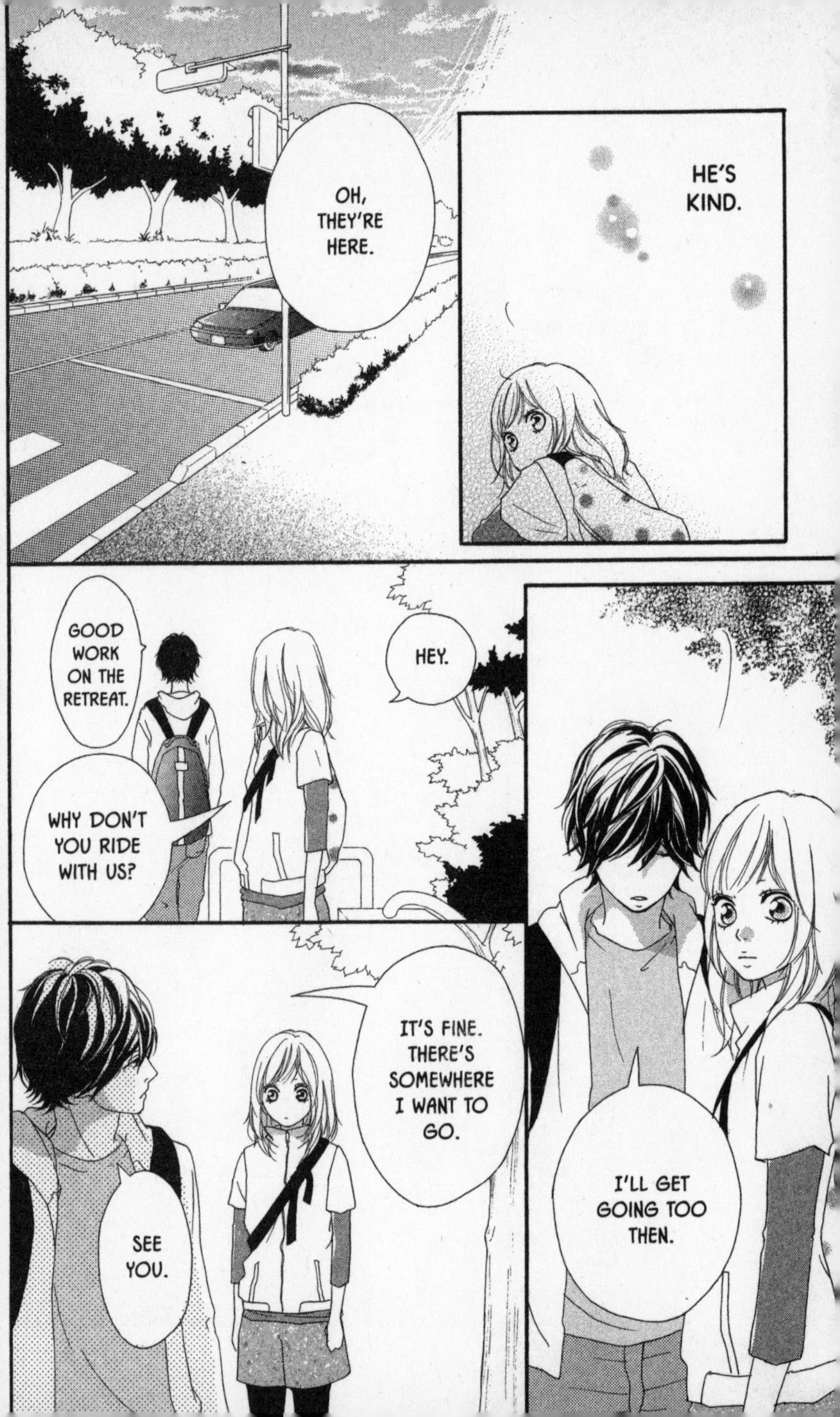
HE'S KIND.
OH, THEY'RE HERE.
I'LL GET GOING TOO THEN.
HEY.
GOOD WORK ON THE RETREAT.
WHY DON'T YOU RIDE WITH US?
IT'S FINE. THERE'S SOMEWHERE I WANT TO GO.
SEE YOU.

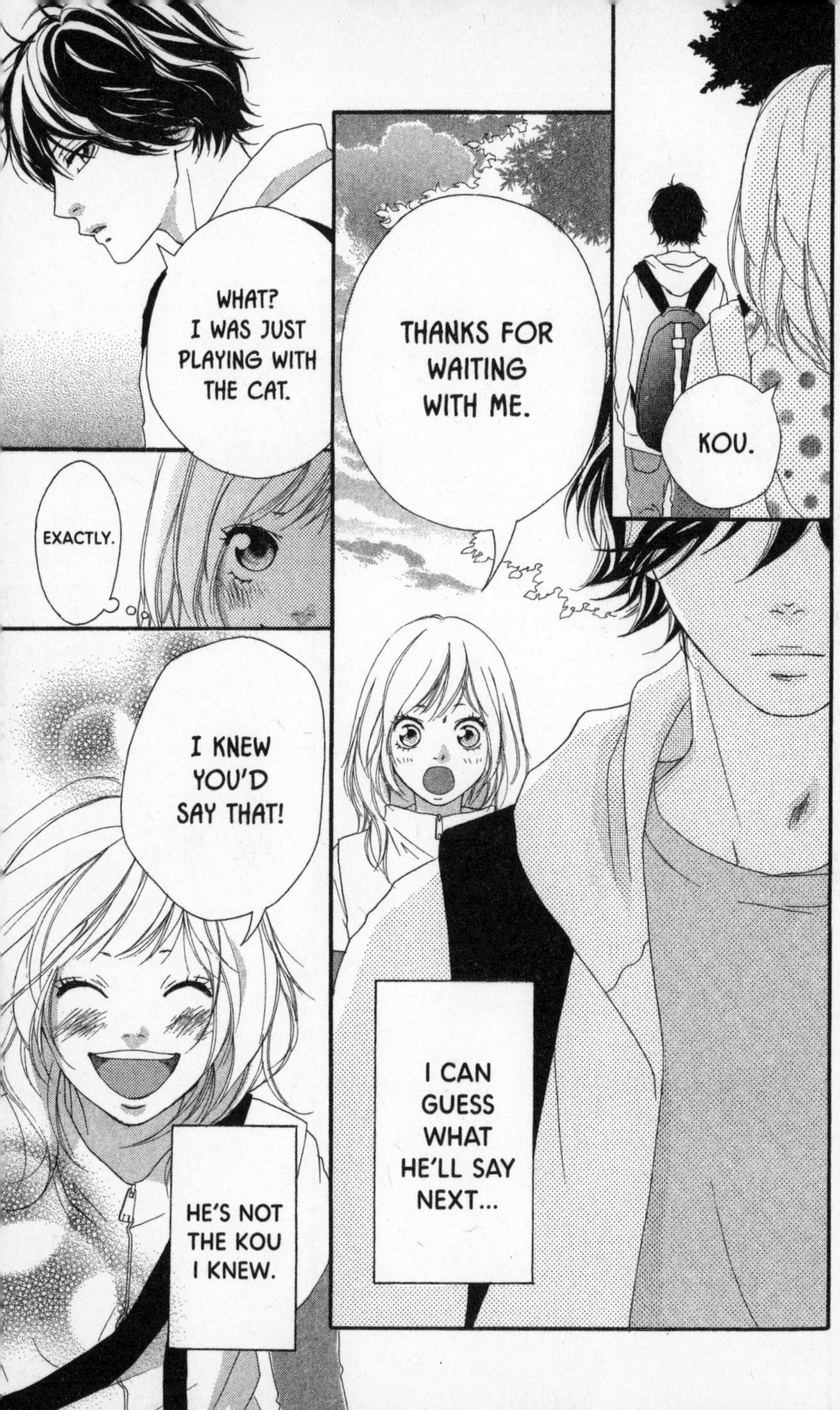
KOU.
THANKS FOR WAITING WITH ME.
I CAN GUESS WHAT HE'LL SAY NEXT...
WHAT? I WAS JUST PLAYING WITH THE CAT.
EXACTLY.
I KNEW YOU'D SAY THAT!
HE'S NOT THE KOU I KNEW.

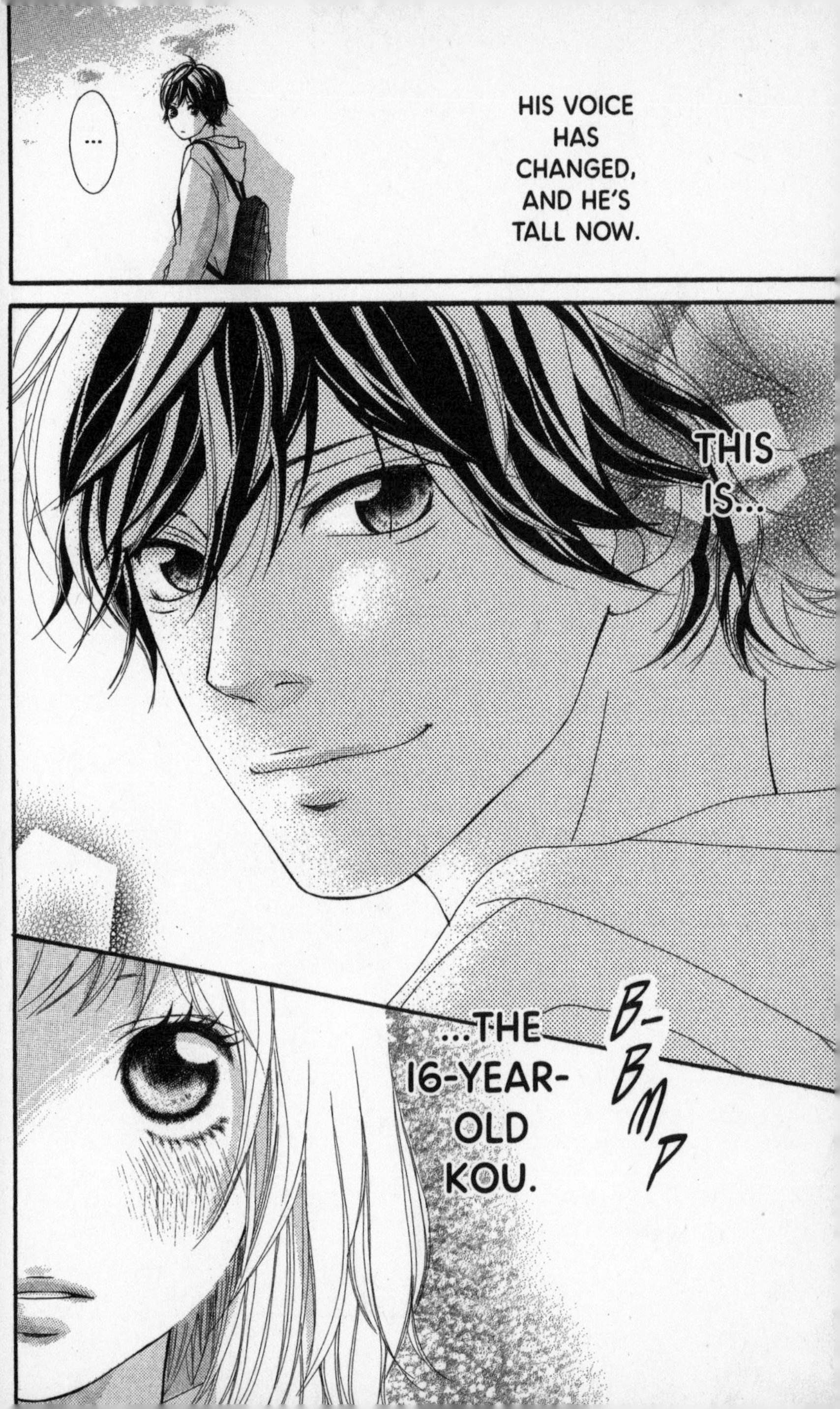
HIS VOICE HAS CHANGED, AND HE'S TALL NOW.
...
THIS IS...
...THE 16-YEAR-OLD KOU.
B-BMP

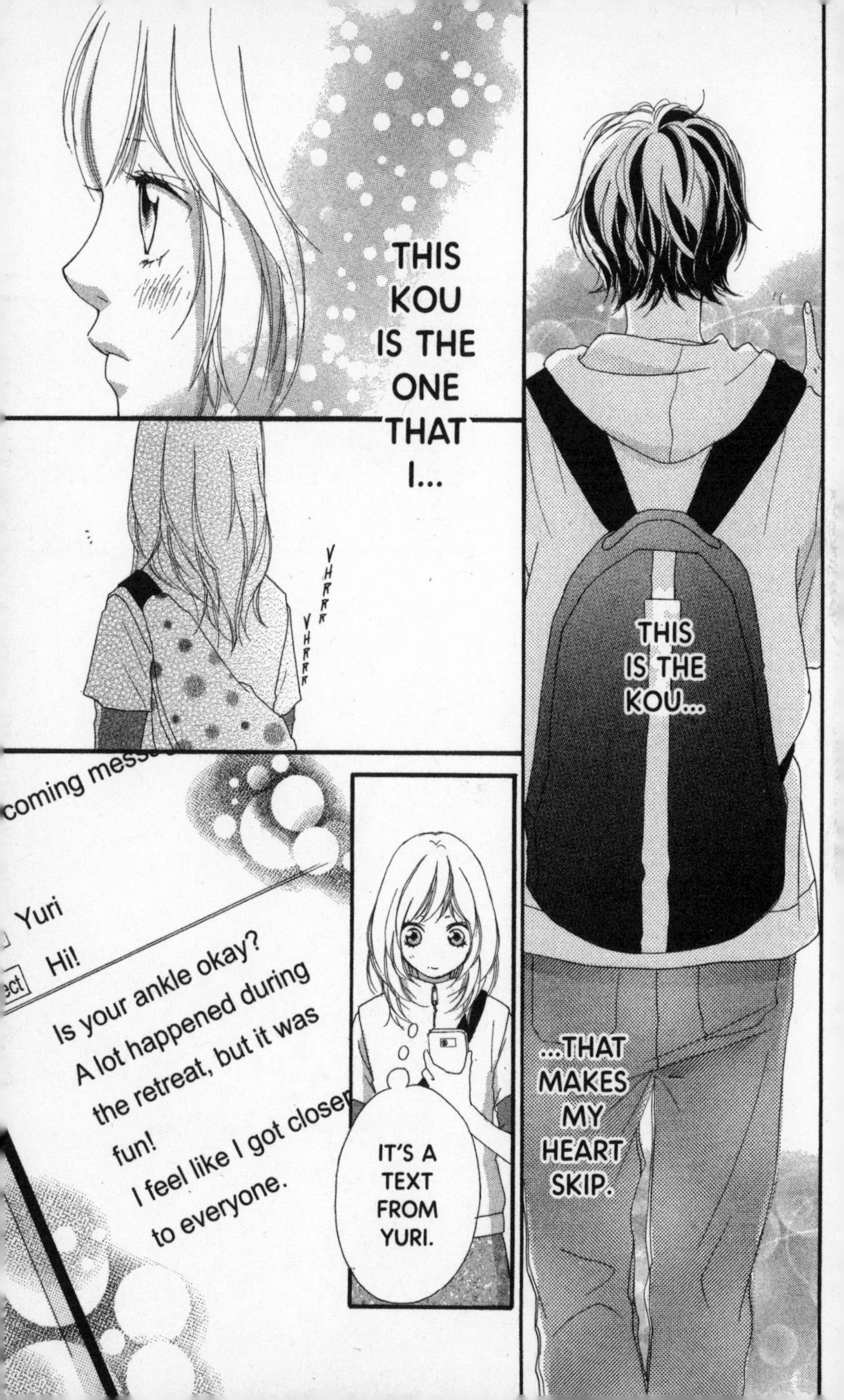
THIS IS THE KOU...
...THAT MAKES MY HEART SKIP.
THIS KOU IS THE ONE THAT I...
VHRRR
VHRRR
IT'S A TEXT FROM YURI.
coming mess
Yuri
Hi!
Is your ankle okay?
A lot happened during the retreat, but it was fun!
I feel like I got closer to everyone.

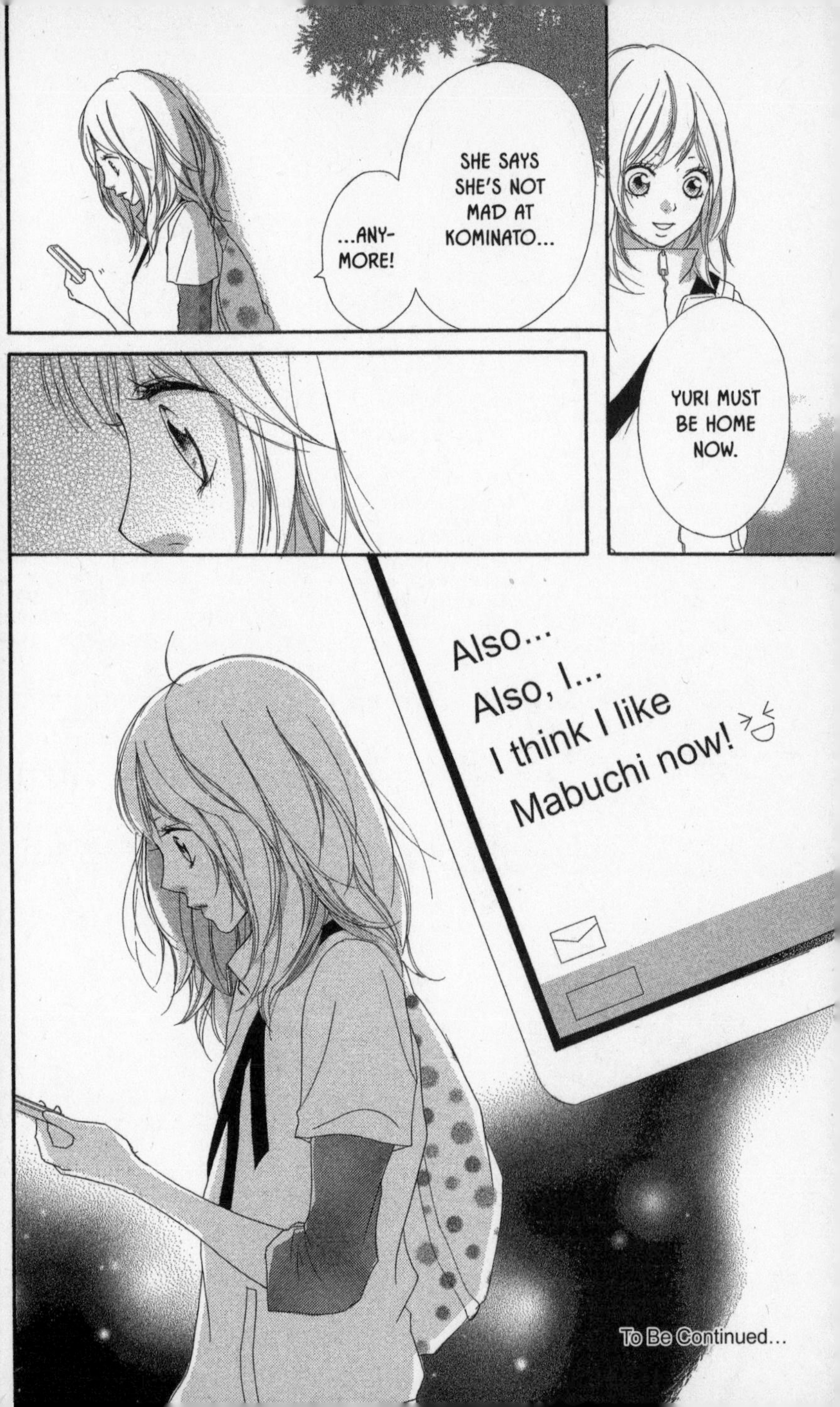
SHE SAYS SHE'S NOT MAD AT KOMINATO...
...ANY-MORE!
YURI MUST BE HOME NOW.
Also...
Also, I...
I think I like
Mabuchi now!
To Be Continued...

←PROFILES OF FUTABA AND KOU
AFTERWORD

AO HARU RIDE CHARACTERS 1

Futaba Yoshioka

- **Birthday:**
  June 19
- **Astrological Sign, Blood Type:**
  Gemini, type A
- **Height, Weight:**
  5' 3", 110 lbs.
- **Favorite Subject:**
  Science
- **Least Favorite Subject:**
  English
- **Favorite Food:**
  Tarako pasta
- **Least Favorite Food:**
  Milk from other peoples' homes
- **Favorite Music:**
  Abe Mao
- **Siblings:**
  None
- **Age When First Crush Happened:**
  First-year in junior high
- **Fun Fact:**
  My bedroom is really girly.
- **Favorite Snack:**
  Galbo Ball
- **Favorite Drink:**
  Tea
- **Favorite Color:**
  White

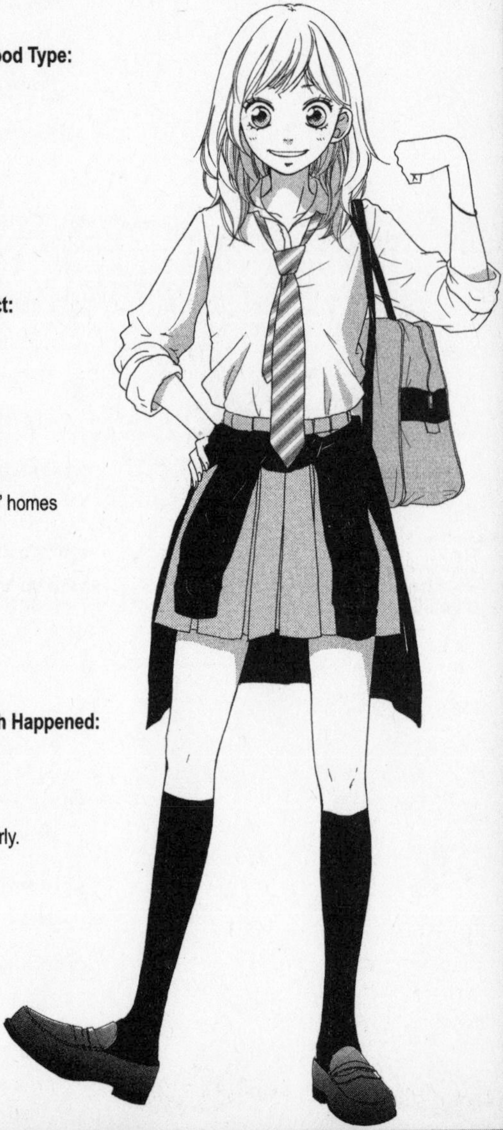

AO HARU RIDE
CHARACTERS 2

Kou Mabuchi

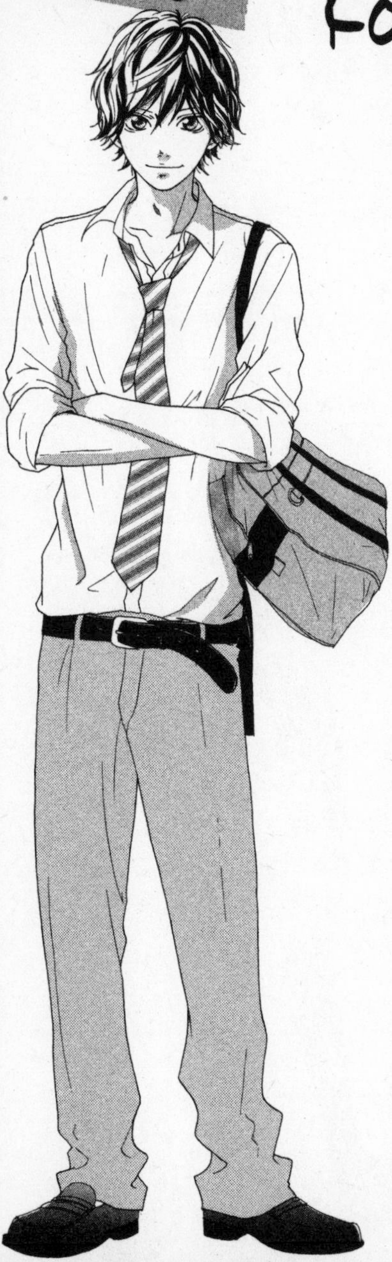

- **Birthday:**
  May 27
- **Astrological Sign, Blood Type:**
  Gemini, type O
- **Height, Weight:**
  5' 9", 128 lbs.
- **Favorite Subject:**
  Social studies
- **Least Favorite Subject:**
  Classical Japanese
- **Favorite Food:**
  Chicken nanban
- **Least Favorite Food:**
  Celery
- **Favorite Music:**
  Dave Matthews Band
- **Siblings:**
  Older brother
- **Age When First Crush Happened:**
  First-year in junior high
- **Fun Fact:**
  My hair is a mix of wiry and wavy.
- **Favorite Snack:**
  Consommé chips
- **Favorite Drink:**
  Coffee
- **Favorite Color:**
  Blue and black

Afterword

Thank you for reading through to the end!

Lately I've been turning in my manuscripts at the very last minute. (I used to always be on time!) When I have a deadline, I often progress from panic to total freak-out to full-on tears. But the moment I finish, I feel such an intense feeling of completion and freedom. It's a feeling I can't describe in words. At that moment, my exhaustion completely lifts away. After the manuscript becomes a book and all you read it and give me feedback, I think about how much I love this work! Now I just need to inch my way back to submitting my manuscripts on time. (I wish there were 30 hours in a day...)

I am lucky and grateful to be doing work that I love, and I will do my best to create stories that are enjoyable. It makes it worthwhile to be holed up in my home to draw. Thank you always for your support! See you next time.

 Io Sakisaka

Until recently, I would go to the convenience store to make copies of my manga drafts. Although it was a pain, it was a good way to get out—otherwise I'd easily stay at home for days in a row.

But, because it was a pain, I eventually gave in and bought a multifunctional printer. Reading the manual was also a pain, and so far I'm using only the copy function.

When did I become so lazy? Apparently I've been this way since I was a kid.

IO SAKISAKA

Born on June 8, Io Sakisaka made her debut as a manga creator with *Sakura, Chiru*. Her works include *Call My Name*, *Gate of Planet* and *Blue*. *Strobe Edge*, her previous work, is also published by VIZ Media's Shojo Beat imprint. *Ao Haru Ride* was adapted into an anime series in 2014. In her spare time, Sakisaka likes to paint things and sleep.

Ao Haru Ride

VOLUME 2
SHOJO BEAT EDITION

STORY AND ART BY **IO SAKISAKA**

TRANSLATION **Emi Louie-Nishikawa**
TOUCH-UP ART + LETTERING **Inori Fukuda Trant**
DESIGN **Shawn Carrico**
EDITOR **Nancy Thistlethwaite**

First published in Japan in 2011 by SHUEISHA Inc., Tokyo.
English translation rights arranged by SHUEISHA Inc.

Printed in the U.S.A.

Published by VIZ Media, LLC
P.O. Box 77010
San Francisco, CA 94107

10 9 8 7 6 5 4 3 2 1
First printing, December 2018

ratings.viz.com RATED T TEEN

PARENTAL ADVISORY
AO HARU RIDE is rated T for Teen and is recommended for ages 13 and up. This volume contains the camaraderie of youth.

VIZ MEDIA
viz.com

Shojo Beat
shojobeat.com

Honey
So Sweet

Story and Art by Amu Meguro

Little did Nao Kogure realize back in middle school that when she left an umbrella and a box of bandages in the rain for injured delinquent Taiga Onise that she would meet him again in high school. Nao wants nothing to do with the gruff and frightening Taiga, but he suddenly presents her with a huge bouquet of flowers and asks her to date him—with marriage in mind! Is Taiga really so scary, or is he a sweetheart in disguise?

RATED T FOR TEEN
ratings.viz.com

viz media
viz.com

STOP!

YOU MAY BE READING THE WRONG WAY.

In keeping with the original Japanese comic format, this book reads from right to left—so action, sound effects and word balloons are completely reversed to preserve the orientation of the original artwork.